Breaking Free

Phoenix Rising Book One

Kat Thrive

To my Love,

Thank you for putting up with me and supporting me through this endeavor. Also, thank you for dealing with the many hours I focused on writing, editing and listening to me complain.

XoXo

Contents

Chapter 1 – Ellianna

"Your flight comes in at one forty-five, right?" I hear my best friend since preschool, Sonja as her voice projects through my car Bluetooth.

"Yup.... I am so glad. You can do this. Pops will be working and Momma has some board thing with the school." I reply as I turn onto my street for the last time.

Sonja quickly responds, *"No problem. I've missed you so much girl. We don't talk enough."*

That stings to close too my heart, not that Sonja knows the whole story yet. I have had to sneak conversations in when I can and they are never that long.

"I'll explain it all tomorrow, if you have time." I inwardly laugh, we'd need a week.

"Drinks after we get you get unloaded?"

My response is a "We will see". I don't think I'll want drinks but who knows, I may need them.

I see my house, really *his* house come into view and know I need to cut the line. Somehow, I've managed to get away with all these calls lately without him noticing. "Babes, I got to go. Thank you. I'll text you tomorrow." I tell her fast.

I click my phone and delete the call history out of habit. Singing gratitude that he didn't make me get an iPhone and have it sync to his iPad like he originally wanted.

I pull in and park my car, really *his* car in the garage and head into the house. I have a game plan and have my things packed in suitcases hiding under the bed.

"ELLIANNA!" I hear Brett yelling as soon as a step from the garage to the mud room. His voice is so harsh and I think back to the night we met. How he was so soft, kind and caring, ready to hand me the world and more.

"Coming Brett....just let me get my shoes and jacket off." I speak softly knowing he can hear me as long as he is in the kitchen.

"You're late!"

Feeling obligated to explain myself to him, I respond "I had to finish a call before I left."

While it's not a lie, it's only a half truth. I was finishing a call before I left work but it was to finalize everything for my new job. It starts in just over a week but tonight I have a flight back home. I also had to do my exit interview with the HR department here before I could leave. Brett doesn't know any of this yet.

Stepping into the kitchen I see Brett hunched over at the island with papers scattered and his laptop in front of him. He looks focused and fierce. There was a time when this view made my heart swell and my panties wet, but that's not the feelings that stir in me now. He's still well defined and attractive but the love and lust that used to be there is gone, long gone. Perhaps, it was only ever lust and infatuation to start with, something that eventually fizzed out.

"Have a good day?" He asks. At least I think it is a question but with his tone I never know if it's a question, statement or a goodbye. He speaks with such a lack of emotion. Anger seems to be the only emotion that I get out of him anymore. Sex happens only because he demands it as a scheduled release. Emotionless. Dry. Unfulfilling. He gets off and I have started to hate myself more and more each time.

"Yeah." I softly respond as I pour us both a glass of wine and set his in front of him.

"What's this for? You haven't even set dinner yet." Brett barely looks up but I can see his brows furrowed together frustrated.

"We need to talk and we may need wine for this talk."

Brett slams his laptop shut and puts his papers in a pile on top before taking a sip from his glass and addressing me. "What did you do?"

Of course, he thinks I did something wrong. I have a list of duties he expects from me as his working trophy wife so if I did not complete something to his taste it would be my fault.

I am not this person. I have never been this person and I can't believe it took me this long to see that I am this person now. I have turned into something or someone that I have always loathed. My strong, independent, fiery personality has moved to the back seat and this timid, eager to please person has replaced it.

It finally hit me when I had seen Sonja again; it had been years since I'd seen her last. When my Grams passed last year, Brett let us travel home for the funeral and we spent a few days. He, of course worked the entire time and could only be bothered when the doting husband rule was public. Everything must look a certain way though, so he had to play the part of the loving husband tending to his wife's grief.

One of the evenings that week, when he was working Sonja and I had drinks. She said to me that my eyes were dull and I lost my spunk. I hadn't even lost my spunk when four of our friends were killed in a car accident in high-school. She was worried because I hadn't been home since Brett moved us to Texas before we got married. She kept asking if was okay through the night and it hit me that I wasn't okay, and it wasn't because my Grams just passed.

"I got a job offer, Brett." Time to break the news.

"Oh well that's good right? Something with less hours or from home? Once I'm through this case, I'll be partner." He says tapping the papers and laptop.

Brett's five-year plan included him becoming partner, followed by babies with trophy wife, aka me, then to run for Senate.

Shaking my head, I answer. "No Brett, the job is back home."

"Then why are we talking about this?" He glares across the kitchen island in my direction.

"I'm going home, Brett"

His voice is emotionless, "Absolutely not. We have a plan Ellianna."

"You, YOU have a plan, Brett. YOU!" I raise my voice.

"You support it. You supported it when we got married and you support it now. It is the plan and that is final." He states like it is merely a written fact.

I sigh, "Sure Brett, maybe at first it sounded great. We would both have everything we wanted but things changed and it became about you and only you."

"WHAT CHANGED ELLIANNA?!" Apparently, we hit screaming match levels.

"You did." I say softly.

"Me! Me? I CAN'T FUCKING BELIEVE YOU!! Ellianna, this is ridiculous!" Brett is livid as he continues screaming across the island at me. I have struck the one nerve that triggers his only emotion in this house.

It wasn't always like this. When we met, he was so caring, loving and supportive of my job. I hated the idea of leaving home and my old job to come with him back to Texas. However, he had already had a job lined up after finishing at Cornell. His family is here too. Old money type but it never seemed like he was cut from the same cloth. He helped me find a job here, super prestigious company but I hate it. The culture is so cold and everyone is cutthroat.

At first everything was wonderful. We got married and bought this house. Everything was basically every American girl's dream. Then little by little I was isolated, trapped and alone. Controlled. He is definitely cut from the same cloth as his family, it's easy to see now, even if it wasn't easy to see then.

"Brett, I have to do this." I softly tell him when he finally quiets enough for me to get a word in.

"FINE. Do this, get your fill. Come back and I'll run for Senate.

Of course, he'd play this off somehow, someway. Tell everyone it was something good and made us a better team or something. Who knows, as long as I fell in line as the loving, attractive wife on his arm what did it matter. I turn away from him rolling my eyes. "I won't come back. I'm taking this job, going home and I am done."

"We are MARRIED. You belong to me. You're not leaving then." He grabs my wrist hard. He's never hit me but I'm a little scared he might. I've never threatened to leave before.

"Brett..." I say softly and with hesitation.

"I love you Ellianna. You can't leave me."

"You don't love me. You love how I make you look."

"Not true. I love you."

"Brett. You knew when you met me that I was independent and a little wild. You tamed me but you pushed me too far, Brett. I am not this person. I am not someone who constantly bows down."

He scoffs and let's go of my wrist. I've brought it up before, that I felt like I wasn't myself. He'd let off for a few days and make promises then it would go right back to how it was. When he turns from me, he throws his wine and glass in the sink so hard it shatters. He goes to the liquor cabinet and pours a glass of scotch. While he might need something harder for this conversation, I know he secretly hates the stuff. It's all for appearance like everything else. "Four years Ellianna, you've been my wife for over four fucking years and not once have you said you were unhappy."

"I have Brett. Many, many times and you don't listen."

"I've given you everything. This house, your car, your clothes, that jewelry, everything."

Now I scoff. "I work too."

I work and he has the money directly deposited into his account. That never sat well with me, we had argued at length about it but eventually he won out. Since all the bills come from one account, he pushed it. Though, I've always put 5% into an account from home he doesn't know about.

"If you leave, you don't take anything."

"I'm taking some clothing and the personal items I brought here, Brett. That is all. I don't want your money, I never did. I just want my life back."

"Your life?!" He laughs out. It's a horrifying sound that I have never heard from him before. "Fuck you Ellianna. Just go then."

"For what it's worth Brett, I am sorry.... I did love you once... I did..." I tell him while I move away from him and out of the kitchen.

"Whatever makes you sleep at night." Brett says as he pours another glass and downs that before pouring a third.

Leaving the room, along with him and my half drank wine, I make my way upstairs to grab the suitcases from under the bed before calling an Uber and coming back down. Brett isn't in the kitchen anymore and I'm grateful as I grab shoes and my purse. I drop my rings and keys in the bowl by the door. Then I step outside and walk to the curb to wait for the Uber. Two minutes away. As I'm counting my blessings and watching the little car dot from the app, Brett comes storming out, slamming doors behind him.

"You'll be back! You are a money hungry whore, you'll be back!!" He screams across the yard.

"Really Brett?! Really? Fuck you if you actually think that about me." I'm losing the calmness I had to keep this plan going. Lucky for me, the Uber pulls up. I open the door to ask for help with my bags as Brett continues to storm across the yard.

"No. Fuck you. You are done. If you think you can leave me and you have another thing coming bitch." Brett hisses out before grabbing my wrist again and tries to pull be back.

"Brett! Stop! You're making a fool of yourself." I yell at him. He pulls me harder and I see the Uber driver looks worried and uncomfortable. When Brett tugs my wrist hard enough to make me lose my balance, I start to scream at him. We are in the middle of the street and I now the neighbors will hear us and start to watch the entertainment. "WHAT ARE YOU GOING TO DO BRETT? HUH? HIT ME? HIT ME IN PUBLIC SO THE WORLD CAN SEE YOUR ABUSE."

He drops my wrist and glares at me. I hit a nerve or two. I don't think he would actually hit me for one, but also his image is so important to him it would look horrible if anyone seen him hit his wife. Plus, he knows this street as well as I do, he knows that Brittney across the street is definitely watching us now.

"Have a good life Brett." I tell him before I slide into the Uber and tell the driver go, leaving Brett glaring us down from the yard. "I'm so sorry you had to see that. He's obviously not taking me leaving well and I apologize."

"No worries ma'am.... Are you okay?" The Uber driver genuinely asks with concern apparent in his eyes.

"Yeah, yeah I think I am." I reply with a smile. A genuine smile for the first time in years. It feels like a weight has been lifted from my shoulders.

I text Sonja and my parents that I'll be texting with a new

number as soon as I get a new phone and number on my long layover. I plan to mail mine back with all the credit cards to Brett. I don't want his money or anything from him. I'm done and I'm cutting all ties. As soon as I'm home I'll be mailing him divorce papers and changing my name back to mine too.

The world looks brighter already.

Chapter 2 - Ellianna

I step out the doors of the airport terminal into baggage claim. This small town has two whole gates in their airport. You can walk through the place in minutes and see the entire baggage claim and all the exits from the hall. "OH MY GOD! YOU LOOK FABULOUS!! GIRL!! YOU GOT YOUR GLOW BACK!!!" I hear Sonja scream across the open baggage claim room.

I giggle and run to her. As soon as I wrap my arms around her, I feel my body release all the tension it built up on the plane. "Girl, I feel good! I feel like myself!"

"You look like yourself! You look so much better than last time, I mean it was a bad time last time but - "

I cut her off. "I know what you mean, and honestly I do. I was not in a good spot; this is where I belong."

Sonja smiles at me. "Let's grab your bags."

"Yes, let me just drop this in a mailer first." I take the package with my phone, his cards and a letter dropping it in the mail slot. The next letter he will be getting will he from my lawyer. Her contact information attached.

"All his shit?" She asks with a big smile.

"Yup, the last of it." I walk back to her and we grab my bags. "Let's go! I want to shower and we definitely need drinks!"

"Are you sure you want to stay with your parents? I have a guest room and I could totally use someone else helping with rent." Son brings up the topic of where I should live again. When I was making these plans, I just wanted out and my parents would always accept me back in my childhood home. No questions asked.

"I really don't want to impose. Plus, I have nothing... just clothes."

"There's a bed in there already. Closet is big and we can find a dresser somewhere cheap later. Plus, you'd have the hall bath to yourself."

"You sure babes? Seriously, I - " I cut my words off when Sonja waves her hands in front of me while we are walking through the lot.

"Look you were my best friend all through school and up until you left. You still are, but also I can barely afford rent right now so honestly you'd be doing me a favor." She is most likely exaggerating, just so I'll say yes. She knows how to play me into a yes after all these years of friendship.

"Okay, if it'll help you."

"That's my girl!" She lightly slaps my shoulder before continuing through the lot with a happy skip to her steps. She helps me load stuff into her SUV and we head to her place. I text my parents on the way, we decided on getting ready then popping in to see them before drinks. I've missed my parents and even my bonehead baby brother. I haven't talked to my brother since Grams, and I barely got to talk with Momma over the phone. To say I miss them is an understatement. I sigh, I can hardly believe that I let myself fall into that trap, being that person. How was there no sign? Maybe there was and I ignored it? Sonja gives me a sad side glance as she drives.

"Sonja, when.... when you met Brett -"

"Did I know this would happen?" She finishes for me.

"Yeah, I mean were there alarm bells, red flags?"

"I don't know Ellie I mean, I met him a handful of times before your wedding. He seemed charming and boy is he handsome. You looked happy enough even when he pulled you down from something you'd normally down. Like at your wedding we would have been doing shots and celebrating but we weren't. Then he took your 4th glass of champagne from you and scolded you about it. You still smiled and said he was right, I figured you were just growing up, I guess. I didn't think...."

"That he'd control my life and isolate me from my friends and family?"

"Yeah Ellie..."

"I am so sorry, Sonja. I thought about you so much and I missed you and I should have tried harder."

"What would he have done if you had? It's okay, honestly I'm just happy you got away when you did."

"Me too." I brush my hair back with my hand out of habit but it is just enough that the sleeve of my sweater comes up.

Sonja starts cussing up a storm and inquiring about it. I look down and sure enough there's a big hand print shaped bruise around my wrist. I noticed it on my layover but it was still faint and I tossed my sweater on to cover it up. "He grabbed it trying to pull me from getting in the Uber. He let go when I asked him if he was actually going to hit me. I don't think he has it in him to hit anyone. He wants control and a certain life and lifestyle but he has morals. He's not a horrible person, we just aren't compatible and I can't be controlled like that anymore."

Son let's out a big sigh. "Ellie. I'm glad you're here. You're safe. Don't ever go back, can you promise me that?"

"Absolutely, I won't be going back." I respond honestly because I know I won't. There's is no reason that I ever would.

"This is home!" Sonja explains as she pulls into a new build duplex house. It is a cute grey blue shade with a pretty white porch. She explained to me how she had to have it but the rent is at the high end of her affordability. Since I start my job next Monday and I have my own savings, I felt fine being that room-mate for her. I can see why already she felt the pull to have this place. Sonja grabs my hand tightly before helping me get suit-cases out of her SUV.

"I'm going to need to buy a car." I state.

"Yup! Good thing your Pops has your back there."

"Oh, for sure! Something American too. Pops about had a stroke when I told him Brett bought me a BMW to drive." I roll my eyes and Sonja laughs.

We walk into a foyer with a coat closet to one side under the stairs, then into a cozy living room with a fire place in the corner. Sonja obviously lives here with her fluffy white couch, big grey pillows and general girly, rustic flair throughout the room. Behind us and tucked behind a wall from the foyer is the kitchen with gorgeous grey blue cabinets, new stainless appli-ances and a large window to the front and a bigger window to the side yard that lets in a ton of light. Feminine, light and classic, just like Sonja.

"This is perfect babe!" I exclaim to her.

"Right! When it was available, I just knew I needed it. It's been tight and I have been putting off getting a roommate by snagging extra shifts."

"Thanks for talking me into helping you." I say as I bump her shoulder. She shows me up to the guest room. It's plain with just a bed and solid blue comforter. Sonja says she didn't know how to decorate it at first, then she planned on a roommate so she left it. We head to the last door in the hall where a small but perfect bathroom is located. A classic white marble van-ity top and black fixtures sits on top of solid wooden drawers for the sink vanity. A modern sliding glass door with black brackets frames the shower and opens up to marbled subway tile and black fixtures.

"It's small, but it's all yours. I have my own bath in the master so I never use this one." Sonja says pulling me from my aweing at how gorgeous her home is.

"It's perfect." I tell her.

"Great, get settled. I'm ordering take-out then we'll go see your parents." She leaves me upstairs and I plop on the guest bed looking around.

Wow, the last 24 hours have been crazy. I mean, I've planned this out for a while but to actually be here, to be home. It feels right. In my new room, I open up my suitcase and put away a few things in the closet. Honestly, it's a big closet and has some built in organizers and drawers so I don't think I'll even need a dresser. While sorting through clothes I pick out an outfit for the night. I have a leather jacket that is still at my parents, I loved it and would match perfect. Brett never let me wear stuff like this and hated the leather jacket but it was my favorite thing. I decide I'll grab it when I'm there. After showering, dressing, light makeup and letting my hair dry natural with a little anti-frizz oil, I head down to find Sonja digging into pizza.

"I've missed thin, crispy, brick oven deliciousness. Texas is just not up to par."

Sonja giggles as she slides the box across the counter to me. The she starts singing her words, "Eat up, I'm getting you drunk!"

I laugh and respond before shoving pizza in my mouth. "Not too drunk, I have appointments with the lawyer, DMV and car shopping all tomorrow."

"Damn girl. You're for real, no breathe time?"

"I can breathe when it's all done and I can pretend like it didn't happen."

"Ellie..." Sonja says softly, concern etching across her face. She sighs, "Maybe you should throw a therapist in there."

"Sonja - " I start but she shakes her head and waves her hand cutting my words.

"You know I work around it babes. Plus, I have one. It's good. We've both been through a lot. I mean look at everything all through high-school, then you went through a whole life of stuff the last 5 years. Just try it is all I'm asking."

I nod, Sonja is a nurse in a rehab clinic part time and an ER nurse the rest of the time. They do inpatient and outpatient care as well as run a lot of different recreational programs. "Anyone you recommend? Non rehab-y?" I joke, but honestly that's the last thing I need is people thinking that I came home because of a habit. It is a small town, wordy gossip like that will get around fast.

Sonja laughs. "I'll get you names, but just because they work with rehab patients doesn't mean that's all they do."

"Gotcha". I respond with a nod.

We finish our pizzas up before Sonja assess my outfit. "Is that what you are wearing? 'Cause Pops will flip if he sees that bruise."

"Yeah, but I have a leather jacket there I'm going to wear."

Sonja's eyes widen. "*The* jacket?" I nod but don't say anything. It's been 9 years and I've been married, plus who knows where he is. It doesn't mean anything anymore but it is still my favorite thing to wear. "Grab a sweater from the hall closet just in case. Don't want Pops freaking out and keeping you home."

Again, I nod at her, "Good idea".

"And Ellie..." Sonja looks at me sadly. I hope that ends soon because I'm not broken. I refuse to be broken and I'm happy now that I'm home. "You know what, never mind. It wasn't important. Let's go." She says shaking her head.

After putting away left-over pizza and grabbing a sweater, we head to my parents. I'm pretty nervous because it has been a while. I feel terrible, I haven't seen them or spoken with them as much as I should have. I am also nervous because now Sonja brought up the history of the jacket and all those memories keep flooding back. I can only hope that it all is just because I am back for good that all those things are coming up. It would really suck for me and my need to come back to myself as a person if they keep attacking my mind. There would be no putting off seeing a therapist if that was the case. Promising myself it is just because I'm home and it'll bury back down, I take a deep breath as we head off.

Chapter 3 - Ellianna

"My Baby!!" Momma screams running from the house. Sprinting to Sonja's barely parked car.

"Hi Momma! I've missed you." I hug her tightly while she practically drags me from the car.

"I've missed you so much baby. I'm so glad you're home."

"Me too Momma, me too."

"Come girls, inside. Ben was fixing coffee." Momma says using her hands to shoo us towards the house.

"Coffee in the evening?" I ask Momma.

"We are old now; we get tired quick." Momma laughs out.

"I'd love coffee, taking this one out tonight to celebrate her homecoming!" Son exclaims.

Momma smiles and hugs Sonja to her. She might as well be my sister since my parents have always accepted her like a daughter and not just my friend. Walking into my childhood home, I immediately cherish the smell. I have missed the scent of cinnamon; coffee and that citrus cleaner Momma has always used.

"Evening girls!" Pops comes around the corner grabbing Sonja in a hug and handing her a cup of coffee before embracing me tightly. "You have no idea how happy I am that you are home Ellie." He says keeping me pulled tight to him.

We talk over coffee, planning out a weekly Sunday dinner since I'll be living with Sonja. All my change of address forms and stuff will still be here though. Pops thinks it is best. He's been filled in on the bare minimum and knows how the divorce will most likely be messy. Momma has told me before that they both speculated more was going on but I don't want them worrying too much. Pops also makes a point that I stop in tomorrow for a car. He insists it will be in his name even if I make the payments. He doesn't want Brett to try to get his hands on anything that is mine. I grab a few things from my old room and pack them into Sonja's SUV. I didn't take everything with me to Texas and Momma wouldn't move or throw anything out. It's helpful now.

"Here it is babes." Sonja says as she pulls the leather from the hall coat closet.

"Oh good! I loved this thing; I look hot in it." I run my fingers over the embedded design in the left sleeve of the leather. It's indented in the shape of a Phoenix rising up off my arm, in high-school I wanted the design tattooed in the same place of my arm but in vibrant orange and red shades. I shrug into it after taking the sweater off. It looks perfect with my tight black ripped up skinny jeans and a strappy crop top that crosses over my ribs and abdomen forming triangular cutouts on my sides and one in the center at the base of my sternum. It still fits perfectly, cutting tighter at my waist and flaring back over my hips and while it smells like leather it's lost its other scents. Letting the memories fade with disappointment.

"You do look hot in it." Sonja excitedly exclaims.

"Brett would never let me wear leather. I got a pair of leather pants that were super-hot once and he lost his mind."

Son laughs, "Seriously? Girl, that should have been your sign right there. Leather suites you."

"Yeah, it does! Ugh! He said it looked washed up and trashy."

"Stuck up prick" I couldn't agree more as Sonja and I laugh together. I feel lighter than I have in 9 years.

"You girls be safe tonight." Pops calls to us.

"Always Pops" Sonja and I say together.

"I'll carry this." He picks up the last bag of random stuff and walks us to Sonja's SUV. "Love you girls, both of you."

"We love you too, Pops" We say together as we each kiss a cheek. It's almost funny how her and I have slid back into our friendship like I wasn't gone for almost 5 years. We pull up to a bar off main, there's a bunch of motorcycles parked which strikes me as abnormal for this town.

"Love this place!" Sonja screams hopping out of the car.

"I just want some tequila and maybe some dancing!"

"They have both!"

It's super loud when we walk in. The floor is full of people and classic rock blasts through the speakers. Now I know why Sonja loves this place. She grabs us two shots of tequila and some tequila grapefruit drink special she says is amazing and we head over to a space by a bar rail that lines the wall.

"This place is so us! When did it open?" I ask.

"Three or so years now."

"Really?!"

I have been so out of the loop from home I didn't even know a place like this was here. It's packed, obviously popular. There are a few rougher looking guys in leather and I notice what looks like a Phoenix stitched on the backs of a few of them. There are also a few girls that could use more clothing but otherwise it's a casual vibe that I dig.

"Let's dance!"

"Yesss babes!" I yell over the music as we make our way to the dance floor. Three or four songs later and we head back to the bar for more tequila. "Babes, I've missed this!" I say, genuinely enjoying myself for the first time in so long.

"Me too" She says and I feel warm knowing my friend still loves me and missed me too.

She grabs my hand tight and grips it as the doors to the bar are thrown open and two tall men in leather step in. Everyone seems to acknowledge them like they mean something in here which I find weird. I don't even know who they are... at least I don't until I see those ice blue eyes scan the room. "Cole...." I half whisper and half choke out as Sonja tightens on my hand. I grab our drinks from the bartender and lead us to the back of the bar far, far away from the only other man besides my soon to be ex-husband, I've ever had an interest for. "Fuck, Sonja. What is he doing back? He fucking dipped, ghosted, disappeared off the face of the fucking earth." I whisper yell at her.

"I was going to tell you, but I didn't think he would be here on a random weeknight." She leans into me so I can hear her.

"How long Sonja?

"Almost four years, it was a few months after you left." She says and my jaw drops as I take in that little bit of information no one found fit to tell me all this time.

"Whatever, in the past. He left, I ran off and got married. Oh well. Drinks up!" I cheers Sonja as she watches me uneasy, not buying a word I said. Hell, I don't buy a word I said. I'm not going to let him rattle me though. The past is meant to stay there for a reason. We go back to dancing a little before we make our way to the bar for round three. Just as Sonja is ordering, I feel a hand grab my left arm.

"WHERE THE FUCK DID YOU GET THAT JACKET?" His voice hasn't changed in 9 years. It's still that low soothing growl that sends chills down my spine and aches my core. Though his tone sounds deadly right now.

I spin to face him, balling my fist at my side. He growled at me about the jacket he gave me and I'm not about to have him pulling shit with me after he was the one that disappeared.

Our eyes meet and I lose my words for a moment. He's searches my face like he has seen a ghost. "You fucking gave it to me Cole, or did you forget when you fucked off to where ever it was you fucked off too?" My voice is low and seething as I hurl angry words at him.

"L?" He breathes out as he drops his hand from my arm and steps back like I burned him.

"In the flesh." I say dryly with a sarcastic smile.

Sonja puts a drink in front of me and I take it while still having a stare down with Cole. Fucking Cole. "If you're good, I'm just going to go back where we were." Son tells me and I nod so she knows I was listening to her whisper in my ear.

"Where's your husband?" Damn small town making everyone know everything.

"Texas."

"Why are you here?"

"Is this 20 questions? Why are you here?"

"This is my bar. Why are you here?"

"Your bar? Wow. Good for you Cole. Now, if you'll excuse me." I growl the words out, my anger that I thought was buried deep, deep down is coming off me in waves. I go to walk away but his hand grabs my arm again. He leans in to my ear to whisper. His sandalwood and leather scent fills my nose.

"Finish your drink and get the fuck out." Is he kidding right now? I scoff and shoot him a "if looks could kill" glare as I make my way back to Sonja. I finally see her and she's chatting with the other guy that came in with Cole.

" Babes!" Sonja yells. "You okay?" She drops her voice to whisper.

I nod and turn to the guy. "I'm peachy, who's your friend?"

"Chris, but most people around here call me Gunner." The guy responds.

He's attractive and reminds me of Cole. He is as tall as Cole but leaner across his arms and chest. Cole has always been tall, lean but solid and wide across the chest. Chris' hair is long, past his shoulders, blond and unruly. Cole's hair is longer than I ever remember him keeping it but falls neatly around his face. Cole's eyes are like the icy blue depths that sunk the titanic, while Chris has bright blues like a clear sky.

"Big difference between Chris and Gunner." I joke back at him. I've always found it odd when people take weird nicknames.

"I've always liked guns, it stuck. Who are you pretty lady?"

"Ellianna, but Ellie to most."

Cole then shouts Gunner loudly over the crowd and music. He still sounds pissed off. "Gotta go. Sonj, I'll call you." Chris winks and walks off.

I turn to question Sonja but she cuts me off immediately. "Don't ask. Things here are a little different since Cole came back."

"I see. Well, he's kicking us out so call it a night?"

"He is not!" She exclaims.

"Sonja, you brought me to his bar. He's not happy I'm here for whatever reason, so he said finish this drink and leave." I say as I shake my glass, mostly ice at this point.

"What an ass. Whatever. I work tomorrow and you have a big day." She finishes her drink and after setting our glasses on the bar we leave. The whole time I felt eyes on me. I can't believe Cole. Who does he think he is coming back after leaving for so long then treating me like I'm the most intolerable person he has ever met? And who is he coming around like he owns the whole town? He says that bar is his but people there treated him beyond that, like he was a king to them is all I can think of how to describe it. I wasn't expecting any of this as my home coming. I also can't believe no one has told me, words will be exchanged over that one.

If it was only a few months after I left for Texas, I wasn't married yet. All I can think on the way home is that I would have come back. I would have come back then for Cole.

Chapter 4 – Cole

"Prez, Tech got a couple of new toys in." I hear Chris say making me look up from the paperwork on my desk. Chris also known as Gunner is my cousin, my best friend, VP and right hand. I met him after my uncle came to town 9 years ago to take me with him to his motorcycle club. I didn't even know then I had family other than my uncle. Once we got back to my uncle's clubhouse, he introduced me to his nephew and my cousin. My mom had a sister too. Someone, I never knew.

Him and I, we just clicked. We were on the same page on things when it came to the club. We loved the thrill of the ride but hated how the prez ran things there. They pulled money from drugs and putting people in the ground, we weren't about that. Not that either of us have clean hands now. I spent almost 6 years learning contacts and getting our plan together while Chris spent 3 of those overseas as a sniper. Finally, we made it out of there. We made it back here to my hometown. The place where my mom raised me before she became an addict; The place where I met L. Now we run things here, just like we had originally planned 9 years ago.

High tech weapons are where the money is, funny thing is most of those contracts go to government, military, police and security firms. Between that and investing in real estate and legit businesses, we do pretty well for the club. We also have multiple new housing buildings here that we had built and we invested in the bar when it was an available store front. They make for easy money covering as well as their own sources of income for the club. Plus, Tech subcontracts to the government on occasion with his computer hacking skills. We are almost as legitimate as they come with pretty expendable income.

I'm proud of what we built and continue to build, no one in the club goes without. Everyone down to the prospects are clean, drug free and well cared for. The community as a whole is thriving, we are actually benefiting this place instead of being a plague.

"Let's go see Tech and test the toys then Gunner." I say standing up from my desk and heading into the locked down basement. Tech, his real name is Paul, he practically lives down there. The dude has some insane skills. He can hack like no one else but knows who to hack and when. As much as we enjoy the extra funds from the government when they call, we don't need to lose Tech to them. When our paths crossed, he was more than happy to come in on our plans and be my left hand. He's also technically a VP, though he takes a more backseat roll with it. Plus, he is our tech guy of course.

"Hawk, Gunner." Tech greets us with a nod as he hops from his computers sprinting to the weapons room.

The basement is his domain. Chris, Paul and I have full access with our fingerprints while the rest of the club can only make it to the security room which doubles as a lockdown shelter. We built into a hill so most of the basement is actually in the hillside and not directly under the house. It is hidden by a false wall; just in case someone gets wind of us and tries to raid us or some shit like that. Funny enough it probably won't be the military or cops since they buy most our stuff, it would be other MCs that want what we have.

"This is cool shit. Came from Italy." Tech says giddy, he's like a damn kid when it comes to new toys he can play with.

Rubbing my hands together I chuckle. "Ahhh Tony, my man got us hooked up again."

"Yeah Prez, all the pieces we need for production of two things. One is a scope with infrared and night vision that also takes account for wind and other objects to make anyone almost as accurate as this fuck here." Tech punches Gunners shoulder.

"No one is as good as me." Gunner complains. Always gun obsessed, I wasn't surprised when they wanted him as a sniper. Worked out since our military contracts are because of his good ins.

"What's the other?" I ask. He did say two items, scope is one.

"Living Armor." Tech replies. Gunner and I share a look at Paul. We look at him like he has extra heads. We deal mostly with guns, minimal explosives and hardly ever armor. We can't make armor high tech and that's our thing. We get the pieces from the Italians, although the Russians have pitched in a time or two. Then we put together, with Tech's touch, the best weapons possible. Paul rolls his eyes at us. "This is tech, let me show you... give me your jacket."

"Absolutely not." I snort out. We all have jackets, it's our thing. Most MCs just have cuts and we do but I've always been a jacket guy. So, we have jackets too and all tend to wear them instead of a vest. Ever since I got L hers it just seemed right to have a jacket. I've had my jacket for as long as L has had hers, mine is worn from the years now with new patches sew in, where she has probably tossed hers but still. Noone touches my jacket. "Gunner, give Tech yours."

"Yeah, whatever man. You are so touchy about your jacket." Gunner says as he slips it off and hands it over.

I shoot him a glare. He doesn't know that much about my life before we met so he wouldn't fully get it. He knows that I originally came back here for a girl named L and that I always planned on coming back for her but that's about it. Once we got here, L was already gone and that changed the plan a bit. The town was getting run down by drugs, businesses were leaving and the community I had left nine years prior was a shell of what it had been.

Tech takes his jacket. "Thanks, Gunner. Now, I'm going to put this chip here and line the inside with this." He says as he holds up a bottle of liquid. He does what he says then lays the jacket on a table under some blue lighted box.

"This is weird, what the hell man?" I say, annoyed.

"Shut up for once, Hawk and give me a minute." Tech shoots a glare before typing on his computer. When he's done, he picks up the jacket hanging it on a target before pulling his Glock and emptying his clip into Gunner's jacket.

"What the fuck man!?!" Gunner yells out.

Paul doesn't say anything, he just pulls the jacket down and gives it back to Chris. It looks like it was never touched.

"Blanks?" I ask, wondering if Tech was just fucking around.

"Nah. Nanotechnology. His jacket is now bulletproof armor. Not all the kinks are worked out yet, but it should last about 6 months or 15 high-powered hits, whichever comes first. I'm working on trying to make it last longer." Tech explains.

"Dope. We can line standard BDUs and help our troops." I respond as Chris is still checking out his jacket.

"That's the goal. Want to get it up to a year and 50 or so hits first."

I'm impressed. "Good keep working. Might as well do all the guys jackets for now just in case. " Paul nods at me. I continue, "We sell the scopes now though, plus we have that Eagle order and the M9s for chief here. Next ship should be the M16s. So, get this shit done. There is too much in my house. Pull Blaze and Jax to help."

"Got it Prez." Tech says. He takes my jacket to do the armor thing then we head back out of the weapons room. I look around Paul's set up at the monitors. A wall of screens that hold all the security cam feeds from our properties and multiple feeds from around the clubhouse. A feed from one of the streets with several of our houses catches my eyes. A flicker if wavy blonde hair, curves and blue ocean eyes that makes my heart stop.... blinking and rubbing my eyes, she's gone. Great, now I'm seeing shit. Every time I get touchy about my damn jacket it happens, maybe I should just toss the thing.

"Anything else?" I ask before ascending the steps.

"Nah." Paul shakes his head.

"I've got rounds to make. Meet you at the bar later? Need to do drop and pickup." Gunner asks.

Nodding, "Fine. Get it done."

....

Parking my bike at the bar I look up to see Chris waiting.

"'Sup Prez."

"Everything good today?"

"Perfect."

I nod in response to Gunner and we walk into the bar doors. I need a drink. My head hasn't focused since seeing that wavy blonde hair earlier.

"Evening boys!" Beck, the bartender and Tech's wife and old lady calls out to us. I've never liked the old lady term but some MC things don't die. Some members as well as Tech and Gunner contribute it to the fact that I didn't grow up in MC life, I grew up and was forced into it later. We make our way around the bar. We scope it out nightly and swap cash in the office. Towards the back of the bar, I catch that wavy blonde hair again. "What the fuck?"

I must have actually spoke out loud because Gunner asks "What?" As he perks up looking around. Before I can answer Brianna plops her ass on my lap. "Hi Baby. I've missed you."

I push her off me and stand. The exact opposite of L. Dark hair, brown eyes. She's attractive enough and we had a decent deal at one point where she came at my call and didn't get pissed when I toss her out immediately. She gets stupid though, like now. I hate people touching me and she thinks she can jump in my lap. I haven't even called her in at least a month. "Not now Bri."

"But it's been forever, Hawk." She wines.

It has been a while; I haven't even wanted to see her face. The last time I was fucking her I kept seeing L in my head. Apparently, I slipped and called her kitten. She got all excited about it and I about died inside. My dick sure as hell went limp and died then. "I fucking said not now Bri."

That wavy blonde hair flashes at the corner of my vision again and I'd know that jacket anywhere. Shoving Bri out of my way again, I push through the crowd to the blonde waves. What the fuck, that can't be L. Someone has her jacket and that's not okay, I'll rip the thing off them. I reach her and grab her arm. "Where the fuck did you get that jacket?" I growl out. I can't help myself; I'm raging inside for two reasons. One, she gave my jacket to someone else. Two, she's fucking gone, she didn't even try waiting. She actually fucking left. Left me, left this town. Left.

Her Grams died last year and I went to the wake, stood back and watched as she cried into some preppy douchebag's arms. Later, I had Tech background her. Married old money, moved to Texas, fancy house, fancy car. Obviously, she's not the girl I loved once. She grew up and changed. Then wavy blonde turns to face me. "You fucking gave it to me Cole, or did you forget when you fucked off to wherever it was you fucked off to?" She is pissed. Feisty as ever. Her bright deep ocean eyes, perfect curves, plump begging lips. Stunned, I'm staring and must have said her name.

"In the flesh." She responds.

Well obviously. Not that I can believe my eyes. I look down and see there's no rings on her left hand. Money wasn't good enough for the little princess? "Where's your husband?" I blurt out, because I can't help but know.

"Texas."

Interesting. Why come back here though? I ask as much and she's still feisty as ever about her answers. Maybe her mouth got her into trouble, the Brett guy seems the type to want his woman one way and one way only. Maybe he got tired of that pretty mouth of hers.

"This is my bar. Why are you here?"

"Your bar? Wow. Good for you, Cole. Now, if you'll excuse me." She avoids the question again. Interesting.

"Finish your drink and get the fuck out." I say wincing after. I don't really want her gone, but I do. I need her gone. I leaned into her and her scent, it's still there. That vanilla and cinnamon sweetness. Now is not the time to try to get involved with her, so I tell her to leave. Maybe it's instinct now, a way of self-protection. She left me. I left too, but I didn't have a choice. I would have come back for her; I did come back for her.

"Fuck!" I step to the bar yelling. "BECK! I NEED A DRINK!"

Beck jumps and pours whiskey in a glass. I never yell at her; I never yell at women actually. I didn't really mean to yell.

"Wanna talk about it?" She asks sliding my drink.

"No."

"When ya do... ya know where I am." She taps my hand and runs back across the bar pouring drinks and taking money.

I look over and see Chris talking with L. Absolutely, not happening. He's been sniffing around Sonja enough and I try to avoid her as much as possible. "GUNNER!" Apparently yelling is my MO tonight.

He rushes back over to me. Fucking good. I don't really want to fight my best friend over L needing some rebound. Although I always thought he was interested in Sonja. Do have to admit though, I've tried pushing him away from her. I just can't look at her know L is gone.

Fuck.

L IS BACK.

FUCK.

Chapter 5 - Ellianna

I'm sitting in the lawyer's office first thing in the morning. It's probably fine that Cole kicked me out of the bar because I was up bright and early ready to go.

"Okay, so looking all this over... you really don't want to try for any of his money Ellianna? You never signed a prenup, it's yours too." Reba says. She's young, if I remember right, she was in Cole's grade. She got into Harvard on a scholarship and came back here a few years ago to settle into the easiness of this town with her young kids. She's more attractive now than in school. She used to be sickly thin, she's filled out and look healthy and happy. Her red hair is still just as long and flowy.

"You can call me Ellie, and no I just want out. Entirely."

"Okay, that should make things easier than. Give me 10 to write up some documents for you to sign then we will send them certified." She says, sorting through papers.

"Also, I need you to send him your contact information. I am using my parents address here and I got a new phone and number. I mailed him back all his cards and phone already. This is the tracking number on that package as well, he has to sign for it."

"You want no contact?"

"None. It's also best if he doesn't know where I am physically living either which is why I'm using my parents address. He already knows where they live and you know Pops will protect his girl."

She looks concerned at me. "Ellie, did he hit you?"

"No." I answer truthfully. "He grabbed me when I was leaving. I still have a good bruise on my wrist." Pulling up my sleeve, I show her and she winces.

"I'm taking pictures of that. Any witnesses?"

"The Uber driver."

"Can I get a copy of his information?"

I agree and we exchange the contacts. She gets her pictures and I sign all the papers. It feels good. "I have to go to the DMV next. Can I change my name back?"

"Yeah, fill this out and I'll notarize it for the DMV too to make it easier."

I fill out the papers like she said, thank her and head to the DMV. Luckily, her office was close enough in town to walk. While you can drive from one end of town to the other in 30 minutes most things are spaced out in that distance. DMV takes forever of course, even for a small town like this. Next stop is to see Pops. Which I should have to call an Uber for because he's on the other side of town, but as I walk out, I am greeted by two friendly faces standing next to a brand new, blacked out Chevy Blazer.

"Big sis, if you aren't the most spoiled. Here I thought the baby always got the best of it." My brother Ry says as Pops smacks him in the back of the head.

"Shut your mouth boy." Pops scolds.

With a laugh Ry says, "See what I mean?"

"Yeah, yeah. Cause Pops didn't pay for your school just for you to drop out." I snicker at my brother.

Ry mocks offense. "Hey now. It's all good. Tech school and doing body work and stuff for Pops in the service department."

"Look at you brother, all grown up." We hug. "I've missed your antics." I whisper to him before letting go.

"I've missed you too sis, I've missed you too."

I hug Pops. "Baby girl meet Betty." He says as he points to the beautifully blacked out SUV.

"Betty huh?" I ask.

Pops laughs. "Well, that first hunk of rust I got you, you named Beatrice so I figured Betty worked for the step up."

"This is mine!?" I squeal in excitement like a little girl.

"Fresh off the lot. Leased in my name. Stupidly good deal from the manufacturer, couldn't pass it up especially when my baby needed a new ride." Pop says.

"Oh my god Pops! This is amazing!"

"Fully loaded and all that."

"Everything for the princess." Ry smirks.

We always had the typical baby brother, big sister relationship. Though Momma always let him get away with all but murder before she'd let Pops step in. Me on the other hand sneezed at dinner and got scolded.

"You see Cole is back?" Ry asks. Honestly, I'm surprised he didn't say anything before, but neither did Sonja.

"Last night." I respond. "Funny that none of you ever told me."

"He's done good for this town." Pops chimes in, not even looking guilty. Apparently, no one felt the need to tell me he's been here the entire time I was married. "I don't know where he went or what happened, but the last 3 or 4 years he's been back he has really got this town and the economy turned around."

"Yeah, well, he left but apparently he thinks I'm at fault or something. He freaked out and kicked me out of his bar last night." I mutter, still pissed off about the bar.

"He did what now?" Pop asks a little stunned.

"It's okay Pops. It wasn't that bad. He just asked me to get out of his bar."

Pops nods at me and rubs my arm before he walks to the SUV, hopping in the passenger seat. I give Ry a look. "What!?"

"The fuck Ry. Pops doesn't need to be informed of such drama."

"Well, we are going to talk about that later."

"Sure, sure. Get in the fucking car Ry."

"Bossy much?"

I roll my eyes as we get in the SUV.

"Pops, this is seriously amazing! Thank you!"

"Can't have my girl hitching rides." He says all smiles. I drive, taking Pops back to the dealership.

"Sonja thinks I should go see a counselor or a therapist." I'm hesitant to Pops reaction but this is something I'd like to hear his thoughts on.

"I think that's a good idea, Ellie. I don't know what all happened but the end of any relationship is hard on the mind and emotions. I only ever want what's best for you baby girl."

"You think I should too then?"

"I know you haven't told your mother or I everything. I think it would be good to talk it out with someone, so yes." I nod as I pull into the parking lot. "Got to get back to work."

"I'm playing hooky Pops." Ry chimes in from the back seat. "Gonna catch up with Princess."

"Fine, but I'll be picking you up at 5 am tomorrow morning."

"Gross Pops. That's a horrible time of day." Ry complains then turns on me. "Princess, you better appreciate me dearly for that torture Pops has planned for me."

"I didn't ask you to stick around. I was just going to go find a gym to member up at."

"Yeah? I got the place. Bye Pops." Ry waves as he takes over the passenger seat.

Pops yells back to us, "Behave! See you for dinner Sunday."

"Thank you Pops! Love you see you Sunday." I reply back and blow a kiss to Pops as he heads into the dealership.

"Spill!" Ry exclaims as soon as I begin to pull out of the parking lot.

"No. Where's this gym?"

"Corner of Crandall and Elm. It's pretty new, has trainers and classes too."

"Sounds perfect. You a member?"

"Yeah! How do you think I rock this bod?! No more football to keep me going. Been boxing there." Oh, my brother, the conceited playboy responds. Rolling my eyes, I nod and turn up the music. I don't want to dish to my brother or my parents. I feel like a failure and am embarrassed that I let things get as far as they did.

"GOING TO IGNORE ME!?" Ry shouts over the radio.

"YUP! Not talking about it!" I yell back.

Now Ry rolls his eyes before he looks out the window until we get to the gym. Ry heads to the desk and signs me in as a guest before grabbing membership paperwork. "Imma run and see if Nick is down for a session."

"Sure. I'll probably just run today. I see they have hot yoga and kick boxing classes though." I say looking at the papers he handed me.

"Two very different things Princess."

"Not really. Strength and flexibility."

We walk down a hall and Ry starts explaining the layout. "Woman's lockers are there. Once you get a membership you can get your own locker, for now your stuff is fine in your bag.

No one will touch it."

"Thanks for this Ry."

He nods and heads to the men's locker. I change into a long sleeve sport crop top. It's loose and flexible but has a crisscross band at the ribs to keep it in place. It came with matching joggers that have the same style banding at the waist and ankle cuffs. Grateful that I even have long sleeve running shirts since I rarely needed them in Texas. I don't need anyone seeing my wrist. That will be a whole conversation I don't want to get into with baby brother. I get back into the hall only to have Ry having a fit. "Jesus Ellie. Could you not?"

"What?"

"Dress like that? Come on!"

"What the fuck, Ry?" I say swatting at his shoulder. He stands a good half foot taller than me, taking after Pop's.

Ry mocks at me again, "God. I hate you. The cardio room is there, I'm just going to pop into the boxing room quick."

"Let me check it out with you. I'm all for the kick boxing class." Ry mumbles fine as he stomps down the hall. Such a child, I roll my eyes and follow him. We walk into a large room with a boxing ring on one side and a large mat on the other. There's a guy hitting a bag on the far side of the room.

"Yo! Nick!" Ry yells. The guy stops punching the bag and looks up. Our eyes meet and he scans my body.

"Ry." He says as he walks towards us, still scanning me. "Who's this gorgeous lady?"

"Dude, my sister." Ry whines but it doesn't seem like Nick is paying attention since his eyes don't leave me.

"Ellie" I state as I reach my hand out. He takes it with a light shake and a wink. He is hot and I feel a little hot about it.

"Nick. Pleasure to meet you Doll."

"She's back home for good and checking out the gym." Ry says dryly.

"Nice, I do personal classes if you're interested." He winks at me again.

Heat blushes across my cheeks, "I might be." I flirt back.

"Don't make this weird. Come on." Ry exclaims.

With a laugh I respond, "You're the one making things weird little brother."

"Little? You're the baby? No wonder you're such a little shit." Nick says as he bursts into laughter and I giggle harder.

"You both suck. I was going to get in a class man, but I think I'm just going to go run."

"Nice to meet you, Nick." I wink back at him and follow Ry to the cardio room.

Ry pouts, "Come on Ellie. Don't fuck around with my friends."

"When have I ever done that?"

Ry rolls his eyes. I've been with two people in my life. Cole and Brett. I can look all I want and neither of them are part of my life now so I can do whatever I want to, if I want to. Though sex seems so unappealing, I do a much better job myself.

"Wanna make a bet?" I say to Ry as I push his shoulder.

He grumbles his response, "On what?"

"I can do 5 miles faster than you!" It's risky, Ry has always been athletic and in shape but I think I've got this.

"You're on for that! What's the stakes?" A smile finally returning to his face.

"Loser buys dinner and drinks! No pizza since Sonja and I had that and the leftovers since I got in."

Ry snorts then holds his hand out in front of him, "Deal. You're losing anyway."

We shake hands, sealing the deal. "Shall see about that!"

35 minutes later I'm cooling down and stretching while laughing at Ry. He was a solid half mile behind me and I really ran out the last mile to beat him almost a mile outright.

"Who knew you kept in shape?" Ry says before finishing his 5 miles and joining me stretching.

"Oh of course. It was the one time of day I got away to myself."

"If it was that bad Ellie. Why did you leave here? Or why didn't you come back earlier?"

I sigh as I keep stretching. "It's complicated Ry. It wasn't bad at first."

"What changed?"

"He did? I did? I don't know. He kept pushing to control me more and more, he would yell for hours if I was late or didn't do something up to par for him. I hated that stupid job he got me and the only time I had to myself was when I could run. That was fine of course because I was meant to be the fucking trophy wife." I'd had my head down stretching my quads while I rambled to Ry. I just kind of let all of it out without meaning to. When I look up my eyes burned into those icy blues across the room. I hadn't even heard the door open. Fuck, did he hear me?

"Shit." I say out loud and Ry looks up like he was about to say something and sees Cole too. Cole turns and stalks out of the room.

"Oh... shit, Ellie. I didn't think." Ry says softly. "Going to chase him or not?"

I get up and run out if the room. I have no idea what propels me to do that, but I do. Looking down both sides of the hall I don't see him. Taking the way away from the lockers I peak into the rooms until the last door, the boxing room. Pushing the door open, it is there I see him. Shirt off, fists unwrapped and hitting the bag like his life depends on it. Slowly I approach him. I don't know what he heard or what's in his head and I don't even know what to say to him. Still, I keep stepping forward.

"Cole." He keeps punching the bag.

I try again. He's still punching, I see his knuckles are breaking open and bruising.

"COLE!!" I scream at him while I reach out and put my fingers on his shoulder.

His body tenses and he finally stops punching. "You're bleeding Cole."

"What do you care, L?" Ouch, well that is a metaphorical dagger to my chest.

"Of course, I care Cole. I've always cared. Even after you disappeared, I still care. I didn't know if you were alive or dead but I had faith you were alive because I knew I would have felt it in my soul if you weren't." Then quietly I say the rest. "At least that's what I told myself to live."

"I was fine, obviously."

"Why did you leave?"

"Had to." He says but he's not looking at me. He's just staring down at his bleeding knuckles with his jaw clenched.

"Who are you pissed at then? Me? Or yourself?"

"Fuck off L!" He yells.

That sparked something in me, I'm angry and I'm ready to fight. "Why!?" I scream pushing at his shoulders. "Why Cole? What the fuck? Why did you fucking leave me?" I'm screaming at him, all the volume I can muster is coming out of my lungs and echoing through the room. All of the anger I have built up in me for the last nine years just pours out.

"Fuck off L!" He screams back at me. His body is tense.

"No! Tell me!" I yell back.

With his voice still raised he responds, stone-faced. "What does it matter? You left too! I came back for you and you were fucking gone!"

I scoff at that. Really, he is pissed at me? "What? I was supposed to just put a hold on my life for you? I didn't even know where you were! You could have been dead! I didn't fucking know where you were!" I hiss the words at him as I shove him in the chest over and over.

"Stop it L! Just fucking leave!" He shouts in my face.

I stop in my tracks; my arms drop to my sides. "Leave?" Tears threaten to come as my vision blurs and I blink them back. I won't cry for him again. "Fine. It's what you're good at anyway. Bye Cole. At least one of us can fucking be courteous enough to actually say bye." I growl the words out before I turn and toss my arm up in a wave.

I hear a thud of something hitting the bag hard again as I reach the door, not turning back I make my way to the lockers to see Ry lingering.

"Take it you two didn't kiss and make up?" He says with a stupid smirk on his face.

"Fuck off, Rylie!" I yell at him using the name he hates.

"Okay Princess. We'll circle back to this over drinks."

I roll my eyes, "I'll text Sonja. You're still buying."

Chapter 6 – Ellianna

After grabbing my stuff from the lockers, we leave the gym. Ry keeps trying to talk to me. I'm seriously not interested in it. I'm seething over my encounter with Cole. He wouldn't even give me a straight answer but apparently, he thinks it's me to blame because I didn't wait? Or my fault he left to begin with. I don't get his rationale for being angry at me.

I sure as hell didn't make him leave and if he came back almost 4 years ago why is he now just showing his face to me. He wasn't even there when Grams died. How can he be mad at me that I left when he left first?

Nine years prior

"Mmm, Kitten. You always feel like heaven." Cole says softly.

Laying in the back of his old beat-up pickup truck, staring at the stars. We are at our spot deep down a dirt road outside of town.

I snuggle tighter to his chest; the night air is cool for summertime and we are only wrapped in a light sleeping bag Cole keeps in his back seat.

"You're done with school officially tomorrow. Now what?"

He sighs as he speaks. "I'm not sure yet Kitten, but you're mine and I'm yours. It'll always be you until all these stars burn out. I'll always find my way back to you."

"That sounds like perfection love." I whisper.

"I think so too." He whispers back as he traces circles on my back. "You have one more year, then what?"

"I don't know. College for marketing, I think. I'd like to travel some, see the world." I respond, snuggling my body tighter to his.

He chuckles at me, "Always so much spunk."

I giggle climbing on top of him. "Always with you." I whisper in his ear straddling his waist I feel him growing beneath me again.

Placing kisses down his neck and chest he grabs my ass and I feel my wetness increase before I feel him gently slide into me.

———————————

"Ellianna!" I hear Ry yell pulling me from my thoughts.

Looking at him, I respond "What?".

"I've been talking to you this whole drive and you're all in your head! What the hell happened?? You need to talk to me Princess." He's practically begging and concern is etched across his face.

"I really don't want to talk about it, Ry." I don't, nor do I want to tell him what I was just thinking about, the memory of the last night I seen Cole before he disappeared. Yeah, that'd be great. Sharing with little brother the amount of sex his sister had in high school. Sometimes, I reflect back and think how lucky we got that I didn't get pregnant. Some shit show that would have been since he left without a word or contact. I texted and called him repeatedly for a full year until someone else got his number and I got an ear full on an answered call.

"Well Ellie, you know what? Fuck him. Fuck men for that matter. You don't need them. We are all a bunch of assholes anyway. Get your life back sis." He says, completely stoneface serious.

I laugh at his response. "Coming from a man, that's gold Ry."

"I'm serious Ellie. Obviously, a lot has happened to you and I just miss my sister."

"You're right Ry. You are right." I sigh. "For now, let's just binge on some food and booze!"

Ry calls in an order of food for delivery after grabbing several bottles from the liquor store and we head to Sonja's. My place now, as weird as it is to say. Sonja and I roomed together at college and shared my rusty old Beatrice car. So, it's nothing new, it's just striking to me how much things have fallen back into place being home. Other than Cole, but honestly what do I even do with that. He's so angry.

Ry is right. I need to focus on myself, and myself alone. I need to get Brett to actually sign the divorce papers and I need to move on with my life as my own person. I know Brett is going to put me through hell about it though, especially since his family is very catholic and very traditional. They care too much about appearances. Maybe I should declare another religion and see if he'll have us annulled based off that.

Thoughts are running through my mind on how to get divorced as I shower and change into lounge clothes, complete with long sleeves. I hope this damn bruise heels fast because I'm running out of clothing options. I should plan a shopping date with Sonja. My Texas attire did not consist of warm clothing I'll need come fall time here. Plus, I could use some decor for this room. Maybe a desk or something. It's a pretty big room considering it's the spare.

"Babes! Food!" Sonja hollers through the closed door pulling me from my thoughts.

"Coming!" I yell back. I'm glad she always got along with my family. Ry is like her little brother too, annoying and all. She's been with him for the last 20 minutes since we got back from the gym and I'm sure he's driven her nuts by now.

I bounce downstairs with the fakest smile I can muster like there isn't a million and one things running through my sad stressed-out mind. My heart aches for Cole more than it did when he disappeared, it doesn't even make sense because it's been so long.

Chapter 7 – Cole

After getting ice packs and taping them around my knuckles, I leave the gym. Punching that bag until it broke only left my knuckles busted up and didn't diminish my anger. Time to ride and clear my head.

All my mind keeps replaying is her talking to her brother. That preppy douche of a husband yelled at her, wanted her to be his trophy wife. She's so much more than that. How could she even let him do that? Obviously, she's not the same person I left here. She was so spunky, so feisty and independent. She glowed when she broke and bent rules but still focused hard on life and school knowing she wanted to make something productive and professional come from her hard work.

She looks the same, smells the same but her glow isn't the same. It's dull. Even when she was angry pushing me the fire that she always had behind her eyes was barely there. She's not the same and I can only be mad at myself. I left her. I broke her. It is all on me, even if it wasn't my choice to leave. I would never purposely hurt her, but I did. I tried to tell her that last night but couldn't. I just wanted to feel her one last time.

So now, I ride. I turn down backroads and let loose on the throttle when I know the road stretches straight long enough to get that rush before I drop to take corners too fast. I just need to feel the wind, the speed, the rush. Center my mind. I walk into the clubhouse. "Prez, beat Nick's ass today or what?" Gunner says.

Taking a look at my knuckles. The ice helped a bit but they are still bruised and cut up. "No."

"I need to take someone out then?" Gunner says excitedly, bouncing on his heels.

"No" I state.

He frowns at me, "What crawled up your ass man?"

"Go away Gunner." I speak walking through the house. He should back off but that's never been Gunner's style.

"Is it that blonde chick? You know her or something?" He says and that makes me stop in my tracks and grab him by his jacket. Pulling him up so he's off balance and I am in control.

"Don't talk about her. Don't look at her. Don't fucking go near her, and do fucking not ever bring her up to me again." I growl out between clenched teeth.

"Okay man. Sorry." Gunner tosses his hands up in defense. I throw Gunner down to the floor and head down to see Tech. I need to know why she's back.

"To what do I owe this pleasure?" Tech pipes out from his computers.

I shake my head. I hate to ask, but I must. "Need a favor. A very fucking quiet favor."

He nods. "Name?"

"Ellianna Turner-Walton."

Tech turns to me and I shoot him a glare that makes him turn around and start typing. "Anything specific?"

"When and why, she came back here."

"Give me a bit. I'll text when I get something." He says, never looking up from his typing.

"Not. A. Fucking. Word. Tech." I growl out at him. Then I head out of the basement and back up to the top floor where the officer suites and my room are located. We built this place when we came here, so it is pretty modern and roomy. We may have stolen a bit to fund it but it was stolen from some shady drug dealing, human trafficking scumbags of MCs.

The top floor like the rest of the clubhouse is modern and clean with a touch of a softer rustic vibe that Beck insisted we needed so it didn't look like a straight up bachelor pad. All of the officer suites have their own bathroom, mine and Gunners are on opposite corners of the floor and are the largest suites with two sets of large windows on each wall looking over the property. On the second floor of the clubhouse are rooms and a couple bathrooms for MC members that stay when they need too. They aren't assigned and it's kind of a first come first serve basis. We have over a hundred members and a handful of prospects but most live outside of the clubhouse. Using some of the homes we have built throughout town so they can live with their families and not in the middle of the chaos that tends to happen in the clubhouse.

Then there is the main floor, it is split in half. Kitchen, dining, and large living on one side for the officers then a bar room with a smaller kitchen and space for a DJ or band and a dance floor. There's also a large meeting room on that floor right beside my office and another office for Gunner.

After a shower my phone pings with a text from Tech so I head down to him. "Anyone else down here." I ask as soon as I shut the door behind me.

"Nah man." Tech responds.

Nodding, "Good. What do you have?"

"Not a lot. Looks like she's been using an account in her and her father's name that she has had since she was 14 to fund her trip back here. She's been depositing about $50 a week in there since she moved to Texas. Plus, some random deposits from her father and a large sum after her grams died. It looks like she was putting money away to run to me. Everything else she had was in her husband's name."

"Brett Walton?"

"Yeah, big shot lawyer, old money, but you knew that already from the last time you had me look the girl up. Looks like he is in the running for partner at the firm he works at soon." Tech carries on.

I tap my fingers on the desk top, "Anything else?"

"Today, she was really busy. Changed everything back to her maiden name. Looks like she's putting everything here under her father though. I know to look around so I did some checking on our cameras throughout town and dug into her parents, that part seemed a little dirty." Tech glares at me.

"They are good people, but I need to know, brother." I respond softly, tapping Tech on the shoulder. Tech nods. I can't blame him for not liking that part. Ben and Sally are a huge part of making this town what it is. They work hard and help everyone that needs it. They have always been well respected, good people.

"Her father leased a blacked-out SUV today but the auto withdrawal is from her bank account and the insurance is in her name. Also, it looks like she's actually living with Sonja Stone even though she's put her parents address on everything."

"That is smart if she's running."

Tech nods. "Also, Ellianna went to see Reba today. Took me a second because it was paid for by her father's dealership. When it popped up, I thought odd right? Why would Ben divorce Sally? So, I hacked Reba's computer."

"Of course, you did." I snicker.

He laughs, "It's too easy since we own the building and I run all the networks there."

"Sure. What did you find?"

"Divorce paperwork. She wants nothing from the guy. Also.... ummmm." Tech rubs his face.

"What?" I growl, he only delays when he doesn't want to tell me something.

"Ummm...well..." Tech is still delaying, I don't know what he's hesitant about but it's pissing me off. So, I'm glaring at him with a death stare. He pulls up a picture of a wrist covered in bruised handprints.

"What the fuck is that, Paul!" I growl out, seething.

Tech stops delaying. I assume it is because now the worst part to tell me has been shown, "Reba's notes say, "Elliana's wrist today after an incident from 2 days ago when she was trying to leave". She noted an Uber driver witnessed the assault. "

"He put his dirty fucking hands on her?" I'm livid. Rage is rolling off me. No one touches her, I'll kill him. "I'm going to fucking kill him. Find everything on that stupid motherfucker, track his every move and if anything points to him trying to come here, I want to know immediately! And cover all that shit of hers up, who knows who he can pay to find her. Hide her." I am yelling as I pace back and forth.

Tech nods agreement but still asks, "You think you're being a little irrational, Prez? Who is this chick?"

"No! And she is none of your business! Do what I say or I'll find someone to replace you."

"You won't, but I get it. Whatever you say, Prez." Tech yells at me as I storm back upstairs.

What the hell was she thinking getting with that man? I'm still seething but I want answers. Throwing on my jacket, tucking my Glock in the side pocket I head out to my bike.

"Need company?" Gunner yells from the side door of the club-house.

"No." I growl at him.

He follows me. "You look like you're going to kill someone. You sure?"

"I'm fine. Go away Gunner." He nods but hops on his bike beside me anyway. I glare at him, "Is everyone forgetting who's in charge here?"

"Nah man, but obviously this is personal. Just making sure you don't do anything stupid." Chris retorts, starting his bike. Chris has always had my back. When my uncle took me from here, not that I can blame him. Since my junkie mom couldn't dig herself out of the hole that she fell in. He took us, she went to rehab so she didn't die and I went to work with him to pay off all her debt. The Prez there was a mean ass man. Chris and I had both been shot by the fuck on several occasions.

Rolling my eyes, I start my bike and take off for Sonja's. Hoping L is there. Pulling up I see a blacked out chevy like the one her father leased today. She's home. I see Chris park his bike a way down the street watching me as I walk up the steps. These duplexes came out really well. I was super proud of the job the crew did on these a couple years ago. I hear music and laughter as I pound on the door. I hear Ry asking Sonja about expecting friends and her no response before Ry opens the door.

"The fuck do you want?" Ry hisses out.

Oh good, the little brother is trying to be protective. "I need to talk to L."

"No." He states and crosses his arms over his chest and blocks the doorway.

"Let me in Ry."

Ry scoffs at me, "No. She's not even here."

"Don't lie to me Ry." I say as he steps out towards me and shuts the door when I hear L ask who it is.

"Listen to me good, Cole. I don't care that you and your friends came into this town like you fucking own the place. That you fixed and built a bunch of stuff and it's actually a nice place to live now, but I don't care man. I'll beat your pretty little fucking face in if you come anywhere near her. She's been through enough." He rubs his face, looking me dead in the eyes and dropping his voice. "You left. You left her and I picked up the pieces. I'm not doing it again." Then he shoves me and I have to step down so I don't lose my balance off the steps. I won't fight Ry. I know he boxes with Nick but I would wreck him, but I wouldn't do that to L's brother. "If you ever loved her Cole, do her a favor and leave her the fuck alone."

I hear the door click open and slam shut as wavy blonde hair and ocean eyes steps towards me leaving me breathless. "Ry, who are you - " her words cut off when she sees me.

"L, I need to talk to you. No more yelling, just talk to me. Please." The word feels foreign on my tongue. It's been at least nine years since I said the word please.

"Ellie, I got this. You can go back inside." Ry says.

"No Ry. It's okay." She says softly. They argue back and forth before L finally says. "It's okay. We can't live in this town yelling in public at each other all the time. It's too small, best to get this dealt with like adults."

"How mature of you." Ry retorts before rolling his eyes and stomping back into the duplex.

"Take a ride with me?" I ask as I hold my hand out. I'm not sure if I want her to take it or not. I want to feel her again but I'm terrified at the same time that touching her will fire something inside me that I won't be able to turn back from.

"Sure." She says as she grabs my hand and my breath catches. Fuck me, she still feels the same 9 years later.

Chapter 8 - Ellianna

After the gym fiasco and my long shower, Sonja and Ry kept me company with that early dinner, a few drinks and blasting music. Ry kept pushing me to talk, but I still didn't want to. Then a song came on. I sang the chorus at the top of my lungs "Let me be sad. Even for a little while. Just a chance to catch my breath. Let me be sad. Even for a little while. Cause it's all that I have left. When all I see are the memories, I don't want to lose a thing. Let me be sad, let me be sad."

The lyrics hit so close to my heart I made Sonja repeat it on her sound system four times and continued with my scream like singing. Sonja joined me by the third repeat and we even started dancing around on the furniture and getting in Ry's face.

Ry sick of us and the song finally said "I get it Princess. I'll back off."

Daylight was then starting to fade. We decided to pick a movie to watch and ease up on drinks since Ry and Sonja both had an early morning. Though picking a movie turned into a fight between the two. Sometimes, you would think they were actually siblings with the way they argue. Halfway through the movie someone was knocking on the door. Ry answered and proceeded to yell from Sonja's porch.

Sonja laughs, "Girl, you've been back like a day and you're already causing trouble."

I roll my eyes at her. "Well, if someone told me Cole was back and I'd be running into him every other turn, maybe I could have avoided this."

She snorts, "You think that's who he's yelling at out there?"

"Who else? But how would he know I'm here?" I ask, cocking my head to the side.

"He kind of owns this town babes. Him and his gang of merry men bikers." Son says with a sigh.

More confused I ask, "What are you even talking about Sonja?"

"You've been gone a long-time babe; a lot has happened." Sonja says. I listen as I stand up from the couch. "Feel free to ride off into the sunset babes."

I wave her off because there still muffled yelling and I've had enough. At this point I'm certain it is Cole, who else would Ry be yelling at. I open the door to start yelling at Ry and drop my own sentence when I get lost in those ice blue eyes. Somehow, he still affects my mind and body, I'll never understand it. After arguing with my brother more I end up on Cole's bike, though I'm hesitant about getting on.

"It's been 9 years Cole." I mumble from beside his bike.

"Bike rides the same. Hang tight and remember to move with me into turns." He says as he hands me a helmet.

I take a deep breath. Taking the helmet from him I slide it on. His hand is still extended so I take it and let him balance me as I swing a leg around to settle in behind him. My face lands close to his shoulder. He still smells the same, that leather and sandalwood scent. He takes off down the street, speeding down the main road and heading outside of town. It's always a rush on his bike, I remember him the first time he was trying to teach me to drive it.

Nine plus years prior

Cole is sitting behind me with his arms around me. His chin resting on my shoulder. "Gas, clutch, break. I'll help you steady your weight while you get the hang of this. My bike has a bit of weight you have to get used to."

"Cole, I'm going to kill us both." I respond, shaking on the bike seat. I drop my hands to my lap.

"You've got this Kitten." He responds kissing the side of my head. Then he takes my hands in his placing them back on the bars and resting his on top of mine.

"Just like this.... easy." He whispers in my ear as he guides my hand over the throttle and the bike moves forward. He keeps his hands over mine. We do this for hours up and down the back road until the sun starts setting.

"You're getting a handle on this Kitten." He says when we finally stop.

Spinning around so I'm straddling and facing him, I wrap my arms around his neck. I whisper into his lips "I'd rather get a handle on you."

"That so?" He says pulling me closer to him, pressing his lips to mine. He takes control and possession of my lips, my body and my soul.

"L?"

I cough a little clearing the memory from my thoughts as I look around and see we are in a field down an old dirt road. Our spot.... My heart skips a beat and my breath catches.

Cole looks at me concerned, "You alright L?"

"Yeah, just been a while since I've been on a bike." I admit while withholding the full truth.

He chuckles. "You used to drive mine and love it. You are telling me you never got your own?"

I shake my head in response looking down. I'm a little embarrassed not that he asks me outright. As much as I loved being on his bike or driving his bike, I couldn't bring myself to do it without him. "What brought you back?" I blurt out the question.

"Getting right to into it?" He asks back. Hopping off the bike, he helps me off. Then he digs a blanket out of one of the saddle bags. Walking over by a tree and puts it down before sitting. "Going to come over here or stand there like a scared deer?"

What an Ass, I think to myself. Though I am glad to see his rough way of being charming is still here. "You and I both know I've never been a scared deer." I retort, but it's a lie and by Cole's expression he knows it is too. Honestly, I was never scared until things with Brett started to hit my breaking points. When I was with Cole, I was fearless, reckless and felt invincible. After he left, I was so broken, and with Brett I was just lost and terrified.

"I think we both know you are a terrible liar as it is, but never have you ever been able to lie to me Kitten." He says soothingly. So, he caught my lie and called me out on it. Some things never change. Taking a big breath, I walk over to the blanket and plop myself beside him. I tuck my knees up to my chin and wrap my arms around my legs.

"What do you know about me anymore, Cole? You left?" I say softly feeling defeated.

He sighs, "It wasn't my choice L."

"You know, you are the only one that's ever called me that? It's always been Ellie or Ellianna." I sigh as well before adding "Well, other than Ry, but we know he calls me Princess because Pops has always loved me more."

Cole smirks and I tighten my arms around my legs. I watch his eyes go to my wrist and his face changes. Realizing, I quickly try to unwrap my arms and pull my sleeve back down but he catches my forearm. "Did your husband to this to you? Is this why you came running home?"

"It's not why Cole." I say, not technically acknowledging who left the bruise.

"So, he beat you? What L? Please tell me." His voice is filled with pain as he pleads. "What did he do to you L?" I let out a sigh and pull my arm back. He was barely holding on to me so he quickly dropped it. I watch him take a few breaths and watch as his face changes from pained to rage and back. That's changed about him, he's never had an uncontrollable anger in him but after what I seen in the gym and watching him now, I wonder what he's hiding that makes his rage flow out.

"This...." I sigh out, raising my arm and pulling the sleeve so he can see the full extent of the bruising. "This is the only time he's touched me with intent to harm." I watch his face again as he takes in my words and his eyes assess the bruise. He seems to collect himself but he doesn't take his eyes off the bruising as pain covers his face. "I hated the person he made me become. He made me bow to his will and isolated me." I admit. "Did you know I hadn't seen or spoken to my brother in a year before today?"

"No. Actually, I've tried to avoid your family." His response is calm and dry.

I burst into laughing. "Jesus Cole." He gives me a confused look with one brow up. "You leave and come back to pretend what? I don't exist? What did I do to you Cole?"

His response comes as he looks at the ground, "It's not like that L."

"Then what's it like Cole? Please, enlighten me " I say dryly.

"Leaving.... I didn't have a choice in the matter. Then... Then I had to do a lot of really bad shit L. Shit I'm not proud of. Shit I don't ever want to talk about. I couldn't show any kind of weakness where I went so, I was trying to protect you. I couldn't contact you, if someone found out you could have been hurt as a way of hurting me. I was going to tell you that night.... but I couldn't bring myself to do it. Honestly, I didn't know what it was going to be like there. I just knew I had to go or worse things would happen. Things to you and my mom. I couldn't let that happen." He never looks up at me, just faces the ground explaining. "Then... Coming back, you were gone. Left to be with someone else. I felt ashamed and at fault and I couldn't bring myself to even look at your family."

"You knew you were leaving?" I say between my teeth, hanging on to the part of the explanation that would have changed everything. Had he just told me he was leaving; things could have been different.

"Yeah....yeah I did..." He says with pain and guilt lacing his voice.

"So instead of telling me you buried yourself in me and made me talk about my future???" I ask and stand-up screaming at him. "What the fuck Cole!"

He cringes as he finally looks at me, "Okay, saying it that way makes it sound really bad."

"It was bad!" Still screaming at him, I pace the ground in front of the blanket.

"I didn't mean to...." His voice trails off and he looks completely defeated.

Stopping the pacing I stand in front of him. "Didn't mean to what Cole? To what? To break me? To terrify me?" Pain flashes across his face. "Cole, I called and messaged you for a YEAR! A YEAR COLE! I would have gone longer but someone else finally got your number and I took it as a hint." I'm still screaming and ranting.

"L..... the last thing I wanted to do was hurt you." He says with sincerity.

With a calmer tone I ask, "Where did you go Cole?"

"I can't really tell you L. I just need you to trust me that I did what I had to and I did it to protect you."

"Trust?" I crack with a laugh. "Cole, our trust broke the second you left."

He sighs and rubs his hand over his face and grabs at his bottom lip. It's something he's always done when he's frustrated. "Listen, my mom got into trouble. A lot of trouble with a lot of scary people. My uncle came and took us both. I had to do work for him and he helped take care of the problem. It took longer than expected and some extra stuff came out of it. When I finally got enough to get out of that mess and come back you were gone."

"Don't put that on me Cole. You left nine years ago it took you almost six to come back."

"Only took you four to leave." He retorts.

I sigh and sit back down. "five actually, four to get over you and move on with my life."

He tenses and rubs his face again. That struck a nerve. "This isn't how I expected this talk to go L."

"Why, because I'm not falling all over you?"

"I didn't expect that version either. I know that I fucked up; I don't expect you to forgive that easily. I did however expect you to be a little more understanding."

That makes me laugh, full on hysterical laughter that brings tears to my eyes. Once I finally settle, I see Cole watching me with those ice blue eyes. "Definitely didn't expect that. You're a little crazy, you know that?" He says softly.

"I've been told a time or two." I giggle. It's unsettling how easy Cole feels. He's like comfort and safety. He feels like home. I have to shake my head at that. It's just familiarity, that's all.

"I suppose that's not the first time I've told you that Kitten." I tense at the name. He always called me "kitten", said it was because I was so little and adorable until my feisty claws came out to play like a little baby kitten.

Cole rubs his face again before asking, "Are you here for good?"

"Yeah, I think so. I'm not going back to Texas that's for sure."

He nods. "That's good L. You deserve better and you deserve to be surrounded by your family."

I nod, he is spot on with what Ry and I talked about today. "Family over everything." I quote something we'd say in high-school, when Cole was my family too.

"Family over everything." He repeats back. He sits in silence as the sun officially goes down and the stars come out.

Breaking the silence, I ask; "How's your mom?"

"Healthy now." He tells me. "Rehab did her good. She moved to Florida with a lady she met a couple years ago."

"That's good...I know how hard it was for you seeing her like that. Especially after everything that had happened."

"Drugs ruin people L. They make people do fucked up stuff. I've made a point to make sure this town stays clean since I've been back." He says with confidence.

"How did you magically appear back with people and funds to buy and rebuild the whole town anyway?"

Cole turns away from me for a moment before turning back to answer. "Made friends. Connections. We were all forced into a situation we didn't want to be in so when we could we spun it for ourselves." He vaguely answers. I'm sure there's more, but if he doesn't want to tell me now then fine.

"Money is power and all that?"

"Power is power." He responds. "You just have to know how and when it's appropriate to use it."

"Very philosophical of you."

"I suppose." He pauses for a moment and his eyes fixate on mine. "I'm not the same person that I was when I left L."

"I can tell." I say softly and look down, breaking our eye contact. "I'm not the same either." We sit in silence again for a while. It's nice really, to just enjoy the comfort of his presence.

"I went to see you when your Grams passed." That got my attention and I turn to watch his face in the darkness, lit only by the moon and stars. "I wanted to see you." He pauses and looks to the sky. "It was the first time I had heard you were back since I came back and I just needed to look at you. I knew how much you'd be hurting and I wanted to be there for you." He pauses again, still looking up at the sky.

"I never saw you." I admit sadly.

He nods like he knew that I wouldn't have. "I watched you at the wake. You were crying but your husband was comforting you. I stayed back. Then, I left before everyone else. I realized you didn't need me." My heart aches as I watch him. He's still looking up but his eyes are pressed closed. If I needed anyone then it was him. Tears threatened at my eyes again and I try to blink back the blur as I turn away. "I didn't mean to make you cry again L. I never wanted to make you cry, ever." He admits and I realize just how in tune we still are to each other.

"It's fine. I just..." I take a breath trying to find the right words. "This is all a little surreal." I turn to watch him as his blue eyes scan my face. "It's kind of funny actually, in a morbid sense." I speak my thoughts. "That you took off because you thought I was fine with my husband."

"It looked that way, I didn't know L." He shakes his head.

I sigh. "Even if you did, what would you have done? Swoop in on your white horse and save me?"

He chuckles. "Black metal horse, but yeah, something like that." He smirks at me.

"Ass." I mumble.

He chuckles again. "I've missed you L." I watch his face. He looks beside himself like he doesn't know what to do next.

"Cole..." He stays quiet, watching my face. "I don't.... I don't know if I'm safe. You can't be involved. Brett isn't just going to sign papers and let me go. That looks too bad for him. Plus, I think in his own weird way he thinks he actually loves me." I take a breath before continuing with Cole watching my face still. "He's going to come eventually. He's going to make this hard for me. He will probably do everything in his power to ruin everything Pops has because he's helping and trying to protect me. I can't let him do that to you too."

"I can handle him." Cole states with complete confidence.

"You don't understand Cole. What you said about power... he has it and he uses it solely for personal gains." I take another breath; I'm speaking my heart out to Cole for some reason but the words don't come easy. "I'm scared Cole." Then I cry. I can't help it, once I admit what I've buried deep it flows out. I'm terrified and not just for me.

Chapter 9 – Cole

"I'm scared Cole." She says and I feel my heart drop in my chest. I have to protect her; this is all my fault. She never would have ended up with that dickhead if it wasn't for me. If I had just told her I'd come back. I reach over to her and pull her to my arms. This is where she belongs. I look down at her as she curls tighter into my chest lightly sobbing, she has always fit perfectly against my side. I hate that she's upset like this though. My girl has never let things get to her like this and I know how badly I've fucked up. I try to soothe her, "Kitten, he can't hurt you and he can't take you. You're not his to take anyway, never was and I'm not going to let him."

"Cole, you can't promise me that. You don't know him." She says softly.

"I have resources and my own power. I can promise all of that and your safety."

She slightly relaxes against me. "I messed up." She admits. "I can't go back to that, I lost myself." I assumed as much; that she must have to let that guy have a hold on her. She was always too strong, spunky and independent.

"What brought the real you out and wanting to come back?" I ask.

"You." She laughs against my chest. "Well, Sonja but her words struck something you used to say."

I look down at her curiously, "Me?"

"I saw Sonja for the first time since my wedding at Grams funeral. We got drinks after while Brett worked, I was interrupting a case with Grams passing, you know?"

"He told you that?" This guy is a bigger dickhead than I thought. She nods her head against my chest and I grip her tighter putting my hand in her hair. If he ever gets close enough, I'm going to beat this guy's face in.

"Sonja and I grabbed some drinks and she told me that I lost my spunk, asked if I was okay. When she said that, it all just hit me. I had lost my spunk and I wasn't okay. You always told me I was full of spunk and light." I bury my nose in her hair, the cinnamon and vanilla scents soothe me. "When she said that it broke my heart all over again, more than when you left. Not only had I lost you, I lost everything you loved about me."

I sigh and try not to curse or get angry. "I never should have left without telling you, this is all my fault."

She lifts up from my chest to pierce my eyes with her ocean blue ones. "Cole. Brett is not your fault."

"He is. You were never his to have. You were mine, always mine, still are mine." She breathes my name. My self-control is gone at this point. I lift her face to mine and take possession of her lips. It's a need right now. I need to feel her lips on mine and she needs to know that she still owns me. I'm hers and she's mine. She releases her control over to me and I press further, possessing her mouth, tasting her.

Mine.

Then my phone rings. "Fuck." I say into her mouth and she pulls away. I feel cold without her. I'm going to kill Chris. "Only emergency calls can come through kitten, I'm sorry." I say before I answer and get up stepping away.

"This better be fucking urgent, Chris."

"Yeah, yeah. Busy with the blonde and all that. This is fucking urgent Prez."

"What did I fucking tell you man?" I lowly scold into the phone. I am going to end up killing him if he keeps this shit up.

"Again, don't care because that's personal. I'll respect you when it comes to the club. Which by the fucking way, is why I am calling. Someone tried to break into the warehouse off west."

"What the fuck do you mean?" No one ever breaks into our shit. It is way to secure. The most action we've had even close to a break in was some kids drinking beer in one of the warehouses. They thought it was abandoned and were trying to be sneaky.

"Exactly what I said."

"Get Paul on it now. Shut down everything, full lockdown. I'll be back in 20." I demand, using Paul's first name instead of Tech because I know L is eavesdropping.

"Yes Prez."

Shoving my phone back in my pocket I turn to L. She already is waiting by my bike with the blanket folded. "Cuss all your friends out?"

"Work actually." I reply.

She rolls her eyes at me, "That doesn't make it better."

"I'm kind of a mean guy." Shrugging, I take a few steps toward her.

With more attitude directed at me she snorts, "yeah, right.". If only she knew. I wrap my arms around her again, mostly because I need to touch her. She calms me and I can't believe she's actually here either. "I've always loved you Cole, but we have a lot to work through before we can get back to that point, if we can get back to that point."

"Mhmmm.... We will." I kiss her forehead before taking the blanket and putting it back in my bag and helping her on my bike.

I manage to drop L off and get back to the clubhouse in just over 20 minutes.

"CHURCH!" I yell walking through the bar to the meeting room. Followed by prospects and members. The officers better be in there already or I'll have to shoot one, just to prove a point I'm sick of the disrespect this week.

"Prez." Gunner greets me.

With a nod I jump right to it. "Gunner, what do you and Tech have?"

Tech answers explaining videos he pulled. 2034 hours someone messed with the power at the warehouse trying to cut the cameras and security. There was only a 30 second lapse of power because the generators kick in. Two guys on blacked out bikes, busted up the print scanner.

"I don't like this, feels like a test run." Gunner says and I agree.

I push orders out. "Double security, put a prospect on the roof, split camera feeds to separate power sources. Prospects, no shots fired. Call in only. Double check all other properties. Back tomorrow. Nine am church. Dismissed."

There's a chorus of "yes prez" as everyone exits to do their jobs.

"Not you two back talking assholes." I announce. Gunner and Tech turn to face me smirking. I run my hand over my face trying to keep myself from beating the piss out of both of them. "We are friends, and you listen when it's work, but you're both getting on my nerves."

"Gonna fill us in on blondie then?" Gunner says and Tech shoots him a side glance. I hate them both.

"Yeah, only because I'll need your help." I admit. We move to my office where they both sit in front of my desk like a pair of giddy school girls. It's absolutely ridiculous coming from two grown men to be acting like this.

"Here to help. Does this mean I can call dibs on her friend now?" Gunner pipes in.

"No shut up."

"Can I talk to Chris about this now?" Tech asks.

"No. You shut up too." I growl. Friends? Who needs friends at this point? I rub my face again.

"Just busting your balls Hawk." Gunner mumbles.

With a sigh, I just put it out there for them both. "She might be in trouble. I fucked up once trying to protect her and just made more of a mess."

"My information is pertinent." Tech states, wiggling in his chair.

"Fine Paul, fucking what?"

"Her husband has been in contact with a PI." He blurts out.

"Great. Fucking great." I mumble. "Paul, I need you to bury everything you can that connects her to her father, same with Reba. Tag shit to me if you have to, I don't care just bury it. That PI and her fucking husband can't find anyone that leads to anyone else. Who knows what kind of shit they will try to pull to ruin people and manipulate her into coming back?"

"Would you two care to explain? Husband? You dickhead, did you steal someone's wife? What the fuck Cole." Gunner pipes in with annoyance in his voice.

"SHE WASN'T HIS TO FUCKING TAKE." Chris and Paul both jump at my outburst. I don't think I've yelled so much in my life as I have in the last 24 hours. My anger is not controlled today.

"Girl has you knotted up Brother." Gunner states with a cold tone.

"She isn't just a girl Chris." I mumble in response then watch as it clicks and his face changes.

He "ooohs" like 4 times and I'm about to reach across my desk as he says. "Ellie. Oh FUCK. She's L." I rub my face again before telling him he's right. "Married huh? You fucked up man." Gunner states.

"You think I don't know this?" I say calmly before the anger takes over again. "He put his fucking hands on her. Broke her spirit first then put his dirty fucking hands on her when she was never his to begin with." I practically hiss out at him.

"The PI move means he wants her back. It won't just be bruises on her wrist this time Cole." Tech is the voice of reason. Also, the computer genius and human profiler.

More sighing from me and I look them both right in the face. "Look, I know and she knows. She's fucking scared. I've never seen her scared of anything in my life but she's scared now. She's terrified he is going to tear apart anyone and everyone that's helping her. That's why I need you both on board with me, not just to protect her but to protect the people around her as well."

"Always Brother." They chorus.

"She's physically safe for now, but we will need a plan if he comes here. Strings from afar we can handle with Tech, but if he's here..." Before I can continue, Tech chirps in. "He's a high-status member of society. You can't kill him and you definitely can't hurt him and leave him alive. We all go to jail then."

"That's why we need a plan Paul." I glare at him.

We end up spending the rest of the night in the basement, filling Gunner in on everything. Then going back and forth on possibilities. We map out possible scenarios and how to handle them, for both L and the attempt on the warehouse. I'm itching to get my hands on someone, but for now we plan. I have to keep L and everyone she loves safe, at all costs even if Chris and Paul disagree with my course of action if all else fails.

Chapter 10 – Ellianna

Back at Sonja's I walk in to find her on the couch with two glasses of wine poured like she was waiting for me. "Hey babes, figured you'd need this." She says raising a glass at me.

"Damn right." I respond taking the glass from her with a big sip.

"Yeah, tall, sexy men on bikes tend to do that." She snickers and I about choke on my second large sip of wine.

"Shut up." I mumble. "You know it's because it's Cole." She nods and lets me know she made Ry go home about half an hour ago. "Lord, I'll have to fix that mess tomorrow."

"He gets it. He's just worried because he's your brother and he's supposed to." She tells me. I sigh as I pour a second glass of wine. Sonja is quietly eyeing me waiting for answers to all her unspoken questions. "We just fall right back into each other. It's like gravity. I'm a weight and he's the center of the Earth."

Son laughs, "That's by far the most ridiculous analogy I've ever heard."

"You know it's true though."

She chuckles and agrees.

"Hey! What about your tall, sexy biker?" I ask.

"What?!" She replies looking mortified.

"That Chris guy from the bar?" I tease her.

"Oooh." She mumbles. "I don't know. He's so hot though right?"

"Not Cole tasty, but pretty tasty." I admit.

"Well, you're a little biased." She says throwing a pillow at me. We spend the rest of the night giggling and drinking wine. Catching up on girl time until it's way too late and Sonja will be regretting it when her alarm goes off early in the morning.

Somehow the next morning, I'm up and wondering into the kitchen for coffee just before Sonja is leaving. "What's your plan while I'm at work today?" She asks grabbing her work bag of snacks, a banana and her travel mug.

"Oh, I don't know. Gym, then maybe see what else has changed around here."

"Oh! Gym. Did you meet Nick? Talk about tall, sexy biker." She exclaims, very excitedly.

"Really? Biker?" I ask. He is covered in tattoos but I wouldn't judge just based on that.

Son nods her head up and down at me, "Yeah, most of the new faces here are. Something with Cole and his connections. He built a big house off the hillside complete with a huge party area. It's like a clubhouse or something, like I've heard of MCs you know? But it's a lot different than what I've heard about so I don't really know what the deal is." She follows up, nonchalantly with, "It's a mystery to me."

My brows furrow, "I had idea; he didn't say anything about it. "

"He came back with secrets babe. I'm sure he's still Cole and I haven't personally seen anything super sketchy." She says before she focuses her eyes directly on me. "Just be careful for me, okay?"

"I will. Don't worry." I say dismissively. "Plus, technically I'm still married."

"Right, well got to go. Have fun today babes!" She says as she walks out the door.

"Work hard!" I shout after her. I make a power smoothie and head to the gym. There's a kickboxing class this morning and I want in on it. Plus, I need to hand over and pay all my membership stuff so I can officially go to the gym.

I walk in greeted by Nick at the desk. "Hey Gorgeous! Ellie, right?"

"Yeah, and you're Nick, right? Does boxing and such?" I respond with a smile. Sonja was spot on with her description this morning.

He smiles. "Yes Ma'am. This place is mine so I do most of the classes."

"Kickboxing, today right? I'd love in on that." I tell him and hand him the filled-out paperwork Ry gave me yesterday.

"Yup! We have about 30 minutes, let me just get your paperwork finished so you're officially a member." He says with a flirty wink.

Smiling up at him I reply. "Sounds perfect.

Nick walks back into a room; I assume it's his office. He took my membership forms and my bank information. They do a quick background check and make sure the auto payments go through for all members as a safety measure. It was on one of the forms I had signed. I smell him just before I feel arms around my waist, his warm breath against my ear as he speaks in a low, deep voice. "Sexy Kitten, to what do I owe this pleasure, seeing you in these tight pants two days in a row?"

I turn in his arms and as much as it pains me, I take a step back. I need a little space to clear my mind. Plus, I really had meant it last night when I said it would take time. "I like this gym."

Cole chuckles. "It's because you found me here."

"Nah, I was pretty settled on it before I caught you beating that poor bag to death." I reply rolling my eyes as he gives me his signature smirk.

"Alright gorgeous, you're officially all set." Nick's voice rings behind me. I watch Cole tense his body and am surprised when

I turn to see Nick looking scared to death. Cole snakes his arm around my waist like he was staking his claim on me. "Uhhh. Shit... Sorry Hawk. Didn't know she was your girl." Nick stammers his words.

His girl? What is he talking about and why is he looking so scared of Cole? He has at least 4 inches on Cole and is way more muscular, plus he teaches the boxing classes. Then there is the question of why the hell is he calling him Hawk? I take a step from Cole, sending Nick and apologetic smile. I take my member card that unlocks the doors here and my locker information from him. "You're fine Nick. I am no one's girl. Thanks for all the membership stuff. See you in class." I tell him and walk down the hall.

Cole yells after me as I walk into the woman's locker room. Sonja was just talking about secrets this morning, she has lived here through these changes that I'm having a hard time understanding. Our town has grown rapidly, which is weird since when I left it was turning into a drug filled dump. The changes it has had all seem to have to do with Cole and a whole lot of secrets. I had already come changed for class but I tuck my bag, change of street clothes and an extra set of athletic wear in the locker before walking back out of the locker room. Pulling my long blonde waves into a high pony. Of course, I walk out and straight into Cole. He is drool worthy in his fitted tank and basketball type shorts. I had noticed yesterday he has collected tattoos in my absence too. Oh goodie, tattoos and secrets.

"Why run from me Kitten?" He asks.

"I'm not your girl Cole. Obviously, you are not the same person you were when I was 16 and I'm not either. We are starting over if anything but I am my own person. I do not belong to anyone other than myself and you have no right to stake any type of claim to me. If someone wants to flirt with me or I want to flirt with them that's my business, not yours." I can tell he doesn't like that response as he does the rubbing his hand of his face thing again, so I decide to walk away to the end room for class.

"L. Come on, we are way past that point." He calls after me.

I spin on my heels to face him. "Are we though? Who's Hawk?"

"I am." I just glare at him. That's exactly my point. He comes back and has a whole new name and everything. I can't deal with all these secrets; he won't even tell me why he didn't come back for so long. I know what he said last night was definitely not the whole story. He is hiding something and until he tells me, I am so not having this. I turn on my heels again and storm toward the large room for classes. "L! Fuck!" He yells after me.

"I'm taking this class Cole." I say waving my hand dismissively.

"Yeah, me too. This conversation isn't over." His tone of voice tells me he is pissed. Too bad for him.

Him following me to class annoys me even more. I roll my eyes even if he can't see them, "That's borderline stalking."

He snorts. "If anything, it is you that is stalking me. I have hit up this class every week since it started and boxing twice a week. Then I'm here for cardio the other days. Basically, I am here every day at some point."

"Whatever Cole. This is my home town too." I grumble out. I am so over his shit. He left first, how is him taking over this town making it impossible for me to do anything here. We walk into class and there's ten other people in the room plus Nick. I'm surprised considering it's a weekday morning and I would have assumed most people would be working at this time. All their eyes turn to us and I instantly feel uncomfortable.

"Great! Last ones, let's get this party started!" Nick yells and claps his hands. "Everyone, newbie to the class is Ellie. Let's be nice." I wave and hear Cole chuckle behind me. "Warm up, then we will show the new girl here how it's done before we go off in pairs." Nick says before instructing us to the mat and through some warm up exercises.

We stretch and everyone finds a jump rope for a few minutes of cardio before Nick and Cole center up in the mat to show through some basic moves. It's like every woman's fantasy seeing these two insanely hot men run through kicks and stances getting all sweaty a few feet from me. I notice the other women here think the same thing. All their eyes are on Cole and I don't particularly like it. "Got it?" Nick asks me. I nod. "Cool. Pair up everyone." He instructs and of course Cole saunters over to me.

"Wanna show me what you got Kitten?" He asks with a wink.

"Pfft. Any chance to kick your ass? Yeah, I'll take it."

I hear Nick snicker to the side of us, obviously finding amusement in my interactions so far with Cole.

"You'll only win if I let you."

"Don't play coy. We both know you'd never lose on purpose. You are entirely too competitive for that." I retort. Nick laughs and mutters something about me being right. We square off in a stance that Nick showed earlier and I find myself falling into an easy pace of taps and kicks. Mostly on the defensive while watching Cole. He swings around me, purposely missing like he and Nick showed earlier. We are to learn in this class, not actually hurt each other. He smirks and I know that's when he's getting cocky. He lounges forward on his right leg and I use the opening to round kick him hard across the shoulder. No play taps for me, I know he can take it and I'm not about to let him pin me.

He staggers a little, caught off guard that I managed to take advantage of the moment and actually hit him. I kick him hard across his thigh while he's still regaining his stance. He drops his leg a bit as he tries to lounge forward again. I catch him with a jab and use the opening to spin him down to a pin. I hear Nick full on laugh to the side of us. "Well now. I think we all know who's really in charge here." He says between laughter, making Cole scowl. "Perfect job Ellie." Nick Praises.

Cole whispers in my ear before letting go of my hips. "I'd lose every time if you're going to pin me."

"Ha. Ha. Very Funny." I say dryly.

"Good class everyone. See you next week." Nick dismisses us. I hop up off the mat grabbing a water bottle and heading to the cardio room. Definitely need to run off the pent-up frustration I have over Cole. Sexual and otherwise.

Chapter 11 - Cole

"She's fine as hell man." Nick says, slapping a hand over my shoulder after the rest of the people from class left the room. I agree, there's no denying it. She has become a woman that is completely undeniable. She is curvier and feistier; her hair has grown longer than she ever kept it in high school. Her face has changed a bit too, her eyes aren't as bright and carefree as they used to be but her lips are a little fuller and her brows arch differently. Her cheekbones are more defined and she walks with a confidence that she never quite had before. Apparently, she is stronger than she ever was too and it makes me wonder if she was waiting for the day when she needed to fight back. I shudder at the thought. "Better figure out how to keep yourself in her good graces, Hawk. She was cut throat and I don't think it was just being competitive."

I shrug Nick off, "She'll come around. She could never stay mad at me long."

"You know her before she came to town? I mean she came in with Ry but figured it was like his cousin or something."

"Sister." I state and Nick looks at me confused. "She is Ry's older sister."

Something registers with Nick. "Oh, Shit. So, you like... know, know her."

"Yeah. Long story. She's mine though, always has been. So, don't get any ideas in that pretty dumb head of yours." I growl back at Nick. I need her to come around and let me publicly claim her and soon, before I have to kill someone for touching her. Her jacket only covers my claim so far and that only works if she is actually wearing it.

"Got it man. You better mark that fast though before someone gets an idea in their head." Nick says just reinforcing my thoughts.

"She's already marked."

"Oh?" He says looking surprised.

"She has her own leather, marked. She's a Phoenix and she's mine." Nick's whole jaw drops which I find hilarious. Only Gunner and Tech really know anything about L, I didn't think she would come back so there was no point of letting the whole club know of my fuck ups. She doesn't even know that she's a Phoenix, she doesn't even know what that even is. Fuck, no wonder she's so pissed at me all the time now. "Put your tongue away you dumb fuck. I need to go run off a fucking ton of frustration."

"My bet would be that you mean that quite literally." Nick says laughing, like I wouldn't put a bullet in him. I probably wouldn't, I like Nick but he doesn't need to know that. I have a rep as prez to keep.

"Fuck Off Nick." I growl out and walk out to the hall. Nick has always been a good guy. I've offered him officer status in the club but he prefers to sideline. He saved Gunner's life overseas and I've always felt in-debt to him for that. He says that we owe him nothing though. We did however, help him get this gym going and then let him keep all the investments. He trains us and helps the prospects learn in return. His loyalty to Gunner and myself runs deep.

I step into the cardio room to the backside of my kitten. I would know that gorgeous, perky ass anywhere. She's running like hell too. This girl is so strong physically and I completely underestimated her on that earlier. She kicks fucking hard and I'll definitely have bruises from that shit.

"Stop staring you creep."

Caught. "Can't help myself." I say stepping on the treadmill beside her and look over. She's already gone two miles in 10 minutes. Jesus, if she keeps running like that she may actually get hurt. "Don't hurt yourself Kitten." I tell her, my tone rather serious.

"I'm fine. Was better before you walked in though." She hisses out. I notice that she isn't even out of breath.

"I don't know, I think you might have missed me." I tease out.

"Keep dreaming Cole. The second you want to fill me in on all your dirty little secrets then maybe we can talk." She taps her phone off pause and music echoes out of her headphones. This is why I always thought of her as my feisty kitten. Her claws are fully out at me and now I need to figure out how to get her to retract them. Also, how to tell her anything else without her running for the hills. I start to run, hard and fast. Pushing all my limits. She has me so wound up since the second she stepped into my bar in her jacket that I feel like I am about to explode.

At some point I see her slow down her pace to a walk and hop off. She takes off out of the room and I just hope she stretches somewhere so she doesn't pull anything. I am partially glad she didn't stretch in here though, there is no way I would have been able to hold myself back from her in that situation. I keep running. Processing. Thinking. Can I really bring her into my world, fully?

Alot has happened in 9 years for both of us, but I have some really shady shit that I've done. She may run far, far away or straight back to that giant clown in Texas of the shit I've done. My phone rings over my music, pulling me from my thoughts and my run. It's Tech, so I answer and head to grab my shit from the locker room.

"What?"

"Bad time? You finally get it back in with Blondie?" He laughs. Bastard, he's being as bad as Gunner.

"Fuck off Tech. I was running you ass."

"We got info on those bikes. Also, our PI friend has arrived in town." Tech stops laughing and turns back to his normal serious and matter of fact self.

"Fuck! I'll be back in 10." I'm just heading out of the locker room and quicken my pace.

"Don't pull your pants back up on my account brother."

"Fuck you, fuck Chris and Nick too. You all fucking suck. You bunch of fucking asshats." Yelling into the phone while I walk by Nick. I tap the phone off and shove it in my jacket pocket.

"Hey now brother, I'm not involved in any of this." Nick yells from the front desk. I shoot him a glare then walk out of the building. Everyone is on my last nerve and running didn't help a damn bit.

Back at the clubhouse I walk into the basement, Tech and Gunner waiting for me. "What do you two have? Also, one more word about L from either of you and I'm shooting you both." I growl out.

"Two bikes matching the two from the warehouse popped up on a red-light cam. I followed them through town then. They took their helmets and face masks off at the stop at Miller Hill. Of course, we have cameras there too. Obviously, they underestimate my abilities to discreetly have eyes across the entire town." Paul explains.

It's a little creepy sometimes to think about, but it's for the safety of the town, as well as to keep the drugs out of this place. Paul has set up small solar cameras at every stop sign, even into the edge of town. They look like they are just the solar boxes for the flashing lights on all the stops to get you attention. The three of us in this room are the only ones aware of them. Most of the time they just record, but in a case like this they come in handy. Tech has some way of getting the computer to trace shit on its own so he only has to pull up what matches. The still from the camera comes up on the large screen and I start cussing across the room and pacing. Fuck this day.

"Did you know he was in town?" Gunner asks.

I snort at Gunner. "Of fucking course not. He was supposed to fuck off somewhere and keep his fucking distance."

"Obviously, your uncle missed you two." Tech mutters dryly.

"Could this be at the worse fucking time?" I growl out, not really directed at anyone. I need to get my anger under control.

"Yeah, because you don't have enough to deal with." Chris says. My best friend is just begging me to end him. I rub my hand down my face.

Tech catches on to my anger and interrupts my thoughts with more information. "The other guy. I sent through facial recognition software, going to see who your uncle is budding up with. My guess is he found friends in a dirty ass hole and they want what we have."

"Of course, he did. He isn't completely stupid. I should have killed him."

"Hard to pull the trigger on family, brother." Gunner says patting my shoulder.

"Anything else?" I ask, though I don't think I want any more news today.

"Just the PI, but you threatened to shoot us, so..." Tech says and turns to his computer.

"Well, obviously the exception would be when it is for her safety. Not these fucking jabs you all think at so fucking hilarious."

"You make it too easy, brother. Plus, Nick already let us know she beat your ass today." Gunner laughs out. I pull my gun and shoot the floor by his feet. I've had enough of the shit today. "FUCK!" Gunner jumps and yells.

"Can we not shoot around the precious and expensive devices, please?" Tech asks. His hands in front of him defensively.

"Fill me in on the PI." I demand.

Tech runs through basic information, pulling up a picture and a record sheet.

"You said he was in town?" I ask.

"Yup. I have all the cameras pinging on his face. Looks like he's staying at the inn off Main. He ordered food in and hasn't left his room much today."

I nod and instruct them to keep tabs before turning to walk out of the basement before I'm interrupted by Gunner. "Can I say something and you not shoot me?" He asks.

I grunt in response and he takes it as an okay. "Uh. So, if this guy is in town to watch Ellie, should you be chasing around after her?" I feel my body tense up at the question. I honestly didn't think about that. I only thought about protecting her and getting her back for good this time. I wasn't thinking about what all that would mean for her if he thought in his fucked-up head that she left to cheat or something. "Brother, if you rub at your face anymore you are going to peel it off." Gunner says to me.

"I FUCKING KNOW!" I yell at him. Gunner and Tech just watch me. Waiting for my next move, clearly unsure if I'm going to completely explode or not. It's been a while since I went into a blackout type rage but the tense anger radiating off me today is putting me dangerously close to that point and they can see it I'm sure. "Anything else either of you fucks want to tell me?" I ask, knowing I need to get away from everyone quickly.

"Maybe..." Tech starts, his voice soft and hesitant. "Maybe you should just tell her. Also, wouldn't hurt to claim her and brand her. It'll ease your mind and keep the club on higher alert when it comes to her. She's the queen here and no one knows it, not even her."

"She's claimed." I mutter. I don't like the idea of telling her everything, I don't think she's going to be all too fond of being branded either.

"I saw her jacket in the bar brother, we mean something more permanent." Gunner says pointing to my compass tattoo I got when I ended up in my uncle's MC 9 years ago. I had it done after I got my patch branded. That shit is covered up now and I have a large phoenix up my backside in its place instead.

"That would mean telling her." I sigh.

"It's time to tell her." Paul says. He's always been the brains. He has also always been way more level headed then either Chris or I.

"Well, that's going to be something." I say out loud but really meant it more for myself. Gunner wishes me luck and Tech makes a joke about needing it since she can kick my ass. "Oh no." I say, glaring at them both. "Both of you are helping me."

They both start complaining and declining, like I'm not in charge here. Appointed by them no less. I pull my gun and wave it around a little. They both change their complaining to a groan and I smile. That's right boys, don't forget who is in charge here.

Chapter 12 – Ellianna

I'm finishing a vegetable lasagna as Sonja walks in from work, she slinks into the kitchen with a huge smile on her face. She loves my veggie lasagna. "Who knew you'd be the best roomie ever!" She says excited. I let out a laugh and pull wine from the fridge as she pulls down two wine glasses. "No Cole today?" She asks.

"Oh... Cole was there today." I say with an eye roll. She raises her brow at me as she scoops a big pile of lasagna on a plate. I explain about the gym today and kickboxing class while we grab our plates and wine heading to the couch. "He's got me so frustrated that I ran 10 miles today." I complain to her.

"Jesus woman. Just ride him and get it over with." She jokes.

I shake my head at her, "He's hiding a whole lot of his past and I'm not going to just fall into bed with him."

Son tries to be serious but ends up just laughing again, "Just saying. It'll do wonders for your frustration. Though you keep kicking his ass and running 10 miles a day, you'll be able to eat and drink anything you want, no problem."

"I'll definitively kick his ass again, but the running will be under 10 miles from now on. My legs are all jelly feeling now, it was too much. I'll be back to work soon and it'll all be good." I say trying to reason with both myself and her.

She nods, stuffing lasagna in her mouth. "If he is not willing to let you in on his secrets, you need to move on babes," her tone actually managing to stay serious this time.

"I know." I say a little sad. It took forever to move on before and look where that got me. Now I'm right back where I was like I didn't actually move on. I just made more of a mess of my life than I ever thought possible. My phone rings interrupting my thoughts. Taking it out from my pocket I see it's Ry. I answer and put it on speaker.

"Hi Brother."

"Make up for last night with drinks?" He says before I even finish my greeting.

"Sonja and I were just going to chill, I think. I ran like 10 miles today."

"I watched you run yesterday. You're fine. Drinks!" Ry demands.

"Son babes, you want drinks with Ry?" I ask here

"YES! I mean you did ditch him yesterday." She replies.

I stick my tongue at her. "I had my reasons. At least, I can show my face at his bar now."

"Yeah, and now everyone knows you can kick his ass too." Sonja yells over me and directly in the phone so Ry hears her.

I hear laughter on the line, *"You kicked Cole's ass?"*

"Kickboxing class today."

"Oh, no shit. We are definitely getting drinks and celebrating that! Get ready! I will be there in ten minutes!" Ry yells much too excitedly into the phone, he doesn't even give me a chance to answer before the call ends from his end.

I look at Sonja but she just jumps off the couch, picking up our plates and glasses taking them to the kitchen. "Hurry! Go get sexed up!" She yells at me. I roll my eyes but do what she says and head upstairs hunting for something to match my jacket.

Finally, I find a red lacy halter top that cuts a low V in the front and is open in the back. I toss it on with a pair of ripped up skinny jeans I found in my closet at my parents. They are a dark wash and sit just right at my hips. Feels good to know I still fit in my clothes from high school. I grab a pair of black boots that lace in the front and stop just above my ankle before heading back down stairs. I wasn't too worried about my hair because it had air dried after my shower when I got home from the gym. My natural waves are a little loose and fluffy but they look fine enough. Sonja meets me in the hall with a huge smile, she has plain jeans and a fitted black t-shirt with some band printed on the front of it. Ry is letting himself in when we get down the stairs. "Jesus. Sis put some clothes on." He complains immediately.

"This is clothing. Don't try to play that game." I snap at him.

"Yeah, well no one will touch you in that jacket anyway so it's whatever." Ry says leaving the door propped open with his foot like he's ready to run.

"What the hell does that mean?" I snap again.

"You should know." Ry says rolling his eyes.

"I don't actually." I snap at him for the third time. I am really tired of people saying things without actually telling me anything.

"Those secrets I mentioned this morning babes." Sonja says. "I didn't connect it until Ry just said it, but he's right. You belong to Cole when you are in that jacket."

I snort. "That's ridiculous. He gave me this jacket when I was sixteen. I really don't think so."

"Whatever makes you feel better, Princess." Ry says quietly. "Let's go." We finally leave and have a quiet drive to the bar. Ry parks and I notice that there are countless bikes parked outside again. When we walk in everyone turns to stare at me again, but it's different from last time I was in here. This time it's half jealous and half admiration and full on just weird.

"The dynamic changed." I whisper to Sonja.

"Small town babes. Everyone knows L is back now." She uses air quotes as she speaks. "That means something here. We flew in under the radar but now Cole has been all over you and people are connecting things."

I mutter under my breath my dislike for this all. "This town got weird." I say out loud rolling my eyes and making my way to the bar. Everyone steps away from me, clearing a path like I own the place or am royalty or something. "So, fucking weird." I say to Ry beside me.

The bartender comes right over to me the second I reach the bar top. She was here last time; I think I overheard someone call her Beck. She's petite and pretty with short brown hair and is covered with bright tattoos. "What's your poison Babe?" She asks with a smile.

"Uh, how about some Tequila shots and two tequila drinks, whatever you make best. Then a Bud for my brother." She winks and steps away pouring drinks. When she comes back, I hand her my card but she won't take it.

"Hawk will actually kill me if I take your money Babe, just put it away." She finally says low and close to me like she's trying not to let anyone else hear what we are talking about.

"Cole is really pissing me off today, please just take my money." I never thought I'd ever say those words, let alone practically beg someone to take my money. Yet, here I am. Begging with a bartender. She smiles at me, winks again and walks away. What the hell is happening here? I down all but one of the shots, I have a feeling I am going to need them. Then I gather the drinks and last shot into my hands and go find Sonja and Ry. They found a booth, with how packed this place is I'm shocked they found an open one. Then I think, maybe I shouldn't be shocked with the way people are acting here. What the hell did Cole tell these people about me? "Scoring booths now too?" I hiss out with annoyance when I reach them.

"Just accept it sis and give me that beer." Ry says dryly like this is all normal.

Once I settle into the booth we finally settle into better conversation. The three of us talk and laugh like I never left. I realized how much I've missed this and realize how light I feel with them. This is where I've always belonged, why I thought Texas was a good idea, I don't know. Maybe, I was just trying to distance myself from here and the heartache this place brought me, but really this is where I should have stayed. I should have been here with my best friend and with my brother. I should have been here when Cole came back. I could have watched the changes happen while the happened, rather than seeing all this after the fact.

I notice we have all finished our drinks and ask if they want another round. I figure, what the hell, it's on Cole right? They both nod at me so I slide out of the booth only to have arms around my waist and the scent of leather and sandalwood filling my senses. "Miss me already Kitten?" He whispers into my ear like he likes to, he's always done that so he can bury his face in my hair for a minute.

"Just figured you wouldn't kick me out twice." I respond dryly.

"We need to talk." He says, using my hips to turn me to face him.

"Yup, only it is more like you need to talk and I'll listen.

He leans close to me so his lips are near my ear again. "You are right." he says softly leaving me a little stunned. Cole Cameron, admitting he's wrong. Well, that's a historical moment. I snuggle into his chest a bit, inhaling the scent that has always been him. He feels and smells like home and all my walls crumble down. Maybe it's the shots of tequila, or maybe it was the realization that I never should have left this town to begin with. Everything just hits me at once like a tidal wave and I suddenly feel extremely vulnerable. He pulls away from me, but tucks me into his side as he talks with my brother. First, they are talking about something irrelevant to me and I tune them out and talk with Sonja. She snuck up and grabbed more drinks when Cole was talking with me.

"Ry, you mind taking Sonja home? I've got Ellie okay?" Hearing them talk about me gets my attention quickly.

"Yeah man, but if she doesn't text me first thing in the morning though, I'm coming for you." Ry responds to Cole like I'm not even here.

Oh no, they do not just plan my time like this. "Cole." I say sternly.

"You've got it Ry." He says to my brother, both of them still ignoring me.

"Cole!" I say louder. This time getting his attention. He turns to me but instead of letting me scold the both of them for trying to control me he picks me up and tosses me over his shoulder. "Fuck! God dammit COLE! Put me down!" He ignores me as he walks out of the bar. This is so embarrassing because I can only imagine the stares considering what everyone looked at me like when I came into this place. I feel the cool night air rush around us and he grabs my hips to set me on my feet. "What the hell do you think you are doing?" I hiss at him. He has one hand holding tight to my hips and he is reaching around me with the other hand for something.

"Keeping you safe with me love." He says softly, putting a helmet on me. "We will talk in the morning when you haven't had anything to drink."

I get on the back of his bike with him and snuggle into his back. "I'm always safe with you Cole." I say softly. I'm only sure he heard me because he reached back to grab my thigh tight before starting his bike and heading off down the road. Eventually, we pull up a long driveway to a huge modern looking house. The whole place is lit up and there are bikes everywhere. He helps me off the bike, then with getting my helmet off. After I start to walk, he picks me up over his shoulder again like he did at the bar. I say his name again but he just ignores me.

"Blondie okay there Prez?" Someone asks, the voice sounds familiar.

Cole responds, "She's fine Gunner. Beck called me earlier after she took a bunch of shots."

So many thoughts start going through my head. Gunner, that's that Chris guy. The one Sonja likes. What is he doing here, and who was he calling Prez? Then there is the Beck thing. She's the bartender and she told on me about shots. I am not a child and I can handle my liquor, if anyone knows that it's Cole. I whine at him again to put me down. He doesn't, instead he just slaps at my ass and calls goodnight to Chris. I watch the ground as we move inside and up steps.

"Cole! At least tell me where we are?" I mumble into his back, giving up on arguing.

"My clubhouse L, where I live. You're safe, I've got you. Just sleep now." He says placing me on a soft bed and pulling my boots off. "We will talk in the morning." I agree and drift off. My last thought is that this bed is extremely comfortable.

Chapter 13 – Ellianna

Light is bright in my face waking me. The end of last night was a little blurry but I remember Cole and I remember him talking with Ry, then that Chris guy when we got here. All I remember is being safe and feeling comfortable in a super soft bed.

I start to become more aware of my surroundings and feel a heavy arm over me. Blinking a few more times to get the last bit of sleep out of my eyes. I am assuming the arm is Cole's, everything here smells like him. All of my senses are overwhelmed with the smell of leather and sandalwood, typical Cole scent. Then I realize I am in my panties and one of Cole's tee shirts. "fuck." I mutter. Cole groans and I try to slide out from under him.

"Kitten." He mumbles.

"I shouldn't be here Cole." I say, embarrassed because I didn't think I was that drunk. Yet, here I am in his t-shirt and not remembering if we did anything. He grabs me and pulls me tight to him so I can't make my escape. I look around the room more, there are two sets of doors on the other side of the room that I can see. I wouldn't have any idea how to get out of here anyway.

He rubs his face in my hair. "You're fine L. Also, nothing happened. You stripped in the middle of the night. I should have known you hate sleeping still in your bra or jeans. I grabbed my shirt from the floor and put it on you." He explains letting me sigh in relief. I've done that to him and Sonja before. Sonja was mortified one morning because she didn't remember what happened and I was completely naked passed out in her bed. "Besides, it's not like this is the first time you've woken up in my bed." Cole chuckles and I scoff. "Stop fretting L"

"Too much, too fast Cole." I tell him. He sighs and rolls on his back, releasing me from his arms.

"We need to talk L. Just hear me out, then you can stay or run away. Your choice and I'll respect your decision and back off if you choose to run."

"Going to fill me in on your secrets?" I ask.

"That's the plan." He says and turns his head to watch me with those blue eyes of his.

I slide up the bed so I'm sitting against the headboard. "Fine. Fill me in then."

He gives me a half smile. "Shower and I'll get you something to eat. I need to take care of something first. Work stuff. Plus, I asked Paul and Chris to join us for some of it. I'm sure you'll have questions and they are better to answer on some things then I am."

I furrow my brows at him. He makes no sense. "Sure, whatever you want Cole."

He gets out of the bed and heads to one of the doors across the room, opening it. "Bathroom, towels are in the first cabinet." He walks to the next door. "Closet. Help yourself. I live with a bunch of other men, so for the sake of my mental health, please find something covering."

I laugh at that, not that he looks amused. Cole, jealous and protective as ever. "Remember you punched Jimmy Martin because you thought he was looking at my ass?"

"He was." Cole states getting into a pair of jeans.

"I doubt it. Jimmy is gay, he and his husband adopted a little girl right before I moved." I inform him. He looks at me in utter shock at that information. "Always so jealous."

He shakes his head, sliding a clean t-shirt on. "Territorial, there's a difference."

"Yeah. Yeah. You better go along and do whatever it is you got to do." I say dismissively, tossing my hand in the air at him before sliding out of his massive, soft bed I could just about live in.

He rubs his hand over his face, though I'm not sure what could frustrate him now. "L." He says making me look at him. "Take your time, and don't leave my room until I get back. Okay?" If this is his house and I'm supposedly safe here, even if he lives with a bunch of other guys why would it matter if I leave his room or not? More secrets of course.

I roll my eyes at him but agree before walking into the bathroom. I'm stunned by it. His room was large with a king-sized bed on a wall between two windows, another large window on the wall across from the door he left out of and a chair in the corner near the closet door, a TV was mounted on the wall across from the bed that had to be at least 60 inches which seems way too big for a bedroom. Then there is this bathroom. Black matte stone counter tops across a double light grey vanity. Light grey cabinets on either side of the vanity, the first holding a bunch of fluffy grey towels. The shower is also black stone tiles with a rain shower head in the ceiling and another large shower head angled off the wall. Clean white tile floors complete the modern, masculine but beautiful room.

How did he afford all this? The secrets just keep piling up. I know for sure his family doesn't have any money; his junkie mother made sure of that.

After I shower, savoring the amazing shower and water pressure, I find a pair of sweatpants and a t-shirt in his closet. He only uses half of the giant walk in with drawers and organizing systems. It's like every female's dream closet and he's only using one side. Typical male. I put on the clothes and look down, I look ridiculous. I am completely swimming in both. I tie the bottom of the shirt in a knot at the front right corner. It makes that look less ridiculous and I roll up the sleeves. Cole still isn't back from whatever it was he was doing, so I put his sweats back where I found them and put my jeans from last night on.

Since he isn't back, I find my phone. He plugged it in for me to charge last night. I text Sonja and Ry that I'm fine and will be home later. Then I scroll through my private Instagram. I made it after I got my new phone at the airport and made sure all my privacy settings are turned up. Even made my name as "El Jade" hoping Brett never thinks to look that up.

I start getting antsy waiting around, Instagram isn't that entertaining. Plus, I've never been one to sit still. I think back to what things were like with Cole before he left. Everything felt so simple for the most part. We were so young. Sure, we suffered loss once together when friends of ours died in a car crash, drugs being the cause of the accident. Then there was Cole's mom, she always had a problem with drinking before she turned to the harder stuff. She was a hot mess, making it all worse with the guys she would bring around. Cole spent way more time at my home with me and my parents than any sixteen-year-old girl's parents would ever allow. I think Pops just understood that it was more about protecting Cole at that point than about his daughter's "innocence". We always had each other. We had my family. We were one. It was just simple.

Then he left and I was completely crushed. Devastated. First, I was overwhelmed with fear. Thinking what if he was dead or hurt. His mom was gone too and the police said they couldn't do anything because his mom was also gone and he wasn't a minor anymore. Two years between us age wise but only a grade apart. My parents, Sonja and Ry all tried their best to comfort me and reassured me he would be back. Nothing worked though, I was miserable and lashed out often. It was selfish of me when I think back, they were hurting too.

Senior year was mostly a blur. I was grieving. I went to college for marketing and business, got my bachelor's degree and got a job right away at a place I briefly interned at. I was completely numb by that point, going through the motions of life. That was when I met Brett.

Charming Brett. He was so handsome and caring. He pursued me for month before I finally gave in. He was finishing up Law School. I met him where I was working since, he was doing some internship for business law. Once I had given into him, he made me feel this happiness that I was missing. It felt like it was the right thing to do, to go with him to Texas. He soothed the ache that Cole left and that was good enough for me.

Only, it wasn't.

Now I'm here. Laying across Cole's bed waiting for him. Debating if I trust him or if I'm just trying to fill the gash in my heart, he left so many years ago. I can't wait around anymore. If I do, I am going to dig deeper into these thoughts and feelings and be a blubbering mess.

I poke my head out the door to look in a hall. This place is huge. Cole's room is at one end by a stairwell but it looks like there's stairs at the other end of the hall too. I see 5 doors on each side of the hall between the stairs. How many people live here to need 10 rooms anyway? The doors are spaced out and look like they would hold almost the same amount of space as Cole's room, maybe a little less. Taking a chance, I step into the hall towards the closest stairwell, just as those ice blue eyes pour into mine.

"Thought you were going to stay in my room like a good kitten." He teases with a smile on his face.

"Antsy. You should know better than to leave me alone that long."

"Can't sit still, I remember." He reaches the step below me. We still aren't eye level; he's always towered over me. He tugs the knot on his shirt so it's back to swimming on me.

"Hey!" I scold him and go to fix it. He just chuckles and asks if I want to have a tour. "Sure, this place is huge. How many people live here?" I respond.

"Depends on the day." He says, holding out his hand for me to take as he explains how we are on the top floor, which are all suite rooms for people that hold status and stay here. His is the largest corner room on this side and Chris as the other on the far side. Then he explains the second floor, it is more bedrooms and bathrooms but these are all basically guest rooms. Basically, if someone needs to live here, they can claim one for the time and will get a key and lock but otherwise they are for anyone that needs a place to crash. Seriously, how many people live here? I think to myself. Sonja said something about a motorcycle club but I thought that was just on TV and in books. Not to mention this place is insanely nice. Aren't MC people like dirty bikers?

"Main floor has the living room and dining room. We can almost hold everyone. This is the kitchen." He says as we take the final stair step into a beautiful modern kitchen. The island has marbled stone that waterfalls off the edge and a raised breakfast bar that holds 10 stools. The cabinets are sleek like the ones in his bathroom but are a darker wood color. The appliances are all high end and chef worthy with two ovens built in plus a large gas stove with an oven. The fridge is massive and there are two sinks, one in the island and one a few cabinets down from the stove.

"This is insanely gorgeous." I state in awe. We move to the dining which is just to the side of the kitchen and you can see a huge patio and deck space outside two sets of French doors. The dining table is a dark wood and seats twenty. The dining room flows into a living space which is tucked behind the stairs and a wall with a large stone fireplace and built ins separate the living room from the kitchen. This room is softer and more feminine with soft grey couches and darker grey chairs. Plus, a giant ottoman and several side tables that all match. Above the fireplace is another large TV that is significantly bigger than the one in Cole's room and if I had to guess it's at least 80 inches.

He walks me back toward the kitchen with a big smile on his face, like he is beyond happy with my reaction to the space. The furthest wall from the stairs and away from the French doors of the kitchen is solid without windows and I see another double door at the one end. Then a single door on the other. "Cole, I definitely have more questions than answers at this point."

"I know. Here, Beck grabbed breakfast sandwiches for everyone while we were in the meeting." He says handing me a wrapped-up takeout sandwich and standing by the counter with me.

"Beck lives here? She's the bartender at your bar?" I ask. Obviously, a bunch of people live here but I haven't seen anyone else yet.

"Not really. She's married to Tech, or Paul. Umm, you've met Chris but he told you he goes by Gunner too and Nick called me Hawk at the gym." I nod eating my sandwich. "You can pick what you are comfortable calling us, but most people do not know us by our given names." He says and I'm still confused he really needs to get to explaining things so I understand what the hell he's talking about. "Anyway, I'll introduce you in a minute. They have one of the suites but they have a house toward town they both prefer living in." I just nod. Yeah, sure. Clear as mud.

"Hey Blondie!" Someone says behind me and I jump a little. The voice sounds familiar and I turn around.

"Hi. Ummm. Chris, right?" I ask and he nods.

"Gunner around here doll, but Cole can explain that."

"He seems to have a lot to explain at this point." I mutter and glare at Cole. He actually seems calm for once though, like this is his element and he can relax here.

"I met Gunner when my uncle took my mom and I away. My uncle was an officer of a MC in Ohio, near Akron. When my mom got in trouble with drug dealers here, both our lives were being threatened. He came to get us. Then took us there, sent mom to rehab and made me work with the MC to pay off her debts and rehab."

I try to just eat the sandwich he gave me but I have been holding in so many questions I blurt out the first thing in response. "So, you two were what, in a gang together?"

"Jesus Blondie, not so damn loud." Chris or Gunner or whatever chokes out.

"Not helping Gunner." Cole scolds him.

"Look, where we were and where we are now are two very different things and you need to keep that in mind when Cole tells you all this Blondie." Gunner says to me seriously.

"So, this..." I start and wave my hands around, gesturing to the house we are in before finding the words and very quietly speaking them. "is your hide out for your gang that's different than your uncle's gang that in Ohio?"

Gunner bursts into laughter as he pats Cole on the back and walks to the giant fridge.

"Sort of but no. Okay, Number one. We are a club. I am the president and Gunner is vice. This is our club house. We are not a gang or a bunch of thugs." Cole says seriously and I nod at him, understanding that part a little better. "We run things completely different than my uncle's club or a lot of other clubs for that matter. Very minimal on the illegal stuff."

Now I burst into laughter almost choking on the last bit of sandwich. No wonder he's all secrets and this and that. He's a criminal. "Cole, Jesus Christ." I choke out.

"L, just let us show you... Please." Cole pleads with me. I hear Chris choke on the water he was drinking.

"Only because you said please. I'm really not amused Cole." He knows how I feel about drugs and running illegal businesses and what not. Drugs ruined our town and now he comes in here acting like he's fixing things when really, he's just a criminal himself.

"Unlike my uncle's MC which by the way, Gunner, Tech and I took care of. They are no longer an existing club." He says and I swallow hard, his eyes softening when he looks at me. "We do not sell or do drugs. We treat women with respect - "

"Speak for yourself Hawk, there's still whores that linger around and get treated that way." Gunner pipes in cutting off Cole.

"What the fuck?!" My eyes get wide.

"Not helping Gunner." Cole hisses out at him.

"I think I should just leave." I say. I mean seriously, what the hell is going on here? Cole is not at all the person I knew. He's a criminal for crying out loud. One that Apparently keeps whores around in his fancy clubhouse and makes everyone in this town think he's such a golden child now.

Cole grabs my hand. "First meet with Tech and see what we really do. We are not criminals or gang member or whatever is going through your mind right now, and I am telling you right now I don't mess around any of the whores that hang out with the members. I don't condone it either but somethings never die."

"He's right on all that. If it makes you feel better, I rarely see him with a woman. He's been stuck on you for years Blondie." Gunner says to me.

"It doesn't, but thanks for that." I mumble out and put my thumb and finger over the bridge of my nose, shutting my eyes and rubbing small circles. A migraine is going to come by the end of the day I'm sure of it.

"Prez, is this still such a good idea?" I hear Gunner say quietly like he thinks I won't hear him.

"Still not helping Gunner." Cole says then takes my arm to lead me to the smaller door that he opens up. It leads to a set of stairs. We head down while Chris follows us.

"L, I've never had to explain this to anyone before. Neither has Tech or Gunner. I don't know what the hell to say or what I'm doing here." His voice is unsteady and he grips my hand tighter like he is scared of me actually running away from him. We come to a metal door with an electronic pad by it. Cole uses his hand on the pad to open the door to a large room full of computers and another guy that is sitting in a computer chair looking like he's been waiting for us.

"Ellie, Nice to finally meet you." The guy says with a smile.

"This is Beck's husband. Paul, but everyone in the club calls him Tech. He is our third in command and also holds a vice title. While Gunner is also our enforcer, Tech handles treasury and secretary positions... He's the brains here." Cole explains.

"Pleasure." I say with a nod and smile. I don't want to be rude but this has already been a lot to try to take in.

"Tech runs the majority of our businesses, especially from the behind-the-scenes aspect. I run the real estate and store front businesses. Gunner handles all the construction and contractor work and company." Cole continues on with his explanations.

I can't seem to help myself with blurting my thoughts out. "Sounds more like you are some kind of cooperate business men or something, less gang like."

"Did you really just let her call us a gang?" Tech says looking mortified.

"I tried man. It's the third damn time. Cole sucks at this." Gunner states.

"You idiots aren't helping." Cole scolds them.

"I really don't understand all the secrets if this is all it is. So, you have a bunch of people that what? Hang out here, ride their bikes, work for you with your legitimate businesses?" I look between the three of them, crossing my arms over my chest.

"Since Cole obviously has no idea how to explain any of this and I'm obviously the brains here, let me explain Ellie." Tech says and so he explains. He tells me about the guns and technology, about the businesses having to also be a cover for the money they bring in, how they funnel money into the community as much as possible and make sure that every member of the club is taken care of as well as compensated for any work they do. They keep drugs and dealers out of our town as well as have alliances with other MCs that want to have a better path. How they have had to kill people to protect themselves, this club and this town. How they skirt the edge of the law on protection and make sure the police here are well equipped and informed of anything sketchy going on and how the police let them handle a good portion of it because they are understaffed and under trained which was why the drugs got so bad here to begin with. It's a lot of information but it really doesn't sound that horrible, even if Cole has blood on his hands, he wasn't doing it because he wanted to. Kill or be killed.

After a moment of me gathering my thoughts on this and the guys letting me have silence, I tell them I have questions. Looking straight at Cole. "Why didn't you contact me when you were in Ohio?"

"They weren't good people there; my uncle isn't a good person and the people my mother got involved with were worse. They would have killed you, or worse yet, kidnapped you and sold you. If they had any idea there was someone out there important to me, they would have made you pay for my mother's mistakes and my debts." Cole tells me, choking on his words several times.

My whole body tenses. "Am I in danger now, because I'm here, if I'm with you?"

"No." All three say in unison.

"You are safest in this clubhouse." Gunner states. "You'll be safer yet outside this clubhouse when you agree to letting you be branded."

"I'm sorry. What? What the fuck?" I look at him, mortified again.

"It's just a tattoo." Quickly, Paul explains. "You'd have our Phoenix tattooed on you and then Cole's name or Queen on you somewhere visible so you're marked as protected."

Cole looks at both of them like he wants to kill them and I feel tense. "I'd protect you with my life, always have, always will." Cole says, tracing my face with his fingers before pushing his sleeve up on his left arm showing a compass in the middle of his forearm. "The only people that knows what this means are in this room."

I look closer and instead of an "N" for north it's an "L" that the compass points to.

I'll always find my way back to you

The words he said that last night play on repeat in my head. I blink away tears and look away from the guys. He was trying to tell me, in his own way. "I just, I need a minute." I walk out of the computer room and head back up the stairs to the kitchen. I catch a few words that carry through the open door and up the steps.

"You going to tell her the rest?" It is Gunner's voice carrying up to me.

Cole's voice responds, "I'll handle it. That is more personal anyway."

I'm not sure my brain can take much more.

Chapter 14 - Ellianna

I grab a water out of the fridge and plop myself down in a chair. Maybe it isn't all so bad, I mean Paul and Chris seem really nice. Cole is, well he is mostly still Cole. Moodier but still Cole.

I can understand why he wouldn't want to tell me. I mean there was a really good chance I'd run for the hills. It's been nine years. Nine horrible years for both of us but he still acts like he loves me, like he has loved me the entire time. It broke him when he came back for me and thought I was moved on. Not that I really was moved on, but how would he have known.

Gathering my thoughts and sipping the water a voice startles me and me from the thoughts going on in my head. "Who are you?"

I look up from the spot I've been staring at on the counter to see a woman with really long and really dark hair. She's skinny and covered in tattoos and a ton of makeup. Her clothing leaves barely anything to the imagination with her short shorts and cropped tank top. I can't tell if she's pretty or trashy. "Uh....I'm Ellie." I tell her with half a smile. Then I wonder if I'm supposed to go by Blondie like Gunner calls me or Queen like Tech explained I was. Not that I really want either of those names.

"Cool. Why are you here?" She asks tilting her head like she is studying me or something.

I really don't know how to answer her or even who she is. "Uh, who are you?" I ask instead of giving her an answer.

"Brianna, girlfriend of the Prez here. So, I'm meant to be here, are you?" She says with a big proud smile. They call Cole Prez, he's the president, he's in charge. She just said girlfriend, right?

Frowning, I still try to be polite, "Excuse me. I just need to get my stuff and leave". Then I head towards the stairs, ready to go straight to Cole's room. I need to grab my purse and phone. I am so stupid, who was I kidding that he was the same and things between us could be fine. His tattoo is just there. Maybe he just hasn't had covered up yet. It couldn't still be a reminder of us if he has a girlfriend here. Brianna, the girlfriend yells at me about not being allowed up the stairs but I just keep going. Even Chris was saying there was more to tell and Cole said it was personal. Yeah, well a girlfriend is rather personal.

I shove all my stuff in my purse and grab my phone off the stand texting Sonja and Ry in our group text to see if either of them could give me a ride as I sprint back down the stairs. I hit the bottom step and come face to face with Cole's freaking girlfriend, again. I just want to leave; I'm trying to hold in my emotions but seeing her again makes it hard.

Of course, he has a girlfriend, I mean I was married it's not like we were saving ourselves or putting a hold on our lives or anything. "Bye then... Maybe I'll see you around." She says sounding happy. I keep my head down while I run past her.

"Doubt it, Bye." I mumble back. I get out the door and outside when my phone pings. It's Ry and he's on his way for me. It's chilly and raining so I pull my jacket out of my purse and shrug it on. Savoring the leather smell until I realize how much it makes my heartache all over again. I make my way down the long driveway just before Ry pulls up.

"You okay sis?" He asks while I climb in his truck.

"I don't know Ry. Just take me home please." He frowns at my response but nods and puts his truck in drive.

10 minutes later and he's pulling into Sonja's drive. I mumble my thanks as I go to hop out but Ry catches my arm. "Ellie, Wait."

"What Ry?" I turn to face him, glancing at his hand on my arm then back to his face.

"Look, I don't know why you are upset again, other than it is probably somehow Cole's fault, but two things okay?" He looks very concerned and serious. Still, I roll my eyes at him. I am not in the mood for a lecture right now. He frowns at me and puts a little more pressure on my arm. "Okay?" He asks again.

"Yeah okay." I respond and sit back in the seat. Ry drops my arm.

"Okay first, you will always be my priority. You are my sister and I love you even if we never say it. What is going to be best for you is always what my interest is going be. You're also my best friend and I really fucking hated you being gone. I won't let anything or anyone get in the way of that ever again."

I tear up. "I know Ry. I hated it too."

He smiles at me a bit but it's only half-hearted reassurance. I really messed up our relationship not just by leaving but by letting Brett keep me from communicating with my family. "Second thing. Cole isn't the same person he was when he left here, but he is not a bad guy Ellie."

Out of everything Ry could have said, that was the statement that shocked me. "I think you may actually be wrong there, brother." I say softly.

He tightens his lips together and I go to exit the truck again. "Did he tell you?"

I sit back again. "Depends on what you're referring to, if you mean his job then yes." I emphasize the job part of my statement.

Ry sighs at me. "You think he's a bad person because of that?"

"Surprisingly, not really." My words are emphasized with a shrug. Ry looks at me with shock showing on his face. "I take it you knew and didn't tell me?"

"Wasn't my place to. I know because this is home for me, I never left, and I don't say that like it is a bad thing, it just is what it is. I know people and I listen to what they say. I figured it out not too long after he moved back and things started changing fast. I necessarily really talk to anyone about it, but sometimes I ask around about it and him."

"I see." I mumble throwing my head back against the seat and sighing. Ry sits in silence with me for a while. "He has a girl-friend." I finally say.

"What was that?" Ry asks, his brows furrowed like I just said the most absurd thing.

"Cole. He has a girlfriend." I repeat clearly.

Ry busts into laughter. "You're joking right?"

"I don't know why you think that's funny, Ry." My face clench-ing with anger.

"Ellie. The guy has loved you since you were kids. I've never once seen him touch other women, let alone date one and I frequent the bar often. I'm sure he's slept around or whatever, guys have needs but I really fucking doubt he has a girlfriend."

Maybe he is good at hiding it, I think to myself then respond to Ry, "Don't know what to tell you Ry. I met her."

"Well, Shit." He says with a sigh and turns away from me. "I didn't mean to laugh. I honestly thought it was absurd." His hands rub along his chin, something he does when he's think-ing about something.

"It's fine. What is absurd is me though, is that I was falling right back into him like he didn't leave me alone for nine years.... even if he claims to have a good reason." Admitting my feelings to my brother, I feel a tear slide down my cheek.

"I am so, so sorry Princess. " Ry says, pulling me across the cab of his truck to hug me.

"Don't. It's fine. I need to get myself back anyway, right?" I mumble into his shoulder before getting him to release me. Leaving the truck as he calls after me to call him if I need him and he loves me. I make my way up the steps to Sonja's duplex wondering how far I can be pushed until I break completely.

Hours later, I wake in my bed to the sound of the front door slamming shut. Grabbing my phone, the time says six pm, so it should just be Sonja coming home. I notice then that I have multiple missed calls and texts from Cole. I ignore them and see there's a text from Ry about keeping my head up. He has grown into such a good man, most of which I missed out on being away.

"Babes" Sonja pops her head into my room.

Looking up from my phone, "How was work?" I ask her.

"Awful, stressful, exhausting." She complains rolling her eyes and plopping on the bed beside me. "You good if I just soak in a bath and go to bed?"

"All good babes, I don't need a baby sitter."

She looks at me and give me half a smile. "You want to tell me why you are mopey?"

With a shake of my head, I brush her off, "I'm good. Go, get some sleep. You do look like shit."

"Thanks. Much appreciated." She teases as she gets up and heads back to the door. "Night babes"

"Love you!' I yell at her. She yells back before I hear her door shut. I figure a nice hot shower will sooth my soul so I head to the bathroom.

It's been a few hours since Sonja got home, I poked my head in her room and she was definitely asleep. I'm antsy and unsettled but not sure what to do. I throw on an oversized sweater and leggings and head out the door. Just remembering to send a text to Sonja I went out in case she wakes up and worries as I reach my car.

"Back for more?" Beck asks me as soon I take a seat in the farthest, darkest corner of the bar rail.

"Just a Corona. I'm just going to hide in this corner of the bar. I'm not actually here. Please don't tell on me." I say, cringing as I remember Cole saying she called him last night.

Beck nods at me. She seems sweet, but I really don't know what lies where with her. "I won't tell, I promise you. I'll even try to keep you hidden over here but there are cameras everywhere in this place. They feed into Tech's office." I nod back at her in understanding. Of course, Cole could have Paul find me if he wanted to. Here is to hoping he's not looking for me. This is really the only bar in town, it is not like I have many options.

"Thanks Beck. I'll owe you." I tell her, she hands me a beer. For the first time, it isn't super busy in here. I take a sip of the beer before setting it in front of me and tapping the sides with my nails. Nervous antsy habit.

"Bad day?" Beck asks.

Shrugging my shoulders, "Something like that."

"Cole can be a pain in that ass but he's a good guy." She says softly in front of me.

I look up at her with half slit eyes. It is really starting to piss me off everyone keeps defending him. "I keep hearing that." I say hearing the venom laced in my voice. She just smiles sadly at me before making her way to the other side of the bar to help someone else.

"Look what the cat dragged in, looking for another hookup?" Brianna asks sitting down beside me. Of course, I should have known that coming here was a terrible idea. Beck, is trying to

defend him and now his fucking girlfriend is here to unknowingly rub it in my face.

"Hi Brianna." I mumble out.

She laughs, I think it's supposed to be a cute giggle but to me
it just sounds like a cat crying. "I know these guys are hunky,
good lays too. So, tell me, who's got your eye?"

That's when I completely break all attempts at being polite.
I turn to her, a glare and an awful grin on my face. "It may
be a hard concept for you, but I don't just spread my legs for
just anyone doll." My voice is dripping venom and I say "doll"
rather drawn out. Definitely meaning the name as an insult. I
am tired of catty games and am really sick of people passing
judgments today. Maybe she is actually a nice girl, but I hate
her and want to stab a hot pointy stick into her eye right now.
She's the last face I wanted to see and it pinched my very last
nerve. "My eyes have only ever been on one person; I came
first and I am permanently imprinted on his body. It's a for life
thing. Now if you don't mind, I'm trying to drink here." I turn
my body away from her and focus back on my drink. Considering the anger, I have right now it is best if I do not acknowledge
her anymore. I feel her glare before she gets off her stool with a
whine and loudly stomps across the bar like a child.

"About time someone other than me put her ass in place." Beck
says handing me another beer. "I only caught the end there, but
she keeps trying to get her claws in your man. Persistent thing
she is, I'll give her that. he always tosses her to the curb."

My eyes widen, "She's not Cole's Girlfriend?" Beck laughs at my
question to the point where she's trying to catch her breath as
she passes a couple guys a few beers. "I'll take that as a no then."

"Did she tell you that?" Beck asks me as soon as she finally gets
her breath back from all the laughing.

Nodding my head slowly, "Yeah, this morning. She was at the
house. She was walking around like she owned the place."

"She always sneaks her way in. She's only allowed in the party room unless she accompanied by a member but she's a sneaky bitch. Finds her way to sneak into the rest of the place."

My heart drops with Beck's explanation. "I fucked up Beck." I tell her.

She wide eyes me then moves across the bar to hand out a few more beers. "Can't be that bad." She walking back to my corner of the bar. I drop my head to the bar top. Cole is probably beside himself and he said he would leave me alone if I ran after he told me all his dirty secrets. "Okay maybe it is." Beck interrupts my thoughts. I groan and she taps the back of my hand. I hear her telling someone to fuck off for five minutes, then brings her attention back to me. "Okay well spill."

Speaking into the bar top I ramble a summary. "He told me today. Well mostly Paul told me and Chris made horrible jokes and Cole looked all pale like he wanted to throw up most of the time."

"Sounds about how I figured it'd go." She giggles out.

I jerk my head up. "Wait, you knew?"

"Course. Made sure they didn't last night and made sure they fed ya this morning too. Damn men would've spilled everything while you were drunk or starving never thinking twice about it. Take it ya didn't take it well though?" She looks at me with sad, loving eyes.

Shrugging again, "Took it okay, I guess. I mean it is a lot of information I was not at all prepared for, but none of it struck me as something that made me want to run away."

"Truth. I grew up around it, so it is not too new to me. Those three idiots, though, they do it different and they do it well truth be told. Plus, they all have pure hearts." She smiles. She obviously cares greatly for them.

Nodding my agreement, I continue on. "I gathered that. That wasn't the problem. I went up to the kitchen to clear my head and get a water."

"Fucking Brianna!" Beck spits out and looks around the bar.

"Yeah, and Cole said if I ran, he'd leave it. Just drop it and not bother me." I say, tears dripping down my face.

Beck rubs my hand. "Sweetie. He's never going to turn you away if you go to him... Now shoo! You need to go get your man!" She takes my beer from me and shoos me out with her hand. Right when I get to the door, she winks at me, "I've got a bitch to take care of."

Chapter 15 - Cole

"You guys think she took that okay?" I ask, rubbing my hands over my face.

"I don't know man; she looked a little shell shocked." Paul says.

He's right she really did; I rub my hand over my face some more. "She just needs a minute to process." I say more to myself than to the guys.

"Sure, but we have to work Prez." Gunner says.

It did take much longer to explain things than I thought it would. When either of these two guys call me Prez, I know it is time to be serious. I make my mind flip into business mode. "Hit me with it, what do you have now?" I ask.

"Your uncle crawled over to the 9s. I confirmed the guy he was with is their enforcer." Paul fills me in on all the details. The 9s don't have as many guys as us, half are drugged up and the other half are either not that smart or barely trained. We would have no issue taking them down, but they have allies.

Shaking my head, we can't risk a shoot-out in town with them or starting a war. "I'm not here for a war. Innocents get hurt in wars." Gunner gives me a side glance, that was touching on a touchy subject on my part. I rub my face again.

"None of us want war man. We just need to keep our defenses up, that's all." Gunner says.

"Fine. Do what needs to be done then." I start to head up the stairs to check on L but Tech has more to say.

"Your PI friend is snooping through some interesting stuff."

Paul calls, making me stop in my tracks and turn back to him.

"Like what?" I ask.

"Graves?" He says, then he pulls up pictures of this PI guy standing in front of four different graves.

The picture makes my blood boil. "Tech, please tell me you know what the hell he's doing there?"

Paul shrugs. "He was writing on his note pad at the last one. I got a still blown up." He pulls up another picture. The pad says "car accident. Blame.".

"Blame? The driver was high and slammed into a tree. What fucking blame?" I'm rambling thoughts and pacing the room.

"You knew who's graves those were?" Gunner asks.

"Yeah. I was 16 so L would have been 14. We were at a bonfire party with half the school. There was always booze and drugs at those parties, but L and I never messed with anything hard. It was there and others did, though. L was supposed to be in that car to go home that night but I made her stay with me. I wasn't about to let her get in that car with a bunch of people high as fuck. Her Pops about killed me when I took her home, it was worth it though. She would have been dead."

I hear Gunner curse and rub my face again. "That doesn't explain what he's doing there."

"Unclear, but he went into the bar shortly after opening and had the balls to talk to Beck." Paul tells us.

"She say anything?" I ask, knowing she wouldn't but asking anyway.

"Nah. You know Beck. She kept it in check too. Didn't punch him. He was asking about you mostly." Paul says.

I nod. "Let them come for me. I'd rather it be me than L." They both look at me like I have multiple heads. "Paul, if it was Beck, you'd do the same."

Paul nods, we all know he would too.

"It's settled then. Keep an eye on that fuck." I order. " Are we done now?"

They both yeah Prez me and I take the opportunity to run up the steps. There is a water bottle on the counter but no L. I shoot her a text before I look in the living room and circle back to the kitchen to go up the stairs. "Hi baby" Brianna's voice makes me want to gag. She slinks towards me. Did she not get the point the other night?

"Get the fuck out. You are not even supposed to be on this side of the house." I growl at her.

She puts her hand on my chest, "But baby, I miss you so much. You look so tense; I can fix that."

"Fuck off Brianna, get the fuck out or you won't ever come back here." I tell her, forcefully pushing her hand off me in the process.

"Is this cause of that blonde bimbo?" She stomps her feet like a fucking child whining.

It takes every ounce of self-control I have to not strangle the girl. Why the hell did I sleep with her again? I think to myself. "Brianna, I don't hit women but if you don't shut the fuck up and get the fuck out. I will not hesitate to break that rule."

"It is isn't it?! What does she have I don't?! She isn't even that pretty and that blonde is so trashy fake." Her voice is like nails on a chalkboard as she screeches.

She breaks the last of my self-control with her insults of L. I pull my gun, hoping L is upstairs and not coming down to me putting a gun in a woman's face. "Fucking leave Brianna. Don't ever fucking come back here. Don't you fucking ever insult this club's queen again either. I fucking promise you that I'm not fucking joking." I growl shoving my gun at her so the barrel is touching between her eyes. She's dumb as fuck and would never know the safety is still on.

Her eyes go wide and she backs away from me before sprinting across the room to the party room door. I strap my gun back into my jacket and rub my hand over my face again. All these problems popping up are really starting to piss me off.

I run up the two flights of stairs to my room. Again no L. Then I notice her stuff is gone too.

"Fuck!" I rub my hands over my face. Clenching my jaw and fists I storm back down the stairs.

I had texted and called L all day, but I did tell her if she knew and wanted to run, I'd let her. So, after hours of no response, I forced myself to stop. I'm not about to break another promise. I've broken her enough for a lifetime already. When I finally head downstairs again, it was only because Gunner had called up, he got a bunch of pizza and wings delivered.

"You've been a raging asshole today man. I get it sometimes the prospects need to get put in line but you were just down-right cold-hearted today." Gunner lectures me and I unkindly tell him to fuck off, just like I had pretty much everyone else today. Not to mention, he is one to talk. The man is brutal to the prospects at times. "Just saying, you can't rip everyone's head off over nothing." He keeps going.

"I already shoved my gun in one person's face today, you want to go for two?" I growl at him.

Gunner puts his hands up and steps back from me. "Damn man, alright. I'll back off. Who got the gun though?"

"Brianna." I state dryly, shaking my head and filling a plate with pizza. I hadn't eaten much today and now of course I'm starving.

"Why the fuck was that whore here?" He asks, almost growling. He has grown to dislike Brianna more and more over time. I fill him in on what happened in the kitchen, by the end Gunner is staring at me weird.

"Something on my face?" I ask him and grab my napkin wiping around my mouth.

"You are so smart but so fucking stupid." Gunner says to me.

Fucking asshole, I think to myself. "What the fuck does that mean?"

"Brianna was here, Blondie is gone. Connect the dots brother." Gunner stares me down, it clicks.

"Fuck dude!" I yell, dropping the pizza that was in my hand back on the plate. I start rushing around the room like a madman. Pulling my phone out of my pocket and grabbing my jacket. Dialing L on repeat, knowing she won't answer but hoping she will so I continue to call anyway.

"Just fucking go man!" Gunner yells at me. I run to the door and pull it open. Stopping in my tracks at the sight in front of me.

"Kitten?" I say softly. He eyes are red and swollen like she's been crying. She is holding her car keys in her hand and her hair is soaked from the rain that started tonight.

"I am so, so sorry Cole! I am so sorry." She cries. Then she leaps at me, wrapping her arms around my neck and clinging to my chest. My arms automatically go around her. "I jumped to conclusions instead of talking to you and I just ran. I couldn't bare facing you and you said you'd leave me alone if I ran. I know I don't deserve your forgiveness but I'm really hoping you will forgive me for leaving."

So, Gunner was right. Brianna, that bitch is going to regret crossing a fucking line today. L is still crying but when I don't respond she starts to pull away from me. That snaps me out of my angry daze. I was too focused on her and my anger to respond. I don't know how she figured it out but I'll thank whatever god send that is later. Now, I just need to take care of my woman, my world, my life. I scoop her up into my arms and carry her up the stairs.

"Well, that was fast." I hear Gunner say with laughter.

Once I get to my room, I kick the door shut and set L on my bed so I'm on my knees in front of her and my hands are on her face. "Kitten, why did you run baby?" I ask her softly, needing to know exactly what happened before I kill someone later.

She sniffles a little but brings her blue eyes up to mine. "That girl, Brianna, she was here. She said she was your girlfriend and she was acting like she belonged in the house and I just believed her." Her eyes search mine looking for answers from me.

"Brianna is nothing. You are the only girlfriend I have ever or will ever have. Brianna is just starting trouble because I kept rejecting her when it had come to anything other than a quick fuck." I admit to L. I can see the sadness clouding her eyes and continue on talking. "I regret sleeping with her, or with anyone else for that matter. Had I known I would have you back at any point I wouldn't have slept with anyone. Nine years is a long time Kitten and I honestly didn't think I would get a chance to have you back after everything." I explain, keeping my eyes on hers. I need her to know that she can always trust me, that I wasn't purposely trying to fuck up anything between us and never would be with anyone else now that I have her back.

"I know that now." She mumbles. I can tell she's trying to keep her voice steady as she speaks so she's keeping her voice down.

"Do you now?" I ask, trying not to laugh.

She smiles a little bit. "Beck told me." Thank fuck, I think to myself with a sigh of relief. I'll have to thank her tomorrow. Maybe she wants a raise, or an extra day off, or maybe I should let them go on a trip. Tech would probably freak out being away from his precious ass computers for a week though. L pulls me from my thoughts again. "I am so stupid. I am so, so sorry. I didn't run because of everything. It was just that and now I know that wasn't even the truth." Now she is full on sobbing. Does she think I won't forgive her for running or something? She's back now, it doesn't matter.

"Don't. L. Please don't cry baby." I kick my boots off as I climb up onto the bed with her. Bringing L up to the head of the bed with me and wrapping her up in my arms. "Kitten, you are it for me. Don't apologize over some stupid miscommunication. You are not stupid either. You are one of the smartest people I've ever met."

"Now you are just sweet-talking me, Cole." She response with a little pout.

"Always baby." I mumble. I push my face into her neck. Placing kisses as I move down toward her chest. She moans a little and tries to say my name with an unsteady voice. I slide my hands under her sweater, running slowly up her sides. I hum into her chest not moving my lips from her skin in response.

"Make love to me?" She asks softly. I pick my head up to see her face. Those ocean blue eyes, I could get lost in them for the rest of my life.

"I love you L. I have always loved you, I never stopped." I tell her. Placing kisses on her lips I sit up pulling her with me so she's straddling my lap. I pull her sweater off over her head and toss it behind me, barely breaking our kiss. I feel her soft hands tugging on my shirt, so I pull that off too trying to keep my lips on hers as much as possible. I can't get enough of her; I don't want to stop tasting her. Her hands are soft, running up and down my abs, setting my body on fire in their path. I reach behind her and unhook her bra. pulling it off her arms and tossing it somewhere behind us. My hands go to her soft, round breasts. Squeezing and kneading.

"Mmm... Cole." She moans out into my mouth, adding to the throbbing in my jeans.

"You are so gorgeous. Perfect." Her pants are some soft, stretch material and I'm entirely too impatient to deal with them. Though, I don't think they would rip for me because of the way the stretch under my hands. "Kitten. I need your pants off. I need to feel you. Clothes. Off. Now." I grunt out.

She hops back from me immediately and pulls her pants off, panties coming with them. I quickly do the same with my belt, jeans and boxers. We both throw them across the room to wherever they end up landing. I grab her waist and pull her tight to me again, planting kisses from her mouth across her jaw and down her neck. My fingers find her wet slit and she arches back. Her arch gives me access to her nipple, I drop my mouth to one, sucking and flicking with my tongue.

I hum my pleasure into her breast, not wanting to give up the taste of her skin. I enter her with one finger, thrusting it in and curling it as I drag it out. She cries out as I tease her center with my fingers. Finding her clit with my thumb, I start rubbing soft circles, repeating my finger thrusts before entering a second. She is dripping wet, and I'm throbbing. We easily could have skipped the foreplay with how wet she is for me already but it feels good to feel her come apart underneath me.

"Cole, I'm... I'm gonna... " She pants out.

"That's it, baby." I tell her. "Cum on my hand." I demand from her. I feel her wetness as she screams. I slow my pace while she comes down before lining myself up to her center. Slowly, I push myself in letting her adjust to me. I grab her ass in my hands and bury my face in the soft space of her neck, licking, sucking and biting at the sick there. I slowly start to thrust into her.

"Fuck, Kitten. You feel so fucking good." I pant out.

She is so tight and hot around my dick; I know I am not going to last long. I feel her hips rocking with mine, trying to match my pace. Needing to be the one in control, I start moving my hips faster and pushing harder into her. Using the grip on her hips to move her with me. I can feel her walls tighten and my cock get harder and throb. I take a hand from her hip and slide it down to her clit. Rubbing circles with my thumb. She tightens hard around me and cries out. Pushing me over the edge as I release into her.

Panting, I shift so we are laying on our sides. Putting my hands in her hair, I pull her face to mine so I can kiss her soft plump lips. "Fuck, I've missed you." I say when I finally break away from her.

"I've missed you too Cole. I promise you; I am here to stay." She better be, I can't go back to life without her again. She's fucking mine and she can't run now.

Chapter 16 – Ellianna

Cole's room is blinding me with light while I try to sleep. I get why Cole doesn't keep blinds on the windows in here, a natural alarm. I roll over expecting Cole in his massive bed with me but his side is cold.

I sigh and take a minute to replay this week and the events of last night. He definitely hasn't lost his touch with me. He knows exactly how to make my body respond to him and what to do to bring me to the edge and back over and over. It was always like that but we were so young and inexperienced before. This was otherworldly.

It was right on the nose when I told Sonja we were like gravity. The pull is too strong, he's part of me and it feels more than just familiarity. It feels exactly like home here, even more so than when I am with my parents or Ry or Sonja. This just feels right.

I grab my phone and see it's still early yet. I can make the gym today still; it'll be the last time before my job starts then I will have to work around my schedule. I see I have texts from Ry and Pops about family dinner tonight. Pops of course says to bring Sonja and I debate if I should ask Cole to come too. He used to be at Sunday dinners every single week, Momma and Pops loved him which is part of why we were allowed to be together pretty much whenever.

As I'm texting Pops, Sonja's face pops up as a call. I sit up against the headboard and answer.

"Hey Babes." I say into the phone.

Sonja responds. Her voice sounding hesitant. *"Hey, so something weird happened."*

Confused and curious, I press for her to continue. "Uh, okay?"

Starting with a sigh, she finally gives me details. *"Some guy cornered me at work. At first, he said he was from some evaluation company getting personal information on employees so that the facility could better the culture, but then he was asking a bunch of questions about you."*

"Me? How would he know me?" That doesn't make sense and it isn't like many people know who I am or that I am back.

"I don't know. It was weird. I called security. He wasn't who he said he was and they made him leave."

The only person who knows I am here or would have any idea who to start asking about me and would is Brett. Now Brett is already going for the people I care about, he is moving faster than I thought he would. "Shit. It probably has something to do with Brett. I am so sorry I put you in that position babes." I tell her, genuinely upset that she had to deal with that because of me.

"No worries on me, I'm worried about you!" She exclaims, her voice raising.

"I'm fine. Maybe, I should tell Cole."

"That's probably a good idea. See you at home later?" She agrees.

"Yeah. Don't forget dinner with Momma and Pops tonight."

"Oh right! It is Sunday. Wouldn't miss Momma's cooking!"

Thinking I should probably find Cole I end the call with Sonja, I'll see her later and we can chat more. "Okay babes, Bye!"

"Bye! Be careful." She says back.

I click off the phone and start hunting for my clothes. I manage to find my leggings and bra. Good enough. I take another of Cole's shirts from his closet. I'm going to have to start leaving clothes in my car if this becomes a thing. My mind is reeling about my call with Sonja as I bound down the stairs. Did Brett really send someone here to ask around about me? What does he gain from that anyway?

As soon as I hit the last flight of steps to the kitchen, I can tell it is different from my first morning here. I hear a bunch of men talking and laughing, chairs moving across the floor and all the noises that would indicate that a bunch of men live here. At the bottom step, I take in the sight ahead of me, there are at least twenty men in jeans, tees and leather jackets. Twenty hella hot men at that; it's quite the sight. I scan the room looking for Cole, but I don't see him, Gunner or Tech for that matter. I do however see Beck in the kitchen slapping someone's hands away from a plate of bacon. "Hey Beck." I greet her with a smile as I lean against the counter. She turns toward me matching my bright smile with her own and pulling me into a side hug.

"Morning babes!! I see you took my advice." Her voice excited and happy.

Nodding, I pull away from her. "Yes, Very good advice. Thank you!"

"Hungry?" She asks me.

I nod again. "Yeah, but I got this call this morning and I kind of need to find Cole."

"They should be back soon, those three never miss breakfast." She tells me. I nod for a third time and pour some coffee for myself. Then I go back to standing back by Beck and asking if she needs help. She waves me off telling me she's about done. She is the one person I know and am comfortable with, so I cling close to her.

Looking around the room, it is a mad house. Men are everywhere. "Is it always busy like this?"

"On Sundays, yes. It's off day for everyone unless there is something pressing, then normally Hawk or Gunner take care of it. Most of them are still probably drunk from last night and just wandered in from the party bar or the guest rooms." She explains before asking me to grab the quiche from the oven and put it on the table with everything else.

I notice there is already a huge pile of pancakes on the table along with cut up fruit, juices, what looks like bloody mary's and a couple bowls of veggies. Beck is making a huge pan of scrambled eggs and finishing up bacon. I do as she asks and while a couple of guys eye me. Most of them avoid looking at me at all, it's a strange thing how they all look at me or away from me. It doesn't make me any more comfortable with being here.

I go back for my coffee and settle into a seat at the bar top instead of the table with the guys as they dig in. Beck appears in front of me with two full plates. "Here" She says, setting a plate on the counter in front of me. "I always save a plate for myself so I made you one too, they are a bunch of animals when it comes to food."

I giggle and thank her. I think Beck and I could eventually be really good friends. I definitely like her, she's a bad ass but also extremely caring. Seeing her like this, she has this whole "mom of boys" thing going on.

"How long have you been with Tech?" I ask her as she settles in beside me.

She finishes her bite of food before answering. "Almost 5 years now. We basically got married right away. It wasn't the best situation at the time but it worked out in the long run." About the same amount of time, I was with Brett, how opposite that went.

I hear doors slam and turn to see my sexy man walking through into the kitchen. He looks pissed as he marches in but as soon as his icy blue eyes meet mine his face softens and he smiles. He beelines right to me and wraps his arms around me.

"Morning Kitten." He says kissing my cheek. "Did the boys behave themselves?"

I laugh and tell him it's all fine. Then Beck chirps in. "Only because I am here! Someone's gotta take care of your girl since you just leave her here with these heathens." She laughs and takes her plate and coffee to over by Tech, plopping herself in his lap.

"I like her." I say to Cole.

He kisses my lips. "Good." He says kissing me again. He keeps touching me like he is afraid I am going to disappear. I push against his chest a little making him pull back from me. "I'm starving, you took all my energy. I'll come right back." He tells me before kissing the side of my head and heads to the table. I watch his back side as he walks. Then go back to digging into my own plate. I hear him joking with all the guys and laughing. They all seem like a big happy family here. I'm almost done with my plate when Cole plops back down beside me.

"I like seeing you here like this." He says, a bright smile across his face.

"Oh?" I ask with a smile and bump my shoulder against his.

He chuckles a little. "This is my house, those guys are my family, but you here... in my shirt again. It feels like home."

"Sweet talker." I say bumping his shoulder again with the smile stuck on my face. "I like this too; it feels good here." He has me all distracted until my phone vibrates on the counter in front of us with a call from Ry. "Something weird happened today with Sonja so I feel like I need to get that." I explain reaching for my phone.

Cole looks at me with worry across his face as he nods in understanding and goes back to his breakfast.

"Hey Brother." I answer the call.

"Hey Princess. Where are you right now?" He asks.

"Umm, Cole's. Why?" My voice hesitant, knowing he is going to have a lot of questions about that for me.

Instead, it doesn't even seem to faze him. *"Can you put me on speaker with him?"*

I ask him to hang on and turn to Cole. "Baby, Ry wants you on speaker with me. I don't know why but he sounds upset."

Cole's face changed before I finished my sentence and started yelling for Tech. He pulls me to his side and takes my phone from me saying something to Ry as he orders Tech to get downstairs. I notice Chris following behind us. Tech uses his hand to get into the room and takes my phone from Cole, immediately plugging it into his computer.

"What the hell is going on?" I ask. Whatever Tech did put Ry on speaker through the entire room, his voice booms back at me.

"Some guy was here. First, he was asking Pops a bunch of questions about the same SUV that we lease for Ellie. Then he started getting personal about it. Dad kicked him out but he came out to the shop and started asking me questions too. First, I thought he was a client, then he was asking about the town and then about Cole." Cole interrupts his explanation, asking what Ry said to this guy. *"Nothing about you. He was asking about the gym before it got weird, so I told him about Nick and classes before I kicked him out too."* Ry tells him.

"What did he look like?" Cole asks.

"Like 50. White. Average. Looked like a plain harmless guy."

Cole starts cussing and pacing.

"Someone asked Sonja a bunch of questions too. She called this morning."

"Why didn't you say anything?" Cole says, stopping his pacing in front of me and running his hand through my hair.

"I was going to, but you just got back and you're distracting. Then Ry called." I explain. The whole conversation Tech is typing away and Gunner looks annoyed in the corner bouncing on his heels. Cole just looks livid.

"You're not leave here L." He grumbles, pulling me to his chest.

I push at him, pulling away. "What? No! We have family dinner tonight and I start my job tomorrow Cole."

"It's for your safety." He says softly pulling me back to him.

I'm not having any of it though as I push away from him again. I hear Ry grumbling about something over the speaker phone but I lash into Cole. "Absolutely fucking not. You are not going to control my life. It is my fucking life and you need to respect my choices. And I am choosing to continue on with my life because I didn't fucking have that option for the last four years!"

I watch Cole's face drop as he realizes what he did. "Shit, Kitten. That's not what " He starts but I cut him off, yelling at him more. Forgetting that my brother is on speaker phone and there are two other people in this room.

"Yo. Fam. Still here. Also, Princess, maybe Cole has a point?" Ry voice echoes through the room speakers.

"You are unbelievable Ry!" I hiss out.

"That place is like a fortress; you are safer there than anywhere else." My brother replies like he is the elder and more reasonable one here.

"I'm not going to be forced to do anything I don't want to do. I am pretty sure we would have all guessed that Brett would either come here or send someone so I am really not surprised." I respond, still sticking to my guns here. I glare at Cole; he's practically scowling at me.

"Fine, but either I am with you or Chris is if you leave here." He orders.

"Fine." I glare back at him, but deep down I know he is just trying to keep me safe.

"I hate you both. See you at dinner." Ry says into the room. *"Oh,*

you better tell Pops that Cole is coming, Princess. Otherwise, he may shoot him." I cringe as Ry hangs up and Tech hands my phone back to me.

"Why would Pops shoot me?" Cole asks. His brows furrowed.

"I wasn't in a good place when you left, you should know how protective Pops is. Plus, he loved you and felt like you betrayed all of us." I explain looking at the floor. "I am sorry about all of this. I was worried it would happen but I am surprised it happened so quickly."

Cole rubs his hand over his face, then closes the distance between us to wrap his arms around my waist. "The guy here is a PI, he's been here a few days."

"Excuse me what?" I scoff out.

Tech pulls a bunch of stuff up on the big screen in front of us. Pictures of a white guy in his 50s around town and writing on a notepad. "I've been watching him. My skills let me hack your husband's financial records and he paid this guy to come here. By the way, I only did that because you told Cole you didn't feel safe, and this is what we do. The only people that know are in this room. I wasn't trying to pry or anything."

"Well, that's just great." I grumble out.

Chapter 17 - Cole

Today has been a total and complete shit show since Gunner knocked on my door this morning at 5 am, it isn't even noon yet and I'm ready to call it quits on the day.

We spent this morning making sure our last delivery was secured and tracking some 9s my uncle has camping just outside town lines. Fuckers should know all of that land; it is our territory. We are going to end up in the middle of a war with these clowns and I'm not looking forward to it. Neither are Gunner or Tech. We had made it out of Ohio free and clear with minimal casualties on our end but it wasn't pretty and it definitely wasn't safe for the locals.

Sundays are supposed to be our rest day and I was planning on making up for some of my lost time with L for the entire day, but nope. Now here we are in the basement tracking this guy's steps so we can figure out what he's looking for. Tech hasn't found anything on Brett so we really need to figure out what this guy is up to, what they want and what they are planning. Nothing has looked promising yet and Tech is the best there is when it comes to this type of thing.

So, like I said, total and complete shit show.

"I'm...I'm just gonna go call Momma and fill her in before I call Pops." L whispers to me, I can see how on edge the thought of some guy tracking her and all her friends and family has her. I pull her tight to me, keeping my hands flat against the small of her back. She's short enough she comes to about my shoulder when she's not wearing heels.

She's perfect. She's smart and knows how to get her way. She has always had her Pops wrapped around her finger but she knows how to play the game too and that includes getting Sally involved. Hopefully, that all leads to me not getting shot. I have been before and it burns like hell. Also, I'm pretty sure Ben knows what I do so he would know that there wouldn't be repercussions if he did decide to shot my dumb-ass.

It was like a hole right through my heart when she explained why Ben would be pissed. Honestly, I've tried avoiding all of them since I got back, with good reason. Holding her tightly I lean down to her to capture her lips with mine. Taking possession of her mouth. Trying to reassure her in the way I know how. Less than a minute into it, she lets out one of her little moans.

"Jesus, you gotta do that here?" Gunner yells from the other side of the room.

I flip him off but L is already pulling away from me. She's all blushed with embarrassment, but honestly, I'm just proud of the fact I still have that effect on her. I pull her back tight to me so I can adjust myself using her as a shield from Gunner and Tech. Of course, she starts giggling. "It's your fault, my feisty little kitten" I softly tell her before letting her go and watching her climb the steps with that perfect ass of hers.

"Put your eyes back in your head, Hawk. We have work to do." Gunner grumbles from beside Tech.

"She's mine. I'll watch her if I damn well please." I growl out, my eyes still not leaving her back side.

Gunner rolls his eyes and I know he's about to say something to piss me off. "Is now the best time to have us babysitting her and her PI? We have our own shit."

I turn and glare at him. "You don't think I don't know we have our own shit to deal with Gunner?"

"Just saying. You haven't seen her in almost a decade man. Now she walks back in with all these problems and you are putting the family that has had your back that whole time at risk over it!" Gunner starts yelling again. I look up the stairs to make sure the doors got closed.

"What the fuck are you saying Gunner?" I step toward him after I know the doors were closed so L can't hear us fighting about this.

"What I'm saying is I think you are being irresponsible and letting your dick get in the way of your fucking job." Gunner states like I'm not going to fucking kill him about it.

For that thought and the fact I've had a shit day already. Then considering I have some anger issues; my fist makes solid contact and a sickening sound with Gunner's face. "She's my fucking family too Gunner. You of all fucking people should know that." I hiss at him, only feeling slightly better now that I punched him.

He wipes blood off the side of his face, I cracked him pretty good across the cheek because there is a decent sized gash. "You know what a war is like, Hawk. You need to think big picture and about your fucking family. Not a little blonde with problems she made for her own damn self." With that last comment he marches up the stairs. I let out a deep breath and turn to Tech who's smirking.

I clench my jaw, "You think this is funny, fucker?"

"Only because I've been there, only because I was on your end of things once and it was you and Gunner against me. I understand man, but you said similar shit to me about Beck." Paul reminds me.

When he and Beck got together it was the worst possible timing, her family were some of the worse people and honestly, I thought Tech was being too good of a guy at the time and Beck was just looking for a way out. "Worked out just fine for you."

"Sure did." He laughs and looks back at his computer. "I think I know what this guy is looking for." I raise my brow, he continues. "Look, when I catch stills of his notebook everything, he is putting down is like a map to you. Other than that car accident, I haven't pieced that part together yet."

"Map to me? Not L but me?" I ask leaning over his shoulder to look at his screen.

"I think he's finding evidence to put you out of the picture. He is either trying to turn Ellie against you or put you in jail."

"Well, neither of those things are going to happen." I snort and lean back.

"She knows everything then?" He asks, giving me a knowing look.

"Been a bit busy Tech, if you haven't noticed."

Paul rolls his eyes. "You might want to, sooner rather than later. She may trust you but that may only go so far if she knows the extent of what you had to do in Ohio. Also, any thoughts on why he's looking into this accident?"

"Not really. I mean, L was supposed to be with them and she wasn't because I flipped out. I saw how fucked up they were and there was no fucking way I was letting her in that car. I mean we had been drinking and I probably shouldn't have driven her home that night either, but they were all fucked up on heroin and acting crazy. I started chugging water after her and I fought, I held her tight to my side until they left then I took her home. Her Pops flipped shit on both of us that night. She wasn't supposed to be at that party or with me so he was pissed she lied. Eventually, he pieced together that I was protecting her and ended up saving her life in retrospect. It was the turning point in my relationship with him where he let me stay with her when my mom was on a bender or whatever." Tech nods through my explanation. "Ben was a fan of me after. He was the closest thing I had to a dad. He has the right to be pissed at me. Tonight, is going to fucking suck."

Tech slaps my back. "Good luck. You'll need it. Now get the fuck out, I have work to do."

Later that evening, we pull up the drive to L's childhood home, I'm driving her new SUV since she insisted that we both wore something "nice". I'm in a suit with my shirt unbuttoned around the collar and no tie. L has this sexy red dress on that cuts a V down her chest. It is otherwise fairly modest, with long sleeves and a tied bow on the side of her hip. It floats around her hips and thighs, stopping at her knees. Her Momma was always a stickler for Sunday Best and L looks amazing, so I'm just dealing not being on my bike, or in my leather.

"You read for this?" She asks.

"Should I be worried still?" I ask back, rubbing my hand over my face.

She smiles at me, "You look good babe, Momma is going to be excited."

Before we step out of the car Ry pulls up in his tuck and hops out. He's also in suit pants and a buttoned-up dress shirt. I jump out of the car and hurry over to the other side to grab L's door for her. She smiles brightly at me as she takes my hand and steps out. God, what that smile of hers does to me. I feel like a giant pile of mush. My "tough guy" exterior is basically not existent when she's around. She calms the anger that rages and the dark thoughts that cross my mind.

"Such a gentleman." She giggles out.

"Only for you." I mumble in her ear.

"Don't you two look dapper" I hear Ry say as we walk toward him.

"Of course, Momma would have it no other way." My girl says. She's practically glowing here. Family was always her every-thing, it pisses me off that fuckhead husband cut her off from

139

them.

"You're right there. Though I'm surprised you got this guy in a suit." Ry punches my arm with a light swing.

"Not about to cross Momma." I tell him. He pats my shoulder with the hand he used to punch me. So far this isn't so bad. It's almost like what it used to be. This was a weekly thing before I left. Dress well, have dinner, pile in the living room and watch sports. They were family and they accepted me as part of it.

"You boys ready to face Pops?" L says breaking me from my memories.

"After you Princess." Ry says with a smirk.

My girl rolls her eyes and grabs my hand before she practically drags me the rest of the way up the drive to the house. No turning back now. We get almost to the house and Ben comes out to stand on the front porch. Of all the fucking things to take me out, it is going to be L's father. I'm basically seeing my life flash before my eyes. She yells for him and let's go of my hand. Bounding up the steps she hugs him tight. I hear him tell her to go help her Momma inside.

Yup, definitely going to die today. Ben Turner is about to have my head on a stake. I swallow hard and try to maintain my ground and some level of confidence here. "Be nice." L scolds him just loud enough for me to hear, before kissing his cheek. She steps to the door; turns to blow me a kiss then prances her perky ass in the house leaving me all alone with Ben. Would it have been too much to ask her to stay as a human shield?

"Whelp brother, nice knowing you." Ry pats my back and starts to walk past Ben.

"Boy, you keep your ass out here too." Ben growls with authority without even speaking that loudly.

Ry stops in his tracks and turns to me looking as terrified as I feel. I've faced some terrifying men and took them out without blinking, but I wouldn't even put up a fight again Ben just on principle. Even so, he may be able to be my ass even if I tried. For an old man he stays in shape and I am absolutely scared of him. Completely scares the hell out of me, I feel like a damn sixteen-year-old kid all over again.

"Cole, I should kick your fucking ass. Right here, Right now. However, my wife as has asked that I don't do that and fortunately for you I love my wife and would prefer to not be on her shit list for the next month over your dumb fucking ass. So, the only reason my fist isn't currently hitting your face is because I enjoy keeping her happy. You should fucking count your blessings and thank that woman." Ben growls the words out; his voice is laced with venom and I know he means every word. Thank god for Momma Sally. "So instead..." He says while closing the space between us. He steps to me until we are eye to eye. I won't stand down or show weakness even if I know I would never hit him back.

"I'm going to tell you this." He seethes out, gripping the collar of my shirt. "I am so fucking disappointed and disgusted with you. Your choices never just affect you and the fact that you did what you did to my daughter makes me fucking sick to even look at you. Especially, considering what that piece of pompous shit of a man she ended up marrying. My daughter may have forgiven you and insists to me you did it for her but I won't be so easy to convince. I find your actions and behavior now even more disappointing. If you cared for my daughter you would have left her alone and let her heal. Instead, I hear you kicked her out of your fucking bar first." Ben stares me down and all I can do is nod as he grips a hold of my shirt tighter and is inches from my face spitting his words out at me.

"Your fucking actions left her broken. My little baby girl was completely fucking broken because you are a selfish dickhead. For fucking years, I helplessly watched my girl grieve over you and you weren't even fucking dead. Then she ran to a worse situation." He drops his hand, but his tone of voice is still seething. "That faking, lying piece of shit, garbage of a boy deserved her even less than you do now. I have no doubts in my mind that my girl is smart and would have seen through his bullshit if you hadn't broken her as much as you did. That boy, that I can't ever forgive you for. Worse yet, you come back into her life like everything is fine and dandy, even showing up here. You got a death wish?" He says looking me dead in the eye. I have no reply to him. Everything he said is right. I am a shit man for leaving, I am a shit man for what I did and had to do once I left and even what I do now. But also, I'm selfish and I can't stay away from her.

After a hard swallow and a low breath out. I realize I had been holding my breath. "You're right, Sir. I have a hard time trying to forgive myself for what I've done as well. I will promise you though, I will protect her with my life, if she wants me apart of hers or not. I will spend the rest of my life making it up to her, as long as she lets me. You Sir have always had my respect and I apologize for what I did to hurt your family and lose your respect in me. You have to believe me when I say it wasn't my choice and if I could change things, I would."

Ben nods at me and rubs his chin for a second. His eyes, I think momentarily softened but it was so quick I could be wrong. Then he turns to Ry and lights into him. "As for you boy, I expect better. Did I or did I not raise you to protect, respect and love your sister?"

Ry visibly pales and I see him swallow hard before barely saying "yes Pops". Then there is a loud smack. When I turn Ry is rubbing the back of his head.

"Some fucking job you've done." Ben grumbles to Ry before stepping back to me. "Now, I expect you to be on your best behavior tonight and show nothing but respect and genuine admiration for my wife and daughter. You don't deserve my daughter and you best be fucking grateful she's come around."

"Always Sir." I say with some confidence. I can most definitely treat Sally and L well, I always have, no reason why I wouldn't now. I hear a car door shut and Sonja yelling out for Pops, before she runs by Ry and I in a flurry of brown hair before wrapping herself around Ben in a tight hug. "It's been forever Pops!" She exclaims while letting go of Ben. He drapes a fatherly arm around her shoulders and guides her in the house talking with her leaving Ry and I in the drive.

"How the hell did I get in trouble of you? Does he not see his precious daughter is insane and would have clawed my damn eyes out if I didn't let her go with you?" Ry complains at me.

I burst into laughter at his little outburst. "Careful how you talk little brother." I manage to get the words out while trying to contain myself.

"You know I am right."

Rolling my eyes, you'd think he'd be more worried about me. "Let's get inside before both her and Sally claw both our eyes out."

"Fair." Is all he says before we walk into the house, I was in more than my own most of high-school.

Chapter 18 - Ellianna

"Momma, Pops isn't going to do anything to Cole right?" I ask my mom in the kitchen after I walk in and give her a hug.

"Between you talking with him and my agreement with him, he shouldn't baby." Momma says rubbing my shoulders. "He wasn't happy even after you explained but he has always liked Cole. He's just gonna put the fear of God in him. You know your Pops."

One would think that's all he'd do but I know Pops is angry. "Momma, he liked Cole before I cried every day in my room for like a year." Momma frowns and changes the subject, asking me to help finish dinner. She went all out tonight. Prime rib, potatoes, gravy, asparagus and scalloped corn. All of Pops favorites and something she only ever put together a few times a year for us.

"There's cheesecake in the fridge for later too baby."

"This is too much Momma." I shake my head while I set the table.

"Nonsense. Welcome home for you and back to the family for Cole. It's just the right amount of stuff for dinner." She says to me, making me smile to my eyes and giving her another hug. She has always been my rock and is always the optimist of us all. She has a gentle giving soul and has always loved and mothered anyone Ry or I brought home.

"Perfect, all my favorite, gorgeous women in one room again." Pops says brightly while walking into the kitchen with Sonja and kissing on Momma's cheek.

"You are too much Pops." Sonja says before coming over to Momma and giving her a hug too.

"Son, could you be a doll and get this gravy in the boat for the table?" Sonja of course complies and leaves Momma's side.

Momma moves to Pops and starts interrogating him. I can't hear all they are saying but they it looks like she's happy with whatever he is telling her. Pops wraps his arm around her and kisses on the side of her head. They have always been extremely loving and affectionate with each other and I can't remember a time of them ever really fighting. If they did it was well hidden from Ry and I. We have however, on multiple occasions walked into the house to an eye burning situation happening before us.

Ry and Cole finally walk in. I feel my face light up in an involuntary smile just at the sight of his ice blue eyes. I notice he doesn't have a scratch on him and that makes me genuinely happier. "Hey Momma." Cole greets my mom and gives her a hug once she steps away from Pops. "Good to see you, you are looking lovely as ever and it smells delicious in here."

"Cole. It's good to see you, now stop sucking up." Momma says and swats him with her hand towel that she carries around on her shoulder when she's cooking.

He chuckles as he comes toward me and lightly puts his hand on my hip. "Just speaking the truth Momma." His fingers lightly circle on my hip. It's subtle and fairly innocent contact since we are in my parents' home. Before when we were here, I'd tell him to stop but now I know he needs it. Even if he came in unscathed from the driveway with Pops whatever was said is bothering him.

"Seats!" Momma yells.

When Momma yells you listen and when she says seats you best find yours and get your ass down. She has rules in this house and you are to listen. Everyone sits around the large dining table. Pops at the head of the table with Momma at the other end. Sonja and I are on either side of Pops with Cole by me and Ry across from him. Luckily dinner conversations flow easily. I was worried after Pops' little chat with Cole but even they are talking and getting along. Cole keeps his hand on my thigh or around the back of my chair so he's touching my far shoulder the entire time. We are going to need to discuss what my father said and soon, since it is definitely bothering him now. After dinner the guys clear the table and do the dishes insisting that Momma, Sonja and I enjoy our wine and relax. We head out to the patio while it's still decently warm out.

"I came up the drive to some real intense tension." Sonja says taking a sip from her wine. I explain their little chat that happened and Momma piped in with how Pops was just trying to look after me. It made me a touch annoyed the way she said it, leading into a full-on argument with between the three of us. "Best throw caution to the wind babe, I mean you did just practically escape your life and marriage." Sonja huffs out.

Shocked she'd say such a thing I glare at her. "Well, I did leave and I am fine."

"Are you though?" She asks, leaving me to continue my glare. I mean, where is she going with this.

"Do you think me being with Cole is a bad idea?" I ask, honestly wanting to know what my best friend and my mother think since they are ganging up on me about him and my life.

"Just seems a little fast. You are different now. He's different now. You've been through hell for years part of which is his fault, yet you are both acting like nothing happened." Sonja softly says while Momma is sipping her wine taking her out from this conversation.

"I haven't forgotten Sonja. Trust me. We have argued and talked and had full on screaming matches and breakdowns about it, and we are still working on it. We are both well aware of the past but we also realize that you can't keep harping on it if you want to move forward." I tell her, trying to keep my emotions in check.

"From the outside looking in perspective, it doesn't look that way." Sonja continues to push her point.

"We've always been connected. Jesus, you both sitting out here have witnessed that. We are soulmates for lack of a less cliche word. We connect deeply and this, what's between us now, even after everything, it is so much stronger. I can't ignore it even if I tried. He has my entire heart and soul and I have his. God, he even has a part of me and us tattooed on him." I speak my heart out, not able to keep my emotions in check about it. How dare she attack my relationship with Cole, especially here in front of my Mom.

"Just doesn't sound healthy is all I'm saying." Sonja says with a shrug and finishes her wine. Maybe something else is going on with her. I try to brush it off. My connection with Cole has always been hard to explain to others, but we both know what we feel. The connection is so strong it almost ate me alive when he left. "Did you fuck him?" Sonja blurts out pouring herself more wine. I hear Momma choke a cough while all I can do is stare at her in shock for asking like that with Momma right here. Of course, my mother knows we have sex, she made sure I was fully covered in high school with all that.

"I think that's an inappropriate question Sonja." I hiss out at her.

Momma chuckles. "It's fine dear. Just catches a mother off guard a bit is all."

"I don't think it matters what we have or haven't done." I state dryly. Now Sonja shrugs at me before suggesting I need to see a therapist again, making Momma look at me with so much concern in her eyes. "Look, I will. I want to get settled into work first, but Cole is a given thing for me. Therapy or not I'm with him and I just think the therapy will be beneficial for other reasons."

Sonja shuts her trap finally and Momma changes the subject. Thank god for Momma. We finally settle into easy conversation and steer clear of my personal life after that. Eventually the guys finish up in the house and come out to join us until the sun sets and the temperature drops to a decent chill.

"We should get going! Tomorrow is a big day, first day of my new job." I say getting up from the deck chair. Cole, Sonja and Ry follow my lead. All of us hugging on Momma and saying byes to Pops before heading down the drive to our cars.

"You coming home tonight?" Sonja asks.

I'm still annoyed with her, but I keep trying to remind myself it's just because she cares and is worried but I don't like her thoughts on the situation. "Yeah, that was my plan since tomorrow is my first work day and all. I'll see you there."

"I'd rather you stay with me kitten, for your safety." Cole says getting in the driver seat of my car.

"I need my own time and I need to sleep. Plus, I have my closet and stuff for work tomorrow all there. I need to settle into a good work flow, you know?"

"I'll stay then." He says.

"Sonja may not be okay with that." I say hesitantly.

Cole rubs his face with his hand, my poor sexy man is frustrated with me. I know he didn't have the best time to start at my parents either. "I'll set up a security detail outside the house then. Gunner is pissed at me so it'll probably be two of the prospects if that's okay?"

"Whatever you feel is necessary love." I say and Cole takes off his suit jacket and puts his leather back on. I know he keeps his gun strapped in his leather; I've felt it against him. I wiggle in my seat and change the music before Cole finally takes off out of the driveway and down the road back into town.

"What did my Pops say?" I ask Cole.

"L..." He says and glances at me quick before looking back at the road.

"I am already guessing it wasn't great. You were fairly quiet and you kept a hand on me at all times. Tell-tale sign something is bothering you."

"Nothing I wasn't expecting and nothing you couldn't guess for yourself. He didn't hit me though which surprised me, I was braced for it."

I shrug, "Yeah, Momma had a fit about it when he suggested it, put him in his place I guess."

"Why's Sonja mad at you?" He asks, obviously ready to change the subject. I don't think he's fully telling me or letting me in as to what Pops said to bother him. He takes my hand and brings it to his lips.

"Turning the table on me and trying to distract me?" I ask. My sweet Cole. His affection has always caught me off guard because to everyone else he is this strong, broody man. Now even more so because he has this deep-down anger in him, I catch it in his eyes at times. Then it's like I get this whole other side, this kind, sweet, loving and affectionate side. "She is just worried; thinks I'm jumping back to you too fast. She thinks I'm not giving myself time to heal from Brett and all that."

He grips my hand tighter, and I see his jaw tense up. "Cole, you have to know that I don't think that, at all. I mean I -"

He cuts me off, " We've been through it all, L. I know baby, I know." I nod and turn my head to watch out the window, this town has changed so much. He pulls up to Sonja's and I notice a truck out front with two guys watching the house.

"Cole, I know whatever Pops said to you has you bothered. You can tell me." I ask him, turning in the car seat to face him.

"L, it's fine. He said what he had to say. I'll work my way back into his good graces and honestly, he loosened up by the end there. He just wants to make sure I'm not going to hurt you again. Which I'm not, he just needs to see it." I scan his face, I'm sure there's more going on in his head but his face tells me that I'm not getting anything else from him. Leaning across the center console and taking my keys from him I land a soft kiss to his lips before hopping out of the car, heading to the front door. "Kitten, wait." He calls getting out of the car. Pausing and turning, he wasn't that far behind me. He places a hand on my waist and tucks some of my wavy blonde hair behind my ear. "Ben just made me feel more guilty than I already do. I love you and I'm going to spend every moment you let me with you making it up to you."

"And I love you Cole, don't send yourself on a guilt trip. What's done is done and we need to move forward from here." He nods and pulls me tight to him. My hands wrap around his neck and his scent of leather and sandalwood fills my senses. "I really do love you Cole. At first, I thought it was just familiarity, but I know it's not just that. It's something deeper that never went away."

"I know baby." He says before he leans down to join our lips in a deep kiss. We break away a little breathless and he sighs. "I'll leave you tonight. The guys will watch the place and I'll see you tomorrow. Call me if you need anything at all and good luck with you first day, Kitten."

I smile and tell him goodnight with another soft kiss on his lips before I turn into the house locking the door behind me. What a crazy day, and tomorrow I start a whole new chapter in my career.

Chapter 19 - Cole

After leaving L last night at Sonja's place, well I guess technically it is her place too now, I couldn't stop thinking about what Ben said to me before dinner. When I left nine years ago, I really thought I was doing the right thing. She needed to be safe and I was a stupid kid. Half of me had figured she would wait for me reading into what I said that last night. Later, I realized that was just hopefulness on my part. The other would have been that she would move on and be happy. As long as she was safe, I didn't care. Not once did I think how it would have affected everyone else around us, or that it would have affected her as badly as it did.

I should have known though. She was as madly in love with me as I was her, at least I had known she was alive, she had no idea what happened to me. I should have told her. I was so worried if I told her she would try to come looking for me or something stupid like that and it would get her killed, or worse. Plus, I was embarrassed by the entire situation.

Once I got to Ohio with my uncle, I knew I had made the right choice to not tell her. Those people were so bad, what they did to people was sickening. There was the human trafficking and then there was the drugs. The other people they dealt with were even worse. Then there were all the people that would drop like flies around us because of small slip ups. Sad how the people my mother got involved with and owed a shit ton of money too were even worse than the people there.

We still haven't been able to entirely track the people my mother owed. Tech has tried a few times. Now though, it has been long enough and they have not come for my mother or I, so I have to think they have moved on by now.

It made me sick and pissed off at myself to even think about what I put L through, and even sicker and even more pissed off that it was still better than if I had let anyone know about her. I am so fucking in love with that girl, I feel like a sappy fucking mush all the time around her. It is highly possible would have gotten us both killed trying to protector.

It is impossible to change the past. It was impossible for me to know the outcomes of my actions and all the possible scenarios are looking at the situation in retrospect. All I can do now is make it all up to her and her family, show her and everyone else that she is my entire world. I'm older, smarter and know this life now. I have the power now and I will kill to protect her.

This morning, I made sure to have flowers sent to her work for her, a little something to congratulate her and wish her luck today, like I said I am a fucking mush. If the guys really knew I would never hear the end of it, I'm going to have to find a balance there somehow. They can't know I'm soft in anyway.

"Yo Prez." I hear Gunner yell behind me. I've been dealing with the warehouse that got broken into by my uncle for the last few hours. Mostly what is stored in here is construction supplies, but we do have some various weapon parts mixed in. It is also where we normally receive shipments until we get them safely moved to the clubhouse. We need to be able to accept shipments here in a few days and my gut has been telling me something is off.

I want to keep the clubhouse as secure as possible but we can't always bring our own shipments in, sometimes they come to us. I'd rather keep everyone but members and prospects out of the clubhouse. Unfortunately, for me the damn members get a say too and there's always random ass people being brought in, especially all the club bunnies or whores or whatever you want to call them that hang around. None of that seems to bother Tech or Gunner as much as it always has me.

The bunnies that live on the property don't bother me as much. Granted, most of them are still constantly half naked and fucking all the members, but we keep them safe. They have come from shitty homes, shitty relationships or drug issues. I make sure they are taken care of and keep clean. In return they take on some jobs, either bartending or cleaning. Beck handles what they are assigned to take care of. It is the one thing that I wish my mom had. Maybe things would have been different if she had a way of being supported.

When they end up in the party room of the clubhouse though, that is a whole other situation, hence the name club whores. Now that L is back and mine; I want her at the club, I mean that is my home, but she's not going to like that at all. I reach up and rub my face with my hand at the thought of L walking into the party room, I hadn't even shown her any of that. Always using the private officer entrance to the kitchen instead. This shit is more complicated than it needs to me.

Gunner keeps talking to me, explaining some of the piles of construction shit in here and how they need them going to different jobs or something. Construction is Gunner's thing, he's a hands-on person. I'll do it if I have to but my heart isn't in it by any means and I prefer handling the businesses and planning. Finally, he stops. "Are you even listening man?"

"Yeah, listen. We need to get a group on a run. At least 10 of us. We need to get the next shipment ourselves and I don't trust shit to not go wrong with the fucking 9's hanging around so my mind is on that." I tell him seriously while looking for the last fucking part on this inventory list that I haven't been able to locate all morning. "Where the fuck is this fucking crate of shit?!" I yell kicking a pallet of sheet rock.

Gunner rolls his eyes. "Gimme that fucking paper." He grumbles and rips it from my hand.

"Mother fucker! If you were anybody fucking else!" I growl at him. I may be a puddle of sap when it comes to L but the fuck am I that type of person any other time.

He mumbles something and walks away from me going from the paper back to a corner of the warehouse. "It's here dick-head." He yells at me pointing at a box. Gunner starts to pry the crate open as I'm walking over to him. "Something doesn't look right." He says explaining why he's opening a crate I had no intentions of opening.

He has the top off when I get to him and we both look in. "What the fuck! What the fuck was supposed to be in here!" I yell pulling my phone out and calling Tech. Crates are supposed to get checked at time of exchange. If the drop is here, they get checked before whoever is dropping takes off. If we go meet our drop then they get checked at the pickup site, most everything here is from drops done right on site. We take the shit we meet for directly back to the clubhouse unless there's lack of room. A rarity, considering the basement to the clubhouse tunnels underground into the side hill and is significantly bigger than the clubhouse. Tech's phone just ringing, it's a weekday in the middle of the day. "Where the fuck is, he?" I yell at Gunner while the phone continues to ring on my second try.

"Prez" Tech finally answers my call, he sounds out of breath for some reason. I look at my smart watch and see it is just past noon. I fill him in and read off the crate numbers. I hear him clicking away at his keyboard and muttering to himself like he does. Gunner is still pacing around the place like that's going to fucking help.

My phone starts vibrating in my hand by my ear, I bring it down to look at the screen. "L" comes across as the contact and her gorgeous ocean blue eyes stare softly into me when a picture of her looking right at me laughing pops up on my screen. I snapped it the other day after I had taken a candid of her and she caught me. She broke into a laugh with her lips turned up and her eyes crinkling at the corners a bit while I snapped a second picture. Of course, I can't answer it right now and that just pisses me off more.

Putting Tech on speaker I send her a text. She must be on her lunch break because she replies right back.

"It's OK, you work too. Thanks for the flowers, you remembered my favorite <3 tty tonight."

All I can think is "Fuck, I miss her." even if it hasn't even been a full day since I last seen her.

Before I can type a response back Tech starts yelling over the line. "This is not good, Prez. Not good."

He knows I hate that. Just get to the point. Gunner stops his damn pacing and comes over by me. "Fucking speak Tech." He yells, as annoyed by the commentary as I am.

"That crate is supposed to have C4 in it. That's why it's in the warehouse." Of fucking course that's what was in here. None of us like explosives in our home, shit sketches us out. Nick handles it mostly because that was part of his specialty when he served with Gunner.

"How fucking much?" I ask looking at the box knowing the answer but hoping like hell I am wrong.

"Enough to take out two thirds of the town, maybe more." Tech tells us. He sounds defeated and I hear a gasp in the background.

"Who the fuck is there, Tech?" I yell. No one needs to know we are missing a fucking ton of explosives and I truly mean no one. The entire town would be panicking.

"Just me." I hear over the phone, the voice belonging to Beck.

"Fuck!! Beck, you can't say a god damn word. This is something even you shouldn't know. Fuck!" I start yelling until I hear her giggling or some shit like this is funny. "And what, do tell is so funny?"

"You know I won't be telling a soul; you are just too on point with you wording." She says. I rub my face with my hand, I did not need to know they were fucking when I called. No wonder Tech didn't answer me right away.

Shaking my head, I get back to the point. "Tech. Figure it the fuck out. This is a big fucking problem, you hear me!" I yell into the phone. "I'm going to have to go on this fucking run tonight." I mumble, knowing I am going to be even more pissed off because of that.

"I'll call Nick." Gunner says beside me and I nod. If there's a ton of C4 just hanging around town, our bomb guy needs to be aware.

"Fucking. Shit. Fuck." I think but must say out loud because Gunner sends me a look across the room.

"It's all the way down to Miami. It'll be days, maybe a week or more. Blondie isn't gonna like that at all. " I hear Gunner point out, like that wasn't already crossing my mind.

"You have a better fucking idea so I can stay here with my wife?!" I yell, not realizing what I said until I said it. The warehouse goes so quiet you could hear a pin hit the floor. "You know what I mean." I eventually mumble out earning a nod from Gunner and a cough from the phone in my hand unable to tell if it was Beck or Tech.

She should be my wife, would have been if things played out differently. Hell, we would probably have a kid by now, or several. I rub my face again, pushing the thoughts of what could have been out of my head. When I close my eyes to rub them with my finger and thumb, I see an image I want for real. L with a round belly, a little girl with blonde curls and a little boy with her ocean eyes and my darker hair.

"Church! Officers only! Fifteen minutes." I scream, then end the phone call. I storm from the warehouse, Gunner hot on my heels. "Fuck! We need Nick too!" I yell knowing Gunner would have heard me. I know Nick doesn't want to be involved much, but he's just going to have to fucking deal with it.

Church turned into a lot of yelling Tech, Gunner and I decided to keep the missing explosives between the four of us, well five since Beck had to be present for that call. Getting explosives out of there would have to be an inside job or at least have inside help. Our warehouses are almost as secure as this clubhouse, not to mention the security feeds that go directly to Tech that are as impossible to hack as he is.

We did however still discuss the breaches of security with the other officers as well as this run and the 9s. It was decided Gunner and I would lead the run, leaving Tech in charge here with Tank as the second in command. Blaze, Jax, Stone, X and Damien would be the other officers with us. Blaze and Jax normally handle runs and have their own crews of six guys each for them. We decided they'd each pick their top two members to round us out. Damien would drive a van with one member from Blaze and X would drive a second van with another member from Jax. The other two guys they pick will ride along with us. Seven on bikes leading with two vans following down. We will change line up and flank the vans on the way back.

Tech thought to split up the guys teams in case one is the traitor, not that the officers know that. They would also have access to shit since it's part of their jobs. A solid portion of our members are military trained, the rest are trained by the others or Nick. When we pulled together enough people from several other MCs as well as my uncle's to take over, the guys willing were like us. They hated the actions and wanted to do better, be better. The guys in this club down to the last prospect were picked because we want to do better and be better than where we came from, we want to make this town better and make a safe, secure hometown for everyone, MC member or not.

That pisses me off more than anything that one of them could be a fucking traitor.

Now, I'm sitting outside of L's pissed off. I have to leave in a few hours and to top it all off I have to leave these two dumb ass prospects to watch over her.

My goal is to convince her to stay at the clubhouse while I'm gone. I'd rather have her somewhere close to Tech. She's going to hate this. I know I fucking hate this. It's not even the run, I love leading runs. It feels good to be on my bike on the open road. I don't want to leave L. Not when I just got her back, not ever again.

I rub my face again before I knock on the door.

Chapter 20 - Ellianna

Waking up this morning I was so excited for my first day at work. It feels like everything is coming together in my life and this is where things were meant to be, where they should have been anyway. I can't help but think that if I had just waited one more year here, if I hadn't have agreed to move to Texas, and if I had stayed here instead, this is where I already would have been in my life. Not to mention I wouldn't have some guy that my soon to be ex-husband paid to come bother my friends and family. To be honest, I am pretty worried about that part. I don't want them going after Cole. I mean what if they find something to put him in jail, I know he's done things so who's to say that isn't a possibility. I pushed down those thoughts and got on with my day. The guys seem to cover themselves well enough and have been pretty insistent on me not worrying.

Shortly after arriving to my new job, getting a tour and short orientation to the building I was shown to my office to settle in and get acquainted with the computer systems and all my sign ins. They told me most of my training is actually done with a few of the programs right from the computer but someone would be around tomorrow to show me the rest of what's expected of me.

Once in my office I see there was a huge bouquet of lilies and wildflowers. Bright pinks, yellows, purples and oranges arranged with some leafy ferns mixed in, all sitting in a large vase on the center of the desk. At first, I thought it was a nice welcome from the company but there was a card. Looking through the card, I see they are from Cole.

He remembered my favorite flowers. I had to push back tears, I couldn't cry on my first day of work here, even if they were happy tears. Cole owned my heart and soul in a way that no one else ever could. Then he does things like this that just reminds me why he's always been the one. Always will be the one.

Maybe, it's my fault that Brett became the way he did. Maybe, I just couldn't love him like I thought I could. I shake my head and smile. Placing the flowers on the long bookshelf against the side wall, I settled in and got to work. I would wait to call Cole during my lunch hour, since I wanted to make a good impression on my first day.

Once I made it home from work, Sonja was still working. The girl works more hours than anyone else, I swear. She is constantly picking up extra shifts in the ER, but covers the rehab clinic three days a week on top of that. I made a quick curry for us. Then took two takeout dishes and two coffees out to the guys watching the house. Just because the guys have to watch me doesn't mean they should suffer for it. They have had eyes on me for almost twenty-four hours now and it is the same two guys. I'm going to have to talk to Cole about that, it is not okay they haven't had a break. They looked so surprised this morning when I took them coffee out to them and even more surprised when I came out with food tonight. I noticed too they were both cautious where their eyes wondered, being sure to not look at me, and almost too polite to me.

Rolling my eyes at the thoughts in my head, I pour a steaming hot bath for myself, complete with relaxing salts and a bubbling bath bomb. Once I settled into my hot bubble bath, I instantly relax in the water with some soft indie rock playing from the little Bluetooth speaker I put in the bathroom.

A knock and the bathroom door clicking open startles me. I must have fallen asleep for a while; the water is rather cold and most of the bubbles have settled. "Kitten." I hear Cole's voice say from the door, he sounds like he's relieved.

Looking up at him, I smile. "Hey baby. " I reply softly and pull the drain plug with my foot.

Cole leans against the door frame. "I knocked, the guys said you were home so I let myself in." he tells me watching me as I step out of the tub and wrap the towel around me.

"I thought I locked the door, is Sonja home?"

He smirks like he's up to something. "Picked the lock babe. We need to get a deadbolt for here."

Gasping a little from shock, I shake my head. Of course, he can pick a lock, I shouldn't be that surprised. Closing the space between us I place a soft kiss on his lips then step around him to my room to find clothes. I really had not meant to fall asleep in there, I must have been more tired from the day than I thought.

"L." I hear Cole say stepping into my room behind me and shutting the door. "We've got to talk Kitten." My heart drops from my chest. Talk, about what? He sounds worried, so now I'm worried. I throw an oversize tee on and turn toward him. He wraps me up in his arms, glides the back of his fingertips across my face and tucks some of my hair behind my ear before explaining, "I have to go out of town for a bit."

"Oh." I say softly and drop my gaze to the floor. I figured there would be time he would have to leave for the club but I didn't think it would be so soon yet. "How long?"

"I'm not sure yet, it could be a week." He says lifting my face up to meet his eyes. "It's not that I want to, it's something I have to do. The club needs me."

"No. I mean, yes. I know, I get it. I knew you would have to be gone at times. I just wasn't thinking it'd be so soon, I guess. I feel like we really just started putting us back together." I say, emphasizing the "us" part.

"I know L, I do. I feel the same way. There are a few things going on right now. Gunner and I both need to go on this run. Otherwise, I'd make someone else do it." His lips are tight and his voice is low. I see the worry shine in his eyes and I can't tell if it's because he's worried about leaving me here or if he is worried about what's going on with the club.

Biting my bottom lip, I put my hands flat on his chest. "Baby. It's okay. When do you leave?"

"Soon. A few hours." He replies. "I also want you to stay at the clubhouse while I'm gone. It's safer and Beck said her and Tech would stay too so that you'd have her around. Please, don't fight me on it." He says the last part with his teeth clenched. He thinks I'd fight him on that. Normally, I would but I was already worried about the guys watching the house.

"I won't fight you on that. Mostly because I don't like that those poor guys have to sit out there and have been watching me for an entire day with no breaks. That's not fair, you can't do that to them. Not to mention the act like they are terrified when I try to talk to them." I say stepping back from him. He has an amused smile on his face for some reason. "Why are you smiling?"

"They act terrified?" Cole says with laughter.

"That's what you're happy about?" I say smacking his chest.

Cole slides his hands to the back of my thighs, picking me up. My legs automatically wrap around his hips. He turns us towards the bed where he drops me laughing. "Yes, I'm glad they are terrified. You're mine, if they fuck up, they answer to me. It means that they are taking this seriously." He says pulling his shirt over his head climbing on the bed, his body finding its way over mine while he keeps his weight rested on his elbow.

"Well, I don't want anyone to be terrified. They can look at me and talk to me without getting in trouble with you Cole." I tell him while my hands find their way up and down his chest.

"Mine." is all he mumbles as he presses kisses along the side of my neck.

I push at his chest. "Cole. I'm serious. Those poor guys. They are young too! Are they even 18?"

He stops his kisses to look up at me. "They are prospects. It's part of the process. They need to earn the club's trust, and my trust. We are hard on them because they have to earn their place with us. They also need to learn. Don't feel bad for them, they knew when they came to us to join what they were getting into."

I sigh. I don't know if I'll ever understand this life of Cole's, every time I try there's something else. Something new that he has to explain to me. "If I stay at the clubhouse, they'll get a break?"

"While you're in the clubhouse, yes."

"I have work, and I need to go to the gym and what about Sonja? And if you're not back Sunday, I still have to go to family dinner." I'm rambling now, for some reason I'm feeling nervous. Maybe because the thought of him being out of town is sinking in. Cole rolls off me, laying on his side. His hands stay wrapped up in my hair. I don't remember him being this touchy with me before. Now it's like every time we are in the same room, he has to have a hand on me.

"You'll need to tell Tech if you are leaving the clubhouse at any time and where you are going. You are to go with him or both of the prospects only, no one else. You're fine at the gym, but the boys will know that. If they know what is good for them, they will train with Nick when you're there anyway." He tells me. The guys that watched me today must be who he means needs to be with me if Tech isn't. They know my work schedule already.

"So, they will follow me to work like they did today?" I ask and get a nod as a response.

"I'll try to get back to you by Sunday, Kitten." He whispers, running his hands through my hair. "I don't want you to stress out about this. He sighs and takes his hand from my hair. Laying on his back he rubs both his hands down his face. "Listen, I just want you safe. Gym, Club and bar all safe. Traveling, work, here, anywhere other than those three places, I don't have any control over. L, if we miss something and you husband ends up here and tries to hurt you, or this PI guy or whatever is here to hurt you." He sits up. "fuck!". He says harshly while running his hands over his face.

Seeing him like that, so worried about me. He'd never forgive himself if something happened when he was trying to protect me. That's why he disappeared without a word to start with anyway was because he was trying to protect me. Even if it wasn't his fault. This week will drive me nuts, but to settle his mind I'll do what he wants while he's gone. It's going to drive me nuts I'm sure, but I'll do it for him. Sitting up and shifting myself behind him, I run my hands up and down his back. His muscles relaxing against my hands with every pass. "I'll do all that. I promise. Don't worry about me, I'll make sure Tech and those two boys take good care of me." I place soft kisses across his shoulder blades, even sitting he towers over me. "What are their names anyway?"

"Matt is the scrawny kid with light hair. Tommy is the dark-haired kid." His tone very matter-of-fact.

I giggle, "No crazy names to remember to call them by?"

"Nah, not everyone gets a name." He shrugs. His body is still fairly tense even under my fingers.

"Why do they call you Hawk?" I ask, I have been genuinely curious.

"I see things most people miss, I guess. When I first got to Ohio there were a bunch of guys in the woods. They were armed and ready to attack, take out the club there. I didn't know who I was with yet, or who would be trying to take them out. No one had noticed but me, I told my uncle and saved the day." His voice is laced with sarcasm. "It stuck. I never told anyone my real name there, no one said it until we came back to this town. Well, Tech and Gunner knew but it was a while after we learned to trust each other. Even now, a lot of the guys don't put two and two together." He finally turns and faces me, pinning my back to the bed again. "I don't like that name coming from you Kitten. Don't call me that unless we are somewhere public or the situation calls for it."

"I won't, you will always be Cole to me. I was just curious." I shrug a shoulder a bit and bring a hand to Cole's face. He leans to my touch.

"Let me love you." He says before kissing me again, taking over my body with the touch of his lips and hands. I let him, knowing it will be days before I see him again. Knowing we will both be worrying like crazy about each other until he's home by my side again.

Chapter 21 - Cole

The longest part about runs is making sure our traveling takes us into neutral or friendly territory. Heading from New York to Florida for most people is long enough of a trip, for us though coming from deep Upstate all the way to Miami it's already been four days and hours upon hours on my bike. There's no way we are going to end up making it back home by Sunday and I'm pissed it's taking as long as it is.

Tech got into contact with a couple of other clubs on the way down that we have been friendly with. Since Gunner and I were both running with this we made a few friendly stops on the way and if anything, positive is coming out of this we are now in contracted alliances with three other large clubs. Their clubs are big and spread out with multiple chapters throughout their regions. Gaining these three alliances doubles our full alliance numbers.

Our club is pretty big, especially considering how new it is. Couple hundred members and a chapter in Ohio we left behind after taking out my uncle's club. Phoenix Rising MC was never even heard of until we went to war with my uncle's club out there. We stirred up a lot of trouble with countless clubs and I've spent a considerable amount of my time fixing relationships with clubs not running drugs. Once the word got out that we are anti-drug running and we are the ones with the best weapons, we gained as many friends as we did enemies. Feels good to have these alliances behind us now, but I'll be damned if I said I liked this trip at all.

I fucking hate it. I hate that L isn't here.

"Hey Prez!" Blaze calls from outside the motel door. We made it into the outskirts of Miami in the early morning hours and decided to rest before meeting our drop. I've been up about an hour now and am suited up. My jacket lined with that bullet-proof nano tech shit that Tech got in a few weeks back, boots laced with a few knives stuffed into them just in case and my 9mm strapped into my jacket with my extra, only for runs, Eagle tucked into the waist of my dark ripped up jeans and a custom set of brass knuckles in my right jacket pocket just for good measure.

Opening the door to Blaze he hands me a large coffee. "Ah, knew you were a good dude." I tell him and sling my bag over my shoulder heading out of the motel room.

"We meet in an hour, it's about 15 minutes from here." He informs me, giving me a run-down of the meeting spot he scouted when we got in.

"Any issues you see on this?" I ask him once he has finished.

"Nah, I've met up with Spider several times for runs. He's lead on their end, should go well." Blaze says as we pack our bikes back up.

I lean against my bike and drink at my coffee as the rest of the guys load up. Feeling my phone vibrate I pull it out to check it. Text from L.

"Miss U. Stay safe."

A sharp ache runs through my chest. She was out of my reach for nine years, yet two weeks she's back and it is physically aching me to be away from her this long. I look around and see Gunner and Blaze are instructing the guys so I decide to call her. She picks up on the first ring, out of breath. "Hi." She practically purrs into the phone.

"Hey Kitten." I say softly, wondering why she was so out of breath answering. "I only have a minute, but I wanted to hear you."

"Mmm... I've missed your voice too." She purrs again, still breathy in her voice. I feel my dick perk up in my jeans and scold myself in my head.

"What are you doing? You sound all out of breath?" I ask, as much as her voice is turning me on, a little voice in the back of my head is ringing in jealous anger. I trust my girl, but she is sexy as hell and I don't trust any guy around her.

"Kickboxing. You're not here to go easy on me." She says with a small giggle, her voice coming back to normal. "When my phone rang after I texted you at a break, I ran to grab it and take it to the hall."

"I hope you are giving Nick hell then. Beat his ass for me." I chuckle. Looking up I make eye contact with Blaze and Gunner; they give me a nod telling me it is go time. "L, we got to go."

I hear her take a sharp breath. "I love you." She says softly, I'd bet she has tears coming to her eyes if I could see her face. "Please come home to me."

Fucking hell, that's a dagger in my chest. I rub my hand over my face. "I love you baby. I'll be home soon, okay?"

"Mhmm..." I hear her, with what sounds like a sniffle after.

"Two days. I'll be back for dinner Sunday." I hang up because the guys are walking closer and I don't know if I can keep a clear head if I hear her upset any longer. Blaze pats my back before walking around me to his bike.

"Don't promise shit, we won't be back by Sunday." Gunner mumbles passing me to his bike.

Clenching my teeth, I ignore Gunner, he's still been pissy with me about L. I don't know what the fuck his problem is. He was fine at first, now he's just being a dick every chance he gets. "Listen up!" I yell across the lot, making all the guys perk their heads up to listen to me. "No fuck ups! Listen to Blaze! We get in, we get out! We get the fuck home!!"

The response is a chorus of "Yes, Prez!" followed by the roar of bikes. We pull onto the road, flanking the vans. I hope like hell this goes right. Pulling into the lot behind this warehouse we are meeting at something feels wrong in my gut. We are a few minutes late and no one is here yet.

Our helmets have coms in them, so I flick my mic on. "Blaze." I growl out, thinking he must have fucked up the time.

"Spider is always here head of time." He says, I feel it as that gut feeling drops deeper.

"Blaze and X. Circle the warehouse. Watch your six. No fuck ups." I order. "Helmets stay on." I say seeing one of the young kids Blaze does runs with start to take his off. Tech has our black with an orange Phoenix wrapping around the side full face helmets lined with some kind of light weight bullet resistant stuff and our coms are wired in so they can hear me. I know most the guys want to go without helmets especially riding, but safety first. Plus, while I'd rather no shots fired, I don't like this and I'm not about to lose a guy because we weren't using the tech we have. I lead the rest of the guys as we park on either side of the vans and hop off our bikes. I pull my 9 from my jacket and have a hand on it as Blaze and X come back to us.

"Warehouse is clear Prez. Empty." Blaze tells me.

"Call your guy Blaze. I want to know where the fuck he is." I spit out, my gut is still feeling uneasy and now I'm just pissed off.

Gunner comes up by my side. "Don't like this."

"Me either." I reply, feeling more uneasy that Gunner is feeling the same.

"Look, sorry for being pissy about Blondie. It's only worries about the club. This shit is unsettling right now though. We need to be in the same head space if something is about to go down." Gunner tells me.

I nod at Gunner. I get it with the being worried about the club, he and Tech built this with me. Together. This is our whole lives and threats to it are threats to us. "Don't worry about it. Just need to know you got my back."

"Always Prez." He says before we both direct our attention back to Blaze.

"Spider didn't answer. Tried his club phone, the bar chick said he left with some guys and a truck hours ago. Their Prez isn't in and she doesn't have a contact number."

"Gunner." I start but he pulls his phone out and nods before I finish, he knows I want Tech on this now. "Saddle up boys. We have a club to get to." Either Spider and his club are fucking with us, which isn't tolerated or someone else got to them on their way here. Whichever case, I'm going to fucking shoot someone today. Fuckers are about to make me fail on a promise.

As we are pulling into the Renegade's clubhouse, Tech calls to tell me their Prez is back here and waiting for me. He also hasn't been able to track Spider and their Prez has no idea where he is either. I'm fuming and so pissed; this is not what I need right now. Gunner, Blaze and I walk into the clubhouse first, it's dead silent. I can see that's normally abnormal here, since there are half naked women laying around and the place is trashed like it is a constant party in here.

We are greeted by a tall, well-built man in his 40s with long, wild red hair. "You must be Hawk. I'm Red."

I shake his hand. "Wish we were meeting under better circumstances. This is Gunner, my right-hand man." I point to my right where Chris has taken up his usual stance beside me. "This is Blaze, My road captain. He normally does these runs and meets with Spider." I say pointing to my left where Blaze has taken up Tech's place beside me. Although it normally ends up Blaze in this spot anyway, since Tech hardly ever leaves the basement.

"Any word on Spider?" Blaze asks.

Red shakes his head. "Best take this to my office." He says before turning and heading down a hallway. The three of us follow with Jax coming in behind us, leaving Damien, Stone and X to watch the two young runners and stay in the bar room.

"Look, I'm sure you are just as pissed off as I am, unless you're the one fucking with me. Though it seems unlikely you'd do that and show up here." Red informs us sternly. I can tell he's a take no shit kind of guy. "We have fucking nothing to go on. Spider is my best fucking guy. Loyal too. I want him found and the fucks that did this tied up in my basement."

I nod at Red before leaning forward in the chair, elbows on my knees. "We are more the types to put people down fast, but for you and for the sake of getting information we will bring them back to you." He nods at me. "Our tech guy is working on it now. Seeing if he can track anything. You got any idea where they were last, we need to check it out."

"Yeah, but I'm going with you." Red informs us. We trade information and make a plan to canvas their warehouse since it was the last known place Spider was at. Tech called to tell us that the last signal from any of their guys phones was there too. He's connected in with Red's tech guy and they have been searching from their end. I'm so fucking livid about all this. I just want to get home to my girl.

Stepping outside before we head out on our search, I call her again, only to get her voicemail. It's afternoon now but she may still be at work. I know sometimes she will have to stay late there if she's working on a project. Telling myself that's all it is, I send her a quick text and pocket my phone.

"I don't have a good feeling about this, Prez." Gunner says quietly as he comes up beside me.

"I don't either, but I'm also worried about L so it's hard to say what my gut is telling me." I tell him quietly and receive a look from him. "I want you with a rifle watching. Shoot to down not kill."

He nods agreement, "It'd be better for someone to get on the roof and I settle on that hillside on top the van."

"Set it up." Is all I have to say before he walks away, I call Tech and give him the plans. I want eyes everywhere and if anyone can get me that it's him. An hour later, everything is sorted. My guys and Red's guys are locked and loaded. We roll out together, but my gut still feels uneasy.

Chapter 22 - Ellianna

Cole has been gone four days now. I will give him credit for constantly checking in with me though, he has been texting or calling multiple times a day. It's been a nice break in my day. Mostly, I've thrown myself in to working. My new job is challenging in all the good ways for me, I'm determined to succeed in this new company. I actually like it and I think it has a lot to do with the people, everyone has been super friendly and welcoming. There hasn't been any of that catty drama and gossip that I've noticed there anyway. I've also been hitting the gym in the mornings and Nick has been working me through some self-defense type training along with the kickboxing.

The guys, Matt and Tommy, have been following me around everywhere like lost puppies. It has been comforting, honestly. They have been joining me out for lunch every day, my treat, since I still feel awful that they are stuck doing this.

Tonight, I am excited though. Beck has another bartender working and is taking Sonja and I out. It was a little forced at first but they eventually ganged up on me and convinced me to stop my self-loathing while Cole is out of town.

"Hey Babes!!!!" I hear Sonja screeching up the steps followed by something else, I think it's Beck but I couldn't quite make it out over the screeches. Before I can open the door to Cole's room it bursts open with Sonja tackling me and Beck following behind laughing. "I've missed you so much! What the fuck! You move in then out in like a week!" Laughing at her ridiculous excitement I try to tell her it is only temporary.

"Ha! I doubt it, Cole isn't going to let you out of his sight now. If he isn't calling you, he's bugging Paul with a hundred questions about where you are and if you are safe." Beck laughs out, making my face bright red.

"We aren't going to suddenly start living together. He'll just have to deal. I need just me and my own space sometimes too." I retort as Sonja finally releases me and starts pulling things out of Cole's closet. There's so much space in that closet, it is practically its own room. I ended up hanging up a bunch of clothing in there that a brought over after Cole left since I promised I'd stay here until he got back.

"Ready to party?" Beck asks with a sly half smile on her face. She is up to something.

Shaking my head, I crack up with giggles. "I feel like I'm going to lose this game of partying tonight. I haven't partied in any meaning of the word in years."

"Babes, you are going to be fine. Now put these on." Sonja scolds and throws clothing at me. "Wait! What's happening with your hair? It's a mess." She says actually looking at me.

It's in a crazy messy bun on top of my head and my waves are frizzed out everywhere. I didn't have time this morning to wash it after class before work so I tried my best to make it okay for work at least. "I'll shower quick and wash it." I tell her rolling my eyes.

The clothing she picked has to be the smallest amount of cloth in my closet. She found some daisy duke like cut off booty shorts that don't even cover all my ass cheek and a shirt with a tattooed Marilyn Monroe that's ripped in slits across the back and no sleeves. It's got the collar of the T still intact but a large section of cut outs from the collar to the center of my cleavage. "Sonja, I can't wear this!"

"You can!!!" She yells as I step out of the bathroom looking at Beck for help.

"Jesus. Sonja, she can't. Cole will actually kill us, and I don't know about you but I like my body bullet free." Beck says looking me up and down. "Not that you don't look hot but only wear that if he's close by."

"See Son, even Beck is uncomfortable with this. Plus, it's fall it gets cold." I complain to her.

"Fine! Ugh, put jeans on instead but leave the shirt!" Sonja says rolling her eyes and flopping on the bed in a huff. Agreeing to that compromise, I run into the closet and put on jeans. The shirt isn't that bad, plus I'll have my jacket on, so the ripped up back won't show as much. Thinking about it now and looking at the closet, I don't remember packing those shorts for here either, Sonja must have taken them from my room at her place. Once I have my boots and jacket on, we are ready to go.

Beck has black boots, black ripped jeans and a white tank under her leather jacket. Looking closer at hers, she has the same phoenix I do, but the back is patched with "Property of Tech" half circled around the top of club's phoenix and "Phoenix Rising MC" half circled around the bottom of the phoenix. The front of her jacket also has some patches and one that says "VP's WIFE". I find it interesting and my eyes keep wondering to the different parts of the jacket.

Sonja has a short red tight skirt with a black tube top and a red leather jacket that's cropped so you see part of her flat abs through it. Her look is finished off with black thigh high boots. She is dressed like a slut and I tell her as much, honesty is part of our friendship. "I don't care. I work all the fucking time and I deserve a good time." she responds to my thoughts on her clothing.

"What about Chris?" I ask, knowing there was definitely something happening there. I know that I struck a nerve with her when her face turns bright red and a large frown crosses her face.

"What about him?" She practically spits out at me. I shrug.

"He isn't here and fuck him anyway. He's such a dickhead. We haven't even slept together; I shouldn't have to deal with shit from him." She admits harshly, then walks out of the room and straight down the steps.

Beck drops a low whistle. "Wow. Was not expecting that."

"Suppose, I should keep my thoughts to myself sometimes." I mumble, a little shocked that she went off like that.

Beck laughs and pats my back before leading me out the door and down the steps after Sonja. "Nah. You are right. She looks like a damn club bunny whore, but if she wants to piss off Chris." Beck ends with a shrug.

I laugh. Beck is right, if jealousy is what Sonja is trying to get out of him, she is definitely going to succeed tonight. Even with Chris and Cole out on their run, they know everything that is happening here. We head to the bar in my SUV but the three of us pile into the back seat so Tommy and Matt could take the front and drive us. I guess that is the perk of having a set of babysitters, built in designated drivers.

From the corner of my eye, I've been checking out Beck's jacket more. I'm still fascinated by it and curious if Cole will want my jacket covered in patches like that. "Don't worry babes, I already have your patches made and ready when it's time." Beck whispers to me and winks.

That sends a strange cold chill down my spine with a wave of nausea. I'm not sure exactly how I feel about my jacket being covered in patches, or to be considered the property of anything, especially another person or to be labeled.

When we pull up to the bar, all my thoughts go out the window. Sonja sprints in and finds what must now be designated as our booth, since it's where we always end up sitting. Again, the crowd parts for us to the bar and to our booth. Beck insisted on handling all the drinks for tonight and that it'd be a surprise. She brings us a tray of orange juice in shot glasses plus three drinks. I raise a brow at her.

"Breakfast shots! They are so good!" She yells passing Sonja and I each one. "To girls' night out!" She yells again, clinking her glass to ours.

I tip mine back, somehow it takes like a breakfast of orange juice and pancakes smothered in maple syrup. "Beck! What magic is this?!"

"Jameson, Butterscotch Schnapps, orange juice and maple syrup!" She says licking her upper lip and grabbing another set of shots. I normally hate whiskey, but this is delicious. We kill the tray, grab our drinks that Beck told us was Jameson and Ginger then head to the dance floor.

All of the guys essentially formed a bubble around us. There was an arm's length from any of the three of us to another person. I find it odd since any other time I've been to a bar or a club, especially with Sonja we end up with sweaty guys grinding all over us. I'm sure part of the distance is me, but there is also Beck. Everyone seems to respect her like the mom of the house even if she's younger than some of these guys. There's also a feeling that I have, that Tech wouldn't hesitate to protect what's his either. He's so kind and quiet, smart in his basement but he has a mysterious air about him, something he hides. It makes me think he wouldn't blink about putting a bullet in someone touching what's his, just as I've heard Cole threaten.

Beck had refreshed our drinks a few times while we danced and I was starting to feel the buzzing effects over my mind as I swayed to the music. "Bathroom quick babes, you good?" I hear Beck say in my ear.

Nodding to her I look around for Sonja before spotting her a few feet off the dance floor wrapped up in some tall, tan masculine body. I giggle and decide to take a break. Our booth was still vacant, at least it was until I sat down. No sooner than planting my slightly dizzy ass in the booth, a brown haired, fake bitch slides in across from me.

"You're still in town?" Brianna says as she leans over the table to get closer to me. Her breasts looking extremely fake from my angle. "Don't you have a husband to get home to?"

Smirking at her comment, it is interesting to me that she has that bit of information. From what Beck filled me in on her, she isn't privy to much and honestly hardly any of this town knew I was married, let alone back. The club knew I was back, but didn't know about Brett. Flatly placing my hand on the table, I turn towards her. Her fake smile matching her fake breasts that she has practically shoved in my face. "I don't actually. The only person I have to get home to is the Prez."

Brianna's face dropped for a moment before she recovered. "Oh, you poor dear. Ruining your marriage for someone who will be bored of you in a few months. You should run back to your husband while you still can. Take what you can get doll."

Unable to help myself I throw out my thoughts, barely containing my laughter, "Funny. I couldn't help but thinking you were the doll here. I mean, you must have enough plastic - " I wasn't quite able to finish my sentence as Brianna grabbed a hold of my hair pulling me from the booth. By her tug on my hair, I can tell she has no strength to fight, I let her pull me while bringing my body up it. It'll be easier for me to hit her without the table in the way.

I grab the wrist that's in my hair with one hand as I stand upright. The other hand I swing for her nose, I am apparently a little drunker than I thought. I make contact with the side of her head instead of her nose, but I still make her scream, "You Bitch!" as she drops the hold of my hair.

Settling back on my feet I make sure I have enough balance before I swing my right hand, this time making its target, directly to her nose while she holds on the side of her head. Blood trickles down her face as the music stops, quieting the bar to only Brianna's screeching. Jesus how did Cole put up with her voice, she's absolutely nothing like me and her voice is like nails on a chalkboard.

Taking advantage of her holding her face, I kick her in the side making her drop to the ground. I step onto her chest, the toe of my boot sitting close to her throat, pressing just enough to make my point and keep her annoying voice from starting up again.

"Listen here, you stupid whore. I am the mother fucking Queen here." I look around the bar. All eyes have landed on us. Beck has this crazy smile on her face and Sonja looks horrified. The guys have a mixture of lust and respect while the other women in the bar look scared or jealous. I feel overwhelmed but oddly full of strength and power. My buzz seems to have settled back to mostly sober. "That goes for all of you, the Prez is mine." I yell louder to the whole bar and press my toe harder into Brianna as she coughs and struggles beneath my foot. I look down at her. "I want you fucking gone. If I see your face again, I'll break it so badly, even the best surgeon can't put it back together *Doll*."

I pull my foot back and take a few steps back from Brianna. She coughs and crawls across the floor to a couple of other plastic, half-dressed girls that help her off the floor and out of the bar. The music turns back on and every went back to normal like nothing happened. Beck runs up and hugs me. "I am so damn proud of you! Oh my god, girl!" She yells jumping up and down around me.

"You are terrifying." Sonja says beside us.

"That bitch deserves it, deserves worse really." Beck retorts still patting my shoulders and hugging me like I just won an Olympic Championship.

I snort. "She is terrible."

"That's just not you." Sonja whispers. I almost can't hear her over the bar noise.

"It is when someone tries to rip my hair out." I scoff at her.

Son looks annoyed and disappointed. "Well, I'm not having fun anymore. I'm going to get a ride home."

I look at Sonja with a frown. "Babes.... no. Look, we'll have the guys take us back to the clubhouse and just chill." I say and see Beck nodding then waving at Matt.

"Fine." Sonja says and heads to the exit.

Beck gives me a sympathetic look and I sigh. Something is wrong with Sonja. I know it's not just me, this isn't how she reacts even if she is trying to be protective of me after everything, I've been through. If anything, I have been feeling like a stronger, more confident version of my high school self before Cole left and the depression settled in.

Something is bothering my best friend.

Chapter 23 - Ellianna

Matt went to bring my car to the back of the bar while Beck went to find Tommy and Sonja. I didn't particularly want to stay in the bar since the encounter with Brianna earned me too many looks and stares to be comfortable. I'm not entirely sure what all the entire bar heard, but I essentially took my place here and within the club without Cole here. I'm going to go out on a limb and say that probably wasn't the smartest idea I've ever had. So, instead of the attention in the bar I found myself outside the back exit, recapping on the evening in my mind. What should have been a fun, easy going night out turned into such drama.

"What's a pretty thing like you doing out here alone?" I heard a raspy voice say to my right. I turn quick, seeing short man in the shadows with a hat and dark coat on. He's definitely not from the club I assess, seeing dress slacks and no leather. Backing away I put my hand on the door handle to the bar, only to feel it hold in place. Locked. "Just want to talk to you little one." the raspy voice says. "See, we have a mutual friend and I think it is in your best interest if you listen here."

I step back as he steps toward me. I can only hope he isn't armed and Matt comes around quickly. "Who?" I ask, trying to keep my voice level and my frightened mind to myself as I wonder if this is someone Brett sent or something to do with Cole.

The guy steps closer so the light hits him just enough to reveal his menacing smile. Bright white teeth that look expensive.

"Well, this mutual friend has much better taste than these trailer trash hillbillies." He says waving one of his hands dismissively at the back of the building.

I snort. One of Brett's guys, he looks familiar I think just before it dawns on me. He's the PI guy. Now I'm angry. Brett thinking he's better than everyone and this sleazy bastard thinking so too, insulting my home. "I'll have you know; those people are my friends and family. I grew up here, this is my home, my roots and if they are trash then so am I." Clenching my fist I raise my voice. "Tell Brett to find someone else."

The guy makes some "tsk, tsk" sounds as he steps closer to me again. "Now, now. A pretty thing like you deserves better than this. Let's just get you back where you belong and make both our lives easier." I laugh and try to think what Tech found on this guy but in the moment, I can't even remember his name. He starts talking again. "Maybe you don't want to come yet but you will. See, your little affair you have here Brett is willing to look past. A small indiscretion while you're obviously having some kind of break down."

Snorting I speak again this time more defensively than angry. "I'm more mentally stable now than I have ever been."

Another weird smile crosses the guys face, he doesn't strike me as a trustworthy guy by any means. More of a sneaky, greasy weasel type. "You may say that now but how well do you really know your little high school sweetheart these days? Hmmm?" He steps closer and I shuffle back more while wondering where the hell Matt is. "Do you know he's a cold-blooded killer? Murderer? Drug runner? Do you know what he likes to do or how he somehow has the funding to buy up half this shit town?"

"I know him well enough to know you're spinning truths into lies." I retort stepping back.

He laughs again, taking several fast steps closer to me. I can smell him; he smells like cigars and cheap cologne. "Pretty thing. You're in such denial, I hate having to do this but time for the hard way." He lounges for me with his last word and grabs at my upper arms. His raised arms give me an opening, I swing my right leg and kick him hard across his ribs. Hearing a satisfying crack, he drops to his knees. "You bitch!" He yells.

I turn to run but he grabs at my ankles, catching one I trip. Throwing my hands out I catch myself on the pavement, palms scrapping and sliding. I feel the loose pieces of gravel embed in my hands, wrist and up my forearms. Wincing I kick back, hoping to catch a sensitive spot but mostly just wanting his hands to release from my ankle. He rolls and takes my leg with him, twisting awkwardly. I scream hoping one of the guys or Matt is close enough to come running.

"Shut up!" He yells. "Shut the fuck up." I feel his other hand grab my free ankle keeping me from kicking more. He tugs at my ankles as he pulls himself to a kneel. My back drags across the pavement, my jacket bunched up in the back and I feel my skin break open and more gravel embed into my backside. "Feisty little bitch. So pretty too. No wonder Brett is going through all this effort for you. I wondered. You were right when you said you were trash. A trashy little whore. Pretty though. Bet Brett wouldn't mind if I took a little taste myself." The guy keeps talking as he uses his arms to keep my legs from kicking out.

As I assess his movements and guess his next move, I fist my right hand. He leans into me, his disgusting groin pressing into mine. I feel his arousal and try to hold back a gag. How disgusting this man is, turned on by a struggling woman. Waiting until his face starts to drop to mine, I throw my fist into his face as hard as I can.

Apparently, it catches him off guard that I can fight back because he pulls back from me. Perfect I think as I feel his weight come off my right leg. Throwing my knee as hard as I can into his already broken ribs, I follow the motion with a left-handed punch and he pulls back from me enough I am able to use my heels and push myself backwards away from him. More gravel tears into the flesh of my back. I'll regret it later but for now I just need to get space and away. My feet clear his body and I swing another kick, this time to his face. I know my body and know my kicks are harder than my punches. I want this slimy weasel to hurt. The guy's head is thrown back from the kick and blood pours from his nose after another satisfying crunch.

Hopping up to my feet I take off, my back to him as I run from the alley to the front of the bar. I see Nick stepping out of the bar wrapped around some girl with a blond bob and hardly any clothing. "Nick!" I scream, hearing the panic in my voice he turns fast to me dropping the blonde as soon as he catches my eyes.

"Fucking Christ. What the hell?" He yells rushing towards me, colliding with me as I run to him and let him wrap his arms around me. "Missy! Don't be a dumb whore, go get someone!" I hear him yelling at the blonde then he starts mumbling how Cole is going to kill him and everyone else. Tommy comes running out of the bar, followed by several other guys in leather.

"He's in the alley." I say pointing, still taking comfort in Nick's strong body. "I think maybe, I knocked him out."

"That's my girl." Nick says patting my back making me wince and flinch back. "Shit. You're hurt?" He asks as Becky and Sonja come flying at me.

"Where did you go!? Where is Matt?! We thought we were meeting you with the car out front but no one came around then we couldn't find you in the bar." Sonja starts rambling on but I think about Matt.

"Matt was getting my car. We need to find him." I say as I take a step toward the parking lot only to be stopped by Nick.

"Nope. The guys will handle it." He says and pulls me toward Beck who's pacing and in front of the alleyway. She's on the phone, I'm assuming with Paul before she notices my hands, gasps and says she'll call back into the phone.

"Your hands!" She exclaims while Nick tells her about flinching when he touched my back. She starts fussing over me along with Sonja all to my dismay. I notice in the alley two of the guys are holding the PI, making him stand with his hands cuffed behind his back. Tommy is beside him taking pictures of his face on the phone, I can see the bruising starting already and the blood still dripping. For some reason though he's smiling. Sick bastard is all I can think.

"You did a good job. Maybe you should be teaching my classes instead." Nick says like a proud father.

"Fucking hell!" I hear my brother yelling before he's in my face, both his hands smushing my cheeks. "Are you okay? What the fuck happened?! Who did this?! I'll kill them!?" Ry rambles and yells.

"I'm fine. If ya'll would stop fussing I'd tell you. First, we need to find Matt!" I see Tommy throw a punch at the PI making him collapse to his knees as the other two let him drop. "Tommy!!" I yell and push away from my brother, Nick, Beck and Sonja. "Tommy! I don't know what happened to Matt!"

That gets his attention, making him look right at me as the other two guys hover over the PI. "Where?"

"He went to get my car. He was going to pick me up at the back door but he never came." I explain and watch as Tommy takes off for the parking lot. One of the guys yells after him, I think his name is Tank. He's one of the officers, enforcer or something maybe. He keeps to himself. He has a room in the clubhouse, but I don't think we've ever spoken. Since Tommy doesn't turn back, Tank tells one of the other members to follow after him. Police lights flash as the chief silently pulls up. He steps out of his cruiser and comes towards Ry and I but Tank intercepts him. I hear Tank say something not questioning me until tomorrow.

"Babes." Beck whispers to me as I watch the chaos around me. Something tells me this chaos would not be happening and things would be more organized with Cole or Chris here. Tank is having trouble keeping things organized but it's probably not something he ever has to do. "Ry is taking us home. Come on we need to get you cleaned up."

"I'll follow you. Hawk is gonna have my head." Nick mumbles as he pushes me towards Ry.

Just as I start to complain, Ry picks me up and tosses me over his shoulder like a sack of potatoes. "Where the hell is Cole, Ellie? I'm so pissed off. Fuck! You're not allowed to leave the clubhouse anymore. Pop's is going to flip shit." Ry rambles on before all but tossing me into the backseat of his truck. Can't ever remember a time seeing my brother as frustrated and mad as he is now. I can't help but feel guilty that I've been gone for so long and I wonder if he also feels guilty about what Brett did to me. I make a mental note to have a heart to heart with him. It's not fair or worth the emotions for him to be frustrated over my mistakes when it's on me.

Beck slides in on the passenger side beside me and Sonja hopped in the front by Ry. We take off leaving the chaos behind and uncomfortable silence falls between us all in the truck. At least it does until we are getting to the drive of the clubhouse. "Ellie." Sonja starts with a sniffle. "I'm so sorry I yelled and took off on you. This is all my fault. I haven't been able to keep my emotions in check the last few weeks and look what happened."

"It's fine, Son." I flash a small smile at her. "I know it's not you. When you're ready to talk though..." I trail off, her eyes flash with something I can't quite catch in the darkness of the truck cab but I know she understands what I'm saying. Pulling up to the private side entrance of the clubhouse I see Tech waiting for us. Phone attached to his ear.

Ry gets to me before I can even get the door open, picking me up out of the truck and throwing me over his shoulder again. "Is this really necessary?" I complain.

"Yes" is the only response I get from him making me shake my head. At this point you'd think he was the older, overprotective brother.

"Put her down. Prez is having a shit fit." I hear Tech scolding Ry as he walks through the kitchen. He settles me on the couch. I hear Sonja asking Beck about first aid supplies and where to go before seeing Beck leading her upstairs. Tech pushes his phone into my hand and sits on the ottoman across from me, leaving my brother standing and hovering over me.

Even though I know it's Cole on the other side of the phone my stomach flips as I say hello. Not only do I miss him but my heart aches at the thought he's not here for this. Then I feel guilty for bringing this to the club's front steps, to Cole's front steps. The PI knew about Cole which means Brett knows about Cole and it takes everything inside me to push back the tears and bile in the back of my throat that raises. "Fuck. L. Kitten. Tell me you are okay." I hear Cole's voice come through the phone.

"I'm okay. Really." I say reassuringly, though I know he won't be happy until he actually lays eyes on me. Cole sighs before asking me what happened. Doing my best to keep my voice level and control my emotions, I explain to him in detail knowing Tech, Ry and Nick are all in the room hanging on every word I say. When I recite the last bit that the guy said to me and before I can explain how I defended myself and got away from him, I hear a string of cusses from the phone and the room before hearing crashing and the line disconnect.

I hand the phone to Tech, who still seems to be the calmest of them all, although he always seems calmer than the rest of them. "He threw his phone, didn't he?"

"Probably... I don't know where mine is, but I need to go see if Sonja will help me clean up this mess before it gets infected." I say showing them my scraped-up palms and standing from the couch.

"I'm sleeping here." Ry says. "I'm not leaving until Cole's back." He explains with a glare to Tech like he's going to argue.

"You know it's against the rules." Tech counters but ends when I shoot him a glaring look. If my brother wants to stay near me, I am not about to argue it. Especially not before I have that chat with him. "Fine, but you both deal with Prez and Gunner later."

I make my way up the steps to Cole's room with Ry following me like a lost puppy. I have to make him stay in the bedroom while Beck, Sonja and I head to the bathroom where Sonja does her best to clean my scrapes. He may be my brother but there is no way in hell I'm about to strip down in front of him. Cleaning hurts like hell as she gets the gravel out and makes me soak in a hot bath with Epsom salts. The she covers me in some kind of ointment and a loose t-shirt of Cole's that Beck pulled from his closet. Again, they all fuss over me. I end up kicking Beck and Ry out of the room. I'm exhausted, both physically and mentally. It feels like it's been a week while it's just been this evening and into the night since all the drama started.

Sonja and I curl up on Cole's huge bed like we used to when we were kids. Taking comfort in each other and our friendship, no matter what we've had each other's backs. We are closer than sisters. Sleep easily comes to both of us as the world and the night fades away.

Chapter 24 - Cole

A twenty something hour drive took me about 16 after I shattered my phone into a million pieces and put my fist through the Renegade's office door. I left their club almost immediately, pausing only long enough to tell Red my old lady was in trouble and I would get his door fixed. He chuckled and dismissed me with a promise to talk once I know she's safe. I knew the rest of the guys would be fine with Gunner, though I was too focused on getting back to L.

We managed to get Spider and his crew back, though almost everyone looks like hell. Blaze took a bullet to the thigh, Jax luckily had his helmet on and while that looks like hell, he's alive. I look like I went a few hard rounds with Nick. It was honestly a little touch and go there for a bit. Gunner saved our asses in the end with a shot to the gas tank of a truck outside, taking the heat off us long enough to take down the last few guys. At the end of it all I was more pissed off to find that the guys behind the bullshit were once again the 9s. Reminding me that my uncle is more of a problem than I ever thought he would be.

Never do I condone killing, but there are times when you are part of a club like ours or hell, while being a damn gun runner, it just has to be done. It leaves a bad taste in my mouth. While our business is mostly legal and often run deals for the police, military and government agencies there are some parts of it that are not so savory. Gunner and Tech look at it like if we were the FBI, we would take out the bad guys as necessary. We are keeping high-powered and high-tech weapons away from the bad guys. Morally, we are doing fine. Not that that eases my mind about it all. Gunner is less phased, but he was a sniper overseas for years. He took lives and seen front line combat. He deals with it too well, sometimes.

While driving I managed to get my high-strung temperament slightly settled after the long hours. Pulling through the clubhouse gate, I know once I see L it'll settle all the way. At least, it'll be settled until I meet this asshole that put his hands on my girl or Tommy and Matt. Those prospects fucked up, they never should have let her out of their sight, yet here we are.

Parking and pulling off my helmet, I am greeted by Tank as he steps out from the party room doors. He keeps to himself most the time though he is one of the best damn tail gunners we could ask for, and he took care of the situation last night.

I nod a greeting as he steps toward me. "Prez." He says with a nod back. "Our Queen is a badass, I'll be the first to vote for her to officially be branded in." I raise my eyebrow in confusion at Tank. He chuckles at me. "You should see what she did to Brianna, not to mention how she staked her claim. Some of the old dogs were a little pissed about that but then she beat that fucker unconscious." He smiles and chuckles again. I'm starting to get a little worried about all this. I don't think I've ever seen Tank smile before. "You should see the piece of shit Prez, she did a number to him. Tommy was the only other one that took a punch at the guy before the Police Chief finally got there to take him in. He wants a word with Blondie, been itching about it but I've kept him off the grounds." Patting his back and thanking him I turn and head into the clubhouse. I need to see my girl.

Opening the door to the kitchen, loud feminine laughter fills the room. Multiple sets of laughs. I follow the noise to the living room, it is packed with Sonja, Beck, L's parents and brother plus Matt and Tommy. Matt looks like hell, his face is dark shades of blue, purple and green. Everyone falls silent as their eyes land on me. All but L, I know it's her from her long blonde waves floating around her back side. "Well, you look like shit." Beck comments. I doubt she's wrong. I haven't slept in well over a day and took several punches to the face the other day.

Beck's comment got L's attention; she turns to see me. Her ocean eyes landing on mine, a little gasp escapes her as she flings herself from the couch straight into my chest. She looks fine and in one piece I think as I wrap my arms around her. She flinches back away from me with a hiss. "Her back is all tore up from getting dragged on the pavement." Sonja says with a tsk. I notice Ben and Ry clench their jaws and Sally has tears in her eyes.

"I'm so sorry Kitten." I whisper in her ear as I bury my face in the side of her neck. Her scent filling my senses like a wave of calm over me. She's mostly okay I remind myself. Few scrapes, it could be worse. Lifting my head to speak to the rest of the room, I keep L tight to my chest. "Have Beck or Tech order dinner for us, we'll do family dinner here. She's not leaving."

Ben starts to say something but luckily Beck breaks in talking about menus and moving the attention off us. Thankfully, she knows me and gets what I really meant from that statement. I scoop L up in my arms and take her up to our room. Ours now, if she thinks she's leaving here any time soon she has another thing coming. Though I know she is going to fight me on it, she belongs here. As soon as she's branded, she won't have a choice. I don't give a fuck if she isn't divorced yet, she's mine and if we have to wait to get legally married that is fine. As long as she's mine in the eyes of the club and the club sees her as one of theirs too that's all that matters to me. By the sounds of Tank though, she already does. Setting her down on the bed I start with the questions brewing in my head. "Tank told me you beat the shit out of Brianna and the fuck head PI?"

I watch her as she nods before explaining the night again, grazing over the bits she already told me on the phone. Can't say

I've ever been prouder of anything than I am of her. No wonder she has won over not just the old dogs but Tank too. Tank doesn't necessarily like anyone. Part of his name too I guess, he's as impenetrable as an armored tank both mentally and physically. Not that I get into the rumors or the gossip much but I have heard when he takes one of the willing club bunnies to bed it's rough on them. They normally end up disappearing for a month or so before showing their face again. He likes to inflict pain, but as long as the girls are consenting it's not my business. When she's finished explaining, she looks at me, guilt and concern washing her features. "Did you really stake your claim as Queen without me here?" I ask with a smile.

Redness floods her face. "Yeah. That was bad huh?" She giggles out, then sighs and looks away.

"Not for you. Everyone knew it anyway, sure there's a whole voting and branding process but from what I heard you got the Old Dogs and Tank on your side so nothing to worry about." I explain before planting a kiss on her lips. What was meant to be a soft show of affection for her turned into a whole different type of show. Just a taste of her and I need more. Considering it's been a week, a week of hell at that it's practically a need. Forgetting her back is wounded, I push her down to the bed and settle my hips between her thighs before she flinches away from me. "Shit. Shit. Kitten I forgot." I mumble over and over after leaping off her and the bed.

"No. It's okay, I forgot too." She says sitting up.

"Let me see." I can tell she doesn't want to show me. Her jaw clenches and she looks away. Her hands are wrapped so I know they are scrapped up good. It is probably a good thing Sonja is a nurse, handling that without her having to go to the Emergency Room. Pulling at her hips, I bring her to me then spin her around.

"Cole, it's fine." She argues.

"I want to see L. I need to know how bad this bastard hurt you."

I say harsher than I meant to while lifting her shirt, which is actually my shirt. I smile at the thought for a second before seeing the road burn like welts up and down the length of her back. They are deep enough that they will most likely scar. "Fuck, I'm going to fucking kill him." I hiss out.

"It looks worse than it feels I promise Cole. It is just tender to touch." Her gentle voice tries to soothe me.

Shaking my head, I let her go and situate herself into a more comfortable position. "It's going to scar. It looks like you crashed a bike with no shirt on."

"You know what that looks like?" She teases me.

I snort, "Course. I do."

"Tell me what happened to your face, then we need to go back downstairs. Though, you must know I've made Tech break a lot of house rules for me in the last twenty-four hours and he's upset about it."

After I explain in minimal detail what happened in Florida, I lead us back down stairs. On the way she explains Tech's distress of letting her brother stay here last night and letting her parents in today during lockdown. It'll get brought up at church, I'm sure but I'll be damned if I care about either of those rules being broken under the context of the situation. Back down stairs, Tech has new phones for both L and I. Putting L in a phone under our account and with a new number. It's not searchable by anyone other than Tech with all his computer shit. We should have probably done that to begin with anyway.

"Seriously? Guys, I can handle getting my own phone." L complains. Tech and I both smirk and head to the door to let one of the guys in with all the food Beck ordered.

"Most of us have a club phone babes, it's nothing. Plus, Tech can track it in seconds." Beck chirps before changing the subject and pulling down dishes to set the table. Half way through dinner the police chief calls me, when I ignore him, he calls through the entire table until Ben picks up Sally's phone.

"Can I help you Marty?" I hear Ben answer the phone. "No. I don't appreciate you interrupting our family meal on a Sunday with your constant calling either...... Next time you feel the need to call my wife, you better think again. Maybe about your own wife." Sally swats at Ben. I hear L beside me unable to hold her laughter. "We'll do so as we see fit Marty.... No, I don't particularly care.... Let him sit there then...... Yup.... Take care now. Don't call again."

"We can go down there after we finish, if you're fine to go then L?" I say to the table, trying to hold in my own laughter.

"Might as well get it over with, probably before he calls Pops again." L responds teasing Ben followed by the table joining in with teasing of Ben and his throwback teases to the rest of us. My heart clenches a bit seeing L's family blending in so well with mine in my home. This is what I want. This is what my life has been missing all these years.

A few hours later we end up at the police station, and by we, I mean half the club along with all of L's family. We have a decent relationship with the police here and a mutually beneficial arrangement. They work with us on occasion but mostly they let us handle things ourselves. In this case though, I'm glad Tech and Tank went with the completely legal route and involved the chief.

L, Tommy and Tank went to give their statements. I caught Nick as he was headed out, he'd just finished giving his statement. He filled me in on his part of the night, mostly just that L ran scared straight to him and then followed them back to the clubhouse and stayed, not that I didn't already know that. As grateful as I am for him and the rest of the guys for making sure they took care of L, I feel anger rising towards them, especially Nick.

They were there, when I should have been. They were comforting her when I was half way across the country. They put their hands on her, even as stupid as it is, I hate that they touched her at all. Tech had showed me the surveillance videos before we headed over here so we could send Marty only what we wanted him to see of course. I watched L run from the alley and leap on Nick, wrapping herself around him. My fist clenches and I have to remind myself to breath before I hit someone who doesn't really deserve it. She was scared and he was there, I wasn't. Only person to blame here is me. She wouldn't have even been in that alley if I was here. I can't even blame Matt, someone jumped him in the parking lot between cars. You couldn't even see the person on the videos other than a dark figure coming out after he passed.

After talking with Nick, I get one of the officers to take me back to the interrogation room with this dickhead PI, sending a text to Tech he knows to hack in and loop their video for us so I can have some of my own time here. He looks up from the table he's cuffed to as I step into the room. As I shut the door behind me, surprise covers his features. "You can't be in here." He comments with a shake to his voice.

"Funny that you think that." I can see the fear flash across his face. Too bad I can't seriously do some damage to him in here. "You look like shit, good." I observe out loud. L did a number on him, and by the way he's holding his side with his uncuffed hand I'd say his ribs look as good as his face does.

"You're going to rot in jail for all the crimes you've committed." He tells me, a little confidence to his voice.

Spinning the chair, I straddle it and cross my arms over the back rest. "Really now? Please, do tell. I'm dying to know what I've done to deserve such punishment." I asking knowing full well what crimes I've committed.

He shakes his head at me. "You're not untouchable. The Walton's are and they want that stupid slut of yours."

I clench the chair back with my fists, the knuckles fading

white with the pressure. "Well, you got one thing right in that sentence. She is mine. Only mine. When you get in touch with your little bitch of a boss, inform him of that will you?" He laughs, I don't think he knows quite how much trouble he and his boss are in. We have a long game plan in the works and they will all fall. "Now Georgie, it is Georgie, right? Or does only your dear mother call you that?" I watch as his face pales out again, that's right George. We know all about you and mommy dearest. "Right, so Georgie. Now that it has been established Ellie is mine, what on earth made you think you could go ahead and touch what's mine?"

He scoffs, "You think you know about me? Don't think so. That little slut of yours must be so sweet though, I just wanted to see what the fuss is all about." George is barely able to spit out the last of his sentence, I'd rounded the table and ripped him from his chair to pin him against the wall with my forearm in his throat. His arm twists and pulls against the cuff in the process.

"You call her anything other than her name one more time and you'll find out if that arm will break before the table or cuffs do." I growl at him, my anger taking over.

He coughs then starts to ramble. "I don't understand why everyone is so obsessed with her. You. Brett. I mean Brett just wants her back. Doesn't matter the cost. You rotting in jail is probably your best option at this point with him."

"Tell me everything."

"Why should I?" His voice whines.

I press harder on his throat and shoulder making his arm twist more. "I'll talk to Chief Peters. Maybe, we can let you out of here. Right now, he has you on two counts of attempted murder and a count of attempted rape. Not to mention the multiple breaking and entering, trespassing and impersonating a federal agent charges that we have you on camera for. You are fairly educated on the law, now that gets you for what? At least fifteen years, right? Plus being a registered sex offender once you're out." He grunts but keeps a straight face so I continue. "Doesn't bother you? Fifteen years that mommy dearest will be alone. Would she still be alive when you got out? Bet you'd have a great time inside too. You willing to take that risk for a paycheck?"

Giving him a minute to think about it I press a bit more on his throat. Finally dropping him, he hits the ground awkwardly since his arm still cuffed. Multiple grunts come from him, letting me know he is in pain. I follow his drop with a swift kick to those ribs he was holding before. I turn to go back around the table, a satisfied smile on my lips. George climbs his way back into his chair. "Fine." He says before proceeding to fill me in on Brett's plan. By the sounds he wants me either dead or in jail, he thinks if I'm gone, she'll run back to him.

It'll be a cold day in hell before that happens.

Chapter 25 - Cole

It has been a few weeks since Florida and the ordeal here with that PI. Things have settled into a nice flow, though I haven't completely convinced L to move into the clubhouse yet, though she stays almost every night. She has really settled into life in this town again, especially with her job.

Blasting music through my Bluetooth headphones, I walk to my section of the large garage. The garage is built off to the side of the clubhouse. My mind races as I think about the past and everything that's happened up until now. My mind sometimes is still processing that L is back. She's here and she spends a majority of her time in my arms like nothing has changed. In reality, everything has, but when she's here and I touch her it feels exactly the same. I feel complete again. She's my soul, without her it was missing.

Fingerprinting my way into the secured garage I stand in front of my collection of cars. I hardly drive them but I've always been a sucker for American classics. When I had come across these beauties in desperate need of restoration, I couldn't help myself. The work of restoring a car has always helped clear my mind.

I grab the keys off one of the hooks for my 1968 Chevy Camaro Z28. When I found it, someone had stripped the interior and a few other parts but the engine was still intact. It took over a year but I put it back together. Now it's a sexy beast of a car, a deep ocean blue like L's eyes with two black racing strips up and over. I once had someone try offering me $70,000 for it, but that was a hard pass. I don't need the money and this car always spoke to me.

Tossing my duffle in the back, putting my extra Glock in the glove box, I hop in and head to L's work. She's off in thirty minutes and a long weekend is here. I had Sonja pack her an overnight bag and sneak it in her car last night. I want to surprise her and sneak us off for a weekend. I need to get away from here and so does she. It's probably a little reckless with everything going on, but Tech and Gunner are the only ones who know where we are going. Tech has already scoped out the place and installed some extra security as well as overriding what was already in place so he is the only person that has access to it.

Once I pull into the parking lot and park by L's SUV I hop out of the car. I unlock her car with the spare key I took from her a few weeks ago and grab the bag Sonja packed from the back. I toss it in next to mine. After relocking her SUV, I stand in front of my car and wait for L to come out.

It's been a hell of a last few weeks, between the damn PI snooping into everyone's life and my uncle creeping around like a panther ready to strike, I've been angry and antsy. I should have put a bullet in my uncle's skull when I had the chance but I just couldn't do it. As much shit he put us through he also saved us in a way, he had loyalty and love for us at some point or he wouldn't have swooped in and rescued my Mom when he did.

Plus, without him I don't think I have met Chris or Paul, or grown this club. Hell, I barely knew motorcycle clubs existed. Things would have been different. Sometimes, I wonder if I had to go through hell, put L through hell, all for this to come out perfect in the end. I can only pray that it comes out perfect in the end.

"Hey Sexy, what are you doing out here all alone?" A soothing purr of a voice brings me out of my thoughts. Looking up I see her. Blonde waves float around her. Her ocean blue eyes are covered by her dark sunglasses but by the smile on her face, I imagine they are bright and full of fire. A dark purple dress with short loose sleeves and a deep V down her chest compliments her skin and curves. It cuts in at her narrow waist with a tied bow on her left hip before it flows back out stopping just above her knees, her legs are toned and her muscles flex as she walks towards me in nude heels. She's a beautiful sight that I will never tire of seeing.

I stand straight and lick my lips as she approaches. "Hey Kitten." I say just as she gets close enough for me to wrap an arm around her waist and pull her tight to me.

"Enjoying the view?" She teases as I run a light finger down the base of her spine and she shutters. Good to know I have the same effect on her as she does me.

"You're so perfect Kitten, I can't help myself." I kiss her deeply, stealing her breath before pulling back. "We are taking a trip."

"Are we now?" She asks, her lashes fluttering while she looks up at me.

"Mhmm..." I let her go just enough to guide her to the passenger door. "Hop in baby." She hesitates and even though I can't see her eyes, I know she's giving me a curious look under those sunglasses. "I planned it all out, even got Sonja to pack you a bag. It's in the back with mine." Giving her my hand to help her in the car, she finally settles in. "You'll like it. We'll get lost on some back roads first though."

She slides her glasses down and smirks at me. Getting lost on back roads was something we did routinely. That's how we found our spot. Our spot, that I now own the property of. It came up for sale last year and I couldn't let anyone else have it. Shutting her door, I walk around to the driver side, looking around to see who's watching. I know that dickhead PI is around somewhere. He didn't take off after our little encounter like I told him too, but he has been keeping his distance. He probably has 100s of pictures of L and I by now. At this point

I'd love to take them and plaster them all over media and news to tell her ex to go fuck himself and sign the fucking divorce papers. I spot him in a Towncar across the corner street. Smiling, I flip him off before hopping in and starting the car.

"Time to lose some assholes, Kitten. Hang on." Was my only warning to her as I throw the car in reverse pulling out of the spot, then punching the shifter into first, peeling out of the parking lot. I hit seventy, slamming through gears, moving our way out of town in a hurry. I look over as L is holding the bar above the passenger door with one hand and switching the new touch radio to her phone. As much as I love my classics, I need the tech and luxuries too so Tech wired it up along with navigation and a satellite communication system that all ties into to the club's system.

Glancing at L, she's so perfect, flawless. It amazes me how comfortable she is with me, anyone else would be yelling at me about my driving by now. It isn't reckless, I know what the hell I'm doing, but it's fast and could be mistaken as dangerous. "You rebuilt this didn't you?" She asks with her voice like silk.

Of course, L would guess right. "I did. She was a mess when I found her."

"Did you pick the paint color?" I nod as I turn off the main road and speed down the first set of back roads. Gravel flying behind us. I'm not taking any chances that PI or my uncle and his new crew follow us. Four turns later and I glance at L. While I've been focused on the roads, she's put her right foot up on the dash and slouched in the seat. Her small fingers tracing lines up and down the inside of her thighs while she's watching me with a smirk.

"Jesus Kitten." I feel my pants tighten harshly at the sight.

"You're sexy as hell when you drive." Her voice is breathy. I should have taken into account the need to fuck her in the middle of making sure no one could find us.

"Fuck!" I hiss out, grabbing her left thigh with my right hand and squeezing. She makes a little whimpering moan and I about lose it. Clenching my teeth, I focus on the road as much as I can. She slides her fingers up her thigh and to her center. She lets out a little moan before she shifts and slides her panties down her thighs and off. "Kitten, it's too risky to pull over yet."

"Suit yourself." She says, making me groan. I try to adjust my pants and unzip to release some of the pain building in my groin. Glancing at her while I'm trying to focus on driving is proving to be difficult. She's teasing me as she pleasures herself with her fingers moaning and writhing in the seat beside me. "Cole!" She screams and pants.

I take the next two turns left, then right. Seeing a dirt road to the left I take that and hear the gravel and dirt flinging behind us. I slow down when I see a wooded area. I find a service path and pull in parking the car. Looking at L before I pop my seat belt off. "You're in so much trouble." I hop out of the car and stalk over to the passenger side. I open the door and pop her seatbelt before pulling her out. She's still fucking smirking, the little tease. Slamming the passenger door, I push her back against it and she instinctively pulls her legs up to wrap around my waist so I'm supporting her. "You did all that on purpose and now you are in so much trouble." I growl out over her neck, watching the bumps rise on her skin every time she feels my breath.

"Maybe." She purrs out. I bite at the soft spot at the base of her next making her moan out my name. Circling the bite with my tongue she shutters in my arms.

"This is going to be fast and hard baby, you ready?" It isn't really a question; I know she is but I want her to know I'm not taking my time with her like normal. This is about me this time, being selfish as fuck. She had hers, I'll get mine now. I drop her legs down and spin her so she's facing the car.

Reaching my hand between her thighs, I smack her soft skin so she parts her legs. She leads forward into the frame of the car for me. Good girl. Since I'm already unzipped at my jeans, I pull them and my boxer briefs down just enough to pull myself out. A quick stroke of her slit with my fingers tells me she's more than ready. I slide my dick between her folds once, covering myself in her juices. Then I shove myself in her center quick and hard.

"Fuck, Cole!" She screams.

"That's my good Kitten, accepting her punishment for being a damn tease." She moans and I pick of the speed of my thrusts, slamming into her over and over. She cries out and wiggles her ass into me asking for more. It's starting to be too much as I feel my balls tighten. I reach around and flick her clit. Once, twice and halfway through the third she comes apart. Her walls tighten as she screams and shutters. That is the end for me and I come harder than I think I ever have before. We both fall into the side of the car before my legs weaken and I pull us both down to the ground with her in my lap. "Fuck L."

She giggles. "I know. I should frustrate you more often."

I grunt, "the fuck you will." She giggles more as I kiss up the side of her neck.

Resting my chin on her shoulder. "I love you, Ellianna."

She tenses for a second at her full name. I never use it, but I want her to know how sincere I am, how much she means to me. "I love you too, Hawk."

Just as I never use her full name, she never uses my club name. She's accepting me for all, I am.

Chapter 26 – Ellianna

Cole is racing down back roads again, post best sex ever. Where ever it is that we are heading seems like it is in the middle of nowhere. It's been hours since we left and all driving other than the quicky in the woods. Honestly, I couldn't even help myself. He looked amazing leaning back on the hood of his car, in his worn out fitted jeans, I mean really the man can wear a pair of jeans. Then his signature black V neck T-shirt and leather jacket. His jacket with the phoenix that I know is embedded on the back matching the one on the sleeve of mine and with "Hawk" and "Prez" scripted on the front. A month ago, when I came back here, I was so naive and didn't have a clue what it meant. I give him props though, the club has a way of being discreet about it all, town doesn't *seem* like it is full of a bunch of bikers that have done some shady stuff.

Watching him, the way he drives. He flows with the car, shifting gears with one hand and palming the wheel with the other. He was made for driving, I know his preferred method is his bike, but I don't doubt for a second that he doesn't have at least a few more cars like this he rebuilt and has tucked safety away somewhere. Now that I'm sated, I am calmly sitting back in the passenger seat with my small left hand resting on his thigh.

Something changed between us in the woods, when he said my full name, I know he was handing his entire self over to me. That's why I called him Hawk saying it back. He needs to know I accept all of him, even the changed part, even the blood I know is on his hands. I accept all of him and I have forgiven him for leaving. Sometimes, things are just meant to have a way. He told me once he doesn't like that name, I'm sure it has to do with the memories of his time in Ohio, but I needed him to know I love him and accept him with all of that included.

Maybe this wasn't the life we planned for us all those years ago, but it's the life we have now. We accept it as it is and we move forward. All that matters now is our future, together. I'm not leaving again and I'm sure as hell never letting him leave me again. I will track him to the ends of the earth this time, he thought he was protecting me, but who protected him? I accept him as he is here and now. He is the other half of me, he is my soul. I would protect him with my life if it came down to it.

Cole pulls off on to a dirt path. A few yards, down the path is gated and I see eight-foot iron fencing going out of sight in either direction of the woods. He puts a code in and the gate opens, after we drive through it closes behind us. "Rather ominous, you think?"

He lets out a low chuckle. "Maybe Kitten, but we needed someplace with the safety and privacy this offers."

A large, gorgeous A-frame style log cabin comes into view. Although cabin is a term I would use loosely, considering the place is massive. The scene is breathtaking, the cabin sits on the highest peak of this hill and looks across a wooded valley and the rolling hills behind it. The sun is beginning to set and the bright red and orange glow that tops the shadows of the hills is beyond any view Texas ever had to offer. "Cole." I breath out his name. "This is stunning."

I see his mouth turn up to an actual smile from the corner of my eye as I continue to take in the view in front of me. He smirks and teases a little half smile on occasion but an actual real smile from him is a rarity. He parks in front of a garage door and grabs our duffels from the back, tossing them over his shoulder, he opens my door and gives me his free hand. I follow his lead to the side door by the garage. He codes in to unlock the door. These guys and their security, I think with an eyeroll, "Tech set this up?"

He nods. "Ours for the weekend, though if you like this place, we'll buy it outright. Tech thinks Beck would enjoy it too and it would be nice to have a safe house that doubles as a getaway vacation home."

"Practical." I state dryly.

"I know it all seems like a lot to you, or overkill on the safety measures but there is always a possibility you're in danger because of me, Kitten." He sighs as he opens the door and leads us into the house before shutting, locking and setting something on another code box on the wall. "I wouldn't be able to live with myself if anything happened to you L."

I lift my free hand to his face and lift up on my toes to kiss his cheek. "I know, but I wouldn't be able to live with myself if anything happened to you either. Been there, done that, not willing to go back again."

He looks at me with sad eyes, lifting his hand to thumb over my cheekbone. "Nothing is going to happen to either of us." His eyes lighten and his mouth turns up on the corners. "This weekend, we enjoy ourselves and not worry about anything else. Let me show you around."

Cole leads me through the foyer into the open living, dining and kitchen area. The living room is gorgeous with a large stone fireplace up one wall and large two-story windows taking up the adjacent wall letting in orange light from the sun setting and a breathtaking view of the mountains around us. The kitchen and dining room are large and functional with wood accents, giving that log home, rustic vibe to the place. There's also a laundry room, bathroom and office on the first floor.

After checking out the downstairs, we head back to the foyer area. There are two sets of stairs there, one leading up and the other leading down. Cole tells me the basement is mostly empty and the owner probably used it as storage. He and Tech has the idea of turning it into a panic room, just in case. Seriously, paranoid over protective men. Though it is sweet they want the club to buy this place, mainly so Beck and I have a getaway spot.

We take the stairs up. The hallway is a loft space that overlooks the living room and has a little nook area with chairs, I could see myself curled up there with a good book. I could see us having Christmas here too, a huge tree in front of the windows and our family gathered. Sharing my thoughts with Cole, he agrees and says we'll talk with Tech about it Monday. Apparently, there is an apartment over the garage that would be great for the club members to crash in, it has four more bedrooms plus a living space and kitchenette.

The first three rooms upstairs are off a hall in the front of the house, windows look over the drive and they all are decent sized guest rooms with a shared bathroom at the end of the hall. There's two master bedrooms up here too. The last one has huge windows on one wall that look over the mountains and a stone fireplace that matches the downstairs. I claim it as our room, making Cole laugh. It has a slate shower and claw foot tub in the en suite as well. The tub calls my name and after the long drive and the last few weeks it sounds like heaven. As if Cole read my thoughts, he gets into one of the cabinets and pulls out my favorite soaking salts with lavender and some rosewater and lavender bath bombs. "Take your time babe, I'll get us unpacked and dinner ready." He says kissing my forehead softly and leaving the room.

This place is an amazing retreat like vacation home. There's even built-in speakers and a touch screen control panel for it. Putting on my favorite relaxing station of Dave Matthews Band Pandora, I fill the tub with hot water and the salts before shedding my clothing and sinking in to the claw tub with a sigh. All my worries of the last few weeks fade away. After my encounter with the PI, the police chief, with help from the Phoenix members, ran him out of town with a warning about returning. I have worried about what information he's taking to Brett ever since that day but Cole has reassured me that it is nothing he can't get handled.

It has been mostly quiet since. I have been settling into my job here and mostly living with Cole. I am not sure why but I haven't officially moved in with him yet. I think part of me still wants some independence, or at least a place to run, not that I think I would ever need to run from Cole. Sonja thinks I have PTSD and I am seeing a counselor that she set me up with middle of next week. More to appease her than anything else. Trying to get my divorce papers signed by Brett though. Why, that is an entirely different type of story. According to Reba neither he nor his lawyers will acknowledge them. He won't even talk to Reba about any of it and only sends minimal information type messages through his lawyers. Which, he doesn't even need. Why he pays someone else to do a job he can do perfectly on his own, I'll never understand.

Reba let me know earlier this week that she will try to push things through the court but most likely it will get denied because we haven't been separated for very long and even that is based only on my choices and the fact that I moved out. There are no legal documents that we are separated at this time. It is annoying and stressful to say the least. He is still controlling my life even from half the country away.

At some point I must have drifted off to sleep, I wake up to cold water. Pulling the plug and sliding myself from the tub, I wrap myself in a large fluffy towel off the rack. The rack that is apparently heated because this towel is toasty warm like at the spa. Smiling with a happy sigh I step back into the bedroom. Cole has laid out clothing for me on the large bed. The dark navy dress and matching lingerie are a stark contrast to the white and blush colored bedding. I slide into the outfit and run some product through my hair letting the soft waves settle down my back the way he likes before heading down the stairs to see if I can find the man himself. It's weird how small things like this, when Cole does them doesn't feel like he's controlling me. It feels loving and caring. I also know that he would never get mad if I decided I wanted to wear something else and not the dress he bought me a set out.

Walking through the living space and to the kitchen, I don't find him. He isn't in the office either. Thinking maybe for some reason he is in the basement; I start to walk that way but get distracted when I hear music coming from outside the large French doors to the patio. We didn't check that part out during our little tour. Opening the door, I'm instantly greeted by the smell of a campfire and grilled seafood. Following the music and smell, I take the patio around the corner of the house. Cole stands with his back to me, looking over the patio to the now dark mountains. He has a fire lit in a stone fire pit that has several chairs and outdoor couches around it. There's also a table set with wine in an ice bucket and a vase of lilies and wildflowers.

As if he senses me admiring him, Cole turns to me with a wide smile. Closing the distance between us he wraps me in his arms, burying his nose in my hair. "Relaxed now love?"

"Very." I reply, rubbing my hands up his chest, across his shoulders and down his arms to his elbows. "Did you do all this?" I ask gesturing to the table.

"Mhmm, I thought you earned a night of my cooking." He says with a smirk, leading me to have a seat at the table.

I giggle, he could never cook before. "You cook now?"

"Beck has taught us guys a few things. Plus, I can use the grill." He informs me, making me giggle at the thought of Beck trying to teach the guys how to cook enough to take care of themselves. I bet most of them barely listened since she still fusses about over them like they are her children. Cole takes my plate and goes to the grill, filling it with salmon, shrimp, asparagus and potatoes that he had wrapped in foil to keep warm. He puts my plate in front of me before doing the same with his. I take over pouring the wine for us both. I mean really, you can't have a perfectly delicious looking bottle of wine sitting here without drinking it.

After we eat and enjoy lighter topics of conversation with each other Cole starts acting nervous. Trying to keep his hands busy by picking up the table, grill, leftover food and getting another bottle of wine. Anything he can keep busy with he does and argues against my wishes to help. "Cole!" I call after him as he starts to fuss over the fire. "Cole, baby stop!" He pauses and looks at me. "What the hell is wrong with you?"

Finally, he plops his ass down next to me on the couch by the fire. "I want to ask you something, but I'm not sure it is the right time." He admits.

"This is why you are fussing around nervous?" I ask and he responds with a nod.

I snuggle into him, trying to calm him. "Well, get it out." I say with a giggle.

Cole takes a deep breath before he digs into his jeans pocket then leans over to pull a box from the little table beside the couch we are on. He puts the box on my lap and grabs my hands. "This is something I should have done years ago." He starts. "Maybe it's terrible timing, I mean you aren't even divorced yet but I don't care. You are mine; you have always been mine. It's time to make it official and really, I just want your approval that we have made it this far and found our way back to each other. I love you and I don't want anyone else but you, you are everything I think about when I think about the future." Cole rambles and I am so confused what he is even talking about. "Open the box."

I pull the top off the box and pull back the tissue paper on top, revealing black leather. "What's all this?" I ask pulling the leather from the box. It's my jacket, the one Cole gave me all those years ago but now it has patches. "Blondie" is sewn into the front in the same place Cole has "Hawk" and "Queen" is above it where Cole has "Prez". I flip it over, guessing correctly what is back there. A Phoenix patch with "Property of Hawk" is sewn into the back, matching Cole's and not just being the embroidered phoenix, I've had for nine years on the back of the jacket.

Tears prick at my eyes. "Really?" I look at him. He has a big smile across his face. "You want me officially as queen? Not just what I yell out in the bar to slut bunnies?"

"Of course, Kitten. I'm serious, I should have done this forever ago." He says before putting the jacket on me and tossing the box in the fire. He moves to a crouch in front of me. "I should have done this a long time ago too." He opens his hand in front of me to a square box.

"Cole is that?" I can't finish my sentence as tears come to my eyes.

"Kitten, will you marry me? I know we'll have to wait to make it legal and all that but I want you marked mine." He rambles on and puts a platinum band wrapped in diamonds with a larger square cut diamond in the center on my left ring finger. I giggle, he just put it on as he rambled not even waiting for me to actually answer him. The giggling pulls him from his rambles. My big strong, sexy, confident biker president is nervous and sweet right now. "Why? Why are you laughing at me?" He asks blankly.

"You didn't let me answer." I say and realization crosses his face. "But yes. My answer is yes." I say with a smile and throw my arms around him. We lose ourselves in each other, ignoring all the problems we still have to face when we get back from the mountains on Monday.

Chapter 27 – Cole

When I had explained to my friends my intentions for this trip, I got three very different responses. Gunner rolled his eyes and said I was crazy. Tech gave a small smile and wished me luck. Then there was Beck, who danced around in excitement. She told me that she had already had the patches made up and everything. Then she proceeded to steal L's jacket from our closet to keep it a secret. It was comical to watch really and it made me happy, Beck is like the sister I never had with Paul and Chris like brothers.

She now has her ring and patched jacket. Once we get back to the clubhouse, Inky will brand L with a Phoenix tattoo and my name. She'll be marked mine forever, as she should have been before anyway. For now, the ring can only be just a promise. One that means, I'll give her everything she wants from life. As soon as she's free from her asshole Ex then it can be more than just my promise. I could give two shits what that asshole thinks too. Maybe he'll get the hint and we won't have to completely ruin his life.

It was a debate the whole drive if I'd actually do it tonight or not. Was it too soon and all that? I mean, she'd only been back about two months now and here I am asking her for the rest of her life. In my heart, I know. It's only ever been her, and always will be only her.

Eleven years prior

"Are you sure you're ready L?" I asked the gorgeous blonde underneath me. Her wavy locks spread around her on the blankets laid

out in the bed of my truck.

"Yes." She replied to me, pulling at the bottom of my shirt until she had it over my head and off me.

We had officially been together a year now and coming to this spot in the middle of nowhere for the last few months since I managed to scrap up the cash to buy this beat-up old pickup. It became our spot since we found it driving around all these backroads.

Neither of us had done the deed yet, though it'd come pretty close here in this exact spot several times. I'd always pulled back, nervous. I know it's going to hurt her but I also hear how much more emotional it is for the girl and I never want her to think I'm taking advantage or anything. It has weighed on me this decision, mostly because I'm two years older than her. I'd wait for her to be ready.

"Seriously Cole. I want this, I want it with you. I couldn't imagine it being anyone else. Only you, always you." She says, a fire burning behind her eyes. After making sure there was no hidden doubt in her eyes, I moved my gaze from her eyes to her lips before capturing them with my own.

Feeling her melt beneath my touch I knew she was serious by her words, and tonight was the first night I made love to the only woman to ever be able to capture my heart.

Snapping from my memories, I recounted the weekend we had together. We spent the rest of the weekend relaxing with each other, watching movies, cooking, cuddling and watching the sunset over the mountains. It was just what we needed.

I don't want to go back this morning. Tech and Gunner already put through the contracts for the house though. It's officially ours and Gunner will be in next week to put in the rest of what we need here. I made that call as soon as she started telling me how she pictured us all here for Christmas. "We'll be back here soon or whenever you want." I tell her packing the car back up. She looks at me gasping before a huge smile crosses her face and she leaps on me, wrapping her legs around my hips. "I told you if you liked it, I'd make it happen. So, I made it happen."

"Thank you." She says before placing her lips on mine.

I pull back from her a little bit, as much as I'd like to keep headed where we were going, we really need to get a move on. "Finish packing baby, we have an appointment when we get back."

"We do?" She looks at me wide eyed.

I nod. "Time for your Phoenix."

"Does it have to be a patch?" She asks, pointing to my back where a large phoenix matching our patches on our jackets has been inked across.

Shaking my head. "I was thinking you could get it up your arm like you wanted that matches the arm or your jacket, then my name somewhere." She smiles up at me and bites her lip. God, you'd think after the number of times I'd taken her over this weekend it wouldn't make me instantly harden, yet I do. I'm convinced though I'll never have enough of her. "What are you thinking Kitten?"

"What if I got a king's crown with a C in it on my ring finger?" She asks softly looking at her hand. My face lights up at that suggestion, I love the idea. I tell her as much with a bit of a smirk I'm not able to hide because I'm going to surprise her with my own new tattoo. Inky could get it done for me fast before hers and she wouldn't even know it until she was done.

After another satisfying but fast fuck against the garage door like the hormonal teenagers that you'd think we were, we hit the road again. Heading back home. Smiles never leaving either of our faces. I was content with her and my life with her now.

Ten years prior

"Do you remember what today is?" L says hoping in my truck after school.

Mom was having one of her bad days. I found her this morning face down in the shower, water had run cold and she was shivering but otherwise passed out cold. Somehow, she didn't drown. I texted L in the morning that I was missing school but would pick her up.

As much as I hate everything mom has put us through, put me through, because of her habit, it tugs too hard at me when I find her like this. I had managed to drag her out of the shower and dress her in sweats and an oversized hoodie before wrapping her up in her bed trying to get her warm.

When she finally became conscious, she screamed and trashed the place. Then she decided that wasn't enough and left immediately after slamming her palm against my face. She's always like that when she starts coming down.

Shaking the thoughts of the day I had and focusing on L, I didn't want to ruin our anniversary. Two years since we were officially together, though she was always mine. One year since we crossed the line and then continued to fuck every time, we had a hidden moment to ourselves this past year. Reaching behind the seat with a smile I pull out the wildflowers and lilies I got for her right before picking her up. "Of course, not Kitten." I say, watching her face light up.

She grabs my shirt collar and tugs me down to her, pressing her lips to mine. "Let's go to our spot." She says when she finally breaks from my lips.

"Thought you would never ask." I reply with a wink, knowing we'd go there I had already packed my truck with everything we'd need for a picnic at our spot.

"What's on your mind?" L asks in the car. We are almost back to the clubhouse now, not taking nearly as long coming back. I didn't feel the need to try to lose people possibly following us.

I smile at her. God, even way back when she was it for me. "I was thinking about our first- and second-year anniversaries." Telling her honestly.

"Those were good ones." She says returning the smile with a blush climbing up her chest, neck and face. "It was always you."

"I know." I say, guilt in my voice. Taking her hand and bringing it to my lips. No matter how good we are now or how much time passes, the guilt that I left her then will plague me, that I am sure of.

"We're home." I say to her pulling through the clubhouse gate.

"That we are. I bet it is time I move all my stuff in, officially." L comments nonchalantly. Her words making the smile that's practically permanent these days grow across my face. "You like that idea?" She asks with a small giggle.

"Thought I was going to have to drag you out of Sonja's and not let you go back ever." I joke, parking the car by the main doors. Hopping from the car I come around to L's door, grabbing it from her and giving her my hand out of the car. "Come on. It's time you seen the main clubhouse." I tell her.

Somehow, I've managed to keep her from the party room and all that comes along with it. The guys are respectful about keeping the living side separate from all the chaos that happens in there. Walking her to the door I hold my breath, she may run seeing whatever hell is happening in there now.

"About time. Long overdue, Queen." Tank hollers across the room as soon as we step in.

We are swarmed with more of the guys and old ladies welcoming and introducing themselves. I notice the club bunnies have made themselves scarce and it's not every day all of the old ladies are here. Beck must have chased the bunnies out and made calls to get everyone here.

"Babes! Oh my god! You said yes!!! Yes!" Comes Beck's loud voice from beside us. Speak of the devil and she shall appear. Tech managing to trail right behind. Beck leaps to hug L.

"You knew?!" I hear L exclaim before Beck tells her about stealing her jacket and the plan.

Tech pats my back with a short congrats but a smile he isn't able to hide. Tank also pats my shoulders. "Don't fuck this up Prez." Tank tells me with a smile before sauntering off back to the bar.

It's still really fucking weird to me, how much Tank has grown to like L. They've stayed up in the living room the few times I've had to handle business outside the clubhouse the past few weeks. Tank treats her like a little sister, very protective and caring. Very unlike Tank with anyone else.

Inky comes in from the church room. Kissing L's forehead, I tell her I'll be back before leaving her with Beck and the other ladies I make my way to him. I want my plan for her first, and have him draw up for her before she heads back with him to be branded.

A decade late, but it's finally happening.

Chapter 28 - Ellianna

"Hey Queen, this means you're really here for good?" I hear Tank say behind me before he appears from the side and hands me a Corona.

I nod and lean my shoulder into Tank, clanking the necks of our bottles before taking a sip and glancing around the room. Everyone turned this place into a party room while I was getting branded. The Club bunnies have even crawled out from wherever Beck had shoved them. The few old ladies and almost all the members are drinking and dancing, from the looks of it they have been going the whole time too. Inky is good, but to get the full phoenix with color around my upper arm it took hours and it's now well into the night. Cole had to step out about halfway through, after showing me his newest tattoo. He matched my crown for him with one for me on his ring finger.

"He'll be back soon. Club business." Tank informs me without me asking. Since the night at the bar with the PI we have been close. He's like a bigger, more over protective brother to me. He reminds me a lot of Ry sometimes, but he has this dark edge about him.

"I still haven't figured out how you learned to read me so well, even my blood brother and best friend since we were babies can't do it." I mumble taking another sip and glancing around the club's party room again.

Tank chuckles beside me and leans on me using my head as an arm rest. The man is tall and it seems to be one of his favorite things to do to me. "They don't observe well. Ry does if it's something he's curious about though. He figured out the club fast and knew not to breath a word. Your brunette friend though, she's too ditsy and self-absorbed."

Shoving my elbow in his stomach he grunts and drops his arm. "She's my friend, speak kindly."

"Just an observation." He grumbles before mumbling something about a pain in the ass and drinking his beer.

I've notice when Tank is with me all of the old ladies and some of the members watch us and the old ladies give me that face like I'm dirt on their shoes. It's worse tonight, either because they have all been drinking or maybe because this is the first time I've been in this part of the club. "Why do they do that?"

"Do what?" Tank grunts grabbing two more beers from one of the club bunnies walking around with a bucket of them.

Taking one of the beers from Tank, I put my empty on the table of them behind us. I've noticed the bunnies that are not rubbing on members are cleaning up after everyone and making sure beers and drinks are passed around. It must be part of the deal for them to be here, earn your keep. Tank explained that they have a house at the corner of the property most of them live in. They would be homeless otherwise; some are recovering drug addicts too and the club helps them stay in their rehab programs and stay clean. Some have just had hard lives. The members give them protection and care, working the bar here is part of their repayment. Of course, some of the club bunnies are just whores that like to hang around.

"Look at us like that? You know, every time they see us hanging out it's like we have eight heads or something?" I say nonchalantly. It doesn't bother me much; I just find it odd.

Tank goes quiet, looking around the room and drinking his beer. Figuring he isn't going to answer me, I also look around the room, searching for Cole. "It's because of me. Because no one here thinks I am any kind of stable. Not that I am, but...." He starts then stares at me before dropping his gaze to the floor. "I'd never hurt you Queen. Never." He finishes before walking away from me, leaving me questioning what happened to him to leave him so hurt and scarred.

I've learned to leave him to his thoughts when he gets like that, he'll come around and fill me in if he feels like opening up later. If he decides he'd rather not talk about it, he'll still come around. He'll just act like nothing happened.

Alone in the sea of members, old ladies and club bunnies, I make my way to the main house doors. I hardly know most of these people and it feels odd not being by Cole's side. Maybe I am getting to be dependent on having him nearby. He's like a comfort crutch.

The main house is eerily quiet compared to the loud party room. Tank said club business, so I make my way down to Tech's basement domain. If they are down here, they know I'm here from the cameras. Tapping on the door they don't answer, figuring what the hell, I'm here anyway I put my hand on the scanner and am surprised when it flashes green with "Queen" and the doors slide open. Six eyes land on me immediately, though the only ones I care about are the icy blue ones that soften as soon as the land on me.

Cole's eyes trail down my body and to my left hand where his ring sits, now with a king's crown with a "C" in the center sitting above it. His lips curl into a smile and he takes a few steps toward me to pull me to him and tuck me close to him, his arm wrapped around my shoulder and across my chest.

"We just let women in here now?" Chris says with a snarky tone.

Tech rolls his eyes and turns back to his computer as Cole tenses beside me. I grab Cole's hand with mine and squeeze it tight before he does or says something to his best friend he regrets. I know Chris is just lashing out because of the stresses around the club. It doesn't help that I think he actually really likes Sonja and for some reason the two of them just can't agree on anything long enough to be in the same room for more than five minutes. "She's one of us now and you will respect her as such. She has access to everything and if she'd like to attend church it is in her rights as well." Cole says and I can tell he's trying to leave the emotion from his voice.

"Beck doesn't attend church." Chris states.

Tech rolls his eyes. "Because she doesn't want to, you know as well as I do that, she has the same access that me, you, Cole and now Ellie has."

I watch as Chris tenses his jaw and fists before releasing them with a breath and running his hand through his hair. "Look, Chris. I don't know what I did to you but when I first got here, I thought we were all friends. If anything, we all want the same thing, I want the same thing."

"Do we though? Because where I am standing you just want an out from your poor choices you don't give a fuck about this club." Chris growls at me in response.

"You are wrong. You are so fucking wrong. I care about this club and the people in it too, including you. I see how much you three love this club, how much you've worked for all this and I want nothing more than to see it grow and continue to be what you vision for it. I didn't want to stay for the longest time, it took a lot of convincing on Cole's part, then Tank's too that it is best for everyone if I stay. I didn't want to put you in harm's way. It's better if we fight this together, and I know there is something else going on here and I want to fight that with you too." I explain. Cole rubs my hand with his and buries his face in my hair for a few seconds as Chris gives a disapproving grunt.

"Okay, well now that the whining part is over and our new Queen wants in let me fill you in." Tech says with a smile before turning to is computer and typing away. "You see, Prez here, and dickhead over there." Tech points to Cole then Chris. "They just couldn't kill their dear old uncle when they had the chance. Nope, they had to be all noble and take the higher ground, or be a bunch of pussies, that's unclear." Tech rambles and throws insults at the two of them. Tech is normally very reserved so I find it hard not to laugh as he explains the seriousness of their uncle being in town and working with some unsavory people. I have a feeling that Gunner irritated Tech enough tonight that I am seeing this fired up and mouthy side of him. "So now, we need to do something about both his uncle and the people he's working with. They are already getting brave and trying to bring drugs into town." Tech finishes, showing a video of what looks to very obviously be a drug deal in the center of town.

I nod before asking, "So what is our next course of action?"

"We haven't figured that out yet, Kitten." Cole says in my ear. "We all have various ideas. I say we burn them all and their compound. Tech thinks we capture my uncle and let Tank have at him until he tells us information and Chris think we play defense until the show up at our doorstep."

"Well Chris, it's not because you hate me but I think you're a little late to play the defense game. They are in the center of town that is our doorstep." I state and watch as Chris rolls his eyes. "Cole, you may be jumping the gun. If their compound is even remotely close to ours then there will be women and possibly innocent children there. You're jumping to fast. However, Tech may not be right either. Paul, can you see who is with him and where they rank?"

"Yeah, he's been with their enforcer mostly. Also a few prospects." Tech keeps typing. "Also, this one guy. He's just a member but he's been around forever and was almost always with their Prez until uncle dearest came to town."

"Of them who would know what the plans were, other than Snake?" I ask and feel Cole's eyes on me.

"The Prez but that would be risky and would automatically mean war, so would the enforcer." Chris breaks down facts.

"That leaves the member. The prospects won't be told shit for shit." Cole pipes in.

"Bingo." I say tossing my hands in the air.

"You're right. No one will automatically start a war over one member, especially if we snatch him while he is on our territory without permission." Tech states as he continues to type away. "Okay, I'm going to watch his every move and will get a team of guys ready for a grab, then leave him and Tank in the far end warehouse."

Cole nods as does Chris all finally agreeing on something. "The next thing is more personal Kitten." Cole whispers to me again before raising his voice to the room. "Tech, how is our other plan going?"

"Ummm.... Well, from my end of things well, mostly." Tech says still typing.

"That doesn't sound promising." Cole states and Gunner rolls his eyes again.

"Let me snipe him and call it a day already." Chris says plainly.

I giggle saying "That's not a terrible idea." earning a small smile from Gunner.

"As fun as that sounds, it won't help and you both know it." Cole scolds us.

Tech finishes typing and spins in his chair. Sometimes, I think he just likes the dramatic flair of spinning around. "Righto, so instead what I've been doing is building several off shore accounts under his name. Now they all link back to him and I have been putting deposits into a large account. He doesn't even notice the amounts going in." Tech brings up multiple foreign bank accounts and Brett's one in Texas our mortgage was a part of. "Did you know how much this asshole is worth,

I mean fucking hell there is over a half a billion dollars in just this account before I started funneling money to him. "

My jaw hits the floor. Not that I was ever with him for the money but he sure as hell didn't ever live like we had million-aire type funds. "Holy fuck." I speak my thought outload as I read through the screen holding the bank statements.

"Okay, so Blondie didn't know she was letting this fuck head keep half a billion when she filed divorce papers. More inter-ested in gold digging now Blondie cause -" Chris starts but cuts off when Cole is suddenly in front of him.

"For fucks sake brother, what the fuck with the insults and blame? Get your fucking head in the game before I am forced to make you step down. You're not doing the club or yourself any fucking favors here. Figure it out or get out." Cole growls into Chris' face.

Tech speaks up then, getting up from his chair and moving to-wards the two men. "Prez is right, Gunner. I'd back and second the vote. I love you man, you're my brother. This is supposed to be us together and you've crossed too many lines and made this harder that it needs to be."

I watch as Chris' face drops in either shame or defeat. "Tell me what you need from me to get done. Otherwise, leave me alone."

Cole wraps himself around me again as Tech sits back in his chair and watches Chris walk from the room.

"I really don't understand what I did to him. Honestly, I thought he liked me; he even gave me a nick name like I was part of you all." My voice breaks as tears break over my eyes.

"Shhh, Kitten. I don't think it's you baby. I'll try to actu-ally talk stuff out with him tomorrow after he calms down. Okay?" Cole tells me and pulls me tighter to him. "Carry on Tech. L may have some extra insight to finish this off."

"Yeah, okay." I hear Tech say before the clicks of the keys start again. "So, these off shore accounts I've been linking them to anything I can find. Even to the 9s and their drug running and human trafficking shit. Several shady politicians and several known Mexican cartel leaders. Anything and everything so when the FBI come raid his house, he'll never see the light of day again."

"That seems extreme?" I look up at Cole who nods.

"Yes, but we don't plan on having the FBI raid unless he forces us to. We just want to show him what we "found" while looking him up." Tech says with air quotes around the "found".

"I see." I say before turning and rubbing my face with both hands. "I don't think the threat would work. He would be confident he could prove his way out of it."

Cole snorts and Tech starts speaking before going back to his keyboard. "Actually. Some of it isn't lies. He has had meetings with Mafia and Cartel guys, defended several in court and his father's entire estate was funded by Cartel money. How do you think he obtained all those funds in your account?"

Again my jaw drops, I never would have guessed any of that.

"Right. I'm just laying things out with a pretty bow for the feds." Tech chuckles out. "Now, where you come in. We need a meeting with Brett."

Chapter 29 - Cole

We spent several hours filling in on the rest of what we found on Brett. He's a scumbag trying to live this persona that he's a saint. He's the worst kind of person in my opinion. A fake, lying hypocrite. She was shocked to find out that her husband was as dirty as they come. He or someone he's hired is really good at hiding his tracks though. Tech just happens to be the best of the best. We decide that she'll call him at Reba's and ask for a meeting there, to talk over things. So, he'll be told anyway. What he won't know is that Tech and I will be there. Tank will have L covered if anything happens, he'll be watching from the next room.

Gunner will be on the roof; just in case things go south. However, we all agree that with his connections and ties to the government and law, as well as cartel we can't just take the easy way out of disposing of the problem. Too much backlash to the club and L. After our discussion I want to call church to get the issue with our uncle taken care of too, but everyone is way too drunk or already passed out from celebrating. "Wow." I hear L gasp beside me with a low whistle.

We just stepped into the party room. I've seen worse, but this is the first time L would have seen this side of the club. I chuckle lowly and step into the room then over a passed out and naked X, face down in the laps of two club bunnies. "Take it this is normal?" L asks with a giggle, grabbing my hand as she follows me over the piles of bodies and around the still conscious people, all in various states of dress.

"Most nights. Though this was a celebration so it's a little more than normal." I tell her as we finally make it to the bar. One of the bunnies, Camie is covering. Passing out shots to Jax and a few others who are still drinking and not taking part in the debauchery that happens in here. "Now you've seen it all Queen. You still want this?" My tone is joking but deep down I know I'm serious and worried she's going to run now.

She laughs, a sweet melody of a sound ringing around the room. "Well, Prez. I could do without seeing half the members dicks, flopping around or buried in one of these slut bunnies but I think I'm sticking around." She says bumping my shoulder then leaning over the counter and asking Camie for four shots of Jameson and four shots of Patron.

Jax comes around the bar to me as L and Camie strike up conversation. If L is to make friends with any of the bunnies Camie would probably be it. She doesn't seem to sleep around with any of the guys and tries to stay out of their sights. They know better than to touch her without permission, but this is an MC and sometimes shit I don't agree with happens. The guys know if they cross lines though, I'll kill them myself. I will not tolerate disrespecting women. Bunnies or not. She's the one I actually trust enough that takes care of the main house as her keep and bartends when Beck isn't. Bunnies don't have permission to go into the main house without escorts. Except for her. I don't know her story but she was in pretty rough shape when she showed up here a year ago. Broken ribs and evidence of rape Doc said when he checked her out, only filling me in because I'm Prez.

She instantly earned our protection and a soft spot I have for her, though I'd never show it. She'd always be welcome here, but the rules say she has to earn her keep, no exceptions. Jax eyes her for a moment before reaching over the bar and grabbing two beers from the bucket on the other side and handing me one. "Wanted to let you know that Gunner tore out of here about an hour ago, after punching that prospect that watches after your girl. Matt, I think? Get the little shits names all confused."

I sigh and run my hand over my face. Chris has done this before. Gone through a mood, but it's been a while. I'm sure it has to do with all the shit he went through growing up around that fucking shit hole of an MC. "You know where he was going?"

"Didn't say. Didn't ask the kid what the problem was either." Jax says.

I try to make it seem like things are fine. That's part of being a leader, "You know Gunner. Was probably just trying to blow off some anger."

Jax snorts. "He wanted to do that he should've asked. Been itching to put my fists through someone's face."

"Soon enough brother. Soon enough." I tell him as L slides back beside me and Camie hands out shots. She's added four for Jax and herself too. I notice Jax's gaze goes to Camie and a blush creeps up her fair skin from her chest to her cheeks the way L's does with me. Something must be going on between the two of them.

"OKAY! End of night shots!" L yells beside me, earning cheers from the few members still conscious and even some attempted cheers from the half passed out ones. Before I realize what, she is doing my Queen is on top of the bar with a shot glass in each hand, her diamond and platinum band shimmering in the light coming from above the bar in a stark contrast to her new tattoo. The Phoenix above shining and glowing in colors being covered in saniderm "To you, the Phoenix Rising MC for accepting me as one of you all. To family and to honor -
"

"If you can't get it in her, get it on her!" One of the guys yell from the back of the room breaking out everyone into cheers and L into laughter as she tosses back one of her shots.

"TO OUR QUEEN!" Tank's gravelly voice yells from the back of the room. L's blush creeps up as the room yells and cheers, chanting "queen" and finishing what shots or drinks they have. I've never felt prouder of L or this club before. She's worked her way in as one of us in a short time and I know from this display every one of them would lay down their life for her if it came to that. A comforting thing considering my uncle would have no problem using her to get to us. A thought that has left an uncomfortable rock at the pit of my stomach.

"CAMIE!" L yells with her voice full of giggles "Get your ass up here!"

The shots have officially hit her I determine as she grabs Camie's arm and pulls her up on the bar with her making her dance with her. It's the first time I've ever seen Camie act this carefree too, L just seems to have this effect on everyone. Her fire and spunky attitude, has come back and she's back to being this light that shines and fills everyone, just like she always used all those years ago before I broke her.

Matt comes in from the back room, limping around the bar and dropping a bunny off his arm into one of the chairs, a pout on her face like she's unhappy and unfinished with him. "Prez." He slides into the seat beside me. I send him a sideways glare. Not because I don't care, I'm rather pissed Gunner beat the piss out of him. His lip is busted as is his nose based off the two black puffy eyes and a large gash is still open with a light run of blood dripping down the side of his face. Prospects aren't allowed to strike members and most definitely not officers. He would have basically been defenseless to Gunners assault. Prospects have to earn their place and know respect and while I'm pissed at Gunner for this I can't slide from my cold and in charge demeanor. "I just wanted to come clean to you before Gunner comes back."

Now the kid has my attention, I turn towards him, my jaw clenched. I watch as his Adam's apple bobs and sweat breaks out on his neck. He's terrified of me.

"I disrespected the VP. He made a comment about Ellie and - "

He must see my body tense more when he calls L by her name instead of Queen. "I mean, umm. Our Queen. And ummm." He gulps again.

"Get the fuck on with it boy before I break your jaw too." I mumble. I wouldn't really but again, sometimes I have to pretend to be the hard ass that is expected of me.

"Right. Prez. Sir. Anyway. I told him to not speak like that about her and that he was being a whiny bitch." The kid finally gets it out and I try not to smile and laugh.

"That all?" I ask, keeping my voice level and tone indifferent.

"Well. So. Also, I didn't know, I swear I didn't." I roll my eyes and glare at him again taking a sip of my beer. This kid is too nervous for me. He gulps before speaking again. "I fucked his girl."

Choking on my beer, I cough and spit half of it out of my mouth onto the bar. It gains L's attention as she scurries down from the bar top and into my arms. "Cole, baby. Are you alright?" She fusses and I nod.

"Apparently, Chris has a girl." I say lowly so hopefully only she hears me over the music.

"WHAT?!" She screams. "Nooooo, WHO!?!"

I shrug before turning back to the trembling prospect. "Well, tell us. Who were you fucking?"

He gulps again and moves closer to L but I can tell he's still trying to keep space between him and I. "Umm. It was your friend. Sonja." He whispers to L but I still manage to hear him.

She gasps and clamps her hands over her mouth. Then bursts into giggles. "Oh sweetie!" She turns out of my arms to grab the prospect into a hug, earning a low growl from me that she waves off. "Is this why your face is all bruised?" She pulls back from him and puts a light hand on the side of his face.

Matt nods before meeting my glaring eyes and taking a step

back from L. "I didn't know she was claimed, I just thought she was your friend and she didn't exactly, ummm.... say she was."

L giggles again. "Oh, sweetie you did nothing wrong. She's not claimed, Gunner is just being a possessive ass. And if I know her at all I'm going to say she practically jumped you?"

The kid blushes. Jesus, I'm supposed to be making these fucking prospects hard as nails and he's blushing because Sonja is a psycho and while I'm sure he wouldn't have declined her, she probably didn't give him much of a choice either. "Okay. Enough." I say sternly and point to Matt. "You. You're on shit duty for a month. Stay the fuck out of Gunner's way and stay the fuck away from Sonja before he kills you. And man the fuck up while you're at it."

He nods. "Thank you Prez. Queen." Then he scurries away the bunny he dumped in a chair earlier chasing after him.

"That was mean." L slaps my chest. "He's practically a kid. I'm a little disturbed Sonja jumped him. Lord, it'd be like jumping my little brother." She says with a gag making me laugh.

"He's a prospect. He has to earn his place. He's fine." I say with her rolling her eyes. "The fuck did I tell you about that?" I sternly whisper in her ear before nipping at her neck then picking her up and putting her over my shoulder as she squeals.

"What the fuck, Cole! Put me down!"

"Nope." I tell her and smack her ass before marching our way to our room, what I'm about to do to her we don't need an audience for.

Much later in the morning hours, I throw open the door to our room bare ass naked about to punch whoever is insistently pounding at it, only to find Chris with a mostly empty bottle of Jack in one hand and the other falling through the doorframe into my face as he follows his hand and lands on me in a heap. "Get the fuck off me man." I growl at him trying to keep my voice low as L is hopefully still sleeping.

"Dude. Why is your dick out?" Chris mumbles and slurs out while I manage to push him in to the chair in the corner of the room.

"Because it's fucking 5 am and we were just getting to sleep Jackass." I growl at him again while picking up a pair of boxers from the floor.

"Oh shit!" He loudly exclaims and starts laughing. "Blondie's naked too then. Fucking dirty bastard." He grumbles and chugs at the last bit of his whiskey.

"Keep your voice down! What the fuck you want?"

"My brother...." He lowly mumbles and looks away. Apparently, we are going to have this conversation at 5 am instead of tomorrow when I planned to fit it in.

Sighing, I tell him not to move as I grab sweats from my closet and cross the room over to L, crouching down at her side of the bed I run my fingers through her hair. She sleeps too lightly to not be almost awake now with Chris's obnoxious noises. I knew it wouldn't take much to wake her. Her eyes flutter open on my second passing stroke through her hair. "What's wrong?" Her soft voice full of sleep and worry crossing her face.

"Chris needs to talk. I'll be downstairs. Okay?"

She sighs. "Need me too?"

I shake my head and lean to kiss her forehead. "Go back to sleep, Kitten" I tell her and hear her practically purr as she shimmies further into the covers and settles back into sleep.

"Cute." Chris mumbles at me when I cross the room, back over to him.

"Shut the fuck up. You're just jealous and pissed you don't have this. Now downstairs. And no more of this shit." My tone stern but my voice low as I grab the whiskey bottle from him and drop it to the floor before grabbing him by the shirt and dragging him out of the room. We are going to get to the bottom of his issues, but first he needs to sober the hell up.

Chapter 30 – Cole

A bottle of water and a couple cups of coffee for each of us and I deem Gunner sober enough to actually discuss things. I've listened to him drunkenly ramble for the last hour while the Jack he drank wore off.

"I love her." He mumbles out looking into his coffee.

I look up at him hoping he's going to continue on but he keeps his head down a I'm almost certain a tear drops down.

A sigh leaves me before I speak. "Sonja I'm guessing?" He gives me a little nod. "Okay man. So, what's the problem? She not interested in you at all or what? Is she what has your damn panties all twisted up? What the fuck man? Talk to me." He hadn't answered any of my questions so I just kept throwing them out at him before giving up and leaning back in the bar chair of the kitchen. Sipping my coffee, irritated I'll be on no sleep today and there's a bunch of shit to do today not including church and a planned boxing session with Nick and L.

Eventually, I try again. In a quiet, serious tone leaning toward Gunner, "Brother, love you man and I'm here for you but you can't keep this up. I need to at least understand what the hell is going on with you. Fuck man. You're taking shit out on everyone around you. You're not keeping your shit together and that affects this club."

Gunner turns away from me and I watch as his body goes from tense and ridged to a deflated sag. He sits like that for what feels like hours to me at this point in our morning since he pounded on my door, but it was probably only a few seconds.

Just as I'm about to yell at him and leave him down here he finally speaks up.

"I'm not and won't ever be good enough for her." He grumbles out.

"You're an idiot." He turns to me, fists and jaw clenched. He's strong and puts up a good fight against me but I've still won every time we've turned to fists so I'm not worried if he hits me. "Let me guess. You're being a dickhead because you won't even try to start anything with her let alone tell her how you feel. Then you find out she's getting involved with other people so you completely lose your shit. All because you feel sorry for yourself because what? Because our uncle and your father were assholes?"

"Because I've killed people! Innocent fucking people!" Chris snaps at me stepping into my face.

Shaking my head, I put a hand on his shoulder. "You did what you were told to do. You did your job either under the government or that MC. The choice wasn't yours and the consequences - "

"I pulled the trigger." He grumbles at me.

"If I asked you to do those things now, would you? Or would you fight me?" I ask and he looks at me. I can see the realization hit his face. The person who he was then compared to now are not the same person. "Don't let guilt and regret keep you from what you want most. Trust me brother."

Gunner nods his head. Slowly at first then with more enthusiasm before pacing the length if the bar island in the kitchen and back. Sipping the rest of my coffee, I try not to laugh as Gunner does his typical Gunner shit. This guy has always been like this. Extreme in whichever way he's swinging his emotions in that moment of time.

"I've got to tell her, brother. I have to tell her. I've got to kill that fucking prospect first though. FUCK! Where is that fucking kid?" He stops pacing and clenches his fists again.

Chuckling. I manage to talk him down from that idea, I actually like the kid. Not to mention he's found his way into L's soft spot and she'd be pissed if he got hurt again, especially for something he didn't even actually do wrong. You can't fault the kid for any of that, most likely Sonja was doing it to get Gunner's attention anyway. If he wasn't so blind, he'd see that too.

Gunner sits back down after pouring more black coffee in both our cups. "You know Cole, Harry being here, back, in town. That just brings everything back, not to mention puts me on edge not knowing what he's planning. Especially, considering we know how sick and demented he is."

"I know, Chris. I know." I say, guilt and shame rising up at the thought we could have killed him but didn't and now all the horrible shit he does is our fault in a way. Snake is a sick, dirty rotten bastard good at manipulation and convincing others he's in the right. He's a lot like Brett in that way come to think of it. We both pause in thought, drinking our coffees on silence. Hopefully, this little breakdown of Gunner's has him back to his normal self and he stops fighting with L along with everyone else in the club.

An angelic voice floats into the kitchen just before soft hands land on my back and even softer lips land on my shoulder. "Good morning boys."

"Morning Kitten." I softly call back as she floats to the coffee maker and Gunner says some smart comment about sex hair that makes L stare him down with a glare that would kill before turning back to her coffee.

"See you're back to yourself or still happily drunk, Christopher." L comments sarcastically.

A snort comes from beside me before a deep breath followed by the words I least expected to hear from Chris leave his mouth, leaving me stunned. "I owe you an apology, Ellie. I was too self-absorbed and too jealous to realize that you were never my enemy or the problem and for that I really am sorry. I hope you can forgive me."

Looking from Gunner to L I can tell he's completely sincere and she's just as stunned as me. The Keurig thing makes its last gurgle into L's cup, pulling us out of our shock. L steps around the bar and wraps her arms around Chris's shoulders before kissing his cheek. I remind myself it's a harmless action and Chris is my brother before I rip his head off for being touched by my girl.

"Of course, Chris. Now treat me like that again and we'll have other words, but I more than forgive you this time." She says softly, patting his arm and walking back around the island to grab creamer from the fridge. "You best be good to Sonja too; she's been my best friend since the sandbox and I have no issue killing or maiming for her."

I smirk, my feisty kitten.

"Yes Blondie, Queen. " Chris says in an honest and non-sarcastic tone for once.

"Good. Now, I know you boys have a lot to do today and I need to get to work. So, behave." L winks at Chris while she comments nonchalantly, grabbing her coffee to take upstairs with her. "I have to leave in an hour, if you can't take me can you get Matt or Tank to? I have to go to Reba's at lunch time then don't forget we have a session with Nick, I think it'd be easier to have a driver today."

She says to me while tapping her mug, rocking on her heels and biting her lip. I know she's still nervous being alone even if she won't admit it. "I'll have Tank go so he can stay with you today, the prospects have shit to do." I tell her as I drop from the bar chair to wrap her in my arms. "We all have you baby. I promise." L nods, I kiss her head just before she escapes from my embrace back up the stairs.

"Fucking hell." Gunner grumbles beside me. "I am such a fucking asshole."

Chuckling, I point out the obvious. "You said it not me."

"She's scared as hell." He states, also pointing out the obvious.

"She tries to pretend like she's not, but other than the cabin and this clubhouse she doesn't want to be alone. She's not comfortable, I can tell. Matt has been hanging out in her office but since you fucked his face up pretty good that's not an option this week."

"Sorry man." Gunner says then slams his fist on the island counter. "Mother fucking bitch ass pussy. I'm going to choke the life out of him."

I stare straight at him. "Stick to the plan. No backlash, but you are welcome to take such fantasies out on Snake and his ban of merry bitches."

"That I can and will gladly do." He responds, downing the last of his coffee before we both go about our morning tasks.

The warehouse has been locked down and relocked down. New security with new feeds funneling to Tech, Gunner and I. One of use has to approve entry to the building, even if it is one of the other of us. Camera feeds cover every inch and Tech even got his hands on these crazy 360 live feed cameras. One on top the building outside getting aerial coverage of the place and one on the ceiling inside getting the same kind of internal aerial coverage. All our goods are back in order and even our other smaller, lesser used warehouse received similar upgrades. Shipments should be smooth sailing in and out from now on and there sure as hell won't be another break in.

We still can't find the C4 and that's bugging the hell out of me but Nick has swept practically even building in town coming back without a trace. There would be no way with the video security upgrades and Tech's facial and item recognition software scanning all the feeds and sending alerts to him with anything flagging. The man has been working endlessly and finally allowed for Tommy, the scrawny ass prospect to help him with all that shit. Apparently, he's just as nerdy and only needs to learn. I wasn't thrilled letting a prospect into such sensitive club stuff but if Tech trusts the kid, I guess I have to, too.

I've been at the warehouse most the morning, loading several vans inside with Matt and X for the next run and making sure everything here checks out. Gunner had some construction projects to sort through and was on a mission to casually make a loop around the 9s little camp the guys found. That left me in charge of this shit. Thankfully, Matt is a hard worker, the kid will make a fine Phoenix one day. X has been busy all morning scratching at his junk and bitching about it burning.

"Fucking hell X! Fucking leave and go see a doctor." I yell at him after turning around to see his hand down his pants, again.

"Dirty fucking club bunnies." He grumbles making Matt chucking and I have to stifle my own laugh.

"Okay dumbass, so number one. Wrap that shit." I scold.

Laughing the kid chimes in. "For real. You're going to get one of those bunnies pregnant. Then what? You're stuck with a whore old lady and a fucking kid that's like you?"

X's face drops. He should really know better, I shouldn't be doing a health class lesson while we are all adults here, loading hundreds of thousands of dollars in weapons into a van.

"Right. Fuck man, even the kid knows." I laugh, unable to hold back. "Secondly, your dirty ass dick needs some antibiotics. So, go see a fucking doctor. And while you're at it, you best be sending the doctor around the club and to the bunny's house with those same antibiotics."

The kid is bent over laughing, trying to catch his breath while X looks like he's going to throw up. "Oh man." X finally mumbles making me laugh.

"It was fucking Brianna. Shit Prez, she was your bitch before Blondie came back to town." X says seriously to me. "I figured she was clean considering that."

"What were you doing with Brianna? I kicked her out and banned her from all club properties for the shit she pulled on L." I ask. More concerned about Brianna being near my kitten and the clubhouse than having some disease from her. L being the only person I'd ever even dream of, let alone think to or trust enough to not use a condom with.

X looks between Matt who's gone completely pale and myself. Confusion littering his face. "Wait what? She was in the clubhouse a couple weeks ago. Fluttering around looking for a hookup. What shit?"

Forgetting X was with me in Florida and assuming that he would have heard about it anyway, Matt and I fill him in on the Queen's fight and banishment of Brianna before I send a text to Tech to figure out how she crawled her way back into our clubhouse. "Let's finish up here. I have a sexy Queen to get back to." I tell them both after X was fully filled in.

Chapter 31 - Ellianna

Tank has never looked as uncomfortable around me as he does right now. He is standing in the corner of my office scanning the room nonstop with his eyes and looking like he wants to be anywhere but here. "Pat, you can hang out outside or literally anywhere. I'm fine, promise." I tell him from my computer. My best attempt to keep my tone steady and put a convincing smile on my face seems to be read for the fakeness that it is by Tank. He eyes soften a little as he looks down at me before crossing his arms over his chest.

"Real cute, Doll. The second that's actually convincing is the second I do that." Patrick Westchester, also known better as Tank tells me. His real name being given to me by him this morning while he drove me to my job. Apparently, outside of the club and clubhouse he'd rather I use his name. His exact words were "You may not be my sister by blood, but you are my sister and no sister of mine needs to call me by my club name." Personally, I think it's his way of apologizing for last night without explaining himself.

"Fine, but at least sit down. You're distracting and I need to finish this proposal so I can submit it for review and head to Reba's." I glare at him still standing in the corner looking like a pissed off secret service man, only covered in leather instead of a fancy suit.

Finally, he nods and takes a seat across from me at my desk. Oddly enough, not a single person at my work has even mentioned or seemly have given any thought or care to the fact that giant men covered in leather have followed me in here and hovered through my work day for the last few months.

Since the incident at the bar with the PI, I haven't been fond of being alone. Add to that learning about Cole and Chris's insane uncle who happens to be creeping around town, Cole's over-protective and smothering ways of me needing a bodyguard at all times seems less insane and more comforting. Of course, we train often and extremely hard with Nick too. I'm a force to be reckoned with, but if that PI guy had been just a little stronger or just a little better trained; things could have gone differently. I shudder at the thought.

After finishing my current task and submitting it to my senior manager for review, Pat and I gather my jacket and bag before heading down to my SUV. I've slowly been gaining more cli-ents and projects at work and I want to succeed there. It's such a better place than where I worked in Texas, just with the cul-ture of the place. I had been good at my job in Texas, but was held down under thumb because I wasn't vicious or cutthroat like the people that seemed to succeed there. I don't think I would have promoted or ever made it to a senior manager position there. Here though, here I could see myself working up through the ranks.

We walk out of the building into the crisp air signaling the beginning of the winter season. Snow doesn't normally hap-pen until after the holiday season that is approaching but the brisk air tells me it's not impossible. Pat remote started my SUV and helps me with my dress and heels into the passenger like a gentleman before climbing into the driver's side and set-ting off across town to Reba's.

"Prez had Reba order lunch so you don't miss out on getting food while we are doing this." Pat tells me after reading his phone.

My stomach flops at the thought of food. Maybe after I make today's call, I'll have settled my nerves, but I haven't heard Brett's voice since the day I left Texas. Conflicting emotions tear through me at the thought of hearing his voice. He always had a soothing way to speak to me after any disappointment or any harsh words he threw at me. He always managed to manipulate my emotions by saying the correct things and getting me to fall back into him. Guess that explains how he has managed to have a shady side life without the rest of the world, myself included knowing.

"Ellianna? Ellie?" Pat's rough hand grabs mine from the passenger door that he has opened. "You okay? You spaced out? We don't have to do this? We can call Prez and figure out another way."

He looks at me, his eyes soft and full of concern. I manage a small smile. "It's okay. I can do this; I need to do this. Face my problems." We make our way to Reba's office. Pat protectively at my side.

"Ellie! Darling, come in. Come in! My receptionist Marilyn is setting up the conference room with our lunches. I hope soup and sandwiches from Baker's Bakery is okay?" Reba says with excitement and a kind smile across her face. Her face only falling when I feel Pat step up behind me after making sure the entrance doors we locked and secured.

"That sounds perfect Reba. Thank you. This is Tank, friend of Cole's and mine. He's with me for support today." My left-hand gesturing to Pat and a large smile on my face that I hope soothes Reba's concerns. Her smile returns a bit before her gaze hardens on my left hand.

"Well, my girl. Please, don't tell me that belongs to Cole." Reba exclaims pointing to my left hand.

A large smile of genuine happiness crosses my face as I put my hand out for Reba to inspect. "It does."

Instead of the excitement everyone else has shown, Reba looks disappointed. Pat sees it too as a low growl comes from behind me. I'd swear the man was raised by animals by the noises he makes sometimes. He hardly speaks to anyone other than me but he often makes grunting or growling noises that reveal his thoughts and emotions.

Reba looks up and meets my eyes. "Well, this doesn't make you look good to any court if anything it will just let Brett get money from you."

"Reba." I say with a cold tone. I feel Pat tense as he steps beside me and puts a protective hand in the middle of my back. "I don't have anything for him to take. He's already taken it."

"No, but Cole does." She says sternly before turning to walk down the hall to the conference room.

I don't follow her, frozen in place at her words. "He can try, but we take care of him before he even gets a chance. Don't worry about it. The whole club has your back." Pat whispers lowly in my ear before guiding me down the hall, his large rough hand pressing between my shoulder blades as he moves us to the conference room. His touch is comforting, but it feels exactly like my brother's or Matt's. Protective and loving but completely platonic. Nothing like Cole's; whose smallest touch lights a fire through my entire body, one that makes my core ache for him and my soul spark.

We enter the conference room to Reba and a petite young girl. She must be Marilyn but with her shoulder length brown hair and sharp features, I never would have guessed that as her name. Pat's hand on my shoulders drops and when I look at him, he has his jaw and fists clenched. Weird, I think to myself as I notice Tank's reaction.

"This is Marilyn. She's started with me recently as I've been getting busier and busier around here. She's going to take notes for me as well today, if that's okay?" Reba asks.

The girl looks up, her grey colored eyes look scared and sad. I can't help but have a sharp ache in my chest wondering what kind of pain she's been through in her years. A better look at her face and she must only be 18 or 19. Pat grunts beside me, his features still tense like he's going to attack. "It's fine Reba. Tank, do you want to sit outside? I can get you if I need you."

"No" is his short cold response as he pulls a chair for me and gets me sitting before moving to stand in front of the door. His face now a mask of no emotions but I notice his gaze lingers on Marilyn as she settles down at a laptop and starts clicking and typing.

"So, today you're going to make a call to Brett. Is that right?" Reba asks pushing the conference phone towards me.

"Yeah, I figured if I call his work from here, he would actually answer. Even if he's not in the office his receptionist should transfer me to his cell." Confidence in my voice but my head has a small nervous nag that maybe he won't talk to me. Reba nods and dials on the phone, putting it on speaker for the room before settling back in her chair, leaning her elbows on the table with her fingers laced in front of her face.

The phone rings. Rings again. A fifth ring and I think no one is going to answer. "Taft law. Brett Walton office, how may I help you?" A high-pitched breathless voice answers then ends her polite phone greeting with a giggle.

My stomach flips as my gut tells me he's not missing me and obviously is having fun with his receptionist. It makes me wonder how often that happened while we were together. I never called his office line but he also hardly answered his cell while he was there unless he was expecting me to call. It would make sense why he was insistent on always using condoms even though I was on birth control and we were married. Not to mention he had a new receptionist, always an attractive blonde female every time I stepped foot in his office.

A shutter runs down my spine. "Hello? Is someone there?" The high-pitched voice calls through the phone breaking me from my disturbing realization.

"Yes. This is Ellianna Walton and I need you to put my husband on the phone." My voice somehow being confident and steady as I make my demand. Pat gives me a quick, small reassuring smile from his place in front of the door while Reba brings her hand to her mouth. Their thoughts matching mine.

"Umm.... well... he's -"

I cut her off not wanting he hear what excuse she's been told to give. "Put my husband on the phone. Now." My anger bubbling and I struggle to keep my tone only stern and not start cussing this girl out. It's not her fault she fell into his games, I fell for them too.

"Yes, Ma'am." She responds her voice wavering. A holding beep echoes through the room as my mind races with thoughts and my heart clenches with emotions. I may hate Brett now, but I had loved him at one time. Or at least trusted and cared for him, yet the more I learn the more I realize how much he fooled me. What a terrible husband he was to me, and yet he wants to try to keep me and own me. He still wants to keep me as his prize when he has no intentions of giving me the same loyalty and never has.

Anger and betrayal tear through me when Brett's familiar voice comes through the phone. "My darling wife, Ellianna. Are you done playing with that dirty motorcycle gang and ready to come home where you belong?"

Knowing my goal is to lure him here, I try my best to level my head and keep on task. Releasing a deep breath, I finally respond. "No, Brett. I told you before I'm not coming back. However, I think we should discuss things in person. I don't think you'll want me back once you see what I've done." Please, just come; don't make this harder for us, I think on repeat while I speak the lines we had decided on.

"Now why on earth would I go to that disgusting town?" He states into the phone.

"Because we need to talk and I'm not coming to Texas. Not to mention that I have very a limited income now and wouldn't be able to catch a plane." I continue on.

Brett's voice struggles to stay calm. I can hear it, it's the same straining tone he would get before he was start to call me all kinds of degrading names. "Now. Ellianna. That's nonsense, you know I'd come get you or pay for anything you need. Just come back, stop playing these games." He's practically seething the last sentence but that seems to go over the heads of everyone here.

"May I speak?" Reba asks softly.

"Who is that?" He asks.

"My lawyer. You don't think I'd actually call you from my own phone, do you?" I respond. If it wasn't for the sound of Brett's breath, I'd assume he had hung up.

"I think it would be best for all parties if you, Mr. Walton, were to come here to New York for a mediation. I mean, all the documents for separation and divorcing were filed here and the order of protection Mrs. Walton gained against you after her assault by an employee of yours was filed and signed with a New York state judge. My next plan of action would be a summons anyway, as I'm sure you would do the same in this type of situation. If anyone would understand the sensitivity and need for you to come here it should be you, or am I incorrect on your pedigree and reputation as one of the best lawyers this country has to offer?" Reba says with a smirk.

I want to clap and congratulate her for her wit and well-played game. A smile crosses my face towards her as she looks up at me. Honestly, I had forgotten the signed restraining order also included Brett since the PI who assaulted me was hired by him.

"Fine. When?" Brett growls out. Anger at being beat at his own game radiating in his voice.

"The Friday before Thanksgiving." I blurt.

"That's this week. Four days from now. You can't be serious Ellianna."

"Oh, but I am. Now, please send Reba your arrival information and she'll arrange what you need as well as for our meeting. See you then, Husband." Sarcasm lacing the last word as the disgusting thought of still being married to this man crosses my mind. I hang up the line and look from Pat to Reba before settling on the timid expression crossing Marilyn's face. My stomach flips again.

He's coming.

Chapter 32 – Cole

Finally, with a break from club chaos, I make it to the gym 20 minutes before L should get there. The perfect amount of time to run off the day and recollect my thoughts. Reba helped L make it happen, Brett is coming here. Our territory gives us an advantage and control in any situation. Now for that meeting to just go well, we need to scare him off for good. My gut has been nagging at me that even if it goes flawlessly it isn't going to work. One can hope though, I worry if we turn to a more violent and permanent solution the backlash to us and the club would land too many of us in jail or worse. We have no idea how deep his ties with the cartel run.

The 9s cleared out of their latest camp site too. We have just been running defensive circles around them and I'm sick of it. Not to mention the more circles we run the greater the chance that Snake will strike. He didn't get his nick name without reason.

Blaze and Jax are taking the next product run, Blaze taking over for X while he sorts out his dick issues, even though he's been on rest since he was recently shot in the thigh. X is a disgusting bastard. I'm nervous for the run now and if I didn't need Gunner and myself here with L to meet Brett one or both of us would be going too. On a plus side they will be taking half the run to a new allied club from our trip to Florida and the rest to Red, now directly allowed to bring the shipment straight to Red's doorstep.

We earned his trust on that trip and in return have been granted open access. He has been insisting on meeting L soon though, he wants to meet the woman that had me throwing fists in his clubhouse and tearing out of there like I was being chased by hellhounds.

Hearing the cardio room door shut while I'm running, I look up to glace around the room. A smile creeps across my lips as blonde waves and ocean blue eyes land themselves in my vision. Those eyes shining brightly. "Hey baby." Her soft voice calls. "Nick's ready for us if you are." Her smile growing as her eyes trace down my shirtless chest and abs.

"Seeing something you like Kitten?" I ask teasingly as I slow down the treadmill. The little bite to her bottom lip did not escape my notice.

"Maybe, but we have a scheduled appointment, so it'll have to wait." L responds with a wink, turning to walk out of the room.

Quickly, I press the off for the treadmill and hop down. I manage to catch her around the waist just before she escaped back into the hallway. "You couldn't possibly think you'd get away from me now, did you?" I whisper by her ear. Her cinnamon and vanilla scent invading my senses. She nods, wiggling her perky ass into my groin but otherwise not moving from my grasp. The little tease. "You know. I can't keep my hands off you when you're wearing shit like this." I inform her, sliding my thumbs under band of her sports bra before snapping it back to her ribs.

She insists on wearing this shit to workout. Just the sports bra, no shirt. My hands travel down her ribs and her solid abdomen to the top of her stretchy spandex pants that rest just below her belly button. My thumbs doing the same teasing snap, earning a little moan from my girl. "You know I've told you not to wear this shit." I remind her again before grabbing her hips to pull her ass tight against my now throbbing hard dick.

My lips making their way to the soft spot of her neck and she whimpers, against my touch. I'm certain she's dripping wet for me and it would be so easy for me to take her against the cardio room door. Just as I'm about to make that thought reality said door flies open and we are greeted with the horrified expression of Ry. L's eyes are closed as she practically pants at my touch, but my head lifted as soon as I heard the door. Chuckling, I loosen my grip and stand back to my full height.

"Oh God!" L gasps making me laugh more.

It takes a second but Ry finally speaks. His face completely reddened, either with anger or horror, I haven't figured which out yet. "Jesus Fucking Christ. In the fucking cardio room? Really? Why? Why! People run in here!" Ry's voice gaining a high pitch at each word, making my laughter more uncontrollable.

His screaming gains attention, Tank pokes his head out from the weight room across that hall. An uncharacteristic chuckle escaping him as he assesses what's happening here. His heavy weight lifting build leaning against the door watching. Nick also found his way to the hallway, his head poking around the corner to look into the door of the cardio room.

"Alright, no fucking in my gym. You've got a class to get to anyway." Nick says as he obviously tries to hide his laughter.

L turns into my chest, burying her face with a groan. Earning another chuckle from me.

"You are all fucking disgusting. This is disgusting. Cole, that's my sister. You can't just be fucking my sister in public places, especially public places I go to. What is wrong with you?" Ry continues on his rant.

I laugh more, tightening my arms around L to walk her from the room while she keeps her face buried in my chest. I can image she's embarrassed at her brother seeing her in such a sexual position with me. "Well, if it makes you feel any better. We weren't fucking yet. Had you been a minute or two later though, you may have something to bitch about."

Ry's mouth drops, speechless at my disclosure. Gaining more laughter from Tank and Nick. "Seriously, you asshole, don't fuck in my gym. That's all sorts of nasty." Nick grumbles.

Little does he know we already have, several times. The most recent being last week and on his desk. My feisty little kitten gets a thrill out of the possibility of getting caught, though I'd never purposely let that happen. I would have locked the cardio door before stripping her down, had Ry not so rudely interrupted. L groans again before letting out a giggle and whispering as much to me, her thoughts reflecting mine.

"Come on lovebirds. We have training to do." Nick calls again making L break free of my arms and heading towards Nick to start our fighting class.

After an hour of training with Nick, I managed to convince L to sneak me into the women's locker room. Making sure to lock the door so I could finish what we started earlier. Fifteen minutes after she snuck me back out of the locker room she finally emerges. Dark ripped up jeans with her favorite fleeced lined leggings showing through the holes. Her hair is back down, flowing around her face and shoulders and a hooded sweatshirt covers her torso with her new leather jacket over top.

"You going to be warm enough to ride?" I ask, knowing the temperature dropped more after the sun went down. I'm going to have to start taking my truck more with L.

She nods and grabs my hand, leading us both out the gym doors. "I'm starving. Take me somewhere with food."

"As you command." I say with a laugh.

She hops on my bike like its second nature to her. I still can't believe she's here with me. She's mine again and every second of every day my love for her grows greater. I would walk through hell for her, take bullets for her and kill anyone who even thought to try to harm her. Calling in a massive Chinese delivery order, I take off for a clubhouse. You can't ever just order delivery for yourself there, times it by ten and hope no-one steals what you wanted for yourself before you get your hands on it.

"I almost forgot!" L exclaims as she climbs off my bike and rushes into the clubhouse without me.

Wondering what has her in such a rush I follow after her, pausing only to tell Matt there's Chinese coming and to make sure he saves L's from the rest of the guys. A flash of blonde waves comes from the doorway to the basement. Confused I follow after her, stepping into Tech's space just before the doors close. "What's the rush?" I ask, getting an amused smirk from Tech.

L clasps her hands and rocks on her feet before finally explaining. "Well, I'm hoping Tech can help us get proof, but I realized a way to very quickly and easily get divorced."

My smile matches hers and Tech's. "Gladly will help with that. How so?" He asks.

She explains how the phone was answered today when she called her shit head husbands office and how Reba had the same thoughts. She also explains how she wasn't supposed to call or show up unannounced and whenever she should show to the office, she would have to wait for him to come get her from security. Several times it was almost an hour of waiting.

"What a piece of shit." I mumble, unable to even imagine cheating on such a stunning woman.

"Well... I mean it all kind of clicked when we heard how he answered the phone. Not to mention it makes things that happened between him and I make more sense too." She says.

What's practically a growl leaves my throat. "What did he do to you L?"

"Nothing." She looks at me, reading the anger coming from me she puts her small hand on my chest. "Nothing, you don't already know about. Just we were married and so sometimes he was weird about things. I always shrugged it off, he was peculiar about a lot of stuff." I stare at her, wanting more details. Only to feed some sick demented part of me that desires the torture of hearing about her with another man. She clears her throat and looks away from Tech and I. "I always had to shower before and after we had sex. He would also. He said he hated the smell of us being sweaty or the scent of our days on us."

"That's fucking weird and he's a fucking bastard." Tech mumbles.

"I have been on birth control since Momma took me for it when I was 14. Religiously taking the pill at the same time every day until I got the IUD a few years ago, which you know anyway. Even with that he always wore a condom. I thought it was strange, I mean we were married and the chance of pregnancy was slim but even if it happened what would it have mattered really? You know? Makes more sense if he was making sure to cover his tracks on the chance, he got something to give to me."

I shake my head, wondering how the thought hadn't crossed her mind before that he's a lying, cheating, shit bag. Though that demented part of me is giddy at the thought there was always a barrier between them and I'm the only one that has completely claimed her and marked her with cum.

"He'd also come home late at least twice a week and often had meetings at one of the hotels in town. I only learned that because I found a bar receipt from there in his pocket while doing the wash."

"Okay. That's enough reasons." I say wrapping my arms around her and pulling her tight to me. "He's not a man. A man wouldn't do such a thing. He was unworthy of even a look from you, let alone a life with you." I whisper in her ear trying to soothe the thoughts of worth I know are creeping into her mind.

Tech rubs his forehead then turns in his chair to start typing at his computers. "I'm assuming his office has cameras, so I'm going to start there. The hotel wouldn't have cameras in the room but would in the bar at least. What was the name?"

"The Omni Rivera" L quickly replies.

Tech nods and types. Chuckling to himself like a lunatic. "For a law firm that helps the cartel they have shit security. I'm already in."

"Really?" L gasps shocked.

I'm not so shocked. They probably have decent security; Tech is just that good. "His office has a camera." Tech says softly. "Do you want to be here while I play through this?"

She nods. "I think I need to confirm today for myself also. Then if you could collect the rest of them yourself for proof to give the judge?"

Tech smiles sadly at her. "Of course, Blondie. Anything you need, always." He promises and I know he truly means what he says. He clicks through and goes to the hour before the call. You see that smug asshole sitting at his desk looking over files. I want to reach through the screen and punch his face in. My grip tightens on L. Tech speeds through 20 more minutes according to the time stamps, then you see a tall, skinny blonde in heels and a painted on short skirt step into the room. His head looks up from his papers and you can see the douchebag practically drooling.

He stacks the papers in a pile before putting the stack in a desk drawer and rolling the chair back from the desk. The blonde slinks through the room, the same type of walk the slut bunnies do through the bar, unbuttoning her size too small shirt as she slinks.

When the blonde finally reaches the asshole she instantly drops to her knees. Putting her hands on the button of his pants and pulling his dick out. The camera is in a corner to the side of his desk so we are getting a pretty detailed view of the whole thing. The blonde starts making a slobbery mess of his dick. He obviously isn't amused with the girls spit because he pulls her off him by her hair with one hand and reaches into his drawer for a tissue with the other.

After drying himself and her drying her mouth he rolls a condom on and pushes her face down on his desk. Her hands going up to hold the edge as he slides into her, still holding her down by the back of her head. "I've seen enough." L states and leaves the room.

I sigh, knowing she'd be upset seeing this. "Paul."

He nods, "You take care of Ellie. I'll sort through this. This gives the judge all the reason he needs to push those papers through." Tech says softly, dismissing me as he turns back to his computers.

I take off after L. I swear, as soon as I can without concern for the consequences, I'm going to kill that stupid fuck with my bare hands for hurting my girl like that.

Chapter 33 – Ellianna

I just couldn't watch any more of that. Any more of watching Brett use a girl that was his ideal look. Blonde, skinny, tall.

I may have been blonde, but I'm not that tall. Fairly short actually, only being about five foot and four inches. I've also always been curvy. My breasts are large and my waist hourglasses in. My hips are wide and I've always had to get at least size 10 jeans because my hips and ass demand it. Not that I have ever minded my figure, but that was always a complaint of his. Run more, work out more, eat less, only drink water, the list goes on.

Funny though, I had asked him several times to be rough with me during sex but he wouldn't. Yet, he slammed that girl's face on to his desk and rammed into her like it was his only desire.

"Hands off X! This is Queen's!" I hear Matt's voice as soon as I step into the main floor. Good boy, protecting my food.

"Prospect, don't make me -" I hear X say before I cut him off.

"You sure you want to finish that sentence?" Both guys turn to look at me, Matt's face lighting up with a smile as X's drops.

Matt takes the container of General Tso's combo and hands it to me. I can see he used sharpie to write "Queen" on it and I giggle. "X, were you really trying to come between a hungry woman and her dinner?"

"Nope!" He says and grabs another container off the island without looking at it and rushing into the dining room, making me laugh more.

"Thank you, Matty. Did you get some for yourself?" I ask.

He smiles. His bruised face looking worse today. "Nah. I grabbed some food at the bar after Prez and I finished up today."

"Okay, as long as you ate. You doing okay?"

His smile drops a little. "Yeah. I mean I kind of liked her too, but..." his sentence trails off.

"She's a lot to handle. I know. Don't worry sweetie, you'll find someone, you'll treat her right and she'll love you back just as much." I tell him, hoping it's true for him. I leave a kiss on his cheek and thank him again before I go into the living room where all the guys are bickering and joking. The guys greet me as I settle into a chair, still starving. I barely had an appetite at lunch from nerves. Now even though I have a lot of thoughts running through my head my nerves are calm and my need for food has kicked in.

I notice X squirming in his chair, a lot. "What is wrong with you, X?"

He turns bright red and all the guys start laughing. Cole comes in with his own container of food and lifts me up to sit in my chair with me on his lap. "His dick burns because he doesn't understand what sexually transmitted diseases are." Cole states trying to hold in his laugh but the rest of the table completely loses it. Even Matt falls out of his chair laughing so hard.

"Well. I hope that's a lesson for all of you." Is all I can think to respond with and try to continue to eat my dinner. It is mean to laugh at him but at the same time these men should know better. The laughter continues for at least 5 minutes and X is tomato red. Standing up, I yell to gain attention. "Okay boys. That's enough! X has learned his lesson, right, X?" I look at him and he slowly nods. "Good. Now think how you'd feel if you were in his situation and your *friends* were laughing at you like this. Easy enough since you all seem to share women and freely put your dicks in between the legs that let you."

The guys seem to take my words to heart and drop their gazes to the table. Mumbles of "Sorry X." And "You're right Queen" are the only sounds in the room. I settle back in my seat on Cole's lap, he grips my waist with a tight squeeze. The table goes entirely too quiet after, and I worry I over stepped.

Then Matty knocks his beer over into his lap. He sends me a wink and I know he did it on purpose to move the attention from X and I. The entire table laughs and makes jokes at Matty before returning to its normal state.

Cole rubs light circles on my hip with his free hand. "You okay, Kitten?"

"Not really, but I will be." I respond to him before joining in a conversation about new shows on Netflix with Matt and a couple other members.

The next night Cole had to handle some club stuff so Sonja, Ry and I, tailed by Tank of course met for dinner at Giovanni's. They have the best brick oven; thin and crispy crust pizza and they are right in town. Tank took off for his own table in the back corner where he could be alone and watch the whole place instead of sitting with us like I had insisted.

I just finished telling Sonja how mortified Ry was yesterday at the gym when he sits down at our table. "It's still not cool Princess. What if I had seen you naked? I mean, what I walked in on was bad enough." He says gagging and ends his statement with a whole-body shake.

"Scarred for life?" Sonja jokes pushing at Ry's shoulder.

"Absolutely. Let's never speak of it again." Ry states.

"What about when they have babies? I mean, you know how babies are made right?" Sonja continues on harassing Ry.

He looks like he's about to either pass out or throw up. Both of which would interfere with my dinner. "Alright. No babies are happening any time soon and we should change the subject. How about, Sonja! Why don't you tell us about your sex-escapades with Matt?"

Ry turns his focus on Sonja. "Yes, please. Let's talk about that." He deadpans, earning a giggle from me.

Sonja turns red and a look crosses her facial expression but I can't quite catch it before the waiter comes over and she paints on a smile. "Sorry if I crossed a line, Son." I whisper to her, receiving a nod and we'll talk later response.

"So, I finish my classes before Christmas and I was thinking of talking to Pops about buying in as a partner with him at the dealership." Ry informs us.

Sonja squeals in excitement. "Really? Oh my gosh look how grown up you are!"

"What do you think Princess?" He asks, turning toward me.

"I think that would be amazing Ry. Pops worked hard to get that dealership built to what it is now. It makes me proud that you want to continue on with Pops, like a legacy, you know." I tell him with a bright smile, wholeheartedly impressed with the idea. "Do you have what he would want for a partnership?"

Ry nods. "I've been saving. My rent is cheap since Adam and I split everything. The only thing I really pay for is my truck and that's just the insurance now. I've been thinking about it for a while. I'd need about 10% of the business worth to put in for partner. Though, I'm not that good at the business side."

"Maybe ask Cole?" I suggest.

Sonja and Ry both look at me curiously. "What?" I finally ask since their shocked expressions are still on me moments later.

"Cole?" Sonja says like a question.

"Umm yeah?"

"What's Cole know about any of that?" Ry asks.

Both of their questioning responses leads me into a fit if giggles before I can answer them. "What do you think he does all day? Parade around on his motorcycle?"

"Well. Yeah." Sonja states dryly leading me to another fit of laughter.

"You guys." I choke out as more laughter escapes me. "Not only does he own and run the bar, but he does all the background stuff on the new buildings and contractor work Chris does. Plus, he handles all the overhead stuff for the motorcycle and parts place that some of the guys run and the gym. Amongst other things."

Ry looks impressed along with shocked. "I suppose he'd be the person to ask, well other than Pops but until I'm ready to have that conversation I'm not about to ask him."

"Right. Plus, it may be good for you two to bond again." I say shoving my shoulder into Ry just before the waiter brings our pizza out to our table. "I don't know about you two, but I'm starving! Nick has me training with him every other day and I'm still running the other days."

Sonja laughs. "I'm sure that's not the only thing burning all your calories."

I wink at her joining her laughter. Ry drops his pizza back to his groaning at the horror thought of his sister having sex. We back off the torment of Ry the rest of the evening. Keeping topics lighter and filling our table with laughter.

"Ry, my darling little adoptive brother." Sonja coos at him, fluttering her eyelashes like her next question is going to be innocent. "When are you going to bring a woman around us? Hmmmm?"

Again, my poor brother looks like he's going to either pass out or throw up. Ry was always a player in high school, being the starting quarterback for football and captain of the baseball team he was always "that guy". He never did bring anyone around Sonja or I though, other than homecoming or prom dates.

"Yes, dearest brother, I think it is time we pried into your love life. Still playing flavor of the week games?" I say teasingly.

Ry swallows. For a second I think he looks scared before he breaks into a smile. Redness creeping into his cheeks. He finally replies, "Definitely playing the field still." The way he says it makes me think it's not true at all though. Before I can question him though, Tank is behind me pulling me from the chair.

"What the hell man?" Ry exclaims also leaping from his chair, Sonja following after us, sliding into her coat and grabbing her purse.

" Ry 's truck. Now. Keys!" Tank growls out, putting his left hand out for the keys. He wraps my coat around my shoulders with an inhumane speed. In a softer tone he instructs the hostess on the way out. "Gigi, send Paul the bill to handle."

I see her nod and write something down. Tank has one arm wrapped protectively around me and his other hand I know is on his gun that's tucked in the inside of his jacket. "Get in. Now." He growls instructions again; I'm guessing to Ry and Sonja. Opening the passenger door, he pushes me in. "Stay down." His tone gentler with me, though still a command.

"What the fuck?" I hear Ry from the back seat.

"Something must have happened. I'm sure it's just an over re-active precaution." I say as Tank slips in the driver seat and immediately takes off like a bat out of hell. "Patrick, what's happening?"

Of course, Tank being the way he is, he merely grunts in response as he continues to drive. Sighing, I settle into the floor of the passenger seat. Luckily, I am small enough to curl up here without being too cramped, especially since we were having dinner at the opposite end of town and it's at least 30 minutes to the clubhouse. Sonja and Ry go quiet in the back seat, abnormal for them. Though, the vibe Tank is giving off right now, I don't blame them.

After what feels like an eternity the truck stops. Tank hops out at the same time the passenger door is ripped open. The scent of sandalwood and leather fills the truck as strong arms wrap around me pulling me from my uncomfortable position and into the cold November air.

"Sorry, Ry. Sonja. Hope you don't mind being stuck at the clubhouse tonight, Beck is getting rooms sorted for you." I hear Cole's deep voice come from behind me, quietly informing my two closest friends of their fate.

We head into the clubhouse; Beck meets us at the door to take Ry and Sonja into the main house. "No. What the fuck is going on, Cole? This obviously involves my sister which involves me. I'm not fucking staying anywhere and neither is she until you tell me what the fuck is going on!" My brother yells at Cole, fury and distrust evident in his voice.

Gunner pops his head out of the clubhouse, most likely hearing Ry. He pauses for a moment seeing Sonja. Shaking his head, he speaks before Cole or I get a chance to. "Kid, unless you're a member this doesn't concern you. Get your ass inside for your own fucking safety."

"Make me a member then. Ellie is my sister; I'll be fucking damned if I don't protect her. I didn't protect her for the last 4 years and look what fucking happened." Ry steps in front of me, between Chris and Cole and looks over me to stare into Cole's eyes. "Don't be the reason I fail her again... brother."

I feel Cole's grip on me tighten. My own tears burning behind my eyes threatening to fall. Knowing that my brother feels like he failed me because of my own choices and own mistakes is completely crushing to my soul.

"Gunner, will you second a vote to under the circumstances

patch Ry in? We were going to vote to patch in Matt and Tommy today anyway, might as well patch in all three." Cole says to my shock, then to my even greater shock Gunner agrees and sends Beck to get the jackets and find one for Ry.

"You'd really do this for my brother? But don't prospects have to do a bunch of shit and earn it? You tell me that all the time when I worry about Matty."

Cole and Gunner both chuckle. Gunner slaps my brother's shoulder and wishes him luck. He then steps back into the clubhouse with Sonja trailing behind him. Cole rubs his hand through his hair chuckling a little more. "Well, since Ry figured out what we do here Gunner and Tech and some of the other guys have apparently been fucking with him." I send him a glare; I know what their way of fucking with people is like and I'm not impressed. Cole's hands go up in defense making Ry chuckle. "I didn't know. I learned that bit shortly after you came back. I was serious when I said I avoided your family; I couldn't handle the reminder of you. I didn't know it was happening. Then, recently, Ry 's been helping us with some jobs."

"You have my brother doing illegal shit!" I yell at Cole then turn on my brother, yelling at him and slapping at his chest. "You been doing illegal shit?"

"No! No. Fucking hell. No." Ry yells defensively trying to duck and avoid my slaps. "Jesus Princess, your slaps fucking hurt."

Cole rolls with laughter before I turn back on him. Instantly straightening himself, he clears his throat and tries to hide his smirk of amusement. "He's not doing illegal shit. Have a little faith in me that I wouldn't let that happen. Just random jobs, helping Gunner move construction stuff, fixing light bulbs, cleaning the vans. No guns, no cash, I promise." He looks up at Ry. "You patch in passes tonight and that changes. You good with that?"

"Yes, Prez." Ry response just like Matty or Pat would.

Worry for my brother consumes me, "Cole." I breathe out.

"Shhh, Kitten. It's no different than me or Tank or Matt. Okay?" He whispers in my ear. It doesn't ease my fears but I can't be upset about one and not the other either. "If this is all settled, we need to get into Church. Shit went down today, and we have new patches to vote on."

Chapter 34 – Cole

I'm stuck in my office catching up on all the shit I've been slacking on now that I have Blaze and Jax all set to take off tonight after the Church vote to patch in Tommy and Matt.

Contracts, paperwork, emails and spreadsheets fill the majority of my job as President and Leader of this club. Keeping things legit means a paper trail, not to mention the bar, motorcycle shop, Gunner's construction business and all the rental properties that pull in a large portion of the club's income all have to be documented and organized well.

It's not the most fun, but it could be worse. Even if I would rather be buried in my feisty little Kitten as she moans out my name and writhes under me. Just the thought has my dick hardening and uncomfortable in my jeans.

The annoying ring of my phone instantly shuts down the discomfort at my groin. Searching through the stacks of papers on my desk, I finally find the damn thing just before it goes to voicemail. I don't recognize the number, but that doesn't mean anything since I get burner phone calls about the guns on the regular.

"This is Hawk. Speak."

"Now, is that any way to greet your favorite Italian friend, Cole Cameron." A heavily accented low voice comes through the line.

"Tony, my man. Apologies, I didn't realize-"

"No worries. Now, I'm calling on a rather personal matter rather

than business. Unfortunately, I don't have much time to rely what I have."

What the hell could Tony have that's personal. I run through everything we know of each other and come up blank. We merely are friendly in business terms. "I'm listening." I reply into the phone, kicking my feet up on the desk.

"Well, you see I debated on what to do here. For some reason I like you and your club. You have been very good business partners and well, you're honorable, loyal and trustworthy. All very admirable qualities that makes me rather fond of you."

"I see. That's quite a compliment, especially coming from you Tony. Thank you."

Who would have thought I had managed to make it into the friendship side of one of the highest-ranking members of the Italian mafia? Not that we go around trying to make friends, or enemies for that matter with any mafia or cartel, but we have run guns with Tony since the beginning. He does provide the best of the best in parts then we make them better.

"Right. As it is, I don't hand those out lightly. I also don't hand out information gathered in business meetings lightly either. Consider this a favor and a gesture of faith and interest in your well-being." He states. This conversation is turning into one I'm not sure I want to be having. Taking a favor from Tony would mean we owe him one. While I think over my options, Tony continues. *"It's about your lovely bella donna. I believe her name is Ellianna?"*

My heart stops. Fuck it, we will owe the Italian's for life and I can regret it later. "I'll owe you, Tony. What about L?"

"I thought you'd say that friend. Don't worry on the favor for now, you wouldn't be the first person I'd call. Now Ellianna, quite the beautiful name for a beautiful girl. Blondes have never really been my type, but there is something about her, no?"

"I don't share well, Tony." I say and manage to catch myself before threatening this powerful man. He chuckles on the other

end of the line and I only hope he finds humor in my posses-
siveness.

*"Again, don't worry friend. I'm not after your girl. Happily mar-
ried, actually and just as possessive. Now, to my reason for calling.
I was in a rather.... interesting... meeting today. You see, I know
many people and even more people know me. Though hardly anyone knows who I work with and no one other than myself knows
where my loyalties lay."* I wonder if I should interject, especially
since he said he was on limited time. I have however learned
that when it comes to Tony he likes to talk to see if people are
actually listening, so I continue to listen to each detail. *"Where
do you think my loyalties lay today?"*

"Since you are on the phone with me after a private business
meeting, I would assume in this case they have fallen on me."
I respond to him, indicating that I'm listening to his every
word.

*"Correct you are, Mr. Cameron. Correct you are. You see, this meet-
ing was called by some associates of mine that happened to catch
that the guns you distribute originally come from me. They figured
they could eventually work their way into my good graces. Though,
I do happen to like those extra goodies you send back, so it would
not happen, but again, they know nothing of me. Cretinos. They
brought me to meet this lawyer. Pezzo de merda."* Tony practically
shouts the last bit of italian.

Trying to keep any chuckling to myself, "Let me guess, Brett
Walton was said piece of shit?"

"Si. Very good. Want to know who else was in this meeting?"

"Considering some of his acquaintances, it would be in my
best interest to be informed. So yes, I'd like to know Tony."

"Harry. Harry Cameron." My heart stops. Shatters. Fails to
pump blood to my brain. *"I wish I was joking or calling with better news friend."*

"What else? What else Tony? I need to protect her, what else was said today?" I ask in an almost panic. This is bad, very, very bad. It means everything I have ever done and put L through was for nothing, because somehow, my uncle knows.

"They are coming. They have something planned to distract your club so they can take her and Harry wants you and Christopher dead. Disgusting man, wanting to kill your own familia. Where is the loyalty?" Tony spits out. You can tell the man thrives off family and loyalties.

"Loyalty never existed in Harry's life Tony. The concept escapes him." I say lowly, my mind turning at the thoughts of what they could be planning.

"I'm sorry I don't have more details friend. I must go. It is bad practice to speak such things discussed in meetings. You understand." He says, with what sounds like sadness creeping to his voice.

"I do. Thank you, Tony. I do owe you one."

"In bocca al lupo."

I chuckle. My Italian is not great but I pick up some things, "Tony, did you really just tell me to break a leg?"

"Si, it is a good luck phrase. Be well my friend." Tony ends the call, leaving me momentarily at a loss for what to do as I process this information.

Then it's like all the emotions I buried for that conversation hits me. "Fuck!" I roar. Smashing my phone and tearing all the papers off my desk. Putting several fists into the office wall before Gunner comes rushing into the room. His quick reflexes and knowing me as well as he does, he catches my flying hand.

"What the fuck Brother?" He asks.

Breaking free from Gunner, I rub my face and push my hands through my hair. "Brett. Harry. Tony. Fuck!"

"The fuck are you talking about? Tony? Like the Italians, has guns Tony?"

"Yes." It's all I can say. Knowing I need to make actions happen and need to get L back here I storm out of the office. "Lock-down mother fuckers! Now!"

My booming voice gains the attention of every single soul in the bar. Club bunnies go scurrying, most likely running to their house at the end of the property that we let them live in. They are still protected on the club grounds but away from me and our business. The members rush up, putting together all the security protocols we have to completely lockdown the grounds.

"Prez, you're locking shit down? Want to fucking fill your VPs in." I hear Gunner as he's following me trying to get my atten-tion but I'm too focused on finding a phone.

"You!" I grab a prospect; I think his name is Cody or something. "Give me your fucking phone."

"Ye-yes Prez." He stutters taking his phone from his pocket. His lock screen a photo of a little girl with curly red hair and a pretty blue-nosed Pitbull.

The picture reminds me that I need to be a little bit human, even if I'm about to crawl out of my skin and want to brutally murder several people. "Could you please unlock it? I need to make a call." He nods and slides his finger on the sensor.

"Thank you." I manage to mutter as I dial Tank's number.

"Why the fuck are you calling me, Prospect?" Tank's gravelly voice full of anger crosses the phone.

Cool, calm, collected. It's time to lead I remind myself. "It's Hawk. Lockdown. Get L back now."

"Yes, Prez." And the call ends. I know Tank out of everyone here will protect her at all costs, and do a damn good job of it.

Gunner grabs me while I'm handing the phone back to the prospect. "What the fuck?" He stares me down waiting for an answer.

"Basement."

Gunner nods and we rush to Tech where I fill them both in on my call with Tony.

"So, we owe a favor to the Italians?" Gunner shakes his head questioning my judgment.

"I, me, not you, not this club. Me, I owe the favor. It was worth it; we won't be blindsided that they are in this together." I respond.

Gunner nods. "We should have shot him in the fucking face."

In retrospect now, we should have. However, it's hard to put down family. Like Tony said on the phone, I have honor and loyalty. Harry is blood and had helped us at one point, even if that help was partially self-serving. I felt I owed him something. Now though, no such luck for him.

He will wish I had killed him then by the time I'm finished with him. Him and that fucking shit head ex of L's. He has passed on his chance of getting out of this a free man. I may not be able to torture then brutally kill him, but I can however tie him up and hand him to the feds. I won't be able to personally kill him but inside, where he has nowhere to run and we have just as many contacts. Well, let's just say he won't make it out in one piece.

"Tech."

"Yes Prez." He responds, knowing I'm in full Prez mode and our friendship is on the back burner.

"Link Brett to children." I state dryly, knowing how awful that is to even think about.

His eyes widen, but he nods, does his dramatic chair spin and gets to work. Tech does his thing and I head upstairs to make sure the lockdown is underway, sending Tommy to the basement to help Tech on my way.

Gunner gets down to business, finally. Commanding prospects and members while handling phone calls and getting the rest of the guys either locked down in their own homes ready to roll at a call or headed here to take shelter on the grounds. Several of the garage buildings have upstairs apartments that most of the guys with families use as needed. Since we been here and have built up to where we are now, with as many buildings as we have and space, this is the first lockdown. I am however, guessing those with families will make use of the spaces.

Seeing Beck fluttering around and making lists for the prospects to get what she needs; I remember that L was with Ry and Sonja. "Hey Beck?" I speak loud enough so I get her attention without yelling and trying to keep my voice calm. She perks her head up from her lists to look at me, concern washed across all her features. "I need space for Sonja and Ry. Also, could you call L's Pops and Momma? Try to get them here. I broke another phone."

"Of course. Any suggestions how to get Ben and Sally here?" Beck asks.

"Be truthful. They will just get upset otherwise." She raises an eyebrow at me. Of course, she only knows we are in lockdown and sees right through me and the idea that Ben or Sally would be okay with just that information.

"Just tell them that the threat is against Ellie and the club only wants to protect them. If that's not enough, find me."

She nods again and puts her phone to her ear, walking way upstairs. I just catch Gunner rushing over to her and whispering in her ear. My guess would be he's going to convince Beck to put Sonja in his room. If he hasn't fixed things with her yet, that wouldn't be the wisest choice.

"You!" I yell at another prospect.

He's new, started around the time Cody did and can't remember his name either. I've been so wrapped up in L, I've missed some shit the last few months. Very unlike me, but I will find balance again after Harry is six foot under and Brett is close to following.

Once he's looking at me and I know I have his attention. "Spread the word. Church as soon as Queen steps foot in this club house."

He nods and takes off, typing on his phone so I know he's alerting those above him.

"Prez."

I turn to face Jax and Blaze.

"Fuck. The run." I say running my hands over my face again tonight. "Gimme one of your phones so I can call Red and explain." There's a lot of shit to be done still and Tank should have L back soon.

Chapter 35 – Ellianna

I started to get nervous as Cole lead us to the large meeting room the club uses for Church. It was about to be my first real meeting as Queen and it wasn't a typical meeting. Not to mention they were voting on
Ry, Matty and Tommy on becoming full members of the club.

"Ry, you gotta wait out here man." Cole directs my brother.

We step into the room; it's packed with members. It's a huge room but I've only ever seen it empty. Now it's stuffed with standing bodies of members and the round table in the center has a Phoenix burned into the solid oak. That is where Gunner, Tech, Tank, Blaze, Jax, X, Inky and two other guys who I know are officers too sit. There is an empty chair at the top of the phoenix that must be Cole's. If memories serves right the other two officers are Ryder and Lucas, they have families and tend to stay out of the clubhouse. There's a third guy at the end who is older and I've never seen him at the club before. Before I can ask who, he is, Cole leads me to him.

"Old Man Bear. This is Ellianna." He says pulling me towards the guy.

If I had to guess I'd say he was in his 60s, his face, though aged and showing wrinkles still holds ruggedly handsome features. His hair is short and grey and he has a long well-kept beard. Tattoos, now faded, peak out from the collar of his T-shirt up his neck and down his arms to his hands.

"Blondie. It's nice to finally meet the woman who has captured not just our Prez but this whole club. It's an honor." He says with a wink taking my hand between both of his. "You can call me Luke. I helped these little shits figure stuff out in the beginning."

I nod and smile, understanding now that Bear is an advisor for the guys which is why he gets a spot at the officer table.

Cole calls for the room to quiet and pulls me down into his lap. "Now before we start with why we are in a full lockdown; we have two prospects and one unconventional prospect sitting in the hall. First, I call a vote for Tommy to be patched in. Is there a second?"

"I second." Tech calls immediately.

"There is a second. Any objections?" He asks and pauses. The room stays quiet. "Good. All in favor?"

The room calls out a chorus of "yays" before Cole asks if anyone votes no and passing the vote that Tommy is now a member.

He moves on to Matt, who's seconded by both Tank and X at the same time. The voting goes the same way and my little Matty is officially a member.

"Okay, the next vote is definitely unconventional. Most of you know Ry, our Queen's brother, and that he's been doing some work for us even though he hasn't technically been voted in as a prospect." I hear the members grunt and shuffle, making my stomach flop, wondering will they disagree with the idea of patching in my brother. "Given the circumstances we currently have and will go into more detail on after the voting process, Ry has approached myself and Gunner about offering himself to the club for our use and to protect our Queen. He has proven himself loyal to this club time and again, including being harassed by a PI trying to get dirt on us."

There are multiple angry grumbles in the room, all seemingly still upset that the PI was looking into us, or perhaps because I had been attacked by him on their territory.

"I move to patch in Ry as a full member, given the circumstances, his loyalty to this club and his willingness to risk his life to protect not just his sister but this entire club." Cole's voice booms over the grumbles of the members.

"I second the vote." Gunner announces.

"I support also." Tank says, getting nods from the rest of the officer table.

"Very good. The officers stand with this vote, but it's still up to the rest of the club. Any objections?" Cole asks.

"Yeah!" A voice from the back speaks up.

The members standing move aside to let the owner of the voice through. I've seen this guy around before, at the bar and clubhouse. Though he has never really said anything to me.

"The rest of us had to go through an entire prospecting process, getting constantly shit on by all of you not to mention all the shitty grunt work we had to do. What the fuck has this kid done other than be related for him to bypass all that bullshit?" The guy yells.

Nick moves forward to face the guy. "He has done all that. He's cleaned up some nasty shit at my gym for me, on several occasions. He's a fighter and even without any ties to this club he has protected us. He has never breathed a word about what we do here even though he figured it out quickly. He's hauled drunk assholes out of the bar trying to touch Beck or one of the Bunnies without permission while you assholes were too drunk to even realize what was happening. I fully support Ry being a member of this club, he has earned that right and privilege more than I have and a hell of a lot more than you, Bruce" Nick ends his speech shoving at the guys shoulders.

My heart beats faster with the disagreements and shoving that has broken out amongst the men, but I can't help but smile at Nick's description of my brother's and his actions.

"Enough!" Cole yells, making me jump. "We aren't fighting each other tonight. Anyone else have anything to say?" He pauses.

"No? Fine. We vote. All in favor?"

To my shock and surprise every member including Bruce says "yay". Tears spring to my eyes before Cole rubs his hand on my hip, under my shirt, soothing my emotions.

"Great. Bring them and Beck in here." Cole calls. Beck busts through the door before Blaze even gets out of his seat. She's bouncing in with three boxes and her smile is across her entire face. Blaze moves to the door around her and I hear him yelling about getting their asses in here.

Matty, Ry and Tommy file in behind Blaze. He stands them at the front of the room. Cole stands taking me with him, Gunner, Tech and Beck to stand between the room and the new patches.

"With honor, loyalty and dignity as well as desire to make things better for those around us, we were founded much like a Phoenix. Rising out of the ashes of all the shit we burned around us. We rid ourselves of those who wanted to do harm to us and harm to innocents, setting fire to them all and rising." Cole takes a box from Beck and gives it to me, then takes another and hands it to Tech.

Cole leans to whisper to me. "Open the box and present it to Ry."

He continues on his speech, opening his box in front of Matty while Tech does the same for Tommy. I follow suit opening my box for Ry. I watch Ry's face go from shock to relief then pride. "Today we extend our family of Phoenix's to three men, each proving their loyalty and devotion as brothers. Welcome to the fucking family boys!"

Shouts erupt throughout the room, echoing in the space. Cheers from the members and the proud faces of my brother and the kid that has worked his way into my heart bring joyful tears to my eyes. I quickly swipe them away before anyone sees.

"Now that that's settled. We have much to discuss, we will party and celebrate when this shit is over!" Cole shouts, making everyone quiet as they shuffle back to where they were sitting or standing.

He launches into a tell all with Tech and Gunner assisting. Explaining everything from our plan to discuss things with Brett, as Cole worded it "kind and politely" to canceling that out because he got an informative call today from an inside source.

None of the three of them would explain their source but trouble is coming and we need a plan to defend our town, this club and me.

Tank pounds his fist on the table at the mention of Snake. Cole and Chris' crazy uncle. Mumbled sounds of anger and displeasure wave through the room as well. Old Man Bear sitting across from me clenches his jaw and fist before dropping his hand to the table and looking at me with sad and concerned eyes.

"Obviously, the first thing is keeping Queen here, under the protection of the club and clubhouse." Jax states from his place across the table.

I snort. "I'm not going to be trapped in my home Jax, also I'm not completely defenseless. I'm sure as hell not going to sit here on my butt while you all march off to possibly get yourselves hurt."

Cole's grip on my hips tightens. Old Man Bear and Gunner both give me smirking nods of approval. "She did beat the piss out of that PI guy." Tommy states before the room erupts in arguments again.

How on earth they manage to get things planned and decided on, I'll never know. The room seems to just be a constant state of arguments.

"Listen up!!" Cole shouts getting the attention of the room

again. "We need to circle back to this, after we decide what to do about Snake and the 9s. They are the biggest threat and one we can take care of on our own."

"What about the ex?" Tanks gravelly voice interjects.

"We can't take him out like you can take care of the 9s, unfortunately. I know him and how he works, I know the lengths he would go to destroy every single one of you for doing so. His connections, which Tech has found run even deeper than I knew of as well as his family would come for all of us." I explain to the room. "Either, I do what he wants and return to him or we find a way to have his entire name destroyed. Remove all his connections and everything he has that keeps him in this place of power. Only then could we strike at him."

"She's right." Tech agrees with me. "He's a whole complicated game of Jenga, but don't worry I'm working on it." He ends with a wink.

"Right. Leave Brett to Tech for now. We need to handle Snake and the 9s." Cole announces over the room which then again turns in to a bunch of arguments on what's the best way to take out the 9s.

"Actually!" Tech yells, which alarms me a bit since Tech doesn't yell. "Blondie had a good idea the other day, we just haven't put it into play yet."

Tech goes on to explain about capturing the 9s member we talked about the other night then using them to get locations and information. He also brings up what he has found out in his research. Tech and Tommy have gathered an impressive amount of information.

The member, Scorpion has been a close friend with the Prez of the 9s for years. On top of that he seems to be informed and allowed in to most meetings. He's also been around Snake a large majority of his time since Cole and Chris' uncle showed up around town.

After a few more arguments and a few more ideas thrown around it's finally voted and agreed on that we get him by tomorrow and get information from him by Friday morning. In the meantime, I'm working my job from the clubhouse and am not to leave.

Friday late afternoon, I'm supposed to meet Brett. According to Tech's information that's still the plan since everything indicates Brett is still in Texas.

I can only hope this goes as planned, if not and if it comes down to me or the club.... Well, I know I'd sacrifice myself for these guys. I would not let harm come to the club.

Chapter 36 - Ellianna

Walking into the main house after the hours and hours long meeting, it's late in the night. Several uncontrolled yawns escape me and I'm a little grateful that I'm calling out sick at work tomorrow until we can sort out me working at home. Fingers crossed my manager doesn't mind and it doesn't look bad against me since I'm just out of my new hire probationary time. Not to mention I actually like my job and the place.

"Ellie! My baby!" I hear Momma's screeching voice full of concern coming around the corner from the living room.

"Momma?" I half question if she's really here as I embrace her. "What? What are you doing here?"

Pops clears his throat beside me, pulling me to a hug. "Your friend Beck called and said you were in danger and we were all being protected here." He explains.

"You're not mad?" I ask. Pulling back from Pops to watch his face. He looks concerned but otherwise fine.

He nods. Though, I notice Momma's features turn sad as Pops talks explains to me, "We know more about this life than you'd think, baby girl. We know you're safe here and we also know if there is a threat against you and you're not available to them they will take the next best thing, most likely us. So here we are." Then Pops looks away from me and a broad smile shows on his face. He steps away, shouting in excitement. "Bear! Well hell, how are you?" Pops then takes off across the room and falls into deep discussion with Old Man Bear like they are the best of friends.

I'm confused and have more questions but my body is becoming more and more exhausted as this night continues on. The energy to ask the questions stirring in my mind is just not there. I do manage to nod my understanding to Momma as I yawn more.

"Oh baby, you have had a day, let's get you to bed." Momma starts to fret until she catches my left hand. "Wait. Is that a ring? And a Tattoo? When did this happen?!" Momma asks excitedly.

"This weekend Momma. I'm sorry, I haven't seen you and all this has been going on."

Momma wraps me in a tight hug, telling me it's fine and she understands, she's just very happy. It's a little overwhelming to me, I wasn't expecting such a response from her, add that on top of my exhaustion my emotions are everywhere. I start to cry, wrapped up in Momma's tight embrace.

When I told them Brett and I were engaged, both Momma and Pops merely asked "are you happy?" Then said "that's good baby." And that was it. Nothing else. Now that it's Cole, Momma is ecstatic and squeezing the day lights out of me.

"Okay baby, you're tired and now I have you crying. Go up to bed and we can tell your Pops tomorrow, okay?" Momma says rubbing my back.

Another nod from me in response. I turn to head up the stairs before I quickly turn back "Wait, where is Son?"

"Oh. She's upstairs, I think. Beck set us up with a room to sleep and said you were on the next floor at this closer end and she was at the other end if we needed anything." Momma replies.

"Thank you, Momma. For everything. Love you." I tell her an continue up the steps.

"Love you too baby. Good night."

I climb the stairs to the third floor and make my way into

Gunner's room. I know he's still downstairs with Cole and the other officers discussing more, illegal actions they didn't want me or the members to be involved in. I'd be surprised if Sonja wasn't in Gunner's room, but I also have a feeling she's not overly happy about it.

"Son, love? You in here babes?" I call into Gunner's dark room after cracking the door.

I hear a low grumble that sounds like Sonja and decide to slip into the room. Headed to the bed, I can barely make out a lump in the shape of her wrapped in the blanket. "Son. Babes. You okay?"

She grumbles again and I know for sure it's her. I curl up on the bed beside her, tugging her to my chest, despite her groans of disapproval. "What's going on babes?"

"Gunner." Is all she says.

"Want to talk about it?"

She sighs and mumbles "no." before cuddling into my chest.

"Okay. Well, I'm here when you do babes. I have your back, always." I say softly, running my hand over her hair.

She quickly falls asleep and I sneak out from under her head, using the pillow behind me as a replacement. Quietly, I step back to the hall. Seeing Beck's room open I pop my head in. "Hey Beck."

"Hey Blondie. What's up?"

"You know what room my brother is in?"

"Course love. He's in the 3rd room on the left coming from kitchen stairwell and your parents are across the hall." She tells me. "Oh! And I dropped a new phone in your room for Cole."

I cringe at that. It's the second phone at least that he's broken since I've been back. It's not like brand new phones, let alone the top-of-the-line new Samsung phones are cheap. "Thank you, Beck. Seriously, you do so much and I really appreciate it.

The guys and I would be lost without you." I tell her getting a smile and "love you babes." In response.

Slipping back down the hall I head to my brother's room. I hear him on the other side of the door talking to someone so I poke my head in catching the last bit of his phone conversation.

"I know but it's what's best.... We'll talk about it when I get home... You're fine, no one knows you mean anything more to me." Ry looks up catching me leaning in the doorway. "Shit. Gotta go." He says into the phone clicking it off. "It's not polite to eavesdrop Princess." Ry scolds.

"It's Queen to you now." I tease. Making my way into the small room and plopping my bottom on the second bed in there.

The room is a lot like a shared dorm room with two twin beds and plain walls. There's a window between the beds with curtains and a night stand between them. Small closets sit on either side of the door. Considering how lavish Cole, Gunner and Tech's rooms are I wonder if the other rooms on this floor are as plain and utilitarian or if there are different rooms for different members.

"It'll always be Princess, Princess." Ry teases back, but worry is mixed in his features.

"Ry, don't be upset or worried that I caught your conversation. If you aren't ready to tell me you have someone special in your life then that's your business. I'm not going to judge or pester you about it either way." I tell Ry honestly, managing to get a small smile from him.

I'd love for my brother to tell me about his personal life. We used to share most things when we were kids. After Cole left, I became distant and was not the best sister in that manner. Then of course Brett happened. I have a lot of making up to do to mend our relationship. We've been working on it since I've been back and we feel closer now than we ever did in high-school even, but I can understand the lack of trust.

"Actually, I want to tell you. I just don't know how to exactly." Ry says looking at the floor.

My curiosity peaks. "Is it something you think I wouldn't approve of? Or something you're ashamed about? Because let me tell you, I take the cake there and can pass no judgments."

Ry snorts. "You do have a point there, Princess." He sighs and runs his hands through his hair. Then he paces in front of me before finally rushing through words. "ImwithAdam."

"Adam, but I've seen you with women? Wait, how long?" I ask softly, because I have. I've even caught him fully unclothed and inside girls from high school on multiple occasions. Adam has always been around and his best friend but I've never so much as seen them touch each other.

He shrugs then sits next to me. "A while. Forever. Since we were like twelve really but recently it's become more exclusive."

I nod, starting to understand. "Okay. So, are you worried about what people may think of you for being gay?"

"No. Yes. Well." Ry rubs his head again then leans his head to rest it on my shoulder. "It's complicated, Ellie. Also please don't label me as gay, Adam is the only guy I've ever even wanted to be with which is part of the complication."

"Okay brother. A soulmate is a soulmate and that's that." I tell him honestly nodding my head and rubbing my hand through his hair, roughing it up before I yawn again. "I should get to bed, I meant to head there over an hour ago."

"Me too. This stays between us, right Princess?" He asks, hesitantly.

"Of course. Goodnight brother." I hug him and head back to my room.

Turning in the doorway, I catch my brother's face looking

troubled. It makes me wonder how much more there is to the complication he talked about. With a sigh and worries running through my head I make my way back up the stairs to mine and Cole's room.

Opening the door, Cole's telltale scent of sandalwood and leather smothers and soothes me. Stripping out of my clothing, I snuggle into our cold bed. Hoping he at least gets some sleep tonight. I know he needs it but also knowing him if he gets any sleep at all it'll only be a few hours that he'll cuddle into me before getting up and going about whatever, it is, he feels the need to do all over again.

Not thinking about it when I finally crawled into bed, I didn't close the room curtains, so at the crack of dawn light creeped into the room and straight into my eyes. Rolling over I open my eyes to an empty bed. By the feel of the ice-cold sheets, Cole never came to bed.

With a loud sigh I toss back the sheets and comforter, climbing out of bed I hunt for one of Cole's t shirts to slip on. Also grabbing a pair of his boxer briefs, I slip the two pieces of clothing on. Who knows who I'll run into on my hunt to find the other half of my soul?

The halls, kitchen and living room are all empty, aside from a passed-out X on one of couches. At least he's fully clothed this time, I think to myself. Wondering to the bar room, I'm surprised to also find it empty.

A thought that maybe he went somewhere crosses my mind, but I don't think he'd do that without telling me or grabbing his new phone. I decide to check his office before the basement, just since I'm on this side of the building. I make my way past the empty meeting room and into Cole's office.

Relief washes over me as soon as I open the door to see him at his desk. He's leaning over papers and has obviously ran his hands over his face and through his light brown hair multiple times. The skin around his eyes is dark and sunken, a concerned frown lines the edges of his mouth and his beard is scruffy.

He's exhausted and stressed. My heart clenches for my man and the toll I can see all this taking on him.

Even so, he's still the sexiest man I've laid eyes on. His sharp jaw line and those icy blue eyes. He's focused on papers, so I can't see his eyes, but I can picture exactly what they look like having stared into them hundreds of thousands of times. His strong chest and arms, covered by his t-shirt and leather jacket, but I know they are solid, lined and defined. His long, jean cladded legs, hidden by the desk and again I know they are just as solid and defined as the rest of him.

I bite my lip and step into the room, closing the door behind me with a flick to the lock. Cole looks up at me with those icy blue orbs I see every time I dream. "Kitten." I hear him call me softly.

"You never came to bed." I step into the room, closing the space between us. "I was worried about you."

As soon as I'm on his side of the desk he pulls me to him. Landing in his lap he tucks me close, breathing in the scent of my hair. "I'm fine Kitten, you should be sleeping."

"You're not fine, Cole. I know you. I know you're exhausted and stressed, I know you refuse to sleep. You need to sleep baby." My voice is soft and calm. My hand goes to his face, resting against his scruff. "Let me help you relax."

I shift in Cole's lap. Moving to straddle him, my hands on either side of his face. His eyes meet mine and I see the fire he gets for me ignite in them. "Kitten." I hear him whisper before I push my lips to his.

We fight for dominance in our kiss. Normally, I'd hand it over, but this morning is about taking care of him. I bite at his lip. A little moan comes from him, parting his lips enough for me to take advantage, my tongue enters his mouth. Another little moan comes from him and I press my center into his. Feeling his hardness, I grind against him and taste his mouth.

My tongue runs across his lips before I move my lips across his jawline and down his neck. "Fuck. Kitten. What you fucking do to me." Cole's voice says in a low, raspy voice.

He grabs at my hips and tries to take control again, but I'm not about to have that. I squeeze my thighs tight at his legs and push him back in the chair with my palms flat. Sucking at his neck, I know I'm going to leave a mark.

My hands go under his shirt, scratching my nails up and down his hard abs and chest before I tug from the bottom up and pull his shirt off him, tossing it on the floor.

I move my lips across his collar and down his chest. Leaving more but smaller marks as I go. He's mine and I'm going to mark my territory if I want to.

Sliding off his lap, I go to my knees on the floor. "Ah, fuck. Kitten." He breaths out again with another one of his little moans.

I love that I can have this effect on him. Heat and wetness flood my own core and I bite my bottom lip. Keeping my eyes on Cole's, I unbutton his pants and tug them with his boxers to his ankles. Earning more panting moans from Cole.

Kissing and sucking from his knees up his thighs, I leave a few more marks. I can tell his dick is throbbing for me. Precum dripping from the tip, a trail of it leaking down the side. "Fuck. L. Fuck, I need you." Cole begs, his hands going into my hair.

He tugs the ponytail out, dropping the band to the floor then laces his fingers in my hair. More heat floods my center at his begging I tease him just a bit more. Running my thumb up the trail of precum to the tip, then circling my thumb around the tip before sticking my thumb in my mouth with a dramatic moan.

"Fucking Christ, L." Cole moans out, throwing his head back in his office chair. One of his hands leave my hair as he brings it to his own to run through. I know he's frustrated and it's taking every bit of effort from him to let me keep control here.

Switching my thumb out for my tongue, I run it along the same trail on his dick. Earning more moans and cusses. I give into his need and take his dick into my mouth. Taking him as far as I can and sucking. Continuing to suck and lick as I move my head, taking him from tip almost to the base again and again. My hands running over his hips and sac. Lightly rubbing and squeezing. After all the teasing, it doesn't take long before he puts both hands back into my hair. I let him take control and fuck my face while I continue to suck. His pants and moans get more and more erratic before he cums down my throat. Still holding my head down, I swallow taking every bit of him.

Cole pulls me up by my hair, ripping his boxer briefs off me as soon as I'm standing. "You fucking tease. Now I'm going to fuck this pussy that I bet is dripping wet for me."

He rarely commands and talks dirty like this to me. I see the fire in his icy eyes and shiver with needy desire for him. His fingers find their way up my thigh to my soaked core. He runs his fingers between my lips, just brushing my clit. Bringing his hand up to his lips, he puts his fingers in his mouth. A breathy moan comes out of my throat as he smirks. "I was right. You naughty girl, you have a needy pussy, don't you?"

I can only nod and bite my lip to keep from moaning again. He grabs at my ass with both hands, lifting me up and setting me on his desk. Pushing at my thighs, he opens my legs wide for him. Trailing up my body he pulls his shirt off me. His eyes travel down my body and I watch as they darken with desire.

Cole leans over me, his again hardened dick pressing and rubbing at my slit. He kisses me, it's needy, deep and passionate. His tongue and mine tangling and tasting. His hands rubbing up and down my thighs.

He moves his lips to my neck, kissing, biting and sucking. Moving to my collar bone he sucks hard until I squirm against him and moan out uncontrollably. I know a huge mark will be there later.

Cole looks up to me, our eyes meeting. With a smile he lines himself up to me then slams his entire length into me. Gasping, my head rolls back against the desk and my back arches.

Relentlessly, he fucks me. Thrusting his entire length in and out of me, wild, needy and hard. It feels exceptional. My core tightens and I know I'm going to cum fast.

"Not yet." Cole breathes out, never letting up on his thrusts. "Not yet, with me Kitten."

"Fuck. Cole. I can't." I can barely manage the half way audible words.

His thumb rubs my clit and I lose all control. My entire body spasms and I clench hard around Cole. Nails digging into his back. He growls as my walls clench hard around him and I feel him releasing. I feel the mix of our hot juices dripping down me and onto his desk.

Cole collapses on his elbows. Putting his weight on them, he drops his head to my chest panting. We are both a sweaty sticky mess and both trying to catch our breath.

Pounding knocks hit the office door. "If you two are fucking done, there's shit going down." Gunner yells from the other side.

Chapter 37 - Cole

"I'm going to fucking kill him one of these days." I mumble into L's chest.

Shaking my head, she giggles. "Could be worse, he could have walked in here."

"Then I would actually have to kill him." I say before I nip at her collar bone then kissing her lips.

Sighing, I manage to pull myself away from her. I don't want to pick myself up off her, or slide out of her. Let alone deal with whatever the fuck Gunner needs. All I want to do is stay here in the warmth of my woman. My crazy, irresponsible, sexy as hell, loving, caring woman. She is the other half of my soul; I instantly feel whole when she's by me and as soon as she's in another room my chest aches like something is missing and it's hard to breathe. I need her like I need air to breathe.

She sits up on my desk, hickies cover her collar and chest. I smirk, knowing I marked her and she's mine.

"Stop that." She teases at me swatting my chest. "I only have a shirt now." She laughs.

After kissing her again, I slide my boxers and jeans up that are still wrapped around my boots at my ankles. "I think, I have extra sweats in here somewhere for when I need to go for a run." I tell her. Rubbing my hands through my hair to try to straighten it out a bit, I move to the sliding closet door. I don't keep much in here and the closet is really just a storage space of shelves but I keep extra stuff if I need it, mostly from before L came back to me. Finding the sweats, I walk back over to her.

She's still sitting on my desk, looking like a goddess. Glowing with her light blonde wavy hair floating around her. Her soft skin still flushed and her ocean blue eyes shining bright. A smile curling up at the edges of her perfect lips. I slide the sweats up her legs and pull my shirt she wore down here back over her head. Kissing her again, getting gaspy, little moans from her.

"Hey. Quit fucking." Gunner yells through the door again. "We have fucking problems."

"You can come in." I yell back.

L's dressed and I just need a shirt, I don't give a fuck if anyone knows what we were doing in here. She's gorgeous and she's mine. I can tell L's embarrassed though so I kiss her again. "I fucking love you." I whisper against her lips.

Gunner flings the door open. "God dammit, would you two stop. We have fucking problems to deal with." He growls out.

L buries her head into my chest giggling and shaking her head. "What's the fucking problem Gunner?" I ask sharply, annoyed that I have to deal with anything when I haven't slept and I just want to be with my sexy Kitten that just gave me the best fucking blow job of my life. One should be happy as fuck after that but I'm overwhelmed with anger at being interrupted.

"Well, Prez. Brett just landed in town. Tech only picked it up because he's been running facial recognition on all the cameras. The fuck has already checked in at a hotel and made himself comfortable." Gunner informs us. L grips my waist hard, still keeping her face buried in my chest. I clench my fists and Gunner continues. "Fucking Snake is with him, but on a good note, Scorpion is in the basement with Tank."

"Why the fuck would you bring him into our fucking house, Gunner?" I seethe, not wanting that filth anywhere near my girl, let alone seeing our basement set up.

"Most secure. Plus, we are in lockdown and Tank is pretty

set on him not making it out alive, no matter what for some reason, so he's here." He glares at me. "You were getting your dick wet and a quick decision had to be made. None of us wanted to come anywhere near this room with the sounds we could hear well across the bar."

"Oh. My. God." L exclaims shaking her head against my chest again, I can feel the heat radiating off her face. "How embarrassing."

"It's fine babe. That was more than worth the whole house hearing." I whisper to her with a little chuckle before addressing Gunner. "You should know better than to bring that shit in our house, Gunner. I expected better decisions to be made by you in my absence."

Gunner glares at me again. "Prez." He seethes out. I can tell he's trying hard to keep his anger under control. Then I remember Sonja is here and, in his room.

"Gunner. Get your emotions in check brother. What's done is done." I sigh running my hand over my face. "Church in 30. Members only. Send Tank to do what he does best for our house guest. We need information and we need it fast."

"You got it Prez." Gunner says, his voice laced with sarcasm. "Put a fucking shirt on, you look like you were mauled." With an eyeroll he leaves, slamming the door behind him.

"Cole." I hear her soft voice tremble, her hands gripping at my sides. "He's here."

"I know Kitten. I know." I tilt her chin up with my hand so I can look at her and see those beautiful ocean eyes. Currently shining from unshed tears and fear. "Go back to bed Kitten. I'll handle this. I've got you, no matter what I've got you."

"But you haven't slept. You need sleep Cole."

Leaning down I put my forehead to hers. "I have functioned on less doing far more dangerous things. Don't worry."

"But -"

I cut her off. "No buts. Please, just this one time, go back to bed." Managing to keep my voice calm but stern, I watch as her eyes flash with anger for a moment before softening.

"On one condition." She states.

"Fine baby, what is your demands?"

"You come take a nap by noon, or else I'm storming in to church or the basement and raising all sorts of hell. Tank has nothing on me when it comes to getting what I want by means of torture." She states. Her tone and expression tells me she means every word too.

"Deal." I agree, because honestly, I'll need to rest before going head first into whatever battle we may plan.

Church had been informative but filled with arguing. It gave me a touch of a headache. It is eleven thirty in the morning and we are just walking out of the meeting room. We didn't even have information from Tank on what Scorpion knows. Yet, around and around we argued.

Not to mention I had to talk Nick and Blaze out of blowing up and setting fire to anything and everything we could find that was owned by the 9s. As devastating as that may be for them, they still have women and children around who are innocent in all this.

L is waiting for me on our bed when I walk into our room. "I thought I was going to be causing all sorts of hell in 30 minutes. Glad you didn't stand me up on our nap date."

I kiss her lips, telling her how I wouldn't dream of standing her up. Pulling my boots, shirt and jeans off I crawl into bed. Wrapping my arms tight around L and letting my body relax to her warmth. "I love you Kitten. You are my world."

"You are my soul, Cole Cameron. I will love you to the ends of the earth and until the end of time."

"And I'll always come back to you, always and forever." I tell her before sleep takes over my consciousness and I'm out like a light.

I wake to slams on the door. I roll over, facing the doorway just before it flies open. An upset looking kid comes storming in yelling. "They took her, they took her." Over and over and over.

"What the fuck prospect!" I yell sitting straight up in bed. My mind is still hazy with sleep and I'm not sure how covered L is so I move my body to block hers.

"What's going on?" She says softly. I feel her sitting up behind me, her arms wrap around my waist and her chin rests on my shoulder.

"They took her, Prez. They took my little girl. You've got to help me. We've got to do something." The kid rambles out, panic through his entire voice.

"They have Emma?" L says, her voice dripping with concern. "Who is they, Cody? How? When?" L asks scrambling out from behind me and rushing to the prospect. I realize she still has a shirt of mine on and my sweats from earlier so she's covered.

How she knows so much about the kid I barely know; I have no idea. Then it hits me that this is the kid whose phone had I used yesterday with the little girl and Pitbull on his lock screen.

"The little girl on your phone?" I ask. Still confused but following L's lead and getting out of bed, pulling my jeans and boots back on.

"Yes." The kid sniffs, obviously trying to hold in tears. "She's my little girl, Prez. We have to get her back. What if they hurt her? What... what..."

L cuts him off. "Shhhh. Cody. We'll get her back. Come on, let's go see Tech." She yells him, wrapping her arm around his shoulders and leading him out of our room. "Meet you down there." She says winking at me.

Her taking control of the situation like this has me hard for her. My Queen took on her role without me having to ask her. For someone who knew nothing about this life until a couple months ago, she has managed to slide right in.

Grabbing a shirt to toss on and mine and L's phones off the bedside table, I follow after them.

Scanning into the basement L has already collected Gunner, Blaze, Jax and Tank, though Tank was probably already down here. A look over his knuckles confirms it as I see fresh blood covering them.

"Cody, sweetie, can you explain to us what's going on so we can help?" L coos at a distraught prospect once I step into the room.

He nods, wiping his face with the sleeve of his jacket. "Emma and Molly were at Emma's grandmother's house. It's her mom's week to have her and all that, but her mother just kind of dumps her off at her grandma's house. I figured she was fine there even though we were locked down. Plus, there's custody shit, my ex is a bitch but she is my baby's mom so I try to get along you know?"

L nods at him, rubbing his arm soothingly and urging him to go on. Once again, I find myself keeping my anger in check that L's touching another man. I fucking hate it, but I also know she means nothing but comfort by it so I'm trying not to tear the kid's arm off over it.

"Anyway. I got a call from Gina, Emma's grandma. Emma was playing in the yard with Molly, Gina heard a Molly growling and barking so she went outside. A man with a black mask on a motorcycle had Emma. Holding his hand over her mouth to keep her from screaming. Gina said he yelled at her. Something about "tell him we are coming for what we want and this is collateral". She called me in a panic and that's all I got out of her." He finishes his story and drops to his knees on the floor. "She's my world. She must be so scared."

Tech asks for the kid's phone and the address for Gina. Then goes about his typing and clicking.

"We'll get her back, kid." I tell him, patting his shoulders. "Jax, could you get him to a room? Get Ry or Matt to sit with him."

Jax nods then grabs the kid under the shoulders, hauling him up from the floor and all but dragging him up the steps.

"Tank, anything?" I ask, hoping for something good we could work with.

He shakes his head. "Not much. He's down a few fingers, toes and teeth. Yet, all I've got is that he's a bastard that likes to hurt women." Tank seethes, clenching his jaw and fist.

"Hurting women? How so?" L's eyes flash anger while her calm voice asks the question.

"You don't want that answer, Queen." Tank states with a growl. He never uses that tone with L.

Her glare across the room states otherwise. That glare could level any man. "I want to know, Tank." Her voice eerily calm.

"Remind me not to fuck with her." Blaze mutters next to me. L must have heard though because her gaze lands on him. He gulps and takes a step back.

Tank looks at me, I shrug. If she wants to know, fine, let her. I'm not about to be on the receiving end of her wrath.

He sighs. "Fine. You want to know, fine, but don't say I never warned you." He runs his blooded hands through his long hair. "Not only does the sick fuck traffic them, he samples the product so to say. Destroying any innocence, they may have. He cuts them, and drowns them only bringing them out of the water to take a couple breaths, just to do it again." Tank pauses, paces a bit. Then with a low, quiet voice that I'm not even sure if I heard him right. "He did it to my sister and my mother before dumping their mutilated bodies in my drive-way the day that I came back from Afghanistan." He looks straight at L. "He said they weren't worth enough to feed long enough to sell them. My sister was only 15."

The room quiets, even Tech stops his typing. None of us had any idea that that's what actually happened to Tank's family. I watch as L takes a deep breath, crosses over to Tank and kisses his cheek. "Take me to him." She whispers.

Chapter 38 - Ellianna

When Tank told us what this disgusting thing that tries to call himself a man had done, my mind just snapped. It was like all the rage at every single thing Brett had done to me, what this guy's crew has done taking Cody's daughter and what they have previously done to who knows how many other women, exploded like a nuclear bomb in my chest.

Just hearing what happened to Tank's mother and sister, my heart dropped and ached for him and them. The torture they had endured before they unfairly died. The torment that Tank has been living with for years, coming back from war with who know what, lingering on his conscious to find that.

It was all too much and this man was about to give us what we want and pay for what he's done.

No more. No more, will I allow this to happen. No more will this man breathe air that he doesn't deserve. No more will these disgusting excuses for human beings continue to take lives and torment women like we aren't equal or worthy enough.

I will walk straight into the lion's den and destroy them from the inside out if I have to, getting Emma back being my first priority. That adorable little girl is only five years old. Her flaming red curls and green eyes are meant to break hearts a decade from now. She's the sweetest little doll of a girl and instantly took to me even though Cody said she was shy with strangers.

After Cole and Tank's protests to let me in the same room as

Scorpion and my relentless insistence they finally took me into a part of the basement I'd never been in. Tank had a setup of tools, knives and other objects lined up on a shelf outside a padlocked door. Opening the door, Tank reveals a bloodied man, hunched over with his stringy long hair covering over his face. His arms and legs are tightly tied to a metal chair. The room smells like copper, piss and bleach.

Walking over to the man, I grab him by his hair, yanking his head back. His eyes snap open and a smirk crosses his face. "Ahhh, sent me something to play with. How kind of you boys." His chilling voice calls to the room while his eyes roam over my body.

I take a step so I'm between his knees. Using the grip, I have on his hair I yank again, then slam his face down as I bring my knee up. The sound of cracking telling the room I broke his nose. Blood pours from his face. I yank his head back and do it again. Another crunching sound echoing around the concrete walls.

One of the guys cusses from the corner and Cole tells them to leave. I know he's watching my every move with a combination of curiosity, worry and pride across his face.

"You fucking cunt." The guy screams out at me. Choking on his blood when I yank his head back again.

I step around to the side of the chair. Holding his head back as far as I can, he coughs and gags on the blood pouring from his nose. "I heard you like to rape and torture women, break them then sell them. Now, tell me that isn't true?" My voice sounding foreign to me, is sickly sweet and doesn't reflect the atomic bomb of anger that's begging to exit my chest.

He gags more, my hand still gripping his hair hard. When his eyes start to roll back, I throw his head forward and release my grip. We can't kill him, yet. We need information from him. Coughing, he spits blood on the floor. "Fuck. You. I'll fucking show you what I do to women." He yells and struggles at the tight restraints, tearing into his skin. Hissing at the rope burning pain he caused himself, he finally settles back.

"I'll take that as a yes then. Good, I won't feel so bad about my next plan of action. Tank, brother, grab me that really shiny knife I seen on my way in here, please?" I look to the guys standing by the doorway. A combination of pride and horror cross all their faces. I'm sure none of them expected their sweet Queen to completely snap, but here we are.

With a nod from Tank, he turns out the door. I look back to the guy. "Scorpion, right?" He glares at me, the side of his lip turned up in disgust but doesn't answer. "Right... so... you see... I strongly feel that men who do the things to women and young girls like you have done aren't men at all. Therefore, I was thinking that when Tank gets back with that pretty little knife I seen, I'll take care of that little detail for you. Making you a more accurate representation of what you really are."

I watch realization hit his face as he snarls at me. "You fucking bitch!"

"Now, now." I say sweetly. "I may reconsider if you answer a few questions for me."

With perfect timing Tank returns with the thin, shimmering blade that caught my eye. He hands it to me then goes back to the rest of the guys, standing with his arms crossed. I twirl the blade around in my hand, keeping my hands in the line of site of Scorpion. Fear flashes in his eyes.

"Where's the little girl?" I ask, still twirling the blade.

"What little girl?"

"Your friends, they took a girl. Where is she?"

"I don't know what you're talking about. You're fucking crazy." He hisses at me.

I smile lightly, maybe I am crazy. I know I'm sick of men thinking they can do whatever they want without consequences.

Well, consequences are here now and I'm coming for them. "Perhaps, you can help me with something else then." His eyes glare into mine before I continue. "Where's Snake and what are his plans, what's the 9s role and all of it?"

He laughs before coughing again on the blood still draining from his shattered face. "You're fucking her, aren't you? Well fuck me, wouldn't that prissy little bitch be shocked that is angel is a fucking psychotic cunt." He laughs more.

I smile again before shoving the blade deep into his shoulder, aiming for the joint space. I know I hit the space when I twist my wrist and his shoulder separates with a pop before I yank the blade out. His arm drops, hanging in place only because his wrists are tied in one place. Blood runs down his arm and to the floor. He screams and I hear a chuckle come from where the guys are. Looking up I see Tank with a proud smile across his face.

Gunner is pale and looks mortified. Jax's looks a little green but Cole's face for once is emotionless and I can't read him.

"I asked a fucking question. Answer it." I demand.

When he says no again, I walk over to the bottle of bleach in the corner. I pick it up and shake it, the bottle must be half full. Going back to Scorpion, I open the bottle up. He starts to ask what I'm doing but I cut him off, pouring it into his shoulder wound, then over his face and hands. He screams like hell. Blood curling, painful screams that fill the entire room.

For a moment my heart sinks and I reconsider my actions, I have never hurt another person other than defending myself with Brianna then the PI. But just as I think I can't do this anymore he stops screaming and starts spilling. Telling us all about their hideouts, where they have the C4, how they were going to use some kids as bombs, because they are sick fucks and even fills us in on where they keep the girls based on their ages. He even tells us how Snake was fucking Brianna before he snapped her neck when she proved to be useless at getting information.

I cringe at that tidbit. I may not have liked the girl but she didn't deserve to die either. When he's finished, I look to Cole. He nods at me and I know they have what they need.

The atomic bomb of anger is still resonating. "Thank you so much for your help. However, you still don't deserve to be a man." I state then shove the blade through his jeans into his groin.

I leave the blade and walk back to the men. Hugging Tank, I say "He's yours now. Kill him as you'd like. I got my anger out." Then I take Cole's hand and let him lead me back up to our room.

He doesn't say a word and neither do I the entire walk through the house. When we get to our bathroom, he picks me up and sets me on the counter. Then he turns to the shower, turning it on and letting steam fill the room. He sighs before stripping his clothes and stepping back to me, pulling off his shirt I still had on from early this morning. It's soaked in blood and bleach, though I hadn't realized that at the time. He pulls his sweats that I also still have on, off my hips, tossing both in the trashcan.

"Are you upset with me?" I ask him, honestly wondering if he's trying not to be mad at me. I know he is ashamed of the blood on his hands and he's probably not thrilled, I just soaked mine in that same blood.

"No." He says, holding his palm against my cheek. "No. Never. Not for that. Not for defending us, this club and yourself."

"It wasn't just that. How could anyone do things like that to those women? To Tank's sister and mother?" I ask softly. "Did you know I remind Tank of his little sister?"

He hugs me tightly and my tears flow from my eyes. The anger that I had disappeared and I'm left feeling drained and my body is trying to cleanse itself from what I've done with tears.

It's like I was on an adrenaline rush and am now coming down crashing. I guess I was really, I let my emotions take control and I became a person a didn't know was a part of me.

I explain all this to Cole. He tells me he understands and knows the feeling. He says he just wants to take care of me. Then he does just that. Putting us both in the shower, he scrubs my skin. The pink water circling the drain with the soapy bubbles until it turns clear. When he's satisfied with that, he washes my hair, massaging my scalp. Then rinses my hair and does the same with my conditioner. Practically purring at him with how good his hands feel I lean into him, my face snuggling into the hallow of his neck. "Thank you, Cole."

"For what Kitten?" He asks softly. His fingers still working their way through my hair.

"For everything. For loving me and taking care of me. For letting me be strong and fierce when I need to be but also letting me fall apart when I've had enough." I tilt my head to look up at him. The shower heads running water over us, I clench my eyes shut remembering how weak I always felt around Brett, how devastated I was those years alone, how broken and worthless I felt so often. Breathing out I open my eyes again, looking into Cole's icy blue ones that make me feel so powerful, "Just thank you. I think I would be in pieces without you, actually I know I would be in pieces without you. You let me feel whole and empower me to fight and to love and to just be me."

Cole drops his hands from my hair to grab my waist, pulling me tight to him. "L, I love everything about you. I love when you fight for what you want and what you believe in. I love how hard you love and care for people, even people you barely know. I wouldn't want to change anything about you, ever. As much as I don't necessarily like when you are feeling down about something, I love that you let me be there to help keep you together. L, I'd completely fall apart without you too. I was a mean and angry, trigger happy asshole, I still kind of am but you level me out baby. You're everything I need. I'm proud of how you handled things today."

He rinses my hair for me before leading me out of the shower and wrapping me in a towel. After drying my hair, he brushes it and braids it down the back. "You remembered how to braid my hair?" I ask him when he's finished.

"Yup. It was one of the things you loved for me to do before you'd pass out for the night. It'd practically put you to sleep and I'd have to tuck a pillow under you so I could slip out of your bed before Pops caught me in there sleeping too." He chuckles, my heart swelling in my chest even more.

Cole leaves the bathroom quick before I can respond. I just finish brushing my teeth when he comes back in, fully dressed and with black leggings and a black sweater for me. "I have to get back downstairs. You're more than welcome to join us but we need to go get Emma back and I'm going to put a bullet in my uncle's head."

I nod in understanding; we took too much time before heading out for Emma. "Cole?" He looks at me after setting the clothes on the counter. "How can we be like this? How can we go from cutting and hurting someone like I just did to being so sweet and sentimental then back to ruthless again?"

He shrugs in response. "I'd like to think it's because we only hurt people that hurt others and are only trying to protect and fight for those we care about."

Leaving kisses on my forehead, I nod. Maybe he's right. I was only thinking about every horrible thing that man had done and getting Emma back.

Chapter 39 – Cole

I struggled letting L handle things how she did. I never wanted her to see that part of this life let alone be a part of it. However, it was what she wanted and I'll be damned if I force her to do or not do the things she wants. I'd tried to reason with her about it but she was bound and determined to make things right and fight for this club and those in it herself.

Part of it was her bond with Tank, that's what pushed her over the edge into being a defensive momma bear. That's the best description of how I saw her in that moment. If she wants to fight, I'll let her. It's her choice. I just may not like it. As long as she's smart about it, I know she is capable. Even if it does mean watching my girl soak her hands in blood when I don't even like the blood that's on my own and that seems hypocritical. It also seems like it would make me a sick fuck, but to me it's just letting my girl be what she wants. She spent so long without that.

I'll pick her up after. I'll follow her to the ends of the earth. I'll always come back to her and that's clearer to me now than ever before. After getting L cleaned up and knowing she'd be okay, I made my way to church. Now that we have all the information we need; I'm sure Tech has processed it all by now. We need to create action.

I bump into Tank, we both headed down the stairs. "It done?" I ask him.

"Will be. He doesn't deserve quick and easy." Tank responds, his voice void of emotions.

Trying hard to not actually cringe at that I nod. The right is his, as L commanded it. We would have let him anyway, after what that man did to his mother and sister. I only know some of it, what Tech and Gunner filled me in on. Tank was local to where we were back in Ohio. He'd gone to war and was injured in the tank he was driving after their convoy hit an IED. He came back to his mother and sister missing, their house destroyed like a robbery.

After police hunts, him calling in favors to various government and military officials he'd made friends with, his sister and mother's bodies showed up mutilated in his yard.

Shortly after that he showed up at the MC's doors. He pledged loyalty to me because of Nick, Tech and Gunner, then barely said a word for years. He helped us take down that MC and rebuild here, I knew I'd have his loyalty for life because of what we stood for and more so what we stood against. That was and is all that has mattered here.

You want to be a Phoenix, must be loyal.

We walk into Church; the room is overflowing like it was last night. Members crowded in, ready to bleed for that loyalty.

"We ready?" I ask at the round table of officers.

The whole table nods. Looking around the room I don't see Cody, Tommy or Matt, even though I see the other prospects and Ry. I wonder what Ry would think of what his sister did less than an hour ago. Tech quickly fills me in on what he got, everything Scorpion said lines up. I know the game plan I'd go with, now the rest of the club needs to agree.

"Listen up!" I yell, the room going silent only immediately. "Church is now is session. This is an urgent matter and you all best be ready. If you're not ready to fight and spill blood for your Phoenix Brothers I suggest you drop you cuts at the door and get the fuck out."

The door flings open, revealing my stunning Kitten. Her long blonde waves still in the braid I did down her back, a few loose strains in the front framing her face. Her legs are covered in black leggings with her black riding boots, a shining glint at the top of those boots tells me she has blades slid in there. Her right thigh bares a holster with a SIG P365 snugly settled in. A loose black V neck shirt covers the rest of her with her Phoenix jacket proudly showing.

She's flanked by Tommy and Matt. Tommy's presence explaining where my little Kitten got her new equipment. Since he's a member now and shadowing Tech, he's been granted access to the weapons room of the basement. L strolls into the room. Smirks of pride cross all the officer's faces while Ry looks beside himself with worry already.

"Sorry, we are a little late, loves." L's voice radiates through the room. She takes her place at my side and I proudly wrap my arm sound her shoulders and take a step back so she's standing almost in front of me at the head of the room. Matt and Tommy stand to the side of the table like protective flanking bodyguards. I almost want to laugh, yet at the same time it just resonates more pride in my chest for this woman.

I clear my throat, gaining the room's attention again, repeating my earlier words. "Now that we are all here, Church is in session. This is an urgent matter and you all best be ready. If you're not ready to fight and spill blood for your Phoenix Brothers I suggest you drop your cuts at the door and get the fuck out."

I feel L tense under my arm as she scans the room. It's hard for me to be concerned that any of these guys would walk out when she's here and just as possessive and protective of this club as I am. No one walks out, the room is so silent I can only here the soft breaths from L.

"Good." I nod my head, tugging L a little close to me so I feel the heat of her radiating on to my side. "Now, one of our prospects had his daughter taken."

The room gasps. "We are going to get her back." L's voice quiets the room's reaction to the news.

"Our Queen here, was able to extract some valuable information from a known member of the 9s. We have known they've been causing problems but haven't been able to pin them down yet. Now, we have what we need to not only take care of them and keep them from being a future problem, but we can also get Emma back as well as be able to rescue multiple sets of women and girls the 9s have taken for trafficking and god only knows what else." The room erupts in angry yells again.

"Quiet!" I yell to get the attention back. "We have a plan. We are here to put it to vote then set out into our plans of attack."

I get into explaining phase one, this is going to be the most difficult phase because we are all going to be split up. We need to hit three places where we know there are women and children and take them to safety. In this case I'm planning to use the police chief and police station but the rest of the members need to agree to this. We should be fine doing it but there's always a risk since we aren't exactly going about any of this is any kind of legal matter.

"Emma is most likely here" I say pointing to a shack in the middle of nowhere Scorpion said they keep the most valuable humans. "We need to get in, get her out with her seeing as little as possible. We also need to get anyone else they have out in the process. Kill any 9s or associates keeping these women, but we don't need Emma seeing that."

"I'll go." L coos. Ry immediately protests and Tank's fist slams the table. L shushes them in a calming tone that somehow only she has. "Listen to me. Emma knows and trusts me. She'll do what I say and come to me. Any women they are keeping, who knows what they've done to them. They won't trust a bunch of men blasting in. There are three places where there are women being kept. I suggest, I take this place where they most likely have Emma. I can defend myself and while it may be where they keep their most valuable or whatever you can see that other than it being isolated there really isn't any protection around. There's no guards outside, you can see it in this drone pic Tech got."

"The place may be rigged with C4 though." Nick steps from the crowd. "You willing to let your girl go on this mission when we don't know where the fuck the C4 is?"

Again, angry shouts fill the room.

"Quiet! Fucking shut up unless you have input that is fucking helpful. We don't have time to argue." I turn L to me quick. "You sure on this?" I ask her quietly.

She answers with a smile and nod. "For this club, anything. For you, everything."

"Nick. You stay with Tech and Tommy. Full eyes on all three sites. If there's an issue you need to walk L and anyone else through disarming. You think you can do that?"

"Yes, Prez." He nods with his jaw clenched. I know he doesn't love the idea of any of this knowing how much C4 is out there.

"If it's anything, our source indicated that they were working on bomb packs in this barn here" I point to the run-down structure outside of town. "They have had to spread out because if they were in one location, they know we'd find them and strike hard and fast. However, we can use this space to our advantage. We will stagger the raids on each of the three buildings in phase one, by 10 minutes. That gives us time to keep things communicating between us but not enough time for them to get back up anywhere."

A chorus of "yes, Prez" greets me.

"The other two buildings, we need women to be present and prepared to help grab these girls. I'm serious when I say it will be worse if there's a bunch of men grabbing at them. They won't know you're trying to help them. I've already asked Beck and Camie, protecting the privacy of church and what's actually going on right now of course, they have both volunteered and Sonja is ready here with Doc to treat anything that isn't surgery serious. If it's agreed on, Doc has suggested bringing a fellow of his in here as well and will have the rest of his staff ready to cover at the hospital if necessary. I don't want anyone hurt but I'd rather we be ready for the worse and not need it." L announces her additions to the plans.

Jax, Tech, Ry and Gunner all start protesting only to shut down by L and her logic. The pride in my chest for my girl swells to a level I didn't even know existed. She's all in on not just me but also this family. Flaws and all, she's in on it for all of us. I can't believe I've missed out on this all these years, missed out on her, on this. Her fire is back.

We continue church, agreements to my plan with L's additions round us out. Tank, Gunner, Matt and Ry are going with L. Jax, Blaze, Ryder and a couple members to the run-down house women are supposedly kept at, taking Camie with them. She's to stay back with Jax until they get the clear from the others.

Myself, X and the majority of the members are raiding the rundown warehouse. If Tank, Gunner and Matt clear the shack with enough time they will meet us while Ry and L bring Emma back to Cody.

Once all three buildings are clear we will meet back at the far end warehouse. After a quick regroup we are raiding the main house and hunting down Snake. Gunner and I have a vendetta to settle. After that, we settle L's. She's ours and what's ours, well it's for life.

Chapter 40 - Ellianna

After final agreements and assignments all the members filled out of the meeting room. Heading to suit up and get ready to roll out. Tech took off to find Beck, no doubt to express the concern he showed in the meeting when I brought in my suggestions.

"I was wrong about you, Blondie." Gunner says, stepping up beside me.

He's similar to Cole in their heights and some of their facial features, like the way his lip curls up when he tries not to smirk. Even their voices at time have similar pitches. It catches me off guard sometimes with just how similar they are, there is no doubt they are related.

"You were, but I won't hold it against you. You hurt my girl though and for that I will." I say throwing a daggering glare at him for a moment, hinting at Sonja and whatever is happening there.

"I'm going to try not to, but let's get through today." Gunner replies before smirking. "Now, I know better than to piss you off, Blondie."

Shoving at his shoulder with mine playfully, though it's really more his upper arm because of our height difference. "Best to remember that."

"What'd you do, Princess? Also, what the fuck was that? Since when are you in charge?" My brother says coming up behind us.

"Learn respect boy. You may be patched now but I will beat

the piss out of you." Gunner says with a growl.

"You'll do no such thing, Gunner!" I glare at him again. "I'm not in charge Ry, Cole is. You need to respect that I can take care of myself even if history may seem like that's not the case. This is my club and family now too; I'm not sitting by when there is a little girl missing and other women in danger and being subjected to god knows what."

Ry looks at me with concern glistening in his eyes. "You can't get hurt, Ellie. You're risking too much."

I hug my brother, tucking my head under his chin while my arms wrap around his waist. "I'm only risking anything for something that's worth it to me. I'm not helpless, plus you're coming to protect me. We have to get that little girl."

Ry's arms wrap around my shoulders and he tugs me tight. I feel his chest release a sigh. "You're so fucking stubborn. Can't just be normal, need to live on the edge and all that. Pain in the ass." He rambles on making me laugh.

Pushing him back, I tell him to go get ready while I seek out Cole. He had gone to get his weaponry. Apparently, though our jackets are lined with some kind of bulletproof stuff. Tommy was filling me in all sorts of things while gearing me up in the basement before we marched into Church.

Brett would have lost his mind had I done something like that in any kind of meeting he had, or even just in general. How crazy it is to me that I could have been so beaten down and controlled to be so docile and accepting of things that bothered me. Then when I'm empowered instead, I flourish into a person that reminds me of my crazy self during high school.

I had no fear but I was protective to a fault. I've managed to break back into that part of me, though a little more reserved and well rounded. Fear still comes and goes, depending on situations. However, I feel safe with any of Phoenix by my side. Maybe, what I'm about to do is stupid. It doesn't feel that way, though. I can protect myself enough and I'll be covered by large, well trained men. It's planned out and scouted. The risk is rather minimal.

I find Cole waiting for me by the doors. "Kitten." Is all he says before he pulls me tight to him. His arms surround me and he leans so his face nuzzles into the side of my neck. "You sure you're okay with this? You'll be safe? Promise me, you'll be safe."

My fingers find their way around him to the back of his neck, tangling in the bottom of his hair. "I'll be safe. I'll always find my way back to you."

"Prez!" someone shouts from outside.

We know it is time to be going, but we are struggling to let each other go. I can feel it in my soul this isn't the last time and this isn't goodbye. We are going to make it back here, safe and together, but I still don't want to let go. "We have to go, Cole" I finally whisper to him.

He lets me go and I instantly feel cold. "Do what you have to Kitten. It'll be okay and I'll be here when it's done."

I nod, he kisses me quick before taking my hand and leading me outside.

"We ride!" Cole shouts. "We follow the plan; we stay on coms. We got it?!"

Another chorus of "Yes Prez" sounds across the driveway. Lines of trucks and motorcycles littering the entire grounds.

"Good! We are Phoenix Rising! Now let's ride!" Cole yells. All the members joining the let's ride showing how proud and united we are here. We may be riding out into planned battles, there will be blood staining our hands by the end of the night but this whole club is loyal and united. I know that I'm in the right place and making the right choice.

Cole kisses my fingers and walks off for his bike. His body is tense and it's all I can do to bring myself to walk the opposite direction to Ry's truck. Any time Cole is tense like that my instinct is to snuggle into him and calm him. That's not what either of us need right now though.

With a shake of my head, I walk off to Ry. Gunner, Tank and Matty are on their bikes ready to flank us as we make our way to this shack. We are headed to a spot about a mile out.

"You good?" Tank asks. A flicker of concern crossing his face, immediately replaced with his serious emotionless expression once I nod.

He revs his bike and I climb in Ry's truck. Ry grabs my hand as soon as I'm in and grips it tight the entire drive. He's keeping me grounded if he knows it or not, I'm sure his death grip on is hand is more for his benefit than mine. I hear the bike's cut their engine as we pull down a dirt lane into trees. They coast into some brushes hiding the bikes and only exposing Ry's truck off the side of the road.

We step out, softly closing the door and checking our coms with Tech.

"Tech? Nick? We good?" Gunner asks running point on this.

"We're good." Tech calls back over the line. "Want to hear Queen, Tank, Ry and Matt."

We respond in succession, clearing checks with Tech. "Okay. I'm going to make my way with Matt to the far side of the shack. Watch for any kind of traps around the land, may be hunting shit or something set up." Gunner tells us. He's headed to a tree that should have a decent view to snipe from and Matt is circling around to cover the back entrance. "Ry. You're on Queen's six the whole time. Tank leads. Got it?"

Ry agrees and Gunner is satisfied with his orders. He takes off through the woods. Tank leads us, using a stick to sweep through leaves for anything trap like. He's slower and more hesitant than Gunner walking through the woods. After a bit of walking Gunner comes through the coms. "There's two men inside. Front left window. Can't verify IDs but clear shot."

"Can you see Emma?" I ask. He responds with a no and we decide to break through. Matt distracting from the back before Tank charging the front.

We get almost to the door, creeping through the brush. I pull the hand gun from its holster, clicking the safety off. Ry does the same while Tank pulls a large knife from his jacket. "Do not enter until it's clear."

"I'm covering your back Tank. Don't demand me otherwise. What if Emma is in there and sees?"

He sighs but nods. Gunner comes through the coms again. "On my count. Matt. 3, 2, 1 go, go, go."

We hear the sound of a door being kicked down and Tank takes off, Ry and I following close on his heels. Shouting inside begins and I can hear two distinct voices. Tank busts through the front door, me tearing into the shack hot on his heels.

Tank catches on guy in a choke hold from behind. Yanking his gun from him. The other guy scrambled after Matty but I was faster, my gun pressing into the back of his skull making him stop immediately.

"Who else is here?" I sternly ask the two assholes trying to run. "You fucking move and I'll shoot you where you stand."

Tank chuckles. "I'd trust her"

My answer was only a glare at Tank. It didn't last long because the guy I had my gun to dropped to his knees and started praying.

"Don't thinks so," I say, kicking his side. "you are too horrible to ask god forgiveness. Where are the children?"

They both stay silent so I ask, "Tank, we only need one yeah?"

Tank grunts a yes. Tightening his hold on his guy and putting his large knife to the guy's throat.

"Woah. Woah. What children?" Tank's guy says, his eyes scanning the room, I can tell he's lying. I follow his eyes to the corner of the room, there's a bunched-up rug.

"Matty, check under that rug, yeah?" Both guys start trembling and I know I nailed it.

"There's a door here, Queen." Matty says.

Gunner comes through the coms, "Kill one, zip tie the other. Just in case."

Tank nods at me, just as I go to pull the trigger a gun goes off from my side. The guy in front of me drops, blood pooling out from under his chest on the floor. "Oh, fuck you shot him, you shot him!" The guy Tank's holding starts chanting, thrashing around in Tank's hold.

Looking beside me, I see Ry. "Why would you do that?" I ask him. Only getting a shrug as response. "I would have done that Ry."

"I'm not letting my sister take a life." Ry mumbles kissing my head and walking over to Matty.

Tank has the other guy hog tied and gagged with a cloth shoved in his mouth.

"Tank, I'm headed to the roof, it doesn't seem like there's any way they'd know we were here but I don't like it. Careful in the basement." Gunner instructs over the coms again.

"Matty, go get the truck. Ry, stay with this guy. I'll check the basement." I say stepping towards the trap door in the floor. Tank cuts my stride off with a hand to my shoulder. He tugs me back and grunts his displeasure at my actions then makes his way down the steps. "I like that idea better." Ry says, keeping his gun aimed at the guy Tank tied up.

"Ellie." Tank calls from the basement, making me scramble down the steps.

It's dark, almost pitch black other than the flashlight that Tank has out. Huddled in a corner are three women, one holding onto a small child. They are dirty and in ragged clothing, what is either dirt or blood stains their hair, skin and clothes in various places. They mostly look uninjured but it's hard to tell.

I put my hand on Tank's arm. "Lower the light brother, keep it on me so they can see me okay?"

He nods agreement so I cautiously step forward. They fall back and huddle closer to the corner. "My name is Ellie. Okay? I'm here to take you all someplace safe."

They watch me curiously but don't say anything. It's hard to see them with Tank keeping the light on me. "El-wee?" A small voice says, coming from the child in the woman's arms.

"Oh, thank God, Emma." I say rushing towards her. The woman hisses at me like she's feral and pulls Emma closer to her and away from me. For all I know these women may be feral, who knows how long they have been here. Taking a step back, I keep my voice as calm and soothing as I can. "Please. I take care of Emma. Her Grammie and dad are worried sick. I've been worried sick. I'm only here to help."

The woman loosens her grip on Emma. "They gave her something."

I nod. "We have a doctor and a safe place, for all of you. What's your name?"

"Sa-sarah." She says.

"Hi Sarah. What's the rest of your names?" I calmly ask as Gunner comes through the coms telling me I'm taking too much time.

The others shake their heads "no" and Emma starts crying. "El-wee, El-wee."

My heart breaks as my name slurs from whatever drugs they

gave her. "I'm here Emma baby. I'm going to get you home to daddy okay?"

She starts to cry again and that seems to break Sarah out of her protective feral-like state. She crawls towards me with Emma still in her arms. When she's close enough she holds Emma out to me. Pulling Emma to my arms she calms and snuggles into me, her head resting in the hallow of my neck. "I no feel good El-wee."

"I know baby. I know." I coo to her, brushing my hands through her snarled hair. "We have to go. It's safe with us, we can protect you, but we need to leave now."

Tech comes through the coms "There's a vehicle moving up the road towards you. You need to get out now."

His words are followed by Cole's voice, who sounds panicked. "Get the fuck out of there! Tank! Get them out of there!"

"Please, Sarah. Emma knows me, she trusts me, she's a child and I'd never hurt her. We need to go, they are coming." I say, turning to the stairs hoping they follow me when I see the panic cross their faces.

Hearing multiple steps coming behind me up the steps before Tank's heavy boots, I sigh in relief. Ry is pacing in the shack when I step up. His face relieved when he sees me holding Emma. "Prez, we have her." He calls into the coms.

"Keep your eyes closed Emma." I tell her, feeling her cuddle into my chest more. Getting into the shack I turn my mic on to speak to Tech. "Emma's been drugged. Have Doc ready. Sonja, three adult females."

"10-4. Now get out." Tech response back.

Rushing out to the truck, Matty helps the women into the back and I hand Emma back to Sarah before climbing into the passenger. Tank climbs in the driver seat and a final shot rings out before Ry steps out of the building and I know that makes two men he's killed today.

Matt, Gunner and Ry pour gasoline through the house and jump into the bed of the truck. "Sarah, I need you ladies to get as far down as you can back there." I tell them, not sure what we are going to meet on the road. Tank pulls out, mud flinging over the shack as he races back towards main roads.

One of the guys throws a lighter into the shack igniting the gas and flames shoot up almost immediately over the run-down building.

"Gunner!" Tank yells out the window, one of the girls sob in the back.

"I see it!" Gunner calls back. Looking through the back window I see Matt and Ry holding Gunner's legs as he's climbed onto the roof of the truck, like that isn't dangerous at all. "Keep fucking driving!" Gunner yells, his voice barely traveling in through the window.

Tank accelerates and finally I see what the issue is in front of us. There are three black jeeps driving at us. Tech and Gunner are communicating through the coms and Gunner gets the okay from Cole to fire. Two shots ring from above us. The center jeep and jeep flanking the left both flip to the right, taking out the third vehicle in a loud, rolling crash. Tank serves and drives around the mess as they fly into the trees. Two more shots ring out before a chaotic explosion. It's like one of those crazy action films happening before my eyes.

"Holy fuck." I breathe out and Tank chuckles.

"Clubhouse. We will send someone after the bikes later." Gunner yells to us before I see the three guys settle in the back of the truck.

"Hey Sarah?" I call soothingly back to the woman. "You can sit in the seats now. We'll be back soon, okay?"

They don't answer but I hear shuffling and see them huddling in the center of the back seat. Sighing. I listen into the coms. They launched part two of our plan. It sounds like it's going about the same as our phase one went. Minimal security, pretty straightforward to our plans for infiltration and rescues. They took a van and will be headed to the holding area of the police station for treatment. The chief was fine with our plan to involve them as long as we supplied everything, of course.

Tank pulls us into the clubhouse drive, pulling in front of the bar room doors. Ry, Matty and Gunner hop out greeting Doc and Sonja at the door. I catch a glimpse of Gunner pressing a kiss to Sonja's forehead before she moves away. The look on Gunner's face is devastating and while I know I can't worry about it right now my heart aches a little for him.

"Sarah, I'm going to take Emma to our Doc okay? Can you follow us in?" She nods handing Emma through the door to me.

Her and Tank help the other two girls out and we head to the clubhouse doors. Cody comes bursting through them. "Emma!" He yells grabbing her from me.

"Daddy!" Emma says, her voice still groggy from whatever she was given.

"Hey Doc!" He's already moving towards me I realize after looking up from the reunited family. "Sorry. I don't know what they gave her. Sarah, do you know what they gave her?"

Sarah shakes her head. The other two girls gripping her arms huddled and shivering. "Maybe. It was a syringe. They gave it to me once after I tried to run, it made me really sick after. Fever and shakes and everything."

Doc pales. "Come Cody. I need to start saline and run some tests. It's too late for Narcan but she's going to withdrawal either way. We need to start trying to flush and get what we can out of her system."

My eyes meet Sonja's, confirming my thoughts. I feel nauseous realizing that they gave a five-year-old child heroin. Sonja comes towards us, her eyes on Sarah and the two other girls.

"My name is Sonja. I'm a nurse and working on becoming a nurse practitioner. I have a room ready and clothes for you. You can come clean up and relax before anything else okay? I'll have some light foods and soups for you too, I'm assuming you haven't had much to eat?"

Sarah nods and steps towards her. Then she turns to me instead and closes the distance wrapping her too thin arms around me. "Thank you." She whispers. Taking the other two girls hands she follows after Sonja. While a small amount of relief settles over me, the majority of my mind and body is still tense.

"Blondie." Gunner calls me from the other entrance. "Phase three has started."

My heart stops. Cole is leading phase three and I can't help but worry. We were going to try to make it to him for this but we didn't have enough time. Holding back tears that I refuse to let fall, I follow Gunner to the basement.

Chapter 41 - Split Points of View

Cole:

Confirmation that L is back at the clubhouse safe and sound lifts a weight off my chest I didn't realize I had been carrying around since church. It's easier to breath and my mind is clearer. That follows with confirmation from Jax that his part is going as planned. Now if only this part goes as planned.

This is their main warehouse and while I have the power of numbers here, I can already tell that it's heavily guarded, unlike the house and shack. Apparently, keeping guards on their stock pile of drugs is more important to them then the women they want to sell.

Scum. That's all these guys are, rotting scum. Worse than dog shit on a pair of new boots.

"Prez." X army crawls beside me. "Miller's got his team on the far side. Shakes has his team set in the western corner. Bobby and Baker are set with their teams in the eastern side. We are ready to raid when you are."

Now would be a great time to have Gunner and his sniper skills, but he wouldn't get here in time. Rescuing Emma took too long, though I expected as much. I purposely sent him with L because I knew he could protect her and have her come out unscathed.

"Beck is back at the vans with the prospects. Ready to storm after we clear." Tech comes over the coms.

"Hawk." Its L's voice in the coms, worry evident in her tone.

"Tech. Keep coms clear. If Jax is on his way to the chief's, we are rolling out." I command. I'm sure it's a sting to L but I can't have her in my ears. I need to focus.

"Got it Prez." Tech calls back and the coms are silent.

"Okay boys. Silencers and blades. Let's roll." I command through the coms.

We need to get into this building as quickly and quietly as we can. Especially, since we are not entirely sure what's in there. X, myself and several other members that normally do runs with X are headed through the front. We creep and crawl, using the fading sunlight to our advantage. The first two guards go down easy. Almost too easy as X grabbed one around the mouth and slit his throat while I grabbed the other.

The next set of guards are right at the door, they are joking with each other and not paying a lick of attention to what's around them. Two more quick blade slips and they drop in a heap at our feet as well.

I look at X, we both exchange a look. This was way too easy. "Cleared." X calls in the coms getting responses from the other teams almost instantly. "This feels off Prez."

"I know, I feel it too." I whisper not wanting the others to hear. Signaling for the door one of the guys bust the lock and shove it open. I peak my head in only to see wires and a timer. "Retreat!" I scream into the coms and take off back to the woods.

It was at fifteen seconds, that's all we have to get all of us as far as possible. It's the only chance of survival. Sprinting and hearing the clunk of boots on the ground behind me it's all I can focus on. Moving forward and moving fast. A noise too loud releases behind me, a force knocks me face first to the ground, my hearing goes, I can only feel pain as everything goes black.

Ellie:

It blew up. The entire warehouse blew up. Cole called for a re-treat and started running. There was a blast then nothing. No com, no video. Nothing.

"Tech." My voice breaks, I feel my legs give out under me and expect to hit the floor. It never comes.

"I got you Blondie." Gunner's voice is rough, his arm strong and protective around my abdomen keeping me upright. "I got you."

"Beck?" I hear Tech say. He sounds far away. "Beck? Can you hear me?"

"Baby? I'm here." I hear Beck's normally soft voice sounding panicked. "Holy fuck. What the fuck happened, the windows of the van fucking shattered and my ears are ringing like a mother."

"The C4." Tech says. His voice raspy like he's trying not to choke on his words. "The fucking building was rigged."

"Fuck." Beck calls, taking over commands of the prospects. "You! You! Go find Prez, He was on this end. You! You, other guy! Get these vans ready, we are moving!"

"Beck, you need to get back to the clubhouse." Tech pleads.

"No Paul. Not until I find everyone." She argues back.

"Beck."

"No."

They continue on and I can't listen anymore. I can't. If Cole could he would contact me, someway somehow. He knew I was watching; he wouldn't purposely let me worry. Pulling away from Gunner, I try to make to the stairs. My legs fail me and I feel myself falling, collapsing to the ground.

"Come on Blondie." Gunner lifts me, one arm under my shoulders and the other under my knees. It's all I can do to put my arms around his neck to help him carry me. When we get to the main floor, I hear the thundering roar of bikes, I look to

Gunner, terror bright in my eyes.

"Fuck." He mumbles, turning to take me back downstairs to the basement.

A slam of the door as it flings open, "Heard you boys needed back up." A booming voice carries through the main floor. "Jesus, Gunner you look like you're about to shit yourself." The guy laughs and Gunner puts my feet to the floor, still holding me with one strong arm keeping me upright.

"Fucking hell, Red. We are at war and you fucking ride up in here." Gunner growls out. Looking at the guy I can see why he's called Red. Red hair and a red beard cover his face. Bright green eyes glow, surrounded by aged skin. He looks strong and wise. Like someone no one fucks with but also gets advice from. "Blondie, Red. Red, Blondie." Gunner introduces us.

I can't place if I should know that but currently my mind is jumbled. Thoughts are just running everywhere.

"Ahhh, been wanting to meet the girl that managed to get Hawk's panties all twisted up so he trashed my office and broke shit." He chuckles again.

I haven't cried yet. I've just felt numb, but for some reason that breaks a dam in my soul and a gut retching sound escapes me. Followed by hysterical cries.

"Oh fuck." Red's voice drops and I hear a cracking and a thud followed by a painful sounding grunt of a man. "Mother-fuckers."

Gunner has me lifted again, moving me. "Shhhh, Blondie. I've got you. I've got you."

I hear Ry calling out to Gunner and then Gunner responding but my mind isn't registering what they are saying. My soul feels shattered, this hurts so much more than when Cole left. The only answer is that he's gone. My soul has shattered because its other half is gone.

More movement, then soft pillows and a soft soothing hand over my forehead and through my hair. "Shhh baby girl. Momma's got you. Shhhh."

A prick in my arm, Momma's soothing voice and I'm out.

Gunner:

Blondie just collapsed in front of Red. She was mostly keeping her shit together all things considered, I'm not sure what happened when Red unknowingly brought up Cole but it was like her mind broke. With the help of Ry, Sonja and Sally we got her in her bed and Sonja gave her a shot of something. I don't know any of that nursing shit but she said it would relax her and help her sleep but that's it.

I trust Sonja and know she wouldn't do anything to hurt Blondie so I let her. We can't have our Queen shattering in front of people right now, not when we have no idea what's happening.

"Sally. Can you stay here and not leave? Text Tech if you need anything and we'll get it but don't leave." I tell Blondie's mom, trying to step into this leading roll I've never wanted.

"I'm not leaving my baby right now." She mumbles and continues watching Blondie.

"Sonja, you need to go back to where you were." Her death glare tells me that she's either not happy with my demand or just generally not happy with me. Unfortunately for me, it is probably the later. "Ry, go find Matt and Tank we have shit to do."

"I'm coming with you." Ben steps forward and meets my eyes, he's determined and pissed off. The anger is radiating off him.

"If you're coming with me to help then fine. If you're coming because you're pissed off about the state your daughter is in, you better fucking stay here." I keep my voice low and directed only at Ben, though I can tell Ry heard because he looks at me wide eyed.

"Cole is just as much my family as he's yours. He didn't let me help him before and I'm not standing by this time. I know more about this life and this shit than you, considering Bear had to help you get started." Ben says to me, putting a finger in my face.

Now I look at him wide eyed. Look at his face and at those dark blue almost black eyes. The same eyes I've seen looking cold, dead and heartless. Then it all hits me, the time frames, the stories, those eyes. "You... You're Bones." I gasp out.

Ben watches my face. Ben. My father's brother. Ben, bones. He ran and hid from my father to protect a woman and start a new life. Bear helped him and never spoke a word about it. Ben, Blondie's father is my uncle.

Well, if that isn't fucked.

He smiles and nods. It clicked for him too. "Hades was your father. Should have realized, fortunately for you, you have your mother's looks. Though you do have your father's hair and I bet his temper."

Ry looks even more bewildered than I do, standing here in Cole's room. Cole, my only blood family that I've ever cared for. Then here's a man and his children that I've grown fond of are actually my blood family too. I cough, clearing my throat as my voice cracks. "We... We have other shit to deal with." I turn and walk out the door but Ben puts a hand on my shoulder.

"I would have protected you for Cole's sake, but this, I'll protect you with my life. I have never been anything like my brother." He drops his arm and walks by me to head downstairs.

Coughing again. "Ry! Fuck! Go do as you were fucking ordered." I scold, then I make my way to the basement to meet with Red and see what Tech has

Step one, gather who we have. Step two, fucking find Cole.

Cole:

A groan comes from beside me. I blink and groan myself. I feel like I've been hit by a fucking truck. My ears are ringing and my vision is hazy and blurry. I can't really feel my legs and I don't remember what happen.

Somehow, I manage to turn my head enough to see what the groaning is coming from. X is laying on his back beside me. Lines of blood run down his ears and he's smothered in black dirt. His torso looks bad, something wet, I'm assuming blood is soaking, his ripped up black shirt and leather jacket.

My eye travel further down him and if I had to guess there's a tree branch through his left thigh.

"Fuck." I groan and try to roll to my side at least.

It starts to feel like a futile effort, but finally I'm able to move my arm and use it to press myself up and flip. Once I'm on my back I think my body is just sore and stunned, nothing necessarily feels broken, maybe some ribs and my eardrums but I can work around those.

"X," I call and cough. Definitely, have broken ribs. My voice is horse and my throat is so dry it hurts. "X." I call again.

"Pr-prez?" His voice shaky.

"Thank fuck." I say. My voice getting a little better. "Don't move man, but keep talking."

"Fuck. This fucking hurts." He coughs.

"Yeah. Fuck, I think we got blown up."

"No fucking shit." He coughs more.

"We need to get out of here." I say, half to myself but also just trying to keep X talking. "It was work to roll but I'm starting to get my bearings back man. I'll get us the fuck out of here."

"I told you it felt wrong." X coughs again.

I groan trying to sit up, broken ribs are a bitch. "I felt it too X. I still opened that door."

It's my fault. Who knows how many guys we lost, my coms are out and I never take my phone out on shit like this? We ran in, guns blazing and I should have known Snake better than that. We hit the place when the sun was just going down and now the moon is high in the sky lighting the field. I've been out hours and no one has found us yet, that's really not good. Something is wrong at the clubhouse. I feel it in my gut, we need to get up and back to them. All of this was a trap to drag us out.

Harsh, raspy chuckles come from the other side of me. "Well, ain't I in luck. Fucking Snake will love this." The man continues to laugh then kicks me in the head.

Everything returns to black.

Chapter 42 - Ellianna

My head is pounding and swirling, it takes all my focus to re-member where I am. The softness of the sheets and bed I'm on, the overwhelming scent of sandalwood and leather. I know I'm in mine and Cole's bed. However, I can't remember how I got here.

Cinnamon, citrus and coffee scents though, that smell doesn't belong here. I try to move but something is draped around my waist and it's impossible to move. I vaguely register a grunt like noise vibrating out of my chest.

"Baby girl, are you awake?" I hear Momma's soft voice ask from beside me.

"Momma?" I question, my throat is dry making my voice raspy. "What? Why?" I ask the question but the memories from earl-ier come back full force. "Sonja drugged me?"

"Just with a little Valium baby. You collapsed and we all agreed it would be best to keep you settled so you could rest." I feel her running her hand over my hair like she used to do when I was sick as a kid.

"How long have I been out?" I ask managing to turn to my side, coming face to face with Momma. "and has Chris or anyone been up with any information?"

Momma shakes her head. "Nothing baby. You've been out, probably five hours or so now. I didn't let Sonja give you much, just enough to get you rested."

Five hours, no one has even been up here in five hours. Sitting up in bed, I gather myself more as my head still spins a bit. Momma gets up and hands me a glass of water she had in here for me. Downing it I start to feel better, especially with my mouth and throat now wet, it doesn't feel as dry and scratchy any more.

My phone is resting on the night stand. I grab it off the charger, Momma must have put it on there as well as changing me into sweats instead of my sweater and legging. No notifications, no calls, nothing. With a sigh I get out of bed and head to the closet, aiming to put on jeans, boots and a shirt with my leather. "Baby girl, what do you think you are doing?"

"I need to find out what's going on Momma. This club needs me, Cole needs me. I am going to find out who did all this and I'm going to kill them." My tone is cold and I can see the concern across Momma's face. Although, I could have sworn I seen something else there first. Pride maybe?

She clears her throat. "You are just like your father." She pauses and clears her throat again; I was thinking she was finished but as I button up my jeans she continues on. "You may be mad at your father and I after I tell you this but you need to know now. I'm not sure if it factors in at all or not but it is time you know now. Please, keep an open mind for me and understand that your father and I kept this secret to keep you and then Ry when he came along safe."

I look up at Momma while slipping my boots on, her mouth is turned down, the light lines that surround her eyes are deeper than normal. She looks tired, worried and like she has aged a few years while I slept. I quickly nod my head and agree I'd keep an open mind before continuing to get dressed.

"I met your father in Ohio as children, we grew up together. We have always told you kids that our parents died before you were both born and we were only children. While our parents did die, your father had a brother." Confused, I tilt my head but keep quiet continuing to listen. "Our parents were in a club there, like this one but dirty and unforgiving. As children we didn't realize it as we were kept away and protected. As we got older, I was still kept away and protected but your father, he was trained and taught by his father. His father was a kind man, a good man and very loving. He didn't like how things were done there but it was part of him, as it was part of his father and his father's father. Ben, he had an older brother though, Henry. Henry was.... well, there was always something off about him, even when we were children. "

"Wait, you and dad? That's why?" I rub my face. "That's why nothing Cole has done bothered either of you and you welcomed him? You know about how things are?"

Momma nods. "There's more though. You see while Ben's father was a kind man, the rest of the club was not as forgiving, including my own father. Since my mother was only able to have me and my father, while unkind, was loyal to my mother, I was the only heir. I couldn't take on the role of president of the club. He wanted me to marry Henry and Henry would take his place and I would take my mother's. Ben's father knew what would happen to me if he let that happen, not to mention I have always loved your father. So, Ben's father reached out to a friend, Bear."

"Our Old Man Bear?" I ask and Momma nods, continuing with her story.

"He got us both new ID's and we changed our last names and ran from the life. When Henry found out he went into a rage. He killed all of our parents and took over the club. He had no sympathy or remorse and he led completely ruthlessly. He opened up all kinds of horrible things, or so Bear told us. He continued to keep us all hidden away. We never thought it would circle back."

"Henry is back?" I ask confused why Momma is bring this up now.

"No. Henry is dead. Cole killed him when he took out the entire MC." Momma replies.

"Henry was Hades? Are you serious?" Momma just nods and I put the pieces I've learned from Cole about Ohio together. "Chris is my cousin, Dad's nephew?" Momma nods again.

"I'll keep you and Pops protected still Momma. There is no way that Snake would know that dad is Hades' brother. Not to mention, he is here for Chris and Cole anyway." I kiss her forehead. "Thank you for telling me Momma. Now I'm going to go kick my new found cousin in the dick for drugging me."

"Ellianna Marie!" Momma yells. "You will do no such thing to Christopher." She scolds me but I'm already headed out the door.

The basement was empty so I make my way to the meeting room. These boys better still be here somewhere or they will have to deal with more than me just being mad at Chris for letting Sonja drug me. Bastard. I probably needed the sleep to settle, sure but I would have recollected myself after the initial shock of everything that happened. Hearing voices on the other side of the door I kick it open and march in.

The room instantly silences and all eyes land on me. Gunner stands at the front of the room looking like he was in the middle of an argument with Pops, Ry, Tank and Red. As soon as my eyes meet Gunner's, he takes a step back. Marching straight to him I grab the sides of his face in my hands and pull his face down so my lips are close to his ear. "I swear to fucking God if you ever, ever order someone to drug me again I will cut you." My voice is a low whisper.

Then just as I lean back from him, I knee him in the groin. He drops as I release him to the ground. Red, who must have heard me starts laughing, it is a deep, booming laugh that shakes his whole body. He doesn't strike me as someone that laughs much so at first, I was a little alarmed at the noise.

My father's expression is unreadable and Ry looks like he

wants to throw me over his shoulder and run. Tank smirks at me and I know he heard me also. The members and officers are watching on in shock, I'm sure they are unsure what to do when their Queen assaults their VP. Turning to Tech I speak again. "Since someone decided it was okay to drug me, does someone want to fucking fill me in now?"

Low murmurs sweep the room, I can tell they aren't happy with Gunner at the moment either. "Fuck Blondie. You collapsed; it was a lot to handle. I thought it was best so you didn't hurt yourself." Gunner says defensively as he collects himself from the floor.

I throw a sharp glare in his direction for a few seconds before Tech clears his throat and speaks. "Now that our Queen is well rested and back with us." I snort at him. "And just as angry as us. Perhaps, she'll have a better idea on handling this now. So, Blondie, let me tell you what I have."

Tech goes on to explain what's happened in the last six hours. We have eight dead members; we will mourn their losses after we avenge them. Eight bodies that Beck and the prospects found while sweeping the area around the blast site against Tech's wishes. We have no video or audio feed at all, the blast took out everything including Tech's two drones. Beck and the prospects also found ten injured members; several are still in surgery. The only two of the twenty guys that were in the blast zone that are unaccounted for are X and Cole.

Beck found X's smashed phone and a bunch of blood soaked grounded surrounded by scuff and drag marks in the dirt. It seems like someone took Cole and X. After regrouping and getting injured members to the hospital, where Beck is taking care of family and well-being communications, the rest of the guys as well as Red and his crew have been in here arguing about what to do next.

"So, let me get this straight. This asshole drugs me, then none of you can keep it together to accomplish anything in my drug slumber?" Venom lacing my voice as anger seems to consume me. Cole. My Cole. The love of my life. My other half. My soulmate. He's out there, taken and nothing has been done to find him, I am fuming. "I am so disappointed and disgusted. Hawk would expect better from every single one of you. So, one of you better have a good idea where the 9s would have taken them, or I'm going to burn everything in my path searching."

Guilty faces surround me. Someone, I don't recognize steps forward from the group of members standing to our side behind Red. His cut tells me he's the Road Captain named Spider. "Hawk came searching for me when I was captured and tortured by the 9s. Blaze got shot in the process of my rescue. You are absolutely right." He drops to his knees and keeps his head down. "For that you have my help and loyalty."

Red nods beside me. "Aye. You got us all Lass."

"Do you know where the 9s may have him?" I ask and Spider looks up.

"Before we rode here, we got word from some nomads that the 9s were seen becoming regulars at a bar three town's over. It's about 2 hours from here but the nomads seemed certain that they were working in the town. They said they used to stop there because it was a decent place, normally a good meal and fuck all that but this last time things were off. Everyone was drugged up and sick looking, the diner had shit food and the bar was pretty dirty and rough." Spider fills us in.

"Tech or Tommy, you wanna take that info and get some recon going?" I ask, though it is more of a demand. Tommy nods and pulls out his laptop, plopping on the floor the clicks and taps soothing my anger. "Thank you, Tommy. Anything else?"

Tank speaks up from beside me. "I want permission to kill Brett."

His question takes me off guard. Mostly because I forgot that he was even in town. "You can't."

He coughs. "He has gone by Reba's and harassed the new girl there." Now I know what this is about, he likes the girl but I know better than to call him out on that in the middle of the meeting room. "Nothing but trouble since he got to town. Best take him out." He grunts.

"Now is not the time. Tech, could you get him back to Texas? Also, could you leak out the pictures of my bruises and statement from that Uber driver too? That should keep him occupied trying to clean up his image back in Texas while we find Hawk and X and kill every single one of these assholes."

Tech nods and sits at the table with his laptop. His fast and furious clicking and tapping matching Tommy's in a soothing rhythm. I turn and address the whole room. "Go rest, eat, recharge. As soon as we have recon and confirmation of the 9s we will reassess. It's been a long day, and we still have a battle ahead of us. I need you all fresh and ready. Red, you and your guys, I'll send one of the bunnies to get you all to rooms, but for now you can use the main house living and dining space."

"Church dismissed." Gunner calls from behind me and everyone starts to file out of the room.

I take the moment to text Camie to see if she'll handle the room situation, I don't really know any of the other bunnies to do that. I also send a text to Beck to check in. She responds right away that things are hopeful on her side.

"Blondie." I hear Gunner behind me again, Tech and Tommy still clicking away. "I really wasn't trying to piss you off. Also, I was handling this meeting."

"Were you? Because all I heard before breaking in here was arguing, not to mention I was out of half a day and still nothing has been accomplished. I don't know about you cousin, but that's not handling shit." I seethe, emphasizing the cousin part to see if he flinches, he does. So does my brother and Pops. "I see I was the last to know that too. Get the fuck away from me, I can't even look at you right now."

Gunner looks defeated "Blondie." he says softly.

"Fucking go!" I yell. I need to get my anger in check, I have never felt so angry before. Although, I've never been in a situation like this before. It's hard for me to comprehend within myself all the changes that have happened to me, not just externally but internally too since I've moved back home. It's only been a few months but I've grown into someone that I really like in these few months.

"Did your Momma talk to you then?" Pops asks.

"Yup. It's not your fault by the way, none of this. Though, I do need you to also go, I need to be away from you all right now." I respond and turn away from him. I hear his footsteps and him mumbling to Ry as they leave the room.

I've felt loved and powerful, strong and cared for. I've felt like I have been given everything I could ever want after spending so many years without the one thing that I wanted most to be in my life. I've physically become stronger and learned how to hold power and when to use it. Cole has given me so much. Even my therapist was impressed in my mental growth since returning here.

Strange how all it takes is one person showing you love and empowering you for you to bloom and grow like I have. I was such a shell of myself after he left and even more of a shell when I was with Brett. Before I left to come back home it was like I was hanging on to a transparent outer bit of me, that was all that was left.

Not now though. Now, I know how strong I am, and perhaps that's why I am so angry. I feel this strength but I don't know how to get what I want back. I will though, I promise that now, I will get Cole back. Even if I really do have to burn down everything in my path.

Chapter 43 - Ellianna

"I've got them!" Tommy calls from his spot on the floor. "I've got them!"

"What? Show me!" I exclaim, running over to Tommy and plopping beside him on the floor.

I have been pacing a hole in the floor for the last hour or so waiting for something. Tech was still working on getting Brett back to Texas. As far as I know he was just putting some finishing touches on things and then it's just a waiting game.

"See!" Tommy turns the laptop so I see the screen too. There are two tall bodies, slumped against a van. Their faces are focused at the ground and they are covered in blood and dirt. "This van pulled up to this run-down garage. They dragged them out, then you can see them carry them inside but you catch Prez's face."

Tommy plays through the feed. It's high quality like what we get from our camera's and drones. We watch as some guys try to drag them inside but Cole spits in the ones face. Then they punch him and drag him by his boots into the garage. "Oh my god." My voice holding on to a sob.

"He's alive still." Tommy says.

"When was this? And what is this feed? It's too good of a quality for a run-down place." Tech says, he's behind me, leaning over to watch the screen, I hadn't even noticed.

"Well, the feed is what lead me here, I was doing a surveillance feed sweep through this area. The usual came up you know an occasional ring doorbell, old school CCTV at the gas station, atm video. Nothing suspicious until it swept up this. Seemed weird being that satellite imaging shows this place as basically a junk yard." Tommy explains. "This was about 20 minutes ago. I skimmed from the last 12 hours. Snake is in there and unless there is a back door somewhere, he's still in there."

"How long to get there? Call Church. It's time to settle this and get our guys back." I stand and head for the doors.

"It'll be an hour at least and that's heavily speeding." Tommy replies.

"Wait. Queen. That's too far. That's leaving things defenseless."

"Not defenseless. I have a plan." I tell him, then scream out the door "Church."

A smile graces my face when all the members and officers come storming in, repeating my words throughout the club-house until everyone is piled back in the meeting room.

Tommy explains what he's found. Then I take over. "I have a plan. Hear me out then you can input your thoughts." I say to the room, after I get nods from Red and Gunner, I launch in my idea.

"They don't know the numbers we have, I'm not sure if they know that Red is here but even if they do, they don't know we have other fighters. They also will most likely be thinking we are in shambles, right? Be we are not. I've spoken with Beck, currently our injured are all out of surgery and they are in the process of being moved here to the club house. We know the defenses here; they will be safe as will our children and families. Everyone will be staying with in the actual clubhouse walls while we are gone. Sonja with my Momma and Beck will tend to those that were hurt and still need care, Doc will come with us." Murmurs already start.

A glare from me silences them. "Prospects will be staying here as well as Old Man Bear, Pops and Nick for protection."

"That's only eight guys! And Cody is still not in -" a member calls out.

"I said let me finish!" Slamming my hand on the table the room quiets again. "Nick has been training the bunnies. They can defend themselves and shoot if necessary. The bunnies will be our defenses."

Shocked gasps and stares cross the room. "You've got to be fucking kidding me!" Another member yells.

"I'm not, and if I can lead us and fight for us, they can defend our clubhouse while we go to get our guys and end this." I state dryly.

"They do fight pretty well. Most of those girls have been through hell and back, they have reason to fight and protect themselves too." Nick tells everyone with a proud smile.

I remember the day that Camie and I went to ask him. He was so hesitant at first but once Camie told him about what happened to her and how she couldn't even try fighting back. She explained how weak she felt because she was still so defenseless and could only hope if something happened, she was close enough to a club member. He was hooked.

Then a few weeks later he was so proud of the work the girls had put in and how much stronger and more confident it could see them all being.

As much as I hated Brianna, I can't say that about most of the bunnies. While I can't say that I love the fact that they whore themselves out to the guys and seem to enjoy it too, I know they all ended up here for shitty reasons and this is their way of survival. The club does take care of all their needs and they get a paid allowance and extra cash off odd and end jobs they do for the club as well.

"Blondie is right. The clubhouse is well fortified, you may not realize it but Ben and Bear can fight just as well if not better than us. With Nick and the prospects here too, they would be well covered. Tommy though should also stay to run tech support here while Tech comes with us." Gunner states.

I can't help but smile that he agrees with my plan. We don't know what we are going to be riding into but we are about to attack what seems to be their main hub, we need all the man power we can for that.

After a minimal discussion everyone agrees. For the second time in twenty-four I'm suiting up for a battle, only this time Cole isn't beside me.

Once we dismiss church with agreement to roll out in fifteen minutes, Tech comes up beside me. "I've been working on a suit for you. Our jackets are lined with bulletproof nanotech and I applied that concept to a riding suit for you."

He takes us down to the basement and into the weapons section. Sliding a hidden wall panel, he reveals a black body suit. A dark orange and red Phoenix tail snakes around the right leg to the back with a Phoenix with open wings covering it. Closer inspection shows me there are hidden slits in the arms and legs for blades to rest.

Tech leaves and lets me slide into it. It's soft and flexible, the sleeves come down to cover my knuckles also, my fingers fitting through the holes made for them and a piece comes around to cover my palms as well. It zips up covering my neck. I slip my jacket and boots back on before stepping back into rest of the basement. Tech is waiting for me with a full-face helmet that matches the rest of the guy's helmets.

"Thought you'd need this too, and these." He says holding out keys. "Cole's mentioned getting you your own bike but then thought against it because he likes you riding with him. Anyway, you should be leading with us and not riding in the van, so these are to Beck's."

I squeal like a teenager. "Oh my god. She's letting me take her SR 1000 RR!"

Tech covers his ears but nods with a smile. I hug him then proceed with skipping up the stairs, helmet and keys in hands with Tech following behind. Walking outside the clubhouse, I see everyone is ready and waiting on us. It's dark out. Being the early morning hours now, the only thing lighting us is the clubhouse's security lights.

Tech heads for a van, I'm sure he loves to ride but he can't use his computers and ride at the same time. Tank wraps me in a bear hug lifting me off the ground. "I have your back the whole time." He says before putting me back on my feet.

We head out.

We cover the entire roadway as we fly through the countryside. Tech told Chief we were moving and to back off before we left so we should have no police issues. I'm riding well over 100 mph, easily taking the corners in this sleek bike of Beck's. It's been forever since I've driven but the memory of how to ride came flooding back easily and the feel of the wind and calm night air is easing my tense body.

"We are 10 miles out. Cut the lights." Tech calls through the coms in the helmets, as he had been directing us through the ride. "No one has gone in or out in the last 30. Last set in was some stumbling guys with girls."

"Try not to injury any of the women, if you have to non-lethal methods." I remind the guys though I'm sure they don't need reminding. Most of them would rather get themselves hurt than hurt a female. "Take them down if it's you or them. Pick you every time tonight. I want everyone back at the clubhouse for Beck's brunch tomorrow."

"One mile out." Tech calls.

We cut our engines, coasting the rest of the way. We line up on the road surrounding the building. "Any eyes Tech?" Gunner asks.

"No. They have no other cameras." He responds.

Gunner pulls his thermal scope out of his saddle and hands it to me, pulling his rifle from its safety spot beside him and flicking at the scope.

"Two guys behind the door. Not much else noticed." Gunner says and instructs Red to head to the back of the building.

Satellite imaging only shows the garage which is kind of small, we are convinced it has something underground. When Red calls back all clear. I head up and knock on the door, it opens and I slice through both throats easily. I wasn't sure if I would be able to do that, Gunner would have picked them off with his rifle if I couldn't, but it was much easier than I thought it would be.

I look down and my stomach twists. Prospects, both young. "Shhh, it's okay. They knew what they were signing up for I promise." Matty says beside me.

Nodding, I look around. We were not to take our helmets off but its dark. I'm worried about peripheral vision. Using the thermal scope Gunner handed me I look around, no heat signals through the rest of the garage space. It's empty. Looking at the ground, it should be all cold. It's not though. Reading the hot temps, I signal to Gunner. We all step in to the garage, only leaving a few members and the van outside in the dark.

"Ain't nothing back here, Blondie. Nothing on this thermal camera back here, either." Red calls in the coms, no helmets, no coms I remind myself not to remove it.

Gunner speaks into the coms, "Check the ground."

"Ehhh. It ain't frost levels." He says.

"Should be, it's November and it has been under 40 all week. Ground should be starting to freeze on top." Tech responds.

"Well, it ain't. It's about the ground temp in Florida." Red tells us.

I ask how far it goes and its quiet for a bit while he looks. "About 100 yards back, same width as the building. They got a football field under us."

"Find the door." Gunner calls and the guys spread out around me. "Red, half your guys keep looking for a back exit or air vent or anything. Other half come around this way."

"Got it, Gunner." Red says back just as Matty finds a slotted door in the floor.

"Got the door. Ready?" I ask.

"I'm going first Blondie." Jax and Blaze both say beside me.

With an eye roll that I know they can't see through the helmet I wave them forward. Their boots clank on metal stairs. Gunner and Matty follows them and I start down behind Gunner. Tank right behind me.

The stairs drop us into a long dark hallway. It's musky smelling and creepy. Like we dropped into the middle of a horror film. "There's a door at the end and a lot of heat behind it. Can't make out numbers. We charge and try to take them by surprise." Gunner says lowly in the coms.

We pile into the hallway; Gunner pulls some devices out of the back and passes them back. They are flat LED lights. "Flick them on. If it is that dark in there we need to see."

The hallway lights up with the bright LEDs. Gunner signals then kicks open the doors, we rush in. Ten startled guys are taken out fairly quietly and easily after being caught off guard like that. They didn't even have time to grab their guns before Jax, Blaze and Matty took two out each with knives and Gunner used his silenced rifle to head shot the others

The guy can shoot, definitely give him that.

Looking around we look to be in a waiting room like space. There are chairs and a few tables but not much else. Two doors are on the far wall at opposite ends. Tech brings up the thermal again, it looks like there are people and rooms around us. "It's a concrete maze down here" Gunner says.

"I've been looking to see about plans or anything but I'm coming up empty. Only thing is maybe a fallout shelter from the 60s." Tech says in the coms.

I'm uneasy about going around in here blind but there's no other choice.

Gunner decides to take the left door, so I take the right. We split the rest of the guys evenly. Then bust through our doors at the same time. My knife finds the neck of a guy to my right, quickly he drops. Tank tackled a man as he went through the door and I see him on the floor by Tank's feet, blood surrounding his head while Tank is choking another man. Matty knives several guys on my left.

There goes another ten men down. The room is similar to the previous but this one has a TV and a kitchenette area. A hallway leans down to the right and we take it. There are four doors on each side, everyone grabs a door and busts in.

Mines a bedroom and I bust in on a naked redhead riding a guy cuffed to the bed. I hold in a laugh until she screams. Running over to her, I wrap my hands around her neck. "Don't fucking scream."

The guy is struggling to get out of his cuffs until Tank is beside me. He hits the guy in the head with the butt of his gun, knocking the guy out. The girl's eyes widen.

"You answer questions and I'll let you get dressed and leave okay?" She nods her head, tears streaming from her eyes. "Good. What is this place?"

I drop my hands from her neck and she gasps falling forward. I grab her by the back of her head and pull her off the guy onto the floor. "Answer." My voice is cold.

"It's... It's a hide-out, I guess. I -I don't want to die." She sobs.

"What's your role here?" Tank asks. His gravelly voice sounding cold and deadly even to me.

"I - I am just a whore. They - they pay me - me and I -" she sobs out, I get the picture so I move on.

"You know the layout of this place at all?" I ask.

"Just. Here. Sorta. You're in the bedrooms, there are more on the other side. I've seen them come and go through the wall at the end. It's weird. That's all I know." She says and starts crying hysterically.

"Get her out of here to Doc first, figure out if she stays with us or goes home." I say knowing the coms are open to Tech.

Gunner comes into our side. "Just bedrooms and a kitchen area. Got about 20 of their guys down, see it's about the same here. Like a dead end."

I shake my head. "The girl talked. She said they go through the wall at the end of the hall. Must be a fake door or something."

We head to the wall. Gunner checks it out, running his hands across the wall. The thermal isn't picking up anything on the other side either. I feel defeated, then it opens. An alarmed looking guy, about 30 just stares at us. Then he puts his hands up defensively and shakes his head. "Don't, don't."

Gunner steps in and grabs the guy, spinning him around so he has him in a choke hold. "Where's Snake?"

"End room." He says pointing down the hall.

"Thanks." Gunner says then pressure points him and the guy drops to the floor. "Someone take him to Doc. We take him back with us."

One of the members nods, stepping forward with the guy beside him. The haul him up and carry him out. "Clear every room till the end. Gunner and I will take the end." I instruct, getting a nod from Gunner.

I'm coming for you Cole.

Chapter 44 - Cole

X and I got dragged from a van and ended up chained to a concrete wall in a completely dark room. I vaguely remember being dragged before I passed out, but the feeling in my back is reminding me all about it.

I hiss when my back scrapes against the rough concrete, sending fresh pain across my back. "Try to save your energy." I hear X mumble beside me. He looks rough, but he's alive. "Snake. Here."

That's all he says. He slumps against the chains. I hope like hell he's just passed out. At some point I must pass out myself because I'm startled awake by a bucket of cold water. "Well, well. Little nephew. Oh, how I've been waiting for this."

Blinking the water out of my eyes, I glare up at my so-called uncle. Harry, also known as Snake. Snake fits him better. He was the man that I trusted so much to take care of my mother and I when we needed it. Considering what I have found out since then and then the meeting between him, Brett and the cartel, well it wouldn't surprise me if he was the one that supplied my mother with all the drugs to begin with.

Disgusting, slithering, piece of shit. How we could even share some DNA I will never understand, not that I had ever met my father, but my mother is a good person when she isn't drugged out of her mind.

"So, fitting that you are here now." He laughs, I do my best to keep my face emotionless and my body indifferent. "It all worked out so well, if I had known that pretty little blonde thing had your attention way back when I definitely would have used that to my advantage, too bad you hid that from me. Did you not trust me?"

I glare. I didn't trust anyone with that information. L was my secret and I'm glad I realized that was best for both of us at the time, even when I had trusted my uncle. "I bet that I wouldn't have ever had to ask for your help if you weren't the one giving my mom drugs to begin with."

He laughs again. "Well, of course I was. I mean not me directly, but you know it was the only way I could keep control of her. She ran away when our other sister died. She thought that the baby she had been carrying died too, but well, we know Christopher is very much alive. You however, ruined him." Snake punches me in the ribs, I have to bite my tongue to not yell out at the biting pain that crosses around my chest. "Pathetic. Both of you. You're too soft. We were supposed to rule, be rich and powerful but you just had to go and ruin everything didn't you?"

Snake is psychotic, there is just no other explanation for the insane thoughts this man has. He continues to throw punches at me, cracking more ribs and tearing apart the skin that is still intact. I feel my lip split open then a cut above my eyebrow, both pouring hot, coppery blood down my face.

When he finally seems to have enough of using me as a punching bag, he takes a few steps back. "You know, when I made sure your friends died at that party, I was really hoping you'd get the blame for it. If only I had realized then who Ben Turner really was at the time. That fucker, covered for you without even realizing it. All because his precious daughter was saved because of you."

"You were the reason they died?" I manage to ask. My throat is dry so my voice is raspy and all I can taste is copper.

"Oh, you know it. Where do you think all the drugs came from for that little woods party? I was wanting you to get busted for dealing, had it all set that who bought from me were to blame you. They did but Ben talked the chief out of it, when they searched your truck and house somehow there was nothing. Your mother used up her stash even. I wanted you in jail, get you hardened up before I came to get you. When that didn't work, well then, I used your mother and her habits. She never could handle herself. Blamed herself for our sister's death and all that." Snake keeps talking, it's like he is proud of himself and his little plans.

He puts a hand under his chin, tapping a long, bloodied finger on his chin. "I did always wonder why you had such a strong will to fight and to live. Now, I realize it was for the blonde. Ironic really, considering who she fell into bed with after you left."

I can't help the glare that crosses my face, staring daggers into the man who was once family. Had I realized then what I know now I would never had trusted him. It's hard to wish things different because without him I never would have met Chris or formed the Phoenix Rising MC with him. Nor would we have managed to build up and save my little home town or all the women we saved taking down his MC in Ohio.

"Now, now." He tsks at me. "Brett, while such a little bitch of a boy, makes a good friend here. His connections and all that. Plus, he offered me a little piece of the blonde if I catch her first. Now that I have you here, that's my plan. I just can't help myself."

Snake rubs his hands together and smiles. It is this cold, dark smile that I remember well from my years with him. "I'm going to get her to come right to me. I bet she will for you. Then, I'll let you watch me fuck her before I kill you."

I thrash around in the chains, expending energy I don't really have. I need to get out of this and kill him. L cannot come here, not ever. I will die before I let that happen. Snake just continues to laugh. Then, the sounds of fighting and gunfire.

It's muffled but that has to be what it is. Shots ringing out from behind the door Snake comes and goes from. It's Gunner, it has to be.

Grabbing knives off a table and pulling his gun from his pants, Snake starts yelling, "What the fuck is this?".

X grunts beside me. I sigh a little, he's still alive. Probably, just barely but he's still alive. Now, I just need to figure out how to get out of here. The door busts down, Red in all his flaming red bearded glory stands in the doorway. "Well hell, Hawk. You look like shit."

Snake starts screaming at him, guys come rushing from a door at the side of the room. Red starts punching, fighting, trying to get the rush of men down. It's chaos in the tight space and I can't see well between my swelling eyes, the darkness of the room and the bodies being thrown around.

Still trying to get my hands out of the cuffs, I feel helpless. They are strung up over a solid metal beam and tight on my wrists. I don't even think if I break my thumb that I would be able to slide out of them. My focus turns to my hands, trying anything, I could probably still fight with a broken hand but I wouldn't be able to hold a gun or knife. If I could break my left hand maybe I could just carry around the rest of the cuff and chain on my right.

A muffled scream breaks me from my focus. A sharp sting through my chest, I know that scream was L. Even X perks his head up and mumbles curses, he knows it too.

The fighting in the room is still going on, Red is still trying to take on six or seven guys himself while it seems like everyone else is still in the larger room. Snake comes back in from that larger room with his arms wrapped around someone's neck. Dragging them in with him. Long, wavy blonde hair, she's still fighting him as he drags her.

He gets close to me but not close enough for me to try to kick him. "Look what I found. Well damn, I didn't even have to try, she came right to me anyway."

L looks up, her bright ocean blue eyes are filled with rage. She meets my eyes and I hold my breath. They soften landing on me and I see the tears swell behind them. I can only image how bad I look; I mean I definitely don't feel great. She is probably seeing layers of blood and dirt, cuts and bruising that covers my face and arms.

"Stop fucking squirming." Snake yells at her, I see his arm tighten around her neck and the alarm in her face.

I try to kick out at him, missing because he's just far enough from my reach. "Don't fucking touch her."

"Oh, I think I'm going to." He pulls a knife out with his free hand, dragging it down the black suit L has on. It doesn't tear or rip, the knife just catches. "What the fuck is this?"

Having to laugh, I do and instantly regret it as my broken ribs protest. Thank you, Tech and all your crazy bullshit. Frustrated, Snake throws L into the concrete wall beside us. I watch helplessly as her head slams into it and she drops to the floor. A path of blood trailing her decent down the wall. "What the fuck did you do!?" I scream at Snake.

A shot rings loud and echoing in the room and Snake hits the ground, blood pooling around his head. Everyone stops fighting. Four more shots and the guys still conscious and trying to fight Red, hit the floor as well. Tank stands in front of me, the kind of rage across his face that means his beast is out. He's not controllable at this point and he starts wrecking the room before storming out to the larger room and disappearing from my sight.

"Well, shit little Blondie." I hear Red say. He's moved over by her while Tank went on a rage. "We gotta get you to Doc, darlin."

She isn't moving, I can't tell if her chest is rising with breath at all. There is so much blood everywhere. "Is she.... Red, is..." I can't even speak the words, but it is like Red knows what I need.

"She's breathing still." Is all he says picking her up and walking out of the room leaving me still chained and not knowing what is happening with L.

An inhumane roar comes out of me, I don't even recognize the noise as something I am capable of making. That gets Gunner's attention, he is instantly in the doorway. His eyes scan the room then land on Snake. I watch him take a big breath. "Fucking serves him right." He mumbles then comes over to me, pulling wire cutters off the table that Snake had pulled knives off earlier. He cuts me down without another word then moves to X. "You look like death man." I hear him say.

All I can do is drop to the floor. L is hurt, bad and I don't know if she will survive. It's all my fault, all of this. Every bit of this. X coughs and mumbles. "Feel like death brother. Let's blow this fucking place."

"You read my mind." Gunner says.

One of the guys comes in, his helmet is still on. Why the fuck didn't L have hers on and why didn't Tank or Gunner. When he speaks, I realize it is Matt. "Doc has Queen. Get Prez and X up to the van. Blaze is readying everything to blow. Someone needs to get Tank to calm down."

"Good, tell Tech we are coming and go get Tank. Everyone out in three minutes." Gunner commands, picking up X and putting him over his shoulder to carry. "Can you walk or I gotta get someone to carry your heavy ass too?"

I grunt and manage to get up to stand. Not sure how but we make it out of the building, the place was underground and the stairs were a bitch to get up in this state.

Gunner leads us to the back of a van, tosses X in and pushes me in too. "Bastard, you could be a little gentler." I grumble but he slams the doors. Looking around I see Doc working over L. It looks like he's already got oxygen running through a tube to her nose and an IV running something through that tube into her arm. He's cleaning and stitching at the back of her head. "Doc?"

He peaks up over his round glasses he uses to see when he's stitching. "Prez. She's got a pretty bad concussion and we need to get her to the hospital for some scans. If the scans are okay, she should be okay." Then he looks back down and gets back to stitching. "X, if you think you'll survive five more minutes, I'll get to you."

X grunts and drags himself up into the opposite bench seat. This cargo van has been set up like a mobile ambulance in the back section that can also be used for some storage. The driver's part is through a partition and has a space for a driver and an area for Tech if he needs to be along for something.

Somehow, I make my way up there, pulling the partition back. "Good to see you Prez. Shit is blowing in about 30 seconds so you need to sit your ass down." Tech says not even looking up from is computer.

Blaze hops in the driver. "Set. Matt is taking Beck's bike back and your driver has his. So ya'll get me."

The revving of bikes roar and echo, then the van starts moving too. As soon as we hit pavement you hear the echoing blast of Blaze's handy work followed by the ground shaking and the sky lighting up behind us. The sun is just starting to rise so the red and orange colors brighten the still grey horizon. Blaze giggles, fucking guy loves fire. Hence his name.

I settle on the floor in the back. My eyes never leaving L. I just watch as her chest slowly rises then falls, then rises again. Doc got her suit unzipped and covered her with a sheet so he could put monitoring stuff on her chest. The slow steady beeping with her slight chest movements let me know she's alive.

That's the only thing I can take comfort in during the excruciatingly long drive back home.

Chapter 45 - Ellianna

Voices fade in and out. A steady rhythm of beeping is always there, singing along in the background of my mind. Everything is fuzzy, black, I can't focus on the voices. My head is throbbing. This painful constant thudding. It's almost in rhythm to the beeping that's still singing in the background. This goes on and on. I have no idea where I am or what's around me. Just beeping, voices and this constant throbbing in my head.

At some point the throbbing starts to dull and the beeping becomes clearer. I hear the voices better but I can't focus enough on what they say. One of the voices finally makes sense to me, "Kitten, wake up gorgeous. I need you; we need you." It's the deep resonating voice of Cole.

I want to wake up, I want to touch him, kiss him, soothe that pain I hear in the tone of his voice. I want to so badly, but I can't seem to open my eyes.

The concept of time escapes me when I'm like this, I don't know how long it has been since Cole was here. Another gravelly voice is speaking to me now though. "Ellie, I don't like people. You broke through that and you made my world seem better, brighter. You remind me so much of Tonya. She was a fighter and a fiery girl too." He chuckles but I hear a sniffle after. Is he crying, I wonder? "I never worried about her because she was brave and never took shit from anyone, but she was so kind too. Her heart was full of love and kindness. She was so much like you. I can't lose you too Ellie. I don't think I could handle my world crashing apart again."

A warm and rough hand touches the back of mine. I'm trying to grab his back but I can tell that my hand doesn't seem to be responding to that.

"Not to mention Prez is losing it without you. He shot one of the prospects in the leg. Harsh even for him. Everyone is trying to avoid him but he seems to pop in and lash out. You just need to wake up, Ellie."

Poor Pat. I hate to see him hurting and he's probably right. To have someone remind him so much of his sister then to let them in only to see them like this. He was so closed off when I first came back here. Noone talked with him and everyone was scared of him. I couldn't imagine the kind of ruthless person he may turn into if he was to lose the one thing that made him a little less scary and a little more human.

Then Cole. My Cole. He's not a mean person at heart, I knew when I came back the anger, he was storing in him, but that's not what kind of person he is in his soul. The soul that fits mine. The other half of me. He's breaking and that is only leaving a trail of anger behind him. I feel a warm, wetness down my cheek. Then another, then the other side. Am I crying?

"Ellie?" Tank calls his warm hand leaves mine. "Ellie? Are you awake? Hey Doc!" He's yelling now, making the throbbing come back. The throbbing starts to drown out his voice again.

No, no, no. I don't want to lose the voices. They fade in and out again, I can only catch words here and there, bits of what's being said. I heard Doc, Tank and Sonja then another voice I don't recognize but it's all clipped.

Something cool runs up my arm and everything fades out again.

The beeping finally comes back into my mind. The throbbing is gone now. I flick my eyes open briefly. Blinding fluorescent lights burn them and I snap them tightly closed. What the hell happened to me? I remember storming the underground bunker, then that's really it. Cole, he was here. We must have saved him.

I need to see him, touch him, know he's here and okay is overwhelming my mind. It's too bright to open my eyes up at the lights, but if I could turn to my side it wouldn't be as bad until my eyes adjusted. My throat is so dry, I don't think I could make words. The thought of words even makes me cringe, it would hurt too much to speak and I don't want to fade back out again.

I can feel my arms and legs, they feel weak and stiff but I think I can make them work. I lift my hand and arm to start to try to turn but stop when a gasp invades my hearing.

"Babes, oh gosh. Don't move." It's Sonja, she's shuffling around, I hear clanking and papers, then her footsteps "Hang on, it's too bright in here." Her hand is on mind, soft small and warm. "Okay babes. Try to open your eyes for me okay?"

I slowly move my head side to side. It's too bright to open my eyes. I can't risk the throbbing coming back. "It's okay the room is dark. Let me see your eyes."

Her reassurance convinces me to open them. At first, she's blurry, then my eyes seem to adjust. She was right the lights are almost off and don't hurt my eyes anymore.

Once the blurriness is gone, I really get a look at her. She looks exhausted. Her eyes are rimmed in red with deep bags under them. Her skin isn't her normal golden tanned tone; she looks pale and pasty. Her hair is a snarled mess, slung in a bun and her face looks puffy, not it's normal sharply angled jawline with well-defined cheeks.

"Oh Ellie!" She hugs me crying. "You're okay"

I nod my head slowly against hers, I'm still afraid to talk, my mouth is so dry it hurts. When she finally releases me, I bring my hand to my throat and motion it down my neck, hoping she gets my drift here. "Water?" She cocks her head to the side.

Again, I slowly nod. She rushes over to a counter and I hear water and ice sloshing into a cup. She brings it right back and helps me sit up and drink it down. I try to gulp it, the cool wetness feels amazing in my mouth and running down my throat but Son urges me to take slow sips instead.

Once she sets the cup down on the tray by the bed, she sits beside me and really looks at me. "We were all so scared Ellie. Do you, what do you remember?" Her soft voice asks, concern crossing her facial features.

"Cole?" My hoarse voice catches in my throat, making me cough a little so Sonja helps me with more water. "Did.... did we get him back?"

Sonja nods. "Good you remember things. You got thrown and you hit your head super hard babes. You had a bleed in your brain. Things were pretty touch and go for a while there."

"Where...where's Cole?" I manage to get out after a few moments of both of us just sitting here.

She shrugs. "I don't know babes. Clubhouse maybe? He's been here nights, sleeping in that chair or watching you or whatever it is he does, but then Matt or Tank come in the morning he leaves." She shakes her head and sighs. "None of them tell me anything. Chris, well, I avoid because he just orders me around all the time. Then Matt runs away as soon as I am even near the room that he's in."

Sonja sighs again and looks like she may cry. "Tank sort of tells me stuff but mostly grunts and says "club business"." She uses her fingers as air quotes as she rambles on. "Ry can't even come around, he came in once and burst into tears then took off before anyone else noticed. Pops has been with Cole a lot and Momma has been here most days. She left a few hours ago."

It's quiet between us again before she lets out a sigh. "I was supposed to call Cole as soon as you woke up but I want time with you. Plus, I figured he'd be super overwhelming for you and really if you're feeling up to it and can walk a bit, we could get you cleaned up and I'll get your catheter out."

I tell her that's a good idea and thank her. She helps me stand, it's harder than it should be and my legs are wobbly. I'm so grateful when I take the first few steps because she had explained that I couldn't have the catheter out unless I could walk assisted to the bathroom.

She fills me in on my health situation and what to do and not do, what to look out for, how I can't wash my hair because the incisions haven't healed enough yet and that they had to shave some of it. I've been out almost three weeks.

As she helps me wash up, she also fills me in at what else has been happening. Brett got word I was in the hospital and showed up here only to be escorted away in hand cuffs by guys in FBI jackets. The media has been blowing up about how I had been abused my him and was in critical care. They really went to town with some wild stories. They also linked him to the cartel along with human trafficking crimes, he will spend his life in jail.

Sonja rambles and ramble, it's nice getting the gossip from what's happened in the last three weeks from her while all I seen was blackness and all I heard was beeping. Once I'm clean, I feel a million times better. I have never been so grateful for a toothbrush in my life and I've had some historically rough hangovers in the past.

We get me settled back into my bed; I'm still limited on basically everything even though I'm awake now. We have to be cautious is what Sonja tells me. The whole time she talked I could tell something is wrong with her, and not just me being unconscious for weeks. When I ask, I know I'm right on the money, her whole body stiffens and she turns a pale shade of grey - green.

"I..... I...." Sonja bites her bottom lip then lands her face on the bed. She answers with mumbles into the scratchy hospital blankets. "I'm pregnant."

That was the last thing, I expected from her. I bite my lip to literally keep my mouth shut and run my hands over the back of her head and hair as soothingly as possible. When she doesn't say anything and the ticking of the clock is all that sounds in the room for minutes I finally ask. "What are you going to do babe?"

Sonja lifts her head up; the red rings of her eyes have grown and wet tears clumped her lashes together. She looks miserable. "It's....well it's early. I only know because I ran a blood test on myself when I couldn't stand the smell of coffee or your mom's lasagna."

Nodding my head, I get it. Those are her two favorite things, with the third being my special veggie lasagna with the creamy sauce. When she doesn't continue, I ask, knowing that the answer may set her off. "Who's the father?"

She stares at me for a moment, then drops her gaze to her hands. "Chris. I'm pretty sure anyway.... I mean it was only once, before...before the lockdown and then you got hurt. He had come over and confessed his love for me and it just kind of happened. Then in the morning he was gone, no sign of him at all, not a text or call or anything. He went back to being such an asshole to me, ordering me about and being his normal commanding asshole self." She laughs but it's more of a sob. "We fought the entire lockdown or he avoided me."

Standing up she tugs her hair and groans, pacing at the side of my bed. "It's him. It has to be. Matt was the only other person and he was so hesitant and careful, like seriously, we used a condom and he still pulled out."

"Son, babes. It's all going to be okay." I pat the bed beside me. She hesitantly sighs but finally sits where I patted. I grab her hands with mine. "I've got you, no matter what."

She smiles a little and nods, then cuddles up to my side, her head resting on my chest under my chin. "I've missed you. I've known for a week and couldn't tell anyone or talk to anyone. You're my best friend, don't ever get hurt again."

I giggle and pull the blanket around her too. "I'll try not to, and I know I slept for like three weeks but I'm exhausted, we should both nap."

She agrees and before either of us know it we are out.

Chair legs scrapping across the floors wakes me, the lights are still low in here so it's dark. Even darker now because the sun must have set and the windows are completely black through the curtains.

A tall, solid figure with shaggy hair is dragging the bigger reclining chair across the floor while Sonja is still passed out on my side. The chair finally stops scrapping and the figure turns and flops down with a sigh. His hair is unkept and shaggy, his beard has grown out past a stubble and the lines and bags under his sunken eyes tells me he hasn't slept in three weeks.

Taking in all his flaws showing how tired and exhausted he is making my heart ache. He's still so handsome though, his sharp jaw line, solid and wide shoulders and chest. Then his ice blue eyes, I've missed those eyes.

I breath out a small sigh, but he hears it. His eyes instantly find mine in the darkness. I can see the relief and love cross them when he meets mine. Cole doesn't hesitate, he's out of the chair and his hands go to my cheeks. "You're awake." His voice is low and emotion filled.

I nod, not wanting to wake Sonja. I know she needs this rest too after our chat earlier. Cole's eyes flicker to her and he sighs. He presses his lips to my forehead.

"Go back to sleep Kitten. I'll be right here." He commands softly.

Cole settles back in the chair and grabs my hand, his eyes never leaving mine. It's like we are having years of conversations, feelings, thoughts and emotions pass between us in that long, soothing eye contact. Eventually, I watch his body loosen, his eyes close and he relaxes into a sleep, letting my mind relax and drift off.

Chapter 46 – Cole

So much bullshit. So many loose ends to tie up. So many projects and deals to catch up on.

Not to mention Thanksgiving has been done, gone, past and Christmas is creeping up on us. Some of guys hate having to work around holiday time, wanting to be with their families and I can't blame them, but if someone bitches about shit one more time, I'm going to completely lose it.

On top of those stresses L has been unconscious for three weeks. Three fucking weeks after everyone just let her roll into that fight like it was hers to handle, no arguments or anything.

Let me tell you, I was livid at that. First Church back after and my anger completely took over. All I could see was red and had an overwhelming feeling to kill someone. A full-on fight with Gunner happened and I beat the shit out of my best friend, of course he fought back. Considering how we looked after I can only imagine how ugly the fight was.

I was covered in blood, both his and mine. I was already beaten, bruised and broken before fighting Gunner, we were both a mess after. I only let off him because a prospect got involved. A prospect that shortly after getting involved got a bullet in the leg.

He's fine now, I did feel bad after finally calming down. I'm not an evil asshole leader like Hades was. I care about my guys; they are my family. L is just my family too, and at the time we didn't know if she'd make it. At this point we still aren't sure when or if she'll wake up. She shouldn't have been there. It wasn't her place.

It managed to make quite the impression on Red though. We will have a lifelong alliance with him, full on brotherhood because of L. He'll always have our loyalty and our backs without question because a feisty little blonde has some way of making every single one of these fucking guys bend to her will.

Knocking on my office door pulls me from my thoughts and this paperwork I'm working on. "Yeah!" I yell through the door, who the fuck is knocking and not just coming in.

"Hey Prez, Reba is here." It's the prospect I shot, no wonder he knocked. He is hesitant to be anywhere near me.

I stand and tell him to let her in. She comes in with her long red hair and pale freckled skin. I remember her from high school, she always stared at me until I looked in her direction. Then she'd turn as red as her hair and look away. She was thin and kind of an ugly, awkward duckling then. Now she's attractive, though I have never been interested. She flushes and steps into the room. "Afternoon, sorry to just pop in. I've been calling but ... ummm."

Cutting her off I apologize; I haven't been bothered to answer the phone unless it's whoever is at the hospital with L.

"Right. So, several things, first is good news." She says, smiling and pulling out an envelope from her purse. "This is Ellie's divorce paperwork. It is all signed, stamped by a judge and official. Ellie is no longer married to Brett Walton."

"That is extremely good news." I say, smiling for the first time in three weeks. Now she just needs to wake up.

Brett had tried to bust into the hospital and demanded to see L. He was physical with security as well as some of my guys, all on camera of course. Also, violating his restraining order. Tech had connected him to a long list of crimes and tipped off his friend at the FBI. I was on my way into the hospital to give the guy a piece of my own mind when I met the agents bringing him out in cuffs. Not as satisfying as it would have been if I put my fist through his face, but joyous enough.

"It is." Reba agrees then continues to her next thing. "The one thing though, his family is trying to counter with a civil suit."

"Can they? Do they have anything?" I ask, I figured they would try something. Old money type families like that don't just lay down and let people walk over their names.

"Possibly, though I think we can handle it. We have too much against Brett that is documented. If Ellie were to tell the full story of his treatment and infidelities to a media source the world would be even more against them." Reba sounds confident enough, I'm glad because I already have too much on my plate.

"I see. You good handling them then?" I ask, she nods. "Good. We'll make sure you are more than compensated. Thank you, Reba."

After thanks, goodbyes and me handing her a check, the prospect walks her out. I lock the divorce paperwork in my safe, taking a quick peek at the documents first. That word "divorce", scrolled across the top of the form make me smile again.

Now L just needs to wake-up. Checking my phone, I see it is getting late. Sonja is with L and Jax is protecting them. Neither have messaged and it makes my mood drop again.

Angry and stressed, I grab my jacket off the chair and storm out of my office into the freezing December air. Still climbing on my bike, I take off. The freezing air keeping me awake and my mood to a dull flame rather than bombs of anger going off.

At the hospital, it's the same routine it's been every day for three weeks. I walk in and have to get buzzed in from the lady that stops everyone at the front desk. The first few times she didn't want to let me in, but once Doc had a conversation with her, she finally put her claws down.

Elevator up to the fifth floor, down a hall then a right turn. I see Jax at the door, he nods and leaves, walking the direction I just came. Even Jax is avoiding me lately. My eyes land on the bed. Sonja is cuddled up to my girl, her head snuggled into L's chest and her also tiny body tucked around her side. Sonja even has one arm and one leg wrapped around L, like she's hanging on to her afraid to let her go. I sigh, I know that feeling too well. As much as I hate that it's Sonja tucked so intimately around L, when it should be L awake and tucked around me like that, I know its harmless. If anything, Sonja needs this just as much.

Something has been off with her; she hasn't seemed to have been handling any of this well. I've noticed but I've been too selfish in my own feelings and loss that I haven't bothered checking on the girl. The chair that I normally sleep in is tucked back in the corner. Seeing it, I walk over to get it, dragging it across the floor I hope I'm not loud enough to wake Sonja. I'm too tired to try to carry the damn thing over, it's not very comfortable but is big and bulky and something for me to sit in and stare at L until my body completely shuts down and my only other option is to sleep.

Same routine, different night. I settle in, dreading the thoughts that I know are about to come. What if L never wakes up, what if she does wake up and doesn't remember anything, what if she hates me now because I didn't protect her, my club didn't protect her, what if she leaves, what if?

A noise comes from the bed, I look up expecting Sonja to have woken and getting up to go home. Surprise doesn't even slightly cover it when my eyes meet those ocean blues I've been missing so much. The feelings in my chest explode, that heart that's barely been there starts beating like crazy and I feel that salty burn of tears start behind my eyes.

Quickly, I jump up and put my hands on her face, never taking my eyes off hers. "You're awake?"

Her response is a smile and a nod. She remembers me, good. Her eyes look to Sonja who is still snuggled in and sleeping soundly, when she looks back to me, I get it. Even just waking up from being unconscious for three weeks my girl still cares about everyone else before herself.

I tell her to sleep, not wanting to upset her even though my mind is racing with questions. Settling back in my chair, I look at her and she looks at me. It's like our souls are speaking to each other, repairing the holes that were left when I was blown up and taken then she was hurt. My world is right, back to its normal spinning. Contentment fills me and eventually I feel myself fading into a deep sleep.

A warm soft hand glides across my cheek, pulling me from a hopeful dream.

L and I were at the beach, her long waves glowing in the sun. A curly haired boy with ocean blue eyes holding her hand and giggling in the salty ocean waves. A small hand was in mine, looking down to see an ice blue eyed girl with her mother's wavy blond hair and full lips smiles up at me. "Daddy!" She giggles as I picked her up and swung her around.

The sight my eyes open up to is as beautiful as the dream. Ocean blue eyes, shining in the light coming from the room windows. Someone has pulled the curtains up letting the light flow in. Sonja is no longer here and L is changed into a long sweater and leggings. Her hair is braided and she looks good, I mean she always looks good but she looks alive. After she has been laying in that bed, pale and unmoving for weeks, this is a good look on her.

"What were you dreaming of? You've been smiling in your sleep for the last thirty minutes at least." Her soft angelic voice is like music to my ears. God, how I've missed that voice.

Smiling, I pull her into my lap. "You." I mumble, nuzzling my face into her neck.

Someone must have brought her soaps when they brought her clothes because she smells like her normal, sweet vanilla and cinnamon. Even her hair smells clean and like her.

Sonja also must have helped her; I know her skull isn't completely healed and they had to shave some of the hair away then they drilled into her brain to relieve the pressure in there from her bleed. It better have been Sonja that helped her anyway.

"I heard you when I was unconscious. I'd get bits and pieces of voices but there were a few times I heard you talking to me, I just couldn't reach out." She tells me, her body leaning into mine as I snuggle my face deeper into her neck, unable to get enough of her.

"How long have you been awake?" I ask curious how I slept through her cleaning up and watching me smile in my sleep for the last thirty minutes.

"It's late for you." She giggles. Fuck, I've missed that giggle, it takes everything I have to make my dick stay down. "It's ten. Matty was here with a bag of stuff for me a couple hours ago, Sonja got up and called him. Then she helped me get myself together before leaving."

I shake my head in her neck, "I would have got you stuff or helped you, why didn't you wake me, Kitten?

"Same reason I didn't let you wake Son last night. You needed that sleep." She pulls back from me, putting her soft hands on either side of my beard. It's long and unkept now, normally I keep pretty shaved or a bit a stubble. "You haven't been taking care of yourself."

"Didn't have it in me. You're the best part of me L. I can't live without you."

"I can't live without you either." She says then presses her lips to mine. Overwhelmed by the taste of her I take over her mouth, possessing her and showing her how much I've missed her.

A booming laugh comes from the doorway, breaking me from L. Her face flushes and she tucks her head into my chest, trying to hide her giggling and embarrassment she always gets at getting caught. "All good darlin'. Glad to see you're awake and seemingly well. Sonja filled me in on your progress overnight, I just want to do some checks then we'll let you go to the clubhouse, but you have to promise me you'll take it easy and rest." Doc says stepping into the room.

"Course, you know she won't be allowed to do anything." I chuckle, glad to hear Doc is okay letting her come home, where she belongs.

He smirks, he knows me well but I'm sure he's learned how uncontrollable this feisty girl can be. "Ellie, seriously, your brain and body still have to heal from the trauma. Take. It. Easy. And call me and Sonja with anything you feel that's different."

She turns in my lap to answer him agreeing. He has her stand for some checks on her balance before he gets her back into the hospital bed to do all sorts of checks. While he's doing all that I check my phone and update Tech and Gunner. Beck is planning a welcome home for her of course, even though I said no, I am betting she won't listen.

"Alright. She's all yours, Prez." He says walking out the door, just before he's gone, he turns with more instructions. "Wait, no bikes either."

I text Gunner quick for a ride before turning to my girl, she's still glowing but I can see she's starting to get tired already. "I have more good news Kitten." She looks at me, her eyes big and bright. "I got papers yesterday from Reba, you are officially a divorced woman."

Her face lights with that big smile as she leaps on me from the bed wrapping her arms and legs around me. "Let's get married! I can't wait another second to be Ellianna Cameron."

"I think that can be arranged Kitten." I say before kissing her with everything I have.

My phone beeps signaling that Gunner is here. Wrapping my arm around my girl, I walk her out of this hospital room. Headed for our home and towards the rest of our lives.

The end.

More of Ellie and Cole will be in the rest of the series, but this is their happily ever after.
XoXo KatThrive

About The Author

Katthrive

Finally submitting the words I have put to paper.

Thank you all.

XoXo Kat Thrive

Phoenix Rising

Book Two coming soon. Stay tuned for
Sonja and Gunner's story.

Breaking Barriers

Plus more of Ellianna and Cole of course.

Made in United States
Orlando, FL
03 February 2023

29402076R00205